PENGUIN BOOKS

FAIRACRE AFFAIRS

Miss Read, or in real life Mrs Dora Saint, was a teacher by profession who started writing after the Second World War, beginning with light essays written for *Punch* and other journals. She has written on educational and country matters, and worked as a script-writer for the BBC. Miss Read is married to a retired schoolmaster and they live in a tiny Berkshire hamlet. She is a local magistrate and her hobbies are going to the theatre, listening to music and reading. She was made an MBE for her services to literature in the 1998 New Year Honours List.

Miss Read is the author of numerous books, which have gained immense popularity for their humorous and honest depictions of English rural life, including, most recently, *The Year at Thrush Green* and *A Peaceful Retirement*. Many of her books are published by Penguin, together with eight omnibus editions. She has also written a cookery book, *Miss Read's Country Cooking,* and two autobiographical works, *A Fortunate Grandchild* and *Time Remembered,* published together in one volume as *Early Days,* with a new foreword by the author.

Novels

Village School Village Diary Storm in the Village
Thrush Green Fresh from the Country
Winter in Thrush Green Miss Clare Remembers
Over the Gate The Market Square
Village Christmas The Howards of Caxley
Fairacre Festival News From Thrush Green
Emily Davis Tyler's Row
The Christmas Mouse Farther Afield
Battles at Thrush Green No Holly for Miss Quinn
Village Affairs Return to Thrush Green The White Robin
Village Centenary Gossip from Thrush Green
Affairs at Thrush Green Summer at Fairacre
At Home in Thrush Green The School at Thrush Green
Mrs Pringle Friends at Thrush Green
Changes at Fairacre Celebrations at Thrush Green
Farewell to Fairacre Tales from a Village School
The Year at Thrush Green A Peaceful Retirement

Anthology

Country Bunch
Miss Read's Christmas Book

Omnibuses

Chronicles of Fairacre Life at Thrush Green
More Stories from Thrush Green
Further Chronicles of Fairacre
Christmas at Fairacre Fairacre Roundabout
Tales from Thrush Green Fairacre Affairs
Encounters at Thrush Green Early Days

Non-Fiction

Tiggy
A Fortunate Grandchild Time Remembered
Miss Read's Country Cooking
The World of Thrush Green

FAIRACRE
AFFAIRS

An omnibus volume containing

VILLAGE CENTENARY
SUMMER AT FAIRACRE

Miss Read

Illustrated by John S. Goodall

PENGUIN BOOKS

PENGUIN BOOKS

Published by the Penguin Group ·
Penguin Books Ltd, 27 Wrights Lane, London w8 5tz, England
Penguin Putnam Inc., 375 Hudson Street, New York, New York 10014, USA
Penguin Books Australia Ltd, Ringwood, Victoria, Australia
Penguin Books Canada Ltd, 10 Alcorn Avenue, Toronto, Ontario, Canada m4v 3b2
Penguin Books (NZ) Ltd, Private Bag 102902, NSMC, Auckland, New Zealand

Penguin Books Ltd, Registered Offices: Harmondsworth, Middlesex, England

First published in Great Britain August 1997
Second impression before publication

Village Centenary first published by Michael Joseph 1980
© Miss Read, 1980
Summer at Fairacre first published by Michael Joseph 1984
© Miss Read, 1984

First published in one volume as *Fairacre Affairs* in
Michael Joseph 1997
Published in Penguin Books 1998
1 3 5 7 9 10 8 6 4 2

Copyright © Miss Read, 1997
Illustrations © John S. Goodall, 1980, 1984

The moral right of the author has been asserted

Typeset in Monotype Bembo
Printed in England by Clays Ltd, St Ives plc

FOREWORD

Those who maintain that nothing ever happens in the country have never visited Fairacre. Its exterior is serene, to be sure, but beneath its life is bubbling.

It was Dolly Clare who added even more excitement to the daily round by pointing out to Miss Read, the headmistress of Fairacre School, that that establishment was now just 100 years old, and what about celebrating its centenary? Dolly Clare herself had been a pupil at the school, and later the infants' teacher until her retirement. She could add first-hand memories to the project. It was decided, therefore, to give a public performance by the pupils, depicting the history of the school's hundred years. It was a busy time. The school's ancient log book was studied for possible dramatic incidents. Parents and friends contributed suitable costumes, and the children squabbled, like any other actors, about the parts they were called upon to play.

All this activity competed with other matters such as the Caxley Spring Festival, the vicar's bee-keeping problems, and the 'flare-up' of Mrs Pringle's leg which kept her from cleaning duties. The fact that her scatter-brained niece Minnie took her place temporarily simply added to the confusion.

But all went well with the main project, and everyone agreed that the centenary celebrations were a triumph.

Summertime at Fairacre was always lovely when this downland village was at its best. The school children enjoyed lessons in the sunny playground, nature walks on the windy downs, and cricket in the neighbouring farmer's field.

In this particular summer, however, Miss Read found plenty to keep her occupied. Joseph Coggs' mother had to go to hospital

and the boy was left alone. Miss Read took him into her school house for a time, and both enjoyed each other's company. Wedding plans for the infants' teacher, a television programme about a Fairacre poet, the annual fete and flower show, kept the village humming. Yes, this particular summer at Fairacre provided plenty of entertainment.

When the Fairacre series ended with *A Peaceful Retirement*, I had scores of letters asking for more. Omnibus editions, such as this, keep these village characters ever-fresh, and I am delighted to know that they give such pleasure.

Miss Read
May 1997

VILLAGE CENTENARY

To
Mary and Victor
with love

CONTENTS

1	January	3
2	February	21
3	March	43
4	April	58
5	May	81
6	June	101
7	July	117
8	August	143
9	September	167
10	October	187
11	November	198
12	December	212

1 January

It was Miss Clare who first pointed out that Fairacre School was one hundred years old.

It was a bleak Saturday afternoon, and we were enjoying hot buttered toast by the schoolhouse fire. Outside, the playground, and beyond that the fields and distant downs, gleamed dully white in the fading light. It had snowed every day since term started over a week ago, and from the look of the leaden skies, more was to come.

The leafless trees stood stark and black in the still air. Distant hedges smudged the whiteness, and a flock of homing rooks fluttered by like flakes of blackened paper.

It looked like a sketch in charcoal from the schoolhouse window. The only spot of colour in this black and white world came from the crimson glow of a bonfire in Mr Roberts's field next to the school. During the day the flames had leapt and danced while a haze of blue smoke wavered about them, but now that the men were homeward bound the fire was dying down – the one warm, glowing thing to be seen.

Indoors we were snug enough. Between us, in front of the log fire, stood the tea tray, the cups steaming fragrantly with China tea. The lamp glowed from the bookshelf behind Miss Clare's white head, making a halo of her silver hair. Miss Clare knows Fairacre School well, for she was both pupil and teacher there for many years, and was serv-

ing as infants' teacher when I was first appointed as head-mistress, until ill health caused her retirement.

Since she was six years of age she has lived in a small cottage in the next village of Beech Green – a cottage thatched by her father, and later by the young man who inherited her father's thatching tools. She lives alone in her old age. Her childhood friend, Emily Davis, shared the cottage with her until she died some time ago, and although Dolly Clare has adapted herself to solitary living with the courage and sweetness of disposition which has charac-terised all her life, nevertheless, I know that at times she is lonely and appreciates a few hours in someone else's company.

I suspect that the winter is a particularly solitary time for her. In the summer, she busies herself in the cottage garden, or makes the jams and jellies for which she is renowned. Friends from neighbouring villages or from the market town of Caxley drive out to visit her, enjoying a country outing. There are more calls around Christmas, with visi-tors bearing gifts and good wishes. But after Christmas, with excitement past and dark evenings, icy roads, and the blight of winter ailments all taking their toll, the long dark nights hang heavily and I try to fetch Dolly occasionally to share my hearth and modest repast, and to give me the inestimable pleasure of her quiet and wise companionship.

'My mother used to say,' said Miss Clare, stirring her tea, 'that once January was over you could look forward to having a walk after tea in daylight.'

'That really is something to look forward to,' I agreed. 'Let's hope we get an early spring. The children haven't had one playtime outside yet, and they are all suffering from the January blues – a horrid disease.'

'It was always so. I expect the first headmistress said much the same thing a hundred years ago. By the way, are you proposing to celebrate the centenary?'

'To be honest, I hadn't realised we were a hundred until you pointed out the date over the door just now. I suppose we'll have to do something to mark such an occasion.'

'We had quite a bustle, I remember, when we were fifty years old in the thirties,' said Miss Clare. 'Mind you, it made a lot of talk. Some people wanted to take the children to London for the day. The Wembley Exhibition some years before had been a great success with the village people, all bowling up in charabancs, and having a marvellous time.'

'Did you go?'

'Indeed I did, and I think the statue of the dear Prince of Wales in butter was the thing that impressed me most!'

'Were there any other suggestions?'

'Oh, plenty! You know what village decisions are as well as I do. There were weeks of discussion – I was going to say *wrangling* – and dozens of ideas, but in the end we just celebrated with a marvellous tea party, and really everyone was happy.'

'I can see I shall have to start thinking about it. You'll have to let me know what some of those ideas were. One thing sparks off another when it comes to sharing suggestions.'

'No doubt you'll find some help in the log book,' said Miss Clare. 'There were lots of meetings held in the school, and I expect some of the decisions were recorded. And I'll certainly rack my brains for possible ideas. It will be fun to have something to look forward to.'

Her eyes sparkled at the thought, and I could not help feeling that my old friend was more enthusiastic about the

village centenary than I was at the moment. No doubt though, I told myself bracingly, once I got down to it I should feel quite as excited about the celebration of our historic century as did my companion.

Later that evening I drove Miss Clare through white lanes to Beech Green. The roof of her cottage was topped with snow. The moon was rising and the sky was pricked with stars. Already the frost had formed, and we crunched our way up to the front door.

We made our farewells and before I returned to the car I turned to her. 'Let's make another date for the first of February,' I said. 'I'll fetch you after school, and we'll have that walk in daylight after tea, as your mother said.'

'That would be lovely,' agreed Miss Clare, and I left her at her door, the light from the cottage streaming out upon the winter garden, and our breath making little clouds before us as we waved farewell.

As so often happens when one's attention is drawn to something, references to the coming centenary came thick and fast.

Mr Willet, who is our school caretaker, church sexton, general odd job man for the village, producer of hundreds of plants for cottage gardens, as well as chief organiser of our village functions, raised the matter one slippery morning when I was approaching the school across the treacherous playground with considerable caution.

'What you needs,' said Mr Willet, holding out a horny hand to steady me, 'is a stout pair of socks over your shoes. No need to teeter along like a cat on hot bricks if you've got summat to foil the ice. Socks is the answer. It's a good tip, miss.'

I promised to remember.

'We doin' anything about us bein' a hundred this year?' he asked.

'I expect so.'

'Well, it ought to be done proper. Stands to reason, us should have a fitting sort of celebration. A hundred's a hundred. Fairacre'll expect summat good.'

I said that I would start thinking about it, and passed through the school door, almost colliding with Mrs Pringle who was advancing with a large wastepaper basket clutched to her cardigan.

Mrs Pringle is our school cleaner, a martyr to unspecified ailments in her leg, particularly severe when asked to undertake extra work, and a thorn in my flesh. While it is always a pleasure to encounter Mr Willet, to come face to face with Mrs Pringle calls for courage, patience and a bridling of one's tongue. Quite often, when my patience is exhausted, as Herr Hitler was wont to say, we have a sharp argument. Mrs Pringle is invariably the victor in these combats as she is quicker-witted, better-prepared and, I like to think, more intrinsically malevolent than I am.

However, she is an excellent worker, and if one can turn a deaf ear to the accompanying grumbles the results of her labours are splendid. I doubt if any other school in the county has such jet-black tortoise stoves, burnished to a satin finish with blacklead and elbow grease. Woe betide any child who is foolhardy enough to sully their perfection, particularly when they have been 'done up for the summer'. In that term, no matter how low the mercury in the thermometer drops, the stoves remain inviolate, and instead we don our cardigans philosophically.

Once a week she switches her attention to my house

across the playground. I can't think that I am really much more slatternly than the majority of working women, but Mrs Pringle soon makes me think so. The odd crumb on the carpet, the splash of grease on the kitchen stove, or a day's dust on the mantelpiece, are seen instantly by Mrs Pringle's eagle eye and magnified tenfold. The day that she discovered a small crust of mouldy bread 'behind, not even in the bread bin' was a red-letter day for the lady, and I have never been allowed to forget it. When Mrs Pringle tells me that she intends 'to bottom the sitting room', I make hasty plans to be away from home for the allotted time. I prefer to be absent when she finds the assorted objects which have hidden themselves at the sides of the armchair cushions. Life is quite complicated enough for a village schoolmistress without seeking further confrontations.

On this particular occasion, Mrs Pringle put the waste-paper basket on the floor and supported herself on her upturned broom. She looked a little like Britannia with her trident, but less elegant.

'Mr Willet tells me there's a lot of talk about us getting to the century. What, if anything, are we doing about it?'

'Oh, something, I hope,' I said airily. 'But of course it will need some thought. I shall have to have a word with the vicar, and the managers. And Miss Briggs,' I added, as an afterthought.

'Humph!' grunted Mrs Pringle. 'A fat lot of use she'll be!'

I was inclined to agree, but could not countenance our school cleaner criticising my new infants' teacher, straight from college and trailing clouds of educational theories which were enough to curdle one's blood. She had only been with me since the beginning of term, and I sincerely hoped that she would soon settle down and do a little plain

teaching instead of what she was pleased to call 'pastoral counselling'.

I decided to ignore Mrs Pringle's interjection, and changed the subject.

'There doesn't seem to be much soap in the wash basins, Mrs Pringle.'

'And whose fault's that?' demanded the lady. 'There was four pieces put out by my own hands when school started, and if them children is allowed to leave it wasting in the water, that's not my affair.'

She picked up the wastepaper basket and made towards the door, where she turned to face me, her three chins wobbling fiercely.

'I'm not made of soap!' she declared, having the last word as usual, and vanished.

The weather continued to be abominable, with icy roads, fresh snowfalls and great difficulty in getting about.

Nevertheless, on my few visits within sliding distance in the village, I had been questioned by Mr Lamb of Fairacre Post Office, our vicar Gerald Partridge, Henry Mawne our local ornithologist, and a number of parents about the possibility of celebrating the school's centenary.

I took evasive action on all occasions. With the weather as it was, there was quite enough to do keeping warm oneself and seeing that the children, the school building and one's own house were protected as much as possible from the devastating cold. Time enough to think about the centenary when the temperature rose, I decided. However, I did consider one or two ideas as I sat close to my fire in the evenings, my feet on the fender courting chilblains.

What about a concert? With songs, or music from each of the ten decades? The fact that the Fairacre children are not particularly musical, and that I am the only one who can attempt to play the piano – preferably compositions cast in the key of C – and that the audience was equally limited in musical knowledge, seemed to make that idea a non-starter.

Or a pageant? It could be based on the log book, with various scenes. But then there were costumes to devise, and we had no stage, and the thought of putting it on in the playground made me realise the many hazards to be faced. Or a display in the school of its hundred years of history? I suppose one could collect photographs, and even a few old exercise and text books, and the children could have theirs on show, as on open days at the school.

I began to think that Miss Clare's recollection of the fifty years' celebration had much to commend it. A mammoth tea party sounded much more festive than my own doubt-ridden ideas. But surely we could do better than that?

Certainly, Miss Clare had fairly sparkled with enthusiasm when she remembered the trip to Wembley and the sight of the Prince of Wales, unforgettable in butter. What about an outing? One of the historic houses within fifty miles of Fairacre, perhaps? But we could do that at any time, and outings were no great treat these days when most parents owned a car. Besides, it seemed silly to go away for a centenary celebration. The whole point of celebrating a hundred years of Fairacre School's progress was surely to have the occasion at the school, by the school, and for the pupils of that school, both past and present.

At that point in my mental meanderings I noticed that the fire needed more fuel, the coal scuttle was empty, and the log basket in the same sad condition. The clock said twenty to ten. Quite late enough for Fairacre folk to be up!

I put up the fireguard, looked out of the front door at the frosty world, and went thankfully to bed.

Miss Briggs, as Mrs Pringle had forecast, was not much help. Since Miss Clare's departure some years ago, I have had a number of infants' teachers, most of them young and very good company.

In a tiny school like ours, with only two teachers, it is essential that the staff is compatible. In most cases we have enjoyed each other's company, although a certain Miss Jackson, some years ago, was a sore trial, not only as a member of staff, but by being so silly as to fall headlong in

love with the local gamekeeper, in the best tradition of
D. H. Lawrence, and so worrying us all to death.

Miss Briggs had left college in the summer before, had
been unable to obtain a post at the beginning of the school
year in September, but arrived at Fairacre to take up her
appointment in January. Her predecessor, a cheerful young
married woman who had driven from Caxley each day, was
starting a family, and I could only be grateful for the year of
hard work and good company the school and I had enjoyed
during that time.

For the first few days Miss Briggs had little to say to me
but quite a lot, and in a loud hectoring tone, to her charges.
The result was a noisy class, but I decided to bide my time
before I interfered. The girl must find her feet, and I knew
that a certain amount of noise – 'a busy hum', as college
lecturers like to call it – was looked upon as downright
beneficial these days. I am all for 'a busy hum' if it can be
halted whenever the teacher so desires, but too often, I
notice, that is not possible.

Then she was unduly anxious to leave school at three-
thirty, when the infants were sent home. Those with older
brothers and sisters usually waited the extra fifteen minutes
until my class was free, and in the normal way, the infants'
teacher was clearing up her classroom, or buttoning
children into garments, in that quarter of an hour.

On several occasions I had seen her car drive away
smartly at 3.31, and found a little knot of restless infants at
large in their classroom awaiting the release of their kinsfolk
in my room. Twice, parents had risked the icy roads to
speak to her about some particular problem after school,
but the lady had vanished, and I had to pass on their
messages.

Clearly, I should have to speak to the girl before many days passed, and I did not relish it. I was fast coming to the conclusion that she was quite without humour, taciturn – perhaps a sulker when crossed – and decidedly lazy. On the whole, I like young people, and had been lucky with many vivacious and enthusiastic teachers in their first job with me. It seemed sad that I could strike no answering spark from Miss Briggs. 'A fair old lump of a girl,' Mr Willet had opined, three days after her arrival.

I was beginning to think that it just about summed her up.

Towards the end of the month, I began to wonder if a new skylight might be the best way of celebrating Fairacre School's hundredth birthday. For all that time, it seems, the skylight, strategically placed over the obvious site for the headteacher's desk, has let in rain, snow, wind, and the rays of the sun.

Throughout the pages of the log books mention of the skylight crops up:

'A torrential storm this afternoon delayed the pupils' departure from school, and precipitated a deluge through the skylight, damaging some of the children's copybooks and the Holy Bible.' So runs one entry in 1894.

Four years later we read the following somewhat querulous entry:

'Was obliged to shift my desk, as a severe draught from the skylight has resulted in a stiff neck and earache, both occasioning great pain.'

Hardly a year goes by without reference to new glazing

or new woodwork needed by this wretched window. Nothing seems to improve it, and I can vouch for the beastly draught which had dogged all the headteachers, and the diabolical way it lets in water.

Mr Willet takes it all very philosophically and quotes irritatingly 'that what can't be cured must be endured'. The wind had been in the north-east, and I was in a more militant mood. If I have complained once about the skylight, during my term of office, I must have complained twenty times. The result has been some sympathy, a little tinkering, and not a jot of difference in improvement.

After three days of howling draught and wearing a silk scarf round my neck, I sat down to write to the office even more forthrightly than usual about my afflictions. On reading it through I was quite impressed with my firmness of tone, which was tempered with a little pathetic martyrdom, and which surely should bring results. I added a postscript about our hundred years at the mercy of this malevolence overhead, and hoped that something could be done permanently. Cunningly, I pointed out what a drain on the county's economy this must have been over the past century. Every little helps when pleading one's cause.

I posted my letter, wondering if it was a waste of a stamp. Time would tell. On the way back, picking my steps through the slushy snow which was taking its time to disappear, I met Henry Mawne, our eminent ornithologist, who has been a good friend to all in the village.

'How's Simon?' was my first question. His young godson had attended my school for a short time, but his brief stay was ended when a rare albino robin, the pride of the village, came to a sudden death at the boy's hands.

'Settling down well at his prep school,' said Henry, 'and I

may as well tell you now, before you hear it on the grapevine, that his father and Irene Umbleditch are getting married.'

'I am delighted to hear it,' I said warmly. 'He's had so much unhappiness, and he couldn't have anyone nicer than Irene. What's more, Simon is so fond of her too.'

'Well, we're all mightily pleased about it,' said Henry. 'No doubt they'll be visiting us before long, and I hope you will come and see them. They've never forgotten how much you did for Simon. And for us,' he added.

We parted, and I returned home much cheered by this good news. David's first wife had been afflicted by mental illness and eventually had taken her own life. It was time that he and poor young Simon had some sunshine, after the shades of misery which they had suffered.

When I entered my house I found a fat mouse corpse on the hearth rug, and Tibby sitting beside it looking particularly smug. Far from being praised, she was roundly cursed as I put on my wellingtons again, collected the corpse by the tail, and ploughed my way, shuddering, to the boundary hedge and flung the poor thing into Mr Roberts's field.

I often wonder if he notices a particularly fertile patch within a stone's throw of the schoolhouse garden. It is nourished by a steady flow of Tibby's victims, and must have made a substantial difference to his crops over the years.

Like most people in Fairacre, my pupils enjoyed feeding the birds during the winter, and our school bird-table was always well supplied with bread, peanuts and fat.

As well as these more usual offerings, Mrs Pringle supplied mealworms which the robins adored. She had first

undertaken this chore when our famous albino robin appeared on the scene. After his death, in the grievous state of mourning which followed, the supply of mealworms ceased, but to our delight a second albino, probably a grandchild of the first, was seen, and the mealworms were hastily added to the menu.

Not that we saw a great deal of the second white robin. It was obviously less bold than its predecessor, and more cautious in its approach to the food we put out. As Henry Mawne had warned us, the robins and other birds of normal colouring would tend to harass the albino. It certainly seemed timid, but was all the more adored by the children on that account. The first robin had frequently come to the jar of mealworms during the day. The second one only came occasionally, and there were days when it did not appear at all.

One afternoon the children were busy making what they term 'bird pudden', which consists of melted dripping mixed with porridge oats, chopped peanuts and some currants. We had melted the fat in an old saucepan on the tortoise stove, and I kept a weather eye on the door in case Mrs Pringle should walk in unexpectedly and catch us violating her beloved stove.

There was a comfortable smell of cooking in the classroom as Patrick stirred the ingredients with my wooden jam-making spoon. The saucepan by now was on the floor. Nevertheless, when the door opened, I nearly jumped out of my skin with guilt.

Luckily it was only the vicar.

'I seem to have startled you,' said the Reverend Gerald Partridge. 'I suppose I should have knocked.'

'Not at all. I just thought you were Mrs Pringle.'

'*Mrs Pringle*?' echoed the vicar. A look of the utmost perplexity distorted his chubby face. 'Now why on earth should you think that?'

'I'll tell you later,' I said hastily. 'Can I help you?'

The vicar put the plastic bag he had been carrying on my desk.

'A friend of mine who is in the publishing business has most kindly given me some children's books. I think he said he was *remaindering* them – a term I had not heard before, I must confess. Anyway, I thought they might go on the library shelf here.'

'Oh, splendid! We can always do with more books.'

He began to haul them out of the bag which bore the interesting slogan: *Come to Clarissa's For Countless Cosmetics*. It seemed an odd receptacle for a vicar to have acquired.

'I have looked them through,' he said earnestly, 'and they seem quite suitable. Really, these days, one can find the most unnecessarily explicit descriptions of deeds of violence, or of biological matters too advanced for our young children here.'

'I am sure your friend wouldn't give you anything like that,' I said reassuringly, 'but I will read them first if you like.'

'It might be as well,' said the vicar. He suddenly became aware of Patrick's activities.

'Whatever is the boy making?'

I explained, the children joining in with considerable gusto.

'Well, I heartily approve,' he said, when he could make himself heard. 'We must do all we can to keep the birds healthy and strong during this bitter weather.'

He began to walk to the door and I accompanied him. He spoke in a low voice.

'Are you sure that mixture is all right? It looks most indigestible to me.'

'The birds lap it up,' I told him. 'They've been doing so for months now so don't worry.'

He smiled and departed. I had barely returned to the stove preparatory to clearing away any mess before Mrs Pringle caught us, when the vicar reappeared again.

'I forgot to give you a message from my wife. Could you come to the vicarage for a drink on Friday at six-thirty? A few people are coming to discuss the arrangements for the Caxley Spring Festival.'

'Thank you. Yes, please, I should love to come,' I said.

He said goodbye for the second time and we set about the stove with guilty speed. Mrs Pringle's name had not been mentioned by anyone in the classroom, but we all knew what lent energy to our efforts.

That evening my old friend Amy rang me. We first met at college, many years ago, and the friendship has survived separation, a war, Amy's marriage and the considerable differences in our views and temperaments.

Amy is all the things I should like to be – elegant, charming, good-looking, intelligent, rich and much travelled. I can truthfully say that I do not envy her married state, for I am perfectly content with my single one, and in any case James, although a witty and attractive man, is hopelessly susceptible and seems to fall in love at the drop of a hat, which Amy must find tiresome, to say the least of it.

'Come and have some supper,' I invited when she proposed to visit me one evening in the near future.

'Love to, but I must warn you that I'm slimming.'

'Not *again*!' I exclaimed.

'That would have been better left unsaid.'

'Sorry! But honestly, Amy, you are as thin as a rail now. Why bother?'

'My scales which, like the camera, never lie, tell me that I have put on three-quarters of a stone since November.'

'I can't believe it.'

'It's true though. So don't offer me all those lovely things on toast that you usually do. Bread is *out*.'

'What else?'

'Oh, the usual, you know. Starch, sugar, fat, alcohol, and the rest.'

'Is there anything left?'

Amy giggled.

'Well, lettuce is a real treat, and occasionally a *small* orange, and I can have eggs and fish and lean meat, in moderation.'

'The whole thing sounds too damn moderate for me. What would you say to pork chops, roast potatoes and cauliflower with white sauce, followed by chocolate mousse and cream?'

'Don't be disgusting!' said Amy. 'I'm drooling already, but a nice slice of Ryvita and half an apple would be just the thing.'

'I'll join you in the pauper's repast,' I promised nobly, and rang off.

2 February

I remembered my promise to Miss Clare and brought her over to tea on the first of the month.

A gentle thaw had set in and the snow had almost vanished. It tended to turn foggy at night and the roads were still filthy, with little rivulets running at the sides, but it was good to have milder weather during the daytime, and a great relief to let the children run in the playground at break. Under the garden hedge a few brave snowdrops showed. I had picked a bunch for the tea table, the purity of the white flowers contrasting with the dark mottled leaves of the ivy with which I had encircled them.

I was glad that I was not slimming like poor Amy, as we munched our way through anchovy toast and sponge cake. After school I am always ravenous, and how people can bear to go without afternoon tea, and all the delightful ingredients which make it so pleasant, I do not understand.

When we had cleared away, we set out on the first after-tea walk of the year. A few early celandines showed their shield-shaped leaves on the banks at the side of the lane, and it was wonderful to see the green grass again after weeks of depressing whiteness.

A lark sang bravely above, and blackbirds and thrushes fluttered among the bare hedges, scattering the pollen from the hazel catkins that nodded in the light breeze. In the paddock near Mr Roberts's farmhouse, sixty or seventy

ewes, heavily in lamb, grazed ponderously upon the newly disclosed grass. There was a wonderful feeling of new life in the air despite the naked trees, the bare ploughed fields and the miry lane we walked.

'I know most people dislike the month of February,' said Miss Clare, as we returned, 'but I always welcome it. With the shortest day well behind us, and the first whiff of spring about, I begin to feel hopeful again.'

'Your mother was quite right,' I told her. 'Everyone should have an after-tea walk on February the first. It's the finest antidote to the January blues I've come across.'

Dolly Clare laughed, and slipped her frail arm through mine. It was sharply borne in upon me how light and thin she had become during the last few years. Her bones must be as brittle as a bird's. Would my old friend survive to see the next spring? Would we share another first-of-February celebratory walk?

I hoped with all my heart that we might.

On the following Friday, I dutifully made my way to the vicarage. I had not heard any more about the Caxley Spring Festival which the vicar had mentioned, and wondered exactly how our small downland village, some miles from the market town, would become involved.

There were about twenty people in the Partridges' drawing room, and only two were strangers to me. Diana Hale, wife of a retired schoolmaster, was there. Their house, Tyler's Row, once four shabby cottages, is one of the show places of our village, and she and her husband are tireless in their good works.

I was pleasantly surprised, too, to see Miriam Quinn who came to live in Fairacre a few years ago. She is a most

efficient secretary to a businessman in Caxley, likes a quiet life, and is somewhat reserved.

Like most newcomers to a village, I know that Miss Quinn was approached by most of the village organisations when she first took up residence at Holly Lodge on the outskirts of Fairacre, for her qualities of hard work and intelligence had gone before her and everyone said, as I find to my cost as a spinster, that a single woman must have time on her hands and enjoy a nice bit of company. Holly Lodge is the home of Joan Benson, a sprightly widow, and she and her lodger seem very happy together. Joan was not at the meeting, and I wondered how it was that Miriam Quinn had been corraled with the rest of us.

It was soon made clear. The vicar, who was acting as chairman, introduced the two strangers as the organisers of the Festival in Caxley, and Miss Quinn as Fairacre's representative.

We all sat back, sherry in hand, to listen obediently.

The Arts in Caxley, one of the strangers told us with some severity, were sadly neglected, and the proposed Festival was to bring them to the notice of Caxley's citizens and those who lived nearby. Let him add, he said (and who were we to stop him?), that he was not accusing Caxley people of *Philistinism* or *Cruelty to Creative Artists*, but merely of *Ignorance* and *Apathy*.

There was a great fund of natural talent in Caxley – and its surrounds, he put in hastily – and there would be two plays by local playwrights put on at the Corn Exchange, several concerts at the parish church, and exhibitions of painting, embroidery and other crafts at various large buildings in the town, and outside.

'What happens to the money?' Mr Roberts, our local

farmer, asked bluntly. Farmers are noted for their realistic approach to life, and ours is no exception.

The speaker looked a little surprised by the interjection of such a materialistic enquiry in the midst of his eulogy about Caxley's artistic aspirations, but rallied bravely.

'I was just coming to that. Any profits will go to three local charities so that a great many people will benefit. They are named in the leaflets which we are distributing at this meeting.'

Mr Roberts grunted in acknowledgement, and the speaker resumed his talk. Miriam Quinn's involvement was then revealed, and she gave a sensible description of her part in the Festival.

'I'm really here to get suggestions,' she said. 'One way of helping, particularly for us in the country, is by opening our gardens. The vicar has already offered to have his open, and so has Mr Mawne. We can arrange a date to suit us all, and in May, when the Festival takes place, our gardens here are at their best.'

'What about the schoolchildren having a maypole? Dancing and singing and all that?' called out someone, well hidden from me.

Miriam Quinn looked at me hopefully.

'I'll think about it,' I said circumspectly. What with the centenary, and the skylight waiting to be repaired, I had some reservations about a May Day celebration as well.

'Beech Green had a street fair once,' said somebody.

'And only once,' said her neighbour. 'The traffic was something awful when Mr Miller's tractor broke down where the road narrows.'

The vicar, adept at handling situations like this, suggested that any ideas might be given to Miss Quinn at the end of

the meeting. He was quite sure, he added, that she would receive every possible support from Fairacre in the part that the village would play in this excellent enterprise.

Were there any more questions?

At this, as always, silence fell upon the gathering. Sherry glasses were refilled, the guests circulated again, and we all knew, as we chattered of everything under the sun bar the matter in hand, that the Caxley Spring Festival would get plenty of attention once the meeting had dispersed.

Amy paid her visit to me one evening when the wind was scouring the downs, whistling through keyholes and making the schoolhouse shudder beneath its onslaughts.

Out in the garden the bare branches tossed up and down, and dead leaves flurried hither and thither across the grass. Overhead the rooks had battled their way home at dusk, finding it difficult to keep on course.

But my fire burned brightly in the roaring draught and Tibby, on her back, presented her stomach to the warmth, paws above her head. We were pretty snug within, whatever the weather did outside.

Amy arrived in a new suede coat of dark brown and some elegant shoes that I had not seen before. She held a bowl of pink hyacinths in her hands.

'Coals to Newcastle, I expect. I know you do well with bulbs.'

'Not a bit of it! Mine are over, and you couldn't have brought anything more welcome, Amy dear. Come in, out of this vile wind.'

She divested herself of the beautiful coat, and exclaimed with pleasure at the fire.

'I've been trying to do without one. After all, the central

heating should really be enough – heaven knows it costs a small fortune to run – but there's something rather *soulless* about the electric fire which I'm forced to put on for an hour or two, now and then.'

'Well, you know me, Amy. I light a fire at the drop of a hat. I can always console myself with the thought that I have no central heating to make me feel guilty.'

'I've felt the cold far more this winter,' said Amy, stroking Tibby's stomach. 'Whether it's *anno domini* or just this slimming business, I can't tell. A bit of each, I expect.'

'How's the poundage going?'

'Much too slowly. If only I habitually drank gallons of beer, or ate pounds of chocolate, I should find it quite easy to cut down the calories, but I eat like a bird.'

'Not worms, I hope.'

'Don't be facetious, dear. You know what I mean. I'm heartily sick of salad and cold meat.'

'Well, that's what you've got tonight. Unless you'd rather have a boiled egg.'

'Either would be delicious,' said Amy, lying bravely. 'Do you know, as a child, I refused to eat salad, particularly tomatoes.'

'My *bête noir* was beetroot,' I recalled. 'Now I love it, and coffee. I didn't touch it until we went to college. I'm sure tastes change as one goes through life.'

'They certainly do. But perhaps it's simply our aging digestive systems, do you think? I used to adore potted shrimps, but these days they go down like greased nails, and I have terrible indigestion.'

'We could have a nice bowl of thin gruel on our laps here,' I remarked, 'if you feel in such an advanced state of decay.'

'Not likely!' said Amy. 'Besides, gruel is fattening.'

'Who was it said that anything one enjoys turns out to be fattening or immoral?'

'No idea, but he knew what he was talking about,' said Amy with feeling.

Over our frugal repast, the conversation turned to Caxley's Festival. I told Amy about Miss Quinn's part in it and our dearth of suggestions in Fairacre.

'Well, in an expansive moment I agreed to have a poetry reading in my house. Do you think anyone will come?'

'The poets will, presumably.'

'That's what I'm afraid of. I mean, shall I be stuck with half a dozen sensitive types, possibly all jealous of each other and with no audience to listen to them? How can I be sure we get a nice, kind, attentive crowd?'

'They'll come,' I assured her. 'Lots of people will simply come to see your house and garden, poets or no poets. Others will be culture-vultures, and game to listen to anything in the cause of Art, and others will feel they can't waste the ticket.'

'And there are bound to be the poets' relations,' agreed Amy, looking more hopeful. 'I wonder if we could organise a group from the evening classes in Caxley? You know the sort doing English Literature? The Beowulf bunch, for instance.'

'"Weave we the warp. The woof is wub" sort of thing, you mean? I don't see why not. English Literature classes should swell the audience nicely, and if you're short, I'll come and sit in the front row.'

'I'm counting on you, anyway,' said Amy, selecting a large stick of celery, 'to pass round the sausage rolls.'

'You'll need something far more spiritual than sausage rolls,' I told her. 'You'll have to have nectar and ambrosia,

and lots of "beaded bubbles winking at the brim" for a poetry evening.'

'We'll have lashings of the latter,' promised Amy, and crunched into the celery.

It was still blowing a gale when Amy left me at about nine-thirty. I saw by the light of her headlamps that a sizable branch had been torn from the horse chestnut tree in the garden, and the path was strewn with twigs and dead leaves. It was going to be pretty draughty sitting under that skylight tomorrow, I thought, if this weather continued.

I sat down by the fire again, and had a belated look at the daily papers. It was the usual conglomeration of strike threats, travel delays, violence, war and sudden death, and the most peaceful reading was the crossword and the obituaries.

The wind howled like a banshee and I found it distinctly unnerving. With Amy for company I had not noticed the vicious elements outside. Now, alone and responsible for any damage done, I became unusually jittery.

A cupboard door by the fireplace creaked slowly open, and I felt my blood pressure rising. Would a yellow clawlike hand with immensely long nails, Chinese fashion, appear round it? Or a black hand perhaps, holding a dagger? Or a white one dangling a knuckle duster?

'You've been reading too many bloods,' I thought, and steeled myself to shut the door firmly. At the same moment, Tibby rose, fur bristling, and advanced towards the kitchen door, growling horribly. I watched her, mesmerised. Could someone have broken in? Had I locked the back door earlier? Probably not, we are a trusting lot in Fairacre, and, under cover of the appalling racket outside it would be quite easy for someone to gain entry.

What should I do? Should I ring Caxley police? Should I arm myself with the poker and fight it out? Reason told me that any burglar, no matter how puny, could easily twist a weapon out of my grasp and use it to belabour me.

Surely I had read somewhere that it was best to offer no resistance. After all, hospitals are severely overcrowded without unnecessary casualties awaiting admission. If it were money that the intruder wanted he was going to be unlucky. I might rustle up three pounds or so, but that would be the most I could find in the schoolhouse at short notice. True, Aunt Clara's seed pearls might be acceptable, but that would constitute the bulk of my jewellery.

I took a deep breath, and flung open the door. The kitchen was as quiet as the grave. Tibby sat down and began to wash her face in the most maddeningly unconcerned fashion.

'Time I was in bed,' I told her, and went.

To my surprise, I had a letter from the office about the skylight. Obviously my pleas had touched some compassionate heart, and the gist of the reply was that this particular item, under 'minor works', would be treated as an emergency, and that Mr Reginald Thorn, of the Nook, Beech Green, had been instructed to call and examine the offending structure.

'Should have thought the office could've found someone with a bit more up top than old Reg,' commented Mr Willet, when I imparted the good news. 'Proper dog's dinner he'll make of it. I reckon I'd make a better job of it meself.'

I too had no doubts on that score, for Mr Willet's handiwork, whether with seedlings, paintbrush or bolts and

screws, is always beautifully done. But the office had appointed Reg Thorn and that was that.

'When do you think he'll come?'

Mr Willet pushed back his cap to scratch his head.

'Now that's asking! I know for a fac' he's making a dresser for that new chap at Beech Green post office, and Mrs Mawne is going up the wall about some shelving he promised her last autumn and hasn't never done yet.'

'He's like that, is he?'

Mr Willet pursed his mouth judicially.

'Well, he's not a bad sort of chap, old Reg, but he's no flier. I mean, he *says* he'll do summat, and he means it too,

but his trouble is he can't say "No" to no one, so the work sort of piles up.'

'So you reckon it'll be the summer before he gets round to our skylight?'

'Now, I'm not saying that. This bein' an office job like, and with forms and that to fill in, well, it might make old Reg get a move on. On the other hand, if all the other people get a bit whacky, and bully him, maybe he'll do their jobs to keep 'em happy. There's no telling.'

He raised his voice to a bull-like roar.

'Get off that there coke, you young devils, or I'll tan the skin off of your backsides, and you can tell your mums and dads why I done it!'

Mr Willet's method of dealing with the young might not find favour with modern psychologists, but it clears the coke pile in record time.

Whether Reg Thorn was awed by the county's official letter, or simply wished for a change of job, thus evading his earlier customers who were breathing fire, no one will ever know. But the outcome was decidedly cheering for me. Reg Thorn arrived within the week just as we were dishing out minced lamb (alleged – I suspected some manmade fibre) and mashed swede.

He was a tall lantern-jawed fellow, and said very little. He gazed up at the skylight with an expression of gloom. I had served all the children, and dispatched the containers to the lobby to await Mrs Pringle's ministrations, before he spoke.

'Rotted,' he said.

I agreed.

He sighed heavily.

'Still leaks?'

'It's been doing it for nearly a hundred years.'

'Ah! Looks like it.'

He remained rooted to the spot, very much in the way of the children returning their plates, but I did not like to say so. At length, he spoke again.

'Best see outside. All right?'

'Yes indeed. Mr Willet's ladder is by the wall if you want it.'

'Got me own. Insurance, see.'

To my relief he vanished, only to reappear framed in the skylight some minutes later. He appeared to be gouging pieces of wood from the window frame, and I only hoped that this operation would not add to the draught trouble.

I served helpings of crimson jelly decorated with blobs of rather nasty artificial cream. It is the children's favourite sweet and I was kept so busy scraping the tin for second helpings that I was quite startled to see Reg again at my elbow.

'Needs a dormer,' he shouted above the clatter.

'Won't that be expensive?'

'Yes.'

'Well, it's up to the people at the office,' I shouted back. 'You can only tell them what you think.'

'Ah!' agreed Reg, and plodded off towards the door.

'My mum,' said Patrick conversationally, 'says old Reg don't get nothin' done in a month of Sundays.'

'That will do,' I replied witheringly. Privately, I feared that Patrick's mum was probably dead right.

Time alone would tell.

There is a widespread belief among town dwellers that remarkably little happens in the country. As any villager

will tell you, the amount of activity that goes on is quite exhausting.

I am not thinking of the agricultural pursuits by which most of us get our living, but of the social side of life. What with the Women's Institute, amateur dramatics, various regular church activities such as choir practice and arranging the flowers, Cubs and Brownies for the younger people, fêtes, jumble sales and whist drives, one could be out every night of the week if one so wished.

As village schoolmistress I try not to take on too much during term time, although I do my best to make amends in the holidays, but nevertheless one has to face pressing requests for such things as two dozen sausage rolls for the Fur and Feather Whist Drive, or a raffle prize for the Cubs' Social.

It was no surprise then, when Mrs Pringle approached me one morning and asked if I would do her a favour. This polite phrase, accompanied by a slight lessening of malevolence in her expression, was the prelude to my whipping up a sponge for some cause dear to her stony heart, I guessed.

I was right, or nearly so.

'I'm helping Mrs Benson with Cruelty to Children,' she announced. 'Could you give us a bottle of something? It's a good cause, this Cruelty to Children.'

I wondered if a bottle of arsenic, or even castor oil, would be fitting in the circumstances.

'Anything, Mrs Benson says, from whisky to shampoo. Or even homemade wine,' she added.

At that moment the children surged in in a state of wild excitement.

'It's snowing, miss,' they yelled fortissimo.

In the stampede, Ernest stood heavily and painfully upon my foot.

'I'll find you something,' I promised Mrs Pringle, as I retired, wincing.

And if ever anyone needs support for the Prevention of Cruelty to Teachers, I thought, nursing my wounds, I shall be in the forefront.

Fortunately the snow was not severe. One or two flurries during the afternoon soon died out, leaving the playground wet but not white, for which I was thankful. It was good to get home again by the fire on such a cheerless day. I was relishing a cup of tea and Tibby's welcoming purrs, when Mrs Willet arrived.

She is a neat quiet little person and renowned in Fairacre for her domestic efficiency. Mrs Willet's sponge cakes and home-made jam invariably take first prizes at our Flower Show, and if there were awards for laundry work and exquisite mending she would doubtless take those too.

She accepted a cup of tea after some demurring and sat rather primly on the edge of her chair. Tibby rubbed round her lisle-clad legs affectionately, and soon Mrs Willet began to look more relaxed.

'Has Mrs Pringle asked for a bottle?' she said at last.

'Yes. I can find her one quite easily.'

This sounded as though I had a cellar stuffed with strong drink, and as I knew that Mrs Willet and her husband were staunch teetotallers I wondered if she would disapprove.

'Then I hardly like to ask you for anything more, Miss Read, but the truth is I've taken on a book stall at this bazaar of Mrs Benson's, and I wondered if you could spare one.'

'You can have a dozen,' I cried. 'Probably two dozen. I'll bring them down during the week.'

'Bob'll do that,' Mrs Willet assured me. 'You put 'em in a sack, and he'll hump 'em home all right.'

I was not too happy about my books – even rejected ones – ending up in a sack, but said I would have a word with Mr Willet when they were ready.

'And what's happening about the centenary?' asked Mrs Willet. 'Any plans?'

'Not *firm* ones,' I prevaricated. 'Do you remember much about the school when you were here?'

'Quite a bit, though I started school in Caxley. We didn't move out to Fairacre until the end of the Great War, some-time in 1918. I had an auntie that lived in one of those cottages near the post office.'

'What brought you from Caxley?'

'Lack of money,' said Mrs Willet sadly. 'My dad was killed in the January in France, and Mum had three of us at home with her. Mum got a good job helping at the Manor here, so we up-sticks and came to Fairacre.'

'A big change for you.'

'We liked it. Mr Hope was the headmaster here then, and a good kind chap he was although he was on the bottle then, poor soul, and that was the ruin of him. Fairacre was a lot different then – more shops and that. There was a smithy and two bakers, as well as a butcher and the stores. I used to have my dinner at the baker's sometimes.'

'Why was that?'

'Well, once a week my mum and auntie had to stay all day at the Manor. I believe Auntie did a bit of dressmaking there, and Mum had to do the windows. Something extra anyway. Most of the children took sandwiches to school,

but there was a lot of horseplay among the big boys and Mr Hope didn't come over to stop 'em, as by rights he should've done. I was fair scared, so Mum made an arrangement that I had two boiled eggs and bread and butter and a cake at Webster's, on the day she was up the Manor.'

'What happened to the other two children?'

'Oh, they were younger, not school age, and went with Mum and Auntie. So they had their dinner in the Manor kitchen. Best meal of the week, Mum said. Always a cut off the joint and vegetables from the kitchen garden, and a great fruit pie to follow, but I wasn't envious. I felt like a queen having my boiled eggs at the shop.'

'With the baker's family?'

'Oh no! Much better than that! There were two or three marble-topped tables for customers. Not that anyone ever came in to eat when I was there, but the Websters did teas for these cyclists that were all about, and ramblers, as they were called before they turned into hikers. Sometimes someone from the village would pop in for a loaf or a pennorth of yeast, and then I'd feel very superior being waited on. My meal cost sixpence, I remember, and I could choose any cake I liked from the window, after the eggs and bread and butter.'

'And what did you choose?'

'Always a doughnut. It was either that, or a currant bun or a queen cake. I reckoned a doughnut was the best value. I had that with a glass of milk. Not bad for sixpence.'

I agreed. Mrs Willet's eyes became dreamy as she looked back almost sixty years.

'There was a lovely picture pinned up on the wall. I think it was an advertisement for Mazawattee tea. There was this lady in a long skirt and a fur stole, with a beautiful hat on top

with her Queen Alexandra fluffy fringe just showing. She was sitting on a park bench, and dangling a little parcel, with "Mazawattee" written on it, from one finger. She had on the most beautiful long suede gloves. I often wondered why she was sitting on a park bench in such gorgeous clothes. It might have dirtied them.'

'Probably collapsed exhausted after carrying a quarter of tea,' I suggested.

'She had a lovely face,' went on Mrs Willet. 'I thought I should like to look like that when I was grown up. But there, it never happened.'

She put down her cup, and began to get up.

'How I do run on! But it's nice to talk of old times. Bob thinks it's a waste of time to hark back, but I enjoy it. That's why I hope you'll be able to think of something for the centenary. We've got a lot to be thankful for in this village, and the school's the real centre of it.'

'It's good to hear you say so,' I told her. 'Never fear! We'll do the thing in style. And I won't forget the books.'

I showed her out into the murky winter dusk, and returned to my fire with much to think about. One day soon, I told myself, I must look through the school log books for some inspiration.

But before I had a chance to do this, Miss Briggs put forward an idea of her own.

'What about dressing the children in the costume of the 1880s, and making the schoolroom much as it was then? We could have copybooks, with pot hooks and hangers, and let them chant their tables, and even have a cane on the teacher's desk.'

I agreed that such a *tableau vivant* would no doubt appeal

to the parents, but wondered if it might be rather ambitious.

'Why?' demanded Miss Briggs.

'Rigging out the children, for one thing. Plenty of parents could make the clothes for one, say, but I can't see big families like the Coggses even beginning.'

Miss Briggs began to look mutinous, and I hastily made amends.

'But I do like the idea, and we'll keep it in mind. After all, any brainwaves we have will probably need to be modified. We must remember, though, that space is limited, and if all the children are present there won't be a lot of room for grown-ups.'

My assistant looked slightly less aggressive, and I began to wonder if this would be a good opportunity to discuss her too-prompt departure after school, but decided to postpone the task, as a bevy of infants swarmed in bearing one of their number with a bleeding knee, all bawling as fiercely as the wounded one. It was not the time for a delicate matter of school discipline, but I determined to broach it before the week was out.

Later that day, Miss Briggs approached me, starry-eyed.

'I've had another idea. Perhaps the vicar would dress up as the Reverend Stephen Anderson-Williams. I see from the log book that he was here for the first ten years of the school's existence, and seemed to pop in daily.'

I hardly liked to tell her, after throwing cold water on her earlier idea, that the reverend gentleman she had named was still remembered by the older generation, as the man who had left a perfectly good wife and six young children at his vicarage to run off with a sloe-eyed beauty from Beech Green. He was never seen again, but it was believed that he and his inamorata made a home together in Belgium.

Somehow, I doubted if the present vicar would wish to portray him in our revels. The Reverend Stephen Anderson-Williams would be better forgotten in my opinion, especially as some of his descendants still lived in the Caxley area.

'It's quite a thought,' I said guardedly, and we left it at that.

There was a sudden lull in the bleak weather, and for the best part of a week the sky was a pellucid blue, and the wind from the downs was warm and balmy. The catkins fluttered in the hedge. Bulbs thrust their stubby noses through the soil, and the birds, bright in their courting finery, began looking for nesting places.

We all felt ten years younger, and the children were as happy as sandboys now that they could play outside. Even Mrs Pringle looked a little less dour and sported a new flowered overall.

'Minnie give it to me for Christmas,' she said, when I admired it. 'I was keeping it for best, but what with the sun and this nice bit of spring, I thought why not wear it?'

'Why not indeed,' I agreed.

'Besides,' she added, 'what's the good of hoarding things? I mean, for all we know we may be knocked down by a bus before we have a chance to use our good stuff.'

This sounded more like Mrs Pringle to me. 'Always merry and bright,' as someone sang lugubriously in *The Arcadians*, but at least she had shown herself momentarily in tune with the spring sunshine around her. One must be thankful for small mercies.

I took advantage of this blessing of early warmth and ushered the children out for an afternoon walk. The rooks

were wheeling about the high trees, and one or two little birds flew across our path, trailing dry grass and moss in their beaks, intent upon their nest building. There was even a bold bumble bee investigating the ivy on the churchyard wall, and someone said the frogspawn might be starting in the pond. Of course we had to go and see, but there was none there.

I looked at my watch. It said almost three-thirty, and we set off for school at a brisk pace. There were several things to put away before Mrs Pringle appeared, and grace to be sung before the end of school at a quarter to four.

As we approached the school gate, Miss Briggs's little car appeared. The children scattered to left and right, but I stood my ground. The church clock said three-thirty exactly, and so did my watch.

Miss Briggs peered from the side window.

'Can you spare a minute?' I said. She looked a little annoyed, but duly reversed into the playground.

The children and I entered the school, tidied up, sang: *Now the day is over* and wished each other good afternoon.

Miss Briggs came into the room as the last of the footsteps died away. It was not quite ten to four.

No time like the present, I thought, and invited her to sit down.

'I oughtn't to stop,' she said. 'I'm picking up a friend at four o'clock.'

'This won't take a minute,' I promised her, and began to point out the necessity of staying until all her children were accounted for at the end of the day.

'But the hours are nine till three-thirty,' she protested.

'Not in teaching, they aren't,' I assured her. 'The children are in your care. What would have happened if one had

injured himself before I got back? There were seven or eight infants under seven left to their own devices.'

She did not appear particularly contrite, or even fully aware of having been at fault, but I made it clear that she must not leave until my children had collected their younger brothers and sisters, and she went off looking more irritated than chastened.

Well, I had said my piece, I told myself, locking my desk drawers. Now it was up to my assistant to profit from it.

3 March

The 'soft weather', as the Irish say, remained with us, and March came in like the lamb rather than the lion. I was pottering about in the garden after tea, admiring the swelling buds on the lilac bushes, when a car stopped at the gate, and out stepped Miss Quinn.

The little I know of Miriam Quinn I like. She is an extremely hard-working and efficient secretary to an eminant industrialist whose offices are in Caxley. So far, she has managed to stay fairly clear of the multitudinous activities in the village, and one rarely sees her.

She and Joan Benson, her landlady at Holly Lodge, are good friends despite their difference in temperament. Joan, since her husband died recently, has taken on all kinds of public work in Fairacre, and her good humour has endeared her to us all.

This visit from Miriam, I surmised, was something to do with the Caxley Festival. I took her indoors with pleasure and offered her a drink, but she shook her head.

'We've just had a farewell party for one of our staff at the office,' she told me, 'and I've had quite enough for one evening, I think.' She went on to explain her visit which, as I had guessed, was about the festival.

'I hope you aren't going to ask me to open my garden,' I said. 'Not that people might be delighted to see more weeds than in their own, but I can't compete with real gardeners.'

She laughed, and I thought how attractive she was when her usually serious expression was lit by laughter.

'Don't worry! It's something far less arduous. We're going to have teas in the village hall, and I'm trying to find out who would be willing to help. Joan's in charge, but would need about a dozen people to make a rota.'

'Oh, I'll willingly help,' I cried, much relieved. 'And if you want a cake, I am rather a dab hand at an almond one.'

'Splendid!' she said, producing a notebook and pencil. I noticed how neat the list was, and how quickly she made her notes. Obviously a treasure in the office at Caxley. No wonder she had been importuned by all the local clubs for help.

'Joan will be so grateful. We've got four names so far, including Mrs Willet who is marvellous, I hear.'

'You couldn't do better,' I assured her.

'What a pretty house this is,' said Miriam.

'I love it,' I said, 'but the snag is, of course, that it's a tied house and I really ought to look for somewhere else for my old age. I keep putting it off, which is quite mad, as house prices get more impossible each week.'

'It's not easy to find a place,' she agreed.

'Would you like to see the rest of it?'

'I'd love to. Houses are a great interest of mine. I was so lucky to find the annexe at Holly Lodge. Nothing in Caxley could compare with it.'

She followed me through the few rooms of the school-house and seemed enchanted with all she saw, pausing at the bedroom windows to exclaim at the superb views which I am lucky enough to enjoy.

'I find this downland country marvellously exhilarating,' she said. 'When I get back from Caxley I feel pretty jaded,

but ten minutes in this air, and with these views, and I'm a new woman. The thought of leaving it fills me with despair.'

'But you don't have to leave it, do you?' I asked, puzzled.

She made a grimace.

'I don't know. It will soon be common knowledge, I expect, so that I don't think I'm betraying confidences. Joan is probably moving nearer her daughter whenever anything suitable turns up. She will sell Holly Lodge then, of course. I suppose I could stay on, but I shouldn't care to live at such close quarters with strangers, and in any case Joan would get a much better price without a tenant in the place.'

'She'll be missed,' I said. 'Let's hope she won't have to go for some time. Isn't she happy here?'

'Very happy. But she's about seventy, and getting less and less fond of driving, and I think her daughter feels she should be at hand if her mother were ill. It's all very sensible and understandable, but I dread her going, and dread house-hunting all over again even more.'

'Well, it was nice of you to tell me, and I won't say anything until I hear from other people that it's known in the village. Not that that will take long, knowing Fairacre,' I added.

Miriam laughed and made for the door.

'No secrets in a village!' she agreed, and departed down the path to the car.

One morning, soon after Miriam Quinn's visit, Reg Thorn appeared again with two men from the education office. They wanted to inspect the skylight again, and to see if the roof would stand a more solid structure built upon it.

This sounded hopeful to me. Could Fairacre School really be getting a proper dormer window to replace our temperamental skylight after a hundred years? I readily gave my permission for them to clamber about on the roof, and they departed.

Luckily, the weather was still fine, and apart from a good deal of thumping overhead which produced a light shower of flaked paint, dead leaves and an assortment of defunct wasps, spiders and earwigs upon my desk, we managed to continue our lessons in comparative peace.

The three vanished just before playtime, and I listened to the children's comments as they imbibed their morning milk.

'I bet them two men was telling ol' Reg the best way to do it.'

'What's a dormer anyway?'

'Do it have curtains like a proper window?'

'My auntie up Caxley says dormers lets in the draught something cruel.'

'D'you reckon we'll get it by the summer?'

'You'll be lucky! What with ol' Reg doin' it?'

It was like hearing their parents talking. Fairacre loves a new topic. The replacement of our skylight was going to keep everyone happy for a long time to come.

But not too long, I fervently hoped. I had a feeling that the fine weather would break the minute the glass was removed.

Mr Willet was of the same opinion. He was surveying the school roof when I went across to my house during the dinner hour.

'That'll never stand nothin' stronger than a skylight, that roof,' he asserted. 'Stands to reason, all that was gone into

when this place was built. If it wouldn't bear the weight then, when them beams was new, what chance will it have now?'

'Perhaps it was too expensive to have a proper window put in then,' I hazarded.

'What, with all the money the Hurleys put up to help pay for it? They'd not grudge a few more quid to make the school ship-shape and Bristol fashion. Always had to be the best for the Hurleys.'

'Come and look at my broad beans,' I urged, anxious to change the subject, and to collect a book of Greek myths to read to the children in the afternoon.

He followed me obediently as I led the way.

He studied my two rows of beans with a serious expression.

'You got blackfly comin' on,' he said. 'And them weeds is doing all right too. I better come up for an hour this evening.'

'Thank you,' I said. 'I'd be glad of your help. Have a look round while I nip in to fetch a book.'

He was still plodding morosely round the vegetable patch when I returned. It was unlike him to look so depressed. Could it be the state of my garden? I had been thinking that it looked unusually tidy. Not that it could hold a candle to Mr Willet's own plot, which was always a miracle of neatness and fertility, but not at all bad by my lowly standards.

'See you this evening then,' I said to the pacing figure.

'Any time suits me.'

'Ah!' answered Mr Willet absently, kicking a stone from the grass on to the garden bed. 'I tell you, Miss Read, that skylight was *right* for that roof. The Hurleys would've

known, and I'll wager old Reg don't. It's not going to be as simple as they makes out.'

So it was the skylight that was casting this unaccustomed gloom upon Mr Willet! I felt mightily relieved.

'Well, cheer up,' I said, making my way towards the playground. 'That's Reg's look-out, isn't it?'

'It'll be mine before the pesky thing's been up a month or two,' forecast my caretaker. 'I'm the mug as always has to clear up other folk's mess!'

As he was still eyeing my weeds, I forebore to comment, but carried my Greek myths across to school in prudent silence.

News of Joan Benson's departure from Holly Lodge was very soon common gossip in the village, as Miriam had forecast.

The first to tell me was the vicar. 'A grievous loss!' he said. 'We were all so delighted when she and her husband and mother arrived, but now we must lose the last of the three. I wonder when she is moving?'

I was unable to tell him, but Mrs Pringle told me an hour or two later.

'Getting down to her daughter's as soon as she can,' she informed me. 'Going to look out for a little place down there. A bungalow, I don't doubt. Stairs get somethin' cruel as you get on, and she's got a touch of arthritis already.'

I said, somewhat shortly, that it was the first I had heard of it.

Mrs Pringle continued undismayed: 'Holly Lodge ought to fetch a good price on the market. Nice garden and that, and you can call your soul your own with that holly hedge

all round. Don't get no busybodies peering in like I do at home.'

This was a side swipe at her immediate neighbour, and I was careful to make no comment. It would soon have got back in Fairacre, and I do my best to steer a steady course.

'I wonder what Miss Quinn will do?' was her next surmise. 'She won't find it easy to find as quiet a place as that little flat of hers, and I don't suppose she earns enough to buy anything outright, do you?'

'I have no knowledge of Miss Quinn's income nor of her future plans,' I said stiffly. Was there no way of stopping this gossip? Evidently not, for the lady continued.

'That little hovel near Miss Waters is in *The Caxley Chronicle* this week for thirty thousand pounds. I ask you! Who'd buy that shack anyway? I can remember when old Perce Tilling bought it for three hundred pounds, and then we told him a fool and his money was soon parted. Not that Perce cared. He'd just won a packet at Caxley races, and his old auntie who kept the shop at Beech Green had just died, and they found over four hundred under the mattress when they lifted her into her coffin, so Perce got that as well. Not fair really, as that daughter of hers, although no better than she should be when it came to American soldiers, did do her best by her mum, and kept her lovely and clean, right to the end.'

'You got a minute?' shouted Mr Willet from the door. Once again he was my saviour, and I escaped thankfully from Mrs Pringle's reminiscences.

Within the week I had been told by Mr Lamb at the post office that it was a great shame Mrs Benson had got to give up. The place was too big for her, no doubt, now her

husband and mother were dead. Still, it should fetch a tidy sum these days. He reckoned anything between thirty and forty thousand.

The butcher, cleaving lamb chops, told me between hacks that it was a pity Mrs Benson's daughter was in trouble of some sort, and such a nice old lady had got to sell up and go to help. On the other hand, this was the right time to sell, and she would probably clear forty or fifty thousand.

Mr Roberts, the farmer, said that we should miss Joan Benson. She'd been a nice body to have in the village, and he was sorry to hear her health was obliging her to leave Holly Lodge. Nevertheless, that was a tidy little property and on a nice bit of rich soil, as his father had always said, a fair treat for root crops. To his mind it should fetch somewhere round fifty thousand.

The price of property in our village has always occasioned the greatest interest. It was obvious that the amount finally given for Holly Lodge would provide Fairacre with an enthralling topic in the future.

It so happened that I met Joan Benson returning from the grocer's shop about this time. She was hurrying along, as round and cheerful as a robin, and put down her basket to talk to me.

'I've just been told,' she said, looking amused, 'that my house should fetch between fifty and sixty thousand pounds. As it isn't even on the market yet, I'm rather tickled. Does Fairacre always rush ahead like this with conjectures?'

'Always,' I told her. 'It's all part of the fun!'

Amy rang up one evening to invite me to dinner to meet the poets who were to take part in the Caxley Festival in May.

'I thought it would be a good idea for them to see where it would be held, and perhaps to meet each other.'

'How many are there?'

'Well, I'm sorry to say I can only rustle up a couple. There were going to be four, but one is having a nervous break-down, poor thing, and the other is touring the United States with his poetry programme. What stamina!'

'Americans are noted for their strength and energy,' I told her.

'Not the *Americans*! The poet, I meant. He looks such a weed too, as though walking up the steps of Caxley Town Hall would finish him off, but there he is – all eight stone of him – bouncing about all over America. I can't get over it. Not that Tim Ferdinand, who will be coming, is much sturdier.'

'How's your weight going?' I asked, reminded of Amy's slimming efforts by these poets' obvious fragility.

'Don't speak of it. I seem to have put on three pounds in the last week.'

'The scales have gone wrong.'

'Do you really think so?' Amy sounded wonderfully cheered. 'I hadn't thought of that. I'll try yours when I come over.'

'Please do, but I warn you that mine are almost half a stone too much, and friends come tottering downstairs looking demented until I explain it to them.'

'I'll remember. By the way, as the poets are so thin on the ground I've found a nice pianist as makeweight, and I'm just wondering if I could ask that marvellous singer Jean Cole who sang at the Fairacre festival some years ago.'

'It's flying rather high,' I said doubtfully. 'I think she only came because she was a relation of Major Gunning's, and he left some time ago.'

'Do you know where he went?'

'I could find out. I've an idea he's in a nursing home or private hotel somewhere not too far away. The vicar might know.'

'Be a lamb and see what you can do. Two poets, a pianist and Jean Cole should fill the bill beautifully.'

I promised to do my best.

'See you on Thursday week then. Long skirt to do honour to my four-course dinner, and make yourself as smart as possible.'

I blew a raspberry down the line to my bossy old friend.

I spent the rest of the evening looking out bottles and books for Joan Benson's bazaar. The bottles presented no problem. I had three bottles of tomato ketchup, a comestible of which I partake sparingly, so two of those went into the basket, and a bottle of homemade lemon essence.

The upstairs cupboard yielded a bottle of shampoo, and another of pungent scent, called *Dusky Allure* which had been given me by one of the children. As the said child had now moved from the district, I felt I could safely donate it. One has to be careful in a village; reputations have been ruined over just such little matters. Not a bad haul, I thought, surveying my five bottles. I only hoped I did not win any of them back again.

But the books occupied me for the rest of the evening. I began in a fine crusading spirit, ruthlessly putting aside half a dozen novels which I told myself I should never read again. It seemed prudent, though, to cast a cursory glance over them, and in no time I was deep in one which I had completely forgotten and found enthralling. I put it back on the shelf to finish later.

Meanwhile, crouched as I was on the floor, I became horribly stiff, and decided to look through the rest in my armchair. At a quarter to ten I realised that I had galloped through most of them, and five were put aside as absolutely essential to my needs. One book alone remained at hand for Mrs Willet's stall. I decided that I had done enough sorting for one evening. Tomorrow I would be firm and start again. It would be a good thing to clear out the bookshelves, but now bed called.

I took a final look at the rows of books. Would anyone read that life of Marlborough? Or that terrible edition of *Lorna Doone* with illustrations presumably executed in weak cocoa? And what about *Whitaker's Almanack* for 1953, and that glossy American cookery book full of recipes about squash and scallions and clams, and every one of them in cupfuls? Any takers, I wondered?

Who would have thought that giving away books would prove so tiring? It would have to wait until tomorrow.

I went to bed carrying my first rejected book with me.

The next morning I determined to find out when Fairacre School had first opened its doors to the children of the village. The forthcoming celebration, once we had decided on its nature, should take place approximately around the same time of year, I felt.

The earliest log book is a battered affair, leather covered and with beautifully mottled endpapers. It weighs several pounds, and the ink has now faded to fawn. The entries make fascinating reading.

I was mightily relieved to discover that the school opened at the beginning of December in 1880. If we were to celebrate the occasion then at least we knew that it must be an

indoor affair. No playground nonsense, wondering if the heavens would open in a summer shower. The longer I live in a village, the more I marvel at the touching faith with which folk organise outside affairs in our climate. June can be cruelly chilly, and I well remember that on Coronation Day on 2 June the most joyful moment was when we lit the bonfire and could huddle round the welcome blaze.

No one would expect anything outdoors at the beginning of December, so that cleared the ground nicely in my opinion. Something in the school must be arranged and, if need be, repeated to accommodate all the parents and friends.

The first headmistress was a Miss Richards, and her sister looked after the infants. Judging by the first entry, the opening of the school had been awaited for some time. The builders had not finished their work in the time allotted. Could some of Reg Thorn's forebears have been employed, I wondered?

The two ladies obviously had difficulty with discipline. There are a good many entries describing canings, and one John Pratt who seems to have been a sore trial and quite unmoved by frequent chastisement. What became of him, I wondered? He was evidently a resourceful boy, for he was discovered 'putting on the Hands of the Clock with the greatest Audacity' in July 1882, and a little later released a frog during the vicar's lesson on the Good Samaritan.

The two sisters resigned in 1885, giving their reason as ill health, but the boisterous spirits of their country pupils must have had something to do with it.

A widow and her daughter came next, and this pattern of a headmistress and woman assistant continued for some years. It was interesting to note that for all its hundred years Fairacre School had remained a two-teacher establishment.

There must have been some odd pairings, I guessed, but probably no more difficult than my present companion-in-harness, Miss Briggs. Two women, thus yoked, must learn to pull together to their mutual advantage and that of the school.

I closed the log book and replaced it in the desk drawer with a feeling of relief. There would be plenty of time to work out something to celebrate our centenary, and at least it would not clash with the Caxley Festival in May, which was showing signs of impinging on our rural tranquillity.

I was slamming back the drawer when the vicar entered. He came to the point at once, after greeting the children and admiring the progress of our hyacinth grown over water.

'As a child I used to grow acorns over medicine bottles,' he told me. 'I had a splendid collection one year.' His eyes grew misty at the recollection, but he returned to the reason for his visit. 'Have you any idea when the school first opened? I confess I can find no reference to it anywhere.'

I told him, with some pride, and his face cleared.

'Ah! That is good news! It gives me plenty of time to arrange a suitable service. Do you think the first Sunday in December, in the afternoon, would be a good idea, or perhaps an evening one during the week?'

I wondered privately whether his parishioners would prefer to forego their Sunday-afternoon nap, or to turn out on a dark December evening, leaving their cosy firesides for the chill of St. Patrick's church. It was difficult to offer advice, and I said so.

Luckily the vicar appeared to make up his own mind. 'On the whole, I think an afternoon service would be best. We want the children to attend, after all, and it would be a great pity if they were deprived just because it was their bedtime.'

I did not like to point out to our innocent pastor that the majority of the children would be glued to their television sets until about ten o'clock or later, imbibing all sorts of dubious knowledge, no doubt.

'There's a lot to be said for a service during the hours of daylight,' I replied diplomatically.

And we left it at that.

'By the way,' I said, as I accompanied him to the door. 'Do you happen to know Major Gunning's address?'

I told him about Amy's hope of inviting Jean Cole to dinner. He looked doubtful.

'She's so much in demand,' he said.

'I know.'

'But I can give you the major's address. He's at a private hotel in Caxley. It's either Ash Tree Hotel, or Elm Court or possibly Hawthorn House. Something arboreal, I know. I will look it up and let you have it, Miss Read.'

He gave a sigh.

'This Caxley Festival is, no doubt, an excellent project, but it does seem to make an inordinate amount of *planning*.'

I agreed, and returning to my class, thought that centenary celebrations shared the same problems.

4 April

Amy's party took place on the second day of the month.

After a boisterous morning which toppled the crocuses and blew the rooks off course, the sun came out, and by the time I set off all was tranquil. The western sky was dappled with little pink clouds as the sun went down, and the air was so clear and still that I could see a range of hills some twenty miles away to the south.

Obedient to Amy's request, I had donned a long black skirt bought at Caxley's most favoured outfitters, and identical to quite half a dozen I had observed on various local friends during the past winter. The blouse that topped it was of black and white silk which I thought looked rather fetching, but as it had a back zip I was resigned to undertaking violent contortions to do it up every time I wore it, and was beginning to wonder how long it would be before such exercises were beyond me.

As usual, I was the first to arrive. Amy greeted me with unusual affection.

'You look splendid! Truly elegant! Come and see the table. I'm rather proud of the flowers.'

She led the way into the dining room, and it certainly was a vision of delight. Daffodils and narcissi scented the room, and in the centre of the table was a magnificent arrangement of freesias and miniature daffodils in shades of cream and gold.

Amy stood surveying it, a look of supreme satisfaction on her face.

'It's perfect,' I told her.

'And that damask tablecloth was my grandmother's. It's a devil to launder, and so it doesn't get used very often, but those Victorians had some good ideas about dressing a table.'

'Do you remember Mrs Beeton's illustration for a simple supper party? Three epergnes of red roses down the centre, and smilax trailing everywhere?'

'Our old edition had a picture of a tray for an invalid,' recalled Amy. 'There were two silver trumpet-shaped flower vases with carnations, as well as two or three dishes complete with silver covers, a coffee pot, milk jug and sugar bowl. I don't think you could lift the thing, let alone stagger upstairs with it. But I must say it looked superb.'

'I pity anyone being taken ill in my house. A plate of toast and a mug of tea would be about my limit.'

'James has occasionally brought me my breakfast in bed when I've been too ill with flu, or something equally horrid, to get up. He can manage very thick bread and butter, with the crusts rather touchingly cut off, and the marmalade pot, and a cup of tea with most of it in the saucer by the time he's negotiated the stairs. But I certainly don't get carnations, and to be honest, I don't think I should appreciate them in the state I'm in when I have to stay in bed.'

'Now tell me who's coming,' I said when we returned to the sitting room.

'The two poets I told you about, and Betty Mason the pianist. Jean Cole is on tour in Belgium. I managed to get in touch with Major Gunning, thanks to you, and he says she'll be back next week and he'll find out her plans.'

'He won't forget,' I assured her. 'He was the mainstay of dozens of our village committees.'

'I invited him tonight, but he says he's become rather too old for parties. A shame really, he sounds a dear.'

'And James?'

'No James, I'm afraid. At a company dinner in South Shields. But I've invited Horace Umbleditch to make up the six. He's giving an organ recital in the church as part of the Caxley Festival, so he'll enjoy meeting some of the others, I hope. And anyway, he's devoted to you.'

'He's nothing of the sort!' I protested. 'I hardly know the fellow!'

'Well, I know better. And he's moved into such a charming house in the school grounds now, and could well do with a wife.'

'Amy, you are incorrigible! You know I have no wish to marry, nor presumably has Horace Umbleditch, and if he had, I'm sure he could find someone younger and keener than I am. Do leave us happy old spinsters and bachelors in peace!'

'Hoity-toity!' cried Amy, as the front-door bell rang. I watched her as she hurried to answer it, admiring the back view of her elegant cream silk caftan. Had she chosen it for tonight's occasion as the perfect complement to her flower arrangements? Knowing Amy, I guessed that she had.

She returned with Betty Mason in tow, a short rather dumpy person wearing black with a sparkling necklace. She had beautifully waved silver hair and a soft, powdery pink and white complexion which reminded me of marshmallows. During the evening I was to discover that she was as sweet and gentle as her looks.

We had scarcely greeted each other when Amy was called

to the door again, and Horace Umbleditch arrived. There was no need for introductions as Betty and Horace knew each other, and were soon deep in discussion about the best choice of music for a country festival.

Then, turning to me, Horace asked if I had heard the good news about his sister Irene.

'Henry Mawne told me,' I said, and then wondered if the good news he spoke of was about the proposed marriage to David Mawne after all. Perhaps it was something quite different – a new post, maybe, or a fantastic win on the pools, always supposing that Irene went in for such things.

However, I did not have to endure suspense for long, as Horace said that the wedding was to be in early June, at a registry office, and no doubt I should see them before then as they proposed to stay for a few days with Henry during the Caxley Festival.

'It is marvellous news,' I agreed, glad to be right for once. 'And where will they live?'

'For the moment in David's flat, but I expect they will move further out sometime. It's not much fun there for Simon in the holidays, and I'm sure Irene will look forward to making a home elsewhere.'

Away from the haunting horrors which that flat must hold for David, I thought privately, and for young Simon who had seen his mother at her most terrifying in those surroundings.

Amy came in and glanced at the clock, which said a quarter to eight. 'I do hope the others haven't lost their way. They are coming together.'

'Tim Ferdinand's usually pretty punctual,' said Horace.

'Oh, you know him! I hadn't realised that.'

'Very slightly. He came to the school one evening to read poetry to the boys. They were remarkably well-behaved.'

No one knew quite how to react to the last remark, and Amy said she must go and check that the crab was all right, conjuring up visions of a sickly crustacean with a bottle of medicine alongside.

'Something smells delicious,' commented Betty kindly.

'I just hope it won't be overdone,' said Amy, setting off for the kitchen. 'It's in a light cheese sauce, and you know how easily that can dry up.'

'Amy is the best cook I know,' said Horace with enthusiasm. 'After school meals, all cabbage and custard, the food here is sheer ambrosia.'

'It's so nice,' said Betty, 'to find people interested in food. I can't bear those who profess to have a mind above it, particularly when you have spent all day and a great deal of money in preparing something you think they will enjoy.'

The bell rang again, and we heard voices in the hall.

'I can't *think*,' we heard a despairing voice say, 'where I went wrong, but we took a short cut and ended up on the downs. It really is too bad the way some of these roads simply peter out into sheep tracks. A hundred apologies, Amy dear.'

'All is forgiven,' said Amy, 'and you really aren't late at all. Come and meet the others.'

She ushered in a short tubby man with a florid complexion set off by a neat white moustache. He could have been taken for a retired colonel or a particularly kindly bank manager. Perhaps he was, I thought, and simply wrote poems in his spare time on the back of Queen's Regulations or the bank's blotting-paper.

'John Chandler,' said Amy. 'He has just published his third book of poems.'

We all gave cries of admiration and welcomed our fellow guest.

'And Timothy Ferdinand. You know Horace, I believe, and this is Betty Mason the pianist, and Miss Read.'

We made more polite noises and I thought how much more like a poet he looked. For one thing, he was painfully thin and pale, as Amy had told me, with a wobbly Adam's apple which showed to advantage as he wore an open-necked shirt above blue jeans carefully fringed at the ankle. I was glad to see he had socks on under the inevitable sandals, and his hands were clean.

He looked a pleasant, if vague, young man, and still seemed to be brooding about the way he became lost on his journey.

'It happens to us all,' I assured him. 'It's those crossroads at Springbourne. Someone said once that it seems to be moved overnight. As a matter of fact, some young people did turn the signpost round one night, and confusion was worse confounded.'

He looked a little happier.

'You're quite right. It was at the crossroads we went wrong. But why not say "No thoroughfare", or "Downs only"?'

'I suppose the reasoning *is* that there is a road for about a mile before it dwindles into a track.'

'Possibly,' said Timothy doubtfully. He took out a rather grubby red and white spotted handkerchief and polished his sherry glass in a preoccupied way. I was glad that Amy was out of the room at the time.

Before long she returned, and we talked about the Caxley

Festival while the most delicious smells wreathed around us.

The attitude of the two poets towards this event varied considerably, although both agreed, somewhat vehemently, that Caxley needed 'to be awakened'. John Chandler looked upon it as a useful way of becoming known to a larger number of readers than before.

'Good publicity,' he said briskly. 'Might even sell a dozen or so extra books. Though one can't help feeling that at these affairs one is preaching to the converted. Still, it all helps.'

Timothy Ferdinand's attitude was less commercial.

'Oh surely,' he cried, 'it is the artist and his work that really matters! He needs an audience to stimulate him, and I think that the festival will do that very well.'

'Let's carry on this discussion while we eat,' said Amy.

We followed our hostess into the pretty dining room and confronted our sizzling ramekins.

'If you don't like crab,' said Amy, 'there is melon ready on the sideboard.'

Only Betty asked if she might change. 'I adore crab, but can't digest it,' she said apologetically, and John rose swiftly to make the replacement.

I thought how sensible Amy was to offer an alternative to one's first course. So often the hostess has gone to no end of trouble to produce something rather exotic, often with shell fish or avocado pear which many people cannot take. I myself have several times been faced with taramasalata which, with the best will in the world, I cannot get down. If only I had been offered a slice of melon or a nice little tot of orange or tomato juice waiting on the sideboard, how much happier I should have been!

Horace Umbleditch sat beside me and John Chandler opposite. They were both exuberant talkers and Amy and I had little to do in the way of keeping the conversation going. Timothy Ferdinand still seemed slightly distraught, at the foot of the table, facing Amy, but gulped down his crab as though he had not seen food for weeks, and nodded abstractedly at Betty's gentle remarks.

Cold turkey and ham with a handsome salad followed the crab, and a dish of mammoth baked potatoes with butter melting in their floury tops. As Amy served us, I was amused to notice that Timothy was engrossed in cleaning between the prongs of his perfectly spotless fork by inserting them busily in the edge of Amy's beautiful damask tablecloth. He seemed quite unaware of anything amiss. His periodic nods at Betty's gallant monologue continued as before, as with eyes on his work he polished assiduously.

Whether Amy saw him or not, I could not say, but she continued serving with her usual charm, whilst commenting on the possibility of getting Jean Cole to attend the poetry reading during the festival week.

Fortunately, the arrival of his main course saw the cessation of Timothy's cleansing operations, and he fell to with a will and did not seem to feel the need to polish anything else during the sweet and cheese courses.

At last he leant back and gave a sigh of contentment. 'What a perfect dinner! I hardly ever sit down to a meal when I'm alone, and certainly never to one as splendid as this.'

'But don't you get hungry?' enquired Amy.

'I suppose I do,' replied Timothy, looking about him vaguely. 'I eat an apple or a biscuit sometimes. Anything that's lying about, you know.'

No wonder he looked so emaciated, I thought.

Conversation then became concentrated upon the form of Amy's proposed evening, and later she took us all into the drawing room to see the best way of arranging things for the great night.

John Chandler appeared outstandingly practical about this, pointing out the best place for the piano with relation to the lighting and the french windows which, with any luck, might be open to admit the warm evening air, scented with roses and stocks. He also suggested seating arrangements which would ensure the greatest number of people being at ease, and reminded me yet again of a military commander deploying his resources to the best advantage.

Timothy did not contribute much to the plans, but sipped his coffee thoughtfully, only surfacing once to remark that it was a blessing no microphone would be needed in a room this size as he had a horror of the things, and had been hurt by falling over one once, and hurt even more by the BBC mechanic's remarks about the accident.

This led to a general discussion about whether it was a good thing to understand machinery, or whether it was better to disclaim all knowledge at the outset of how to deal with the objects, and to let someone else tackle the problem.

Eventually the delicate task of allotting time for each artist's performance was undertaken, and it was agreed that roughly half an hour, give or take five minutes, for each, should ensure a full evening's pleasure, and that it was up to each performer to rehearse his own contribution to fix the time it would take.

By eleven o'clock the company had dispersed, looking happy and well fed.

Amy turned down my offer to help with the washing up. Evidently, unheard by me and probably by everyone else in Amy's beautifully soundproof house, her daily help had been hard at it and the kitchen awaited the morrow as spotless as ever.

'Do you think it went well?' asked Amy, on the doorstep.

'Everything – but *everything*,' I assured her, as I let in the clutch, 'was absolutely perfect.'

I was delighted to have a letter from the office, a day or two later, to inform me that work on the new window to replace the present skylight would begin at the end of term and should be completed before the beginning of the summer term.

This was good news indeed, although I should have preferred to read '*will* be completed' rather than that cautious '*should* be completed'. However, it was better perhaps to face the probability of a half-finished job than to be disappointed later.

Mrs Pringle shared Mr Willet's doubts about Reg Thorn's ability to do the job at all, let alone to a deadline even as vague as this one.

'What he done to my poor sister-in-law in Caxley you'd never believe,' she assured me. 'You'd think he'd feel downright sorry for a widow woman as suffers something so cruel with arthritis in her hands that she hasn't done her back hair for years now. She told me herself as Reg promised faithful to have her straightened up by last Easter. He'd only got the porch to put to rights. Bob Willet would have done it in two days flat, but Reg hung it out, just when the wind was in the east, fairly scouring out Peg's hall with the front door off, and the bill – which came pretty smartish, I

can tell you – was twice the estimate, and give poor old Peg indigestion for a week.'

'Let's hope he's improved since then,' I replied.

Mr Willet, who had joined us, snorted with disgust.

'We'll be lucky to get that dratted dormer by next winter, and then I don't reckon it'll work. If there ain't trouble with the roof I'll eat my hat.'

I refused to be depressed by my two Job's comforters. Nothing could be worse, I felt, than the present ancient skylight. I acknowledged the office's letter in enthusiastic terms, and looked forward to seeing the workmen on the job before the Easter holidays.

I felt less enthusiastic about Miss Briggs's progress in the infants' room. To be sure, she did not rush away at three-

thirty as she had done previously, but I rarely saw her smile, she shouted at the babies who, naturally, became noisier than ever, and she made no response to any of my overtures. Mr Willet's early summing up of the young lady as 'a fair old lump of a girl' was true.

It was difficult to know how to improve matters. Over the years, I had worked with dozens of infants' teachers with just the screen between us. Some had been shy, some bold, some flighty, but all had been fairly cheerful, and some outstandingly gifted. A two-teacher school must be harmonious. There is no getting away from each other, which is possible in a large establishment, and I was at a loss to know how to overcome the girl's sulkiness.

Was she ill perhaps, I wondered? Was she in love? Was she homesick? Or had she realised that she was in a job she disliked, and worried about how to get out of it?

As far as I could find out, she had few friends in Caxley and had not joined any clubs or societies. She must be lonely, I felt, and her digs, though adequate, were not particularly comfortable, I gathered.

I should have to have a word with her sometime, I supposed gloomily. Only a week or two of the present term remained, and she was having a holiday in France at Easter. With any luck she would return with more zest to Fairacre School.

I did not need much persuading to put off this problem until her return, telling myself – not for the first time – that things might sort themselves out. My faith in the power of destiny to resolve my problems is touching, but usually misplaced.

The April weather, which had been kindly, now switched

to the other extreme and became violently windy, with sudden vicious storms which scoured the countryside, dowsing newborn lambs and tossing the daffodils to the ground.

The skylight dripped steadily during these onslaughts, and the worst of the storms always seemed to coincide with playtime, so that the children were obliged to spend their break indoors, much to everyone's annoyance.

Several new puddles appeared in the playground, and on the rare occasions when the children spent a few minutes outside a new game had been devised, called, I gathered 'Splashem'. This involved jumping in the deepest part of a puddle just as someone passed, preferably an infant too small to retaliate and likely to get more of him drenched, and then to enjoy not only the victim's discomfiture, but also the hilarious glee of the onlookers.

It was a game I did my best to stamp out promptly, but not before several cross mothers had called to complain about sopping clothes and squelchy shoes.

On one of the stormiest days, the dinner lady slipped over in the playground, all the gravy was spilled, her knee was badly grazed and her tights ruined. Miss Briggs took care of the school while I rendered first-aid in the school house. She seemed more agitated about the loss of the gravy than her own injuries.

'I could easily pour some of Beech Green's into a jug for you,' she offered, as I dabbed at her knee with TCP.

'Don't worry, it won't hurt us to go short for once. This skirt is soaked. Would you like to borrow one?'

The offer was accepted, and she went off dry if not particularly elegant, and full of apologies.

Mr Annett, the headmaster at Beech Green, and also

choirmaster and organist at Fairacre, called on choir night to tell me that Miss Clare was staying with them.

'She's not too bad,' he began, shaking a wet umbrella energetically, 'but Isobel found her with a heavy cold yesterday when she called, and persuaded her to have a day or two in our spare bed.'

'You are good Samaritans,' I said.

'Not a bit. But come and see her if you can.'

'I'll come tomorrow if it suits you.'

'Fine. We'll look forward to it.'

He sprinted churchwards, and I went indoors out of the beastly wind. This was no weather for poor frail Dolly Clare, I felt, but was comforted to think of her in such safe hands at Beech Green.

If anything, the weather was wilder still when I drove the few miles from Fairacre to Beech Green. The windscreen wipers could scarcely keep pace with the torrent of rain which lashed the car. Young leaves and scraps of early blossom littered the leafy road as though it were an autumn evening. A fast running rivulet ran each side of the lane, and every puddle sent up a shower of drops, reminding me of 'Splashem' and my naughty boys.

The few people I passed on the road were well wrapped up in waterproof garments ranging from sou'westers to wellingtons. I only saw one umbrella, and that was causing its owner considerable trouble. In rough weather, our downland winds can soon rip such a thing to pieces, and it is wiser to have one's hands free to tighten a headscarf or to turn up a raincoat collar against the onslaught.

I found Miss Clare sitting by a cheerful fire. She was dressed, and had a pretty lacy shawl round her shoulders.

'Isobel had to go out,' she told me. 'She is giving a talk over at Springbourne and I wouldn't let her put it off. Really, I'm quite rested now after two nights and one whole day in bed.'

She certainly looked very well, though as thin as ever, but her eyes were bright and I think she was enjoying the company of the Annetts.

'They are so kind,' she went on. 'And the more I know of them the more I am reminded of my early teaching days when Mr and Mrs Hope looked after me so well.'

'Was that the headmaster who had to leave Fairacre?'

Miss Clare nodded sadly. 'He was a gentle soul, and very musical like the Annetts, but they lost their only child when she was twelve or so, and he never got over it. He took to the bottle, you know, and left soon after the Great War in 1919, if I remember rightly.'

'You remember the war well enough,' I said.

'Too well,' she said. 'Not only because I lost my dear Arnold in France, but because of the appalling number of young men from here who never came back. One of the saddest sights in Fairacre School was the black armbands worn by so many of the children. And the tears! You would see some little mite busy writing, and then the pen would stop, and the head would go down and the crying begin. It was dreadful to feel so helpless in the face of such sorrow. Mr Hope felt it all terribly. Sometimes I wonder if that was another reason for his taking to drink.'

'He didn't drink in school?'

'No, thank goodness! He made up for it at home, and was simply morose and befuddled in school towards the end. He

still worked hard though, and did a great deal to help the war effort, and saw that the children helped too. Why, I remember that even the youngest babies were set to fraying pieces of white cotton and linen with a darning needle to make field dressings. And of course we all put as much as we could spare – which wasn't much, in those days – into War Savings stamps.'

'But at least you were spared bombings and rushing into air-raid shelters in that war.'

'We saw practically nothing of the war in Fairacre,' agreed Miss Clare, 'and I think, despite the horror stories in the newspapers, that there was less real hatred towards the Germans. We prayed every morning for the war to end, and I daresay we realised that German children were doing the same. We *disliked* them, of course, and *intensely* and I remember Mr Hope taking a grammar lesson at the other end of the classroom. He was trying to get the children to stop using the word "got" – with small success, as you might imagine. He wrote it on the blackboard, and crossed it through. "Got, got, got," he cried. "A horrible word! It must be German! Simply leave it out, and say: 'I *have* a pen! I *have* a new nib!' Understand?" And one of the Bryant boys, a real little gipsy said: "I ain't got neither, sir!" and everyone broke into laughter, including Mr Hope.'

'He sounds a good chap,' I said. 'A pity he had to leave.'

'A tragedy,' agreed Dolly. 'He was as much a casualty of war as my dear Arnold.'

She fingered the gold locket which hung under the lacy shawl. She wore it constantly, and I knew that it contained a photograph of the red-haired young man who had shared the fate of thousands of others whose names were written

upon country memorials, and in the hearts of those who loved them.

'Heard the latest?' enquired Mr Willet the next morning. 'About the vicar?'

Elevated to rural dean? Broken a leg? Off on holiday? All these dramatic possibilities leapt to mind before Mr Willet spoke again.

'He's going to keep *bees*. I only hope he knows what he's letting himself in for. My old gran had three of those straw skep hives on an old table by her bottom hedge, and by gum, you didn't dare go near 'em to scythe the grass or pick a few runner beans nearby. Fair vicious they was.'

'I expect he's gone into all that.'

'I doubt it. Mr Mawne's been eggin' him on, and got him a couple of hives from some chap over at Bent who's giving up. Seen the light, I reckon. Why, I remember getting some of my gran's bees up my jersey as a kid, and havin' swellings like pudden basins.'

'They tell me that's good for rheumatism.'

Mr Willet snorted.

'Them old wives' tales! My gran had rheumatics something terrible and I bet she was stung often enough. She still told them old bees all that went on, like you hear about. She told 'em about Grandad dying in Caxley Hospital of the dropsy, and about the grandchildren being born. Funny really. People says bees are wise, but the more I hear about 'em the more I wonder. Did you know they goes for people dressed in blue?'

'Never heard of it.'

'No, nor I bet you haven't heard as they don't like compost heaps or bonfires or mowing the grass and a lot of

other things you finds in a garden. Pesky little objects! I
don't envy the vicar, that I don't!'

'But think of all the lovely honey,' I said.

'Bet you a dollar they'll be getting rape honey. Mr
Roberts usually has a good field of that – you know, that
blazin' yellow stuff.'

I said I knew what rape looked like. I had not lived in the
country all these years without –

Mr Willet interrupted me.

'All right, all right! All I'm saying is that the vicar will
have to take his honey off smartish if it's rape, or it'll gum
up the whole works. Terrible stuff to extract, as my old
gran could tell him, if she'd been spared. No, he don't know
what he's letting himself in for, and I only hope he's got a
blue bag for banging on the stings.'

'Can you still get a blue bag?'

'I doubt it,' said Mr Willet. He sighed and moved off.
After a few steps he stopped and called across the play-
ground:

'Hope you aren't thinkin' of startin' bees,' he shouted.
'That's one thing I'm not helping you with, I can tell
you.'

During the last day or two of term, I turned over in my
mind the snippets of history that I had heard from Dolly
Clare. Somewhere here there was the theme for our
centenary celebrations, I felt sure.

To give Miss Briggs her due, the idea of dressing the
children in the costume of 1880 had some merit. Perhaps we
could have just two children in costume telling Fairacre
School's story in each decade? Or, more practically, a boy
and girl of each of the five reigns – six, if you included

Edward VIII – through which the school had passed, suitably apparelled for their particular narrations.

It would be best if we could let the whole school take part, and perhaps a song or poem typical of each period could intersperse the narration. I discussed my nebulous ideas with Miss Briggs, who seemed remarkably co-operative for once. Perhaps her impending holiday in France was having a stimulating effect.

'Have you fixed a date?' she enquired sensibly.

'Sometime in the first week in December,' I told her. 'And for two performances definitely, otherwise we shan't have room for everyone. I thought parents of infants one afternoon, and the others the next.'

'What a good idea! And perhaps we could combine it with the tea party the children usually give at Christmas.'

'That's a thought,' I agreed.

The Christmas party for parents, with the children acting as hosts, is a long-standing tradition in the school. Sometimes we are hopelessly overcrowded; dividing the party into a two-day event might help considerably. I looked at my assistant with new respect. At times she was quite bright, I thought.

'Of course, there's heaps of time for making arrangements,' she said.

'We'll have to start pretty early,' I assured her. 'We must know what we propose to do next term so that the mothers can think about costumes, and it looks to me as though the whole of the autumn term will be devoted to rehearsing, whatever we decide upon.'

'Let's hope the dormer window will be done by then,' said Miss Briggs, watching a steady drip dropping into a bucket by my desk.

'It had better be!' I said grimly.

Mercifully, the rough weather subsided as suddenly as it had arrived, and the last day of term ended in a clear, serene evening.

Its blissful tranquillity matched my own feelings. The empty school basked in the golden rays of the setting sun. The rooks' cawing was the only sound above the tidy playground, and Tibby and I sauntered in the garden relishing our solitude. The narcissi wafted heady draughts of fragrance towards us. The grape hyacinths were a sea of blue in the shrubbery, and some fine scarlet tulips, straight as guardsmen, towered above them. What if the groundsel and dandelions and chickweed were making steady progress? With the holidays ahead I could soon root them out.

The hooting of a car horn brought me back to earth, and I found Amy at the door.

'I've been shopping in Oxford,' she said, 'and thought I'd call on my way home. Is it convenient, or are you having a cocktail party or anything?'

'Don't be funny,' I begged her. 'Whenever have you caught me preparing for a cocktail party?'

'You never know,' replied Amy vaguely. 'How pretty your garden looks.'

We strolled happily around my small plot, enjoying the unusual calm and warmth.

'Do you want to see my new purchases?' enquired Amy, as we made our way back to the house.

She dived into the car and emerged with two exotic-looking dress boxes which she carried into the house. There seemed to be half a hundredweight of tissue paper in each one, but at last the garments were revealed. One was a set of

glossy underwear, petticoat, knickers and brassiere in what was called, in my youth, oyster satin. The other was a stunning three-piece in silk jersey, cream in colour with delicate gold decorations at hem and neck.

'Well!' I exclaimed. 'They are all truly gorgeous!'

'So they should be at the ghastly price I had to pay for them. Now I'm beginning to wonder if they are a trifle young for me.'

'Rubbish!' I told her. 'You're a very good-looking woman, as well you know, and can wear anything. You always could.'

'So could you, my dear,' said Amy kindly. 'You were really quite pretty at eighteen when we first met.'

'Everyone is quite pretty at eighteen,' I retorted. 'A few decades later it is really quite enough to be clean and respectable, and I only hope I'm that. Anyway, I have no doubt that you would soon tell me if I weren't.'

Amy laughed, and began putting the clothes back among the tissue paper.

'Are you going away?' she asked.

'Not this holiday. At least, I haven't booked anything. I might slope off to Devon for a few days and hope to find bed and breakfast somewhere.'

'You'll be lucky! You really should organise yourself better. I'm always scolding you about it.'

'You are indeed,' I agreed, pouring her a glass of sherry.

'You know, even the *simplest* holiday needs to be arranged well in advance. James and I are having a few days in the Scillies at the end of next month, and we booked the hotel and the helicopter flight across from Penzance, way back in January.'

'Well, you're well-organised people, and I'm not.'

'With James so terribly busy we simply have to plan things, or we'd never get a break together. We propose to sleep, sunbathe, birdwatch and eat.'

'Sounds heavenly,' I said. 'I'll do it myself one day, when I can get round to arranging a holiday six months ahead.'

'I hope to live to see the day,' said Amy, putting down her empty glass. 'Well, I must be off. I'm glad you approve of my purchases.'

She looked rather sadly at my cardigan. 'How long have you had that shapeless garment?'

'About six years. And don't suggest that I give it to a jumble sale. It's pure wool, and hand-knitted by dear Mrs Willet. What's more, it's got *pockets*, which mighty few garments have these days, and I shall wear it till it drops into rags.'

'That won't be long!' Amy assured me, and drove off.

5 May

This is easily my favourite month and I greeted its arrival by remembering to say 'White Rabbits' aloud before uttering another syllable.

This childish superstition, told me first by a fellow six-year-old, is supposed to bring you luck for the rest of the month. When discussing such matters now, I tend to pooh-pooh the whole field of folklore, astrology, horoscopes and the rest of it, but I find myself hastily throwing spilt salt over my shoulder, dodging ladders and, if not in polite company, spitting in a ladylike way if I see one magpie.

Fortified by my 'White Rabbits' incantation, I got up and hung out of the bedroom window to relish the perfection of a May morning. The copper beech was in tiny leaf, which spread a rosy gauze over the tracery of bare branches. Dew shimmered on the grass, and drops of moisture on the hawthorn hedge sparked a hundred miniature rainbows.

Out in Mr Roberts's clover field a pheasant squawked. It was probably an anxious mother warning her chicks of the dangers that lurked around. Somewhere, high above, a lark was vying with another in the distance, the song pouring down from the blue in drops of pure music.

The air was cool, and deliciously scented with hyacinths and narcissi from the garden bed below. Later, it would be hot, and with luck I should be able to take my tea tray into

the garden, after my day's work, and relish the joy of growing things. I remembered, with immense pleasure, that there was nothing in the diary for the evening of May the first. What bliss!

As I dressed, I pondered the problem of loneliness. I receive a great deal of unnecessary sympathy for my single state, and am touched by kind people's concern for the fact that I live alone. If they only knew! I find it much more exhausting to share my home with friends who come to stay, much as I love them, and the places I visit I remember much more clearly, and with keener affection, when I have visited them alone. I suppose that this is because one wanders around, looking at objects which are of particular personal interest, and absorbing their aspect and history without the distraction of a friend diverting one's attention to something which she has discovered.

No doubt, it tends to make one extremely selfish, but such solitude has its compensations. For one thing, it is possible to pursue a train of thought, or to carry out a piece of work, unmolested. I heartily sympathise with widows and widowers who are used to a shared life, and suffer horribly when that is shattered. The fact that so many of them adjust relatively quickly to the situation is indicative of their bravery; the fact that others never really recover is understandable. But, as a spinster, I have never been called upon to try to mend a broken life, and I am deeply grateful for that mercy. Amy's many attempts to marry me off have failed, I like to think, largely because of my contentment with my lot. It would be insupportable, of course, to think that the men were lukewarm!

The postman arrived as my egg was boiling. He brought a six-page document from the office about the necessity for

Stringent Economies in Schools, and a glossy circular exhorting me to invest in a gold pendant which could be mine for rather more than two months' salary.

The latter went into the wastepaper basket, and the former I resigned myself to reading when I felt stronger. But not this evening, I told myself, taking a refreshing look at the shimmering glory outside.

The first of May was going to be devoted to savouring its hope and beauty.

The Caxley Festival began to loom large. An enormous amount of organisation had gone into its arrangements and *The Caxley Chronicle* carried copious advance notices of the pleasures in store and the absolute necessity of sending early for tickets, not forgetting the stamped addressed envelope for their return.

Although Fairacre was only on the edge of these stirring events and was spared the feverish activity in the market town itself, yet even so we had our small part in the excitement. The gardens, which were to be open on the first Saturday and Sunday of the month, were being tended with unnatural fervour. Mr Willet, whose garden is always in a state of perfection, was somewhat scathing about these unseemly efforts.

'There's no call for panic,' he told me, 'if you keeps the hoe going regular. Some of these people is going fair demented! Why, I heard as that new couple up the other end of the street, is planting out their geraniums, pots and all, from the greenhouse! Just to make a show! It's a scandal, I reckon, and if there's a sharp frost, as can often happen in May, they've lost the lot.' He puffed out his moustache in disgust, and moved off about his business.

Mrs Pringle was equally censorious when she arrived.

'Never saw so much fuss in all me borns,' she said, chins quivering. 'Did you know as Mr Mawne borrowed Mr Hales's electric shears to tidy up his yew hedge, and nearly killed hisself by cutting through the cable?'

I expressed my concern.

'Oh, he's come to no harm,' shrugged Mrs Pringle. 'But if he hadn't got into this fever it would never have happened. And they say the vicar's now worrying about people disturbing his new bees, and wishing he hadn't offered to open the garden at all. These 'ere festivals can cause a mint of trouble it seems.'

'They sometimes raise a mint of money,' I pointed out, and waited for the expected answer.

'As my dear mother used to say: "Money isn't—"'

Linda Moffat burst in upon Mrs Pringle's mother's well-known maxim to tell us that the youngest Coggs had locked himself in the lavatory and was yelling for help.

I went to supply it.

So often was my attention drawn to the Caxley Festival that I was not in the least surprised to hear Amy's voice on the telephone, and confidently awaited the news about some festival plans.

I was surprised to find that it was something entirely different that she had in mind.

'Am I right in thinking that in these decadent days you get a whole week's holiday around what, in our youth, was known as Whitsun?'

'That's right. Spring Bank Holiday is its official name, Amy, and it starts some time at the end of the month, and I

believe we go back to school on Monday the third – maybe it's the fourth. I've mislaid my diary.'

'*Mislaid your diary*?' squeaked Amy, profoundly shocked. 'What on earth will you do?'

'It'll turn up,' I said vaguely. 'I may have chucked it into the wastepaper basket with some other rubbish, or I may have left it in the post office. I shall have a look today some time.'

'I have never met such a wholly lackadaisical person in my life,' scolded Amy. 'Why, if I were so careless as to lose my diary, I should be absolutely *daunted*! Life would have to stop until I'd found it again.'

'My life will tick over quite well without it for a day or two,' I assured her. 'What's the news?'

'Not very good, I'm afraid. James has muddled his dates, and now finds it is impossible for him to come to the Scillies at the end of the month. He has some engagement in Canada then, and we both wondered if you would like to come with me instead. What do you think? We were to go on the Sunday, stay overnight at Penzance, then fly across on the Monday morning. Do say you can come!'

'It sounds blissful! How long for?'

'We had planned to come back on the Thursday or Friday, so you'd have time to do any chores before school started again, if that's in your mind.'

I thought rapidly. I could not think of any particularly pressing engagement during that week, but without my diary it was difficult to be sure. I said as much to Amy, thanked her sincerely for an exciting invitation and promised to set about searching for my missing diary immediately.

'I'll ring you the minute it's found,' I assured her.

'And make the answer Yes,' said Amy, and rang off.

The first two or three days of May had been deliciously balmy, and we all told each other how lovely it would be if it lasted over the weekend.

Visions of suntanned visitors in summer frocks saunter-ing about the newly spruced Fairacre gardens kept most of us happy, but one or two pessimists shook their heads sadly. To my alarm, Mr Willet was one of them. He is such an accurate weather prophet that I viewed his forebodings seriously. The sky was cloudless on Friday afternoon and I only hoped that this time he might be wrong in his weather forecast.

But, sure enough, when I watched the weather man on television that evening, some ominous whirligigs, like well-spun spiders' webs, hovered unpleasantly near the west coast, and would bring rain and strong winds to the entire country. It was small comfort to learn that the weather would be more severe in the north than the south. The hardy types up there can take it, I thought callously, turning to our own dispiriting outlook which affected my feelings much more sharply.

I woke very early on Saturday morning. It was about five o'clock, and sure enough, a steady rain splashed along the gutters, and dripped from the trees. From the look of the garden, it had been pouring for several hours. Half a dozen sparrows splashed energetically in a large puddle by the box edging. The bird bath was full to the brim, though not being used for its right purpose by any of my bird friends.

The trees glistened, the roof tiles dropped miniature cas-cades on to those below, and some of the roses already

drooped their heads, heavy with moisture. I decided to make myself a cup of tea and take it back to bed. Delicious Saturday morning, despite the rain, when I could call my time my own!

Tibby burst through the cat flap on the kitchen door, as I poured my tea, and rubbed her sopping-wet bedraggled body round my bare legs, ignoring my vituperation in an ecstasy of love. To salve my conscience, and to give myself time to get safely upstairs with my precious cup, I hastily put down some Pussi-luv, and hoped that she might mistake it for liver.

Hunched comfortably against the pillows I surveyed the streaming window over my cup. Would this rain stop? If not, would it be possible to postpone the opening of the gardens? And if so, how could it be advertised? I knew that a lot of people had planned to come from some distance to support the project. It was too bad.

I remembered that Irene Umbleditch and David Mawne were to be among our visitors, and looked forward to hearing their news. My mind went back to the time when David's unhappy little boy, Simon, spent a short time at Fairacre School. He would be away at boarding school now, and I wondered if we should ever meet again.

The rain continued all the morning, and by noon a nasty little wind had got up and was blowing the rain diagonally across the countryside. The sky was of uniform greyness. It was like being in a canvas tent, and the chances of a break in the clouds seemed non-existent.

The gardens were to be open from two o'clock until eight on both Saturday and Sunday, and I knew that several coachloads of people were expected from Caxley. At two o'clock, I donned wellingtons, my stoutest mackintosh and

a rain hat which made me look like a witch, and set off bravely to do the rounds, or until exposure sent me home again.

It was heartening to see how many other people were doing the same. We met under umbrellas, in porches, under trees, anywhere to escape the relentless rain, and admired the dripping and battered beauty before us. A wonderful sense of camaraderie united us, as we sloshed our way around, and I was delighted to meet the Mawnes, their nephew and his bride-to-be, Irene, acting as hosts to the brave visitors in their garden.

They gave me good news of Simon.

'He's settled down very well now, and may move up next term. He's made friends with a pair of twins, two solid matter-of-fact youngsters who are marvellous ballast for our volatile Simon,' said David. 'We hope to take all three away in the summer, if their parents agree.'

Henry Mawne espied Miriam Quinn alone in the distance, and hurried to bring her over to meet his nephew. Once they were in conversation over a rare shrub of Henry's, I excused myself and splashed my way homeward.

To my surprise, the clock said four-thirty. It was no wonder I was wet. My expensive mackintosh had let water through the shoulders. My hair was plastered to my head by pressure from the ugly rain hat. My feet were soaked, as the rain had run down my legs into my wellingtons, but I was aglow with a sense of duty well done.

In this complacent and self-congratulatory state I decided to treat myself to a small fire on such a cheerless day. Whether the chimney was damp, which was understandable, or whether the wind was in the wrong direction, no one could say, but the result was unpleasant.

Clouds of acrid smoke blew into the room. My vision of

'the small but bright wood fire' beloved by novelists vanished in three minutes flat, as I set about opening windows, holding up newspapers over the fireplace to assist in the right sort of draught, and cursing generally whilst my smug feeling of virtue rapidly evaporated.

Trust Fate to deflate one's ego!

The rain continued throughout the night. By morning, sheets of water covered the roads and some of Mr Roberts's fields. But slowly it improved, and by early afternoon a watery sun was visible fleetingly between the scudding clouds. It looked more hopeful for visitors to Fairacre's gardens, I thought.

Having done my duty the day before, I decided to do my ironing, polish my few pieces of silver, write some letters, and generally catch up with some long-neglected household jobs. But as I was about to switch on the iron, I saw that a bird was fluttering madly at one of the schoolroom windows.

I put down the iron, took the school key from its hook, and went to the rescue. As anyone who has been engaged on such an errand of mercy will know, the fact that every available window and door is open seems to make no difference to the demented captive, which dashes itself wildly against all the closed apertures. After ten minutes' pandemonium the wretched sparrow darted out of the door, and I sank thankfully into my chair.

It was suddenly and blissfully peaceful. A shaft of watery sunshine illumined the classroom, a few dusty motes disturbed by the bird's and my agitation floating in its beam of light. A little breeze stirred one of the children's pictures pinned to the partition, but otherwise nothing ruffled the tranquillity of this ancient room.

It must be full of ghosts, I thought, or at least of memories. I found the idea comforting. How many children had sat in this place, imbibing knowledge both good and bad, observing the quirks of their neighbours, forming their own judgements, growing into the adult people they would be in a few years?

These same walls had seen the gamut of emotions from hilarity to despair. I remembered Miss Clare's remark about the celebratory tea party in the thirties, and the grief of children left fatherless in the First World War. This building had weathered sunshine and storm, peace and war. It had sheltered many who grew to be good men and women, and a few felons too. How far, I wondered, did the influence of this ancient school spread? All over the world there must be men and women who remembered something of the things taught them here, or were told of them by their forebears who knew the old school.

It came to me, with a poignancy I had not felt before, that I was an insignificant part of a worthy and long heritage. It was a humbling thought. Here was the heart of the matter, the spirit of the place, the unifying thread which ran through a hundred years. If only something of that spirit could be transmitted during our centenary celebrations!

I rose to return to my neglected kitchen tasks. As I locked the school door, holding that same ancient key which had chilled the palms of so many of my predecessors, I thought with keener appreciation of the centenary story which was to be told. Would it be possible, I wondered, to express that feeling of continuity which had enveloped me in my silent schoolroom?

I had been busy with thoughts of Amy's kind invitation,

and decided that I should love to go with her to Tresco in the week's holiday ahead. My diary turned up within ten minutes of our earlier conversation, but I had been unable to reach her on the telephone..

'I can only have been in the garden,' she assured me, when at last we made contact, 'and I can't tell you how glad I am you can come.'

'Not as glad as I am to have been invited. I've always wanted to see the Scillies, and never got round to it.'

'You won't be disappointed. Now, I think our best plan is for me to pick you up about eleven on the Sunday. We'll stop for a pub lunch, and then take our time getting to Penzance. We should be there in good time for a nice dinner. We're booked in at the Queen's, and the food is always good.'

'Perfect,' I said.

'Have you found that diary?'

'Of course I have!'

'No "of course!" about it,' said Amy severely. 'But put down these arrangements while you remember them.'

'I'm not *quite* senile,' I protested.

'And don't forget my poetry reading on Wednesday. I'm counting on you to lead the clapping.'

'I'll be there,' I promised her, and we rang off.

But Fate decreed otherwise.

A week or so earlier, a sizeable chunk of stopping had dropped out of a back tooth. As it had not hurt, and I already had an appointment with the dentist within a month, I had ignored the gaping hole, except for wiggling at it with my tongue now and again.

Wednesday's school dinner consisted of rissoles, mashed potato and peas, followed by a sticky treacle tart which was

welcomed rapturously by the children. Without thinking, I tackled my slice, only to be smitten with the most piercing pain in my damaged tooth.

I was obliged to leave the children to Miss Briggs's care and rush to the schoolhouse for first aid. The oil of cloves bottle, well hidden behind cough mixture, alka seltzer, aspirin tablets, and a particularly sinister bottle labelled 'The Mixture' – for what malady I had completely forgotten – was found to have about two drops of thickened syrup at the bottom which I did my best to apply with a wooden cherry stick wrapped in cotton wool.

If anything, this treatment seemed to aggravate the pain, and I hastily mixed a solution of my old friend TCP with warm water and tried again. But this time the pain was throbbing in my ear as well. By dint of holding warm TCP solution in my mouth, a slight diminution of pain resulted, but it was obvious that I could not take a class with my mouth bulging with water.

I tottered back just in time to see Mrs Pringle arriving for the washing up.

'Why, you do look bad!' she greeted me, with much satisfaction. 'You mark my words, that face'll be up like a plum pudden in an hour or two. You wants to tie a stocking round your jaw, and my auntie in Caxley always swore by some mustard in the tooth to keep it warm.'

I felt unequal to replying, and watched Mrs Pringle make for the lobby with a heavy limp. This was a sure sign that she was affronted, had taken umbrage, and was in her martyred mood. By this time, my tooth hurt so much that I was beyond caring if Mrs Pringle slit her throat with one of the school knives, although she would have had to be pretty determined in the face of such uncooperative bluntness.

I stuck it out until playtime when I confessed my plight to
Miss Briggs, who proved sympathetic and willing to cope
with the school for the rest of the afternoon, while I
returned to the schoolhouse and rang the dentist.

'Aren't you lucky?' said his receptionist, and while I was
recovering from this remark, she added, 'We've just had a
cancellation. If you can get here by a quarter to five, Mr
Bennett will see you then.'

Kind Mr Bennett! Dear Mr Bennett, I thought gratefully!
I was positively longing to see him. Usually the thought of
going to the dentist – even one as humane as Mr Bennett –
casts a gloom over my life for days ahead. Now, crazed with
pain, even with a mouthful of hot TCP, I viewed my trip to
Caxley as a drowning man must view a lifeboat.

I went across the playground to apprise Miss Briggs of
events and to lock up my cupboards and desk. The children
were blissfully quiet, as they usually are in a crisis. The
dividing door was propped open, so that the infants' teacher
could keep an eye on them, and I returned to get wrapped
up when I remembered Amy's party.

There was nothing for it but to cry off. In my present
state, I could not have sat through a commercial television
jingle, let alone two or three hours of Caxley culture. Amy
was wholeheartedly sympathetic, and magnanimous about
my defection.

'You poor old darling! Take as many painkillers as you
can, and a warm bath, and crawl into bed as soon as you get
back. I'll ring tomorrow to see how you are, and tell
you how it went tonight. Now, tie something round your
face before you venture out, or you'll have earache as
well.'

'I have already. And Mrs Pringle suggests a stocking.'

'Mrs Pringle is a fool!' said Amy forcefully. 'Nylon's useless. You want a silk scarf.'

Wonderfully cheered by hearing Mrs Pringle denounced in such a forthright manner, I rang off, and went upstairs to swathe myself as directed.

I fairly galloped into Mr Bennett's presence when summoned. He looked astounded at the speed with which I clambered into the dreaded chair and displayed my raging tooth. Usually he is obliged to lead me to the seat murmuring soothing noises as grooms do to nervous horses.

'We'll soon settle that,' he said. 'Just temporarily, of course. I'll give you a shot, and a temporary filling, and we'll make an appointment to do the job properly when the inflammation has gone.'

I surrendered myself to his ministrations with only an occasional yelp and whimper, and was home again within half an hour.

I took Amy's advice and went to bed. Tibby followed me, and we snuggled down together, the cat on top, pinning the bed clothes down uncomfortably, but I was past worrying.

It was bliss to be in bed before six o'clock, and comparatively free from pain. My final thought was of Amy's concert, and all the hard work she had put into providing a successful evening. What a broken reed I was!

Nevertheless, despite my guilt, I fell asleep within minutes, and only surfaced when the alarm clock called me to face another day.

Amy was as good as her word and rang me after school the next day. After kind enquiries about my temporarily quiescent tooth, she told me that the evening had been a huge success.

'And you were *much* missed,' she added. 'Everyone enquiring after you and desolated to hear about the toothache. Do you know, we made nearly sixty pounds?'

'Marvellous,' I said, suitably impressed.

'Including the raffle, of course, and some records Jean Cole sent as she couldn't come herself. And the food seemed to suit everybody.'

'I bet it did, knowing your usual efforts.'

'Do you know, there were some veal patties left and Tim Ferdinand asked if he could have them to take home! What a strange man he is! Not that I minded. He's so emaciated I was glad to provide tonight's supper as well as yesterday's, but I must say I felt that I was making up a doggie bag as I packed the remnants.'

'It's probably because he's a poet. His standards of behaviour are quite different from normal, no doubt.'

'Yes, well, there it is. The veal patties have found a kind home evidently. For two pins I believe he would have taken the dregs of wine too. He was looking rather keenly at the bottles as he left.'

Amy reminded me about our holiday plans. I promised to be ready in good time, and we exchanged farewells.

The few days before that longed-for holiday were spent in reading-tests, a school medical inspection, patching up my tooth, and in writing a letter to the office pointing out that work on the skylight had still not begun, and why not?

But on Friday we broke up, and Sunday morning dawned clear and bright. Here was May at its best, and I carried my case downstairs with a glad heart.

Amy was punctual, refused coffee, complimented me upon my neat appearance, and we set off westward. After ten minutes' secret anxiety about whether I had switched

off everything switchable, whether I had left out the tin-opener for Tibby's Pussi-luv which Mrs Pringle was kindly giving her, and whether I had shut the pantry window which usually gets forgotten, I gave myself up to the enjoyment of the drive. Time enough to worry if I returned to a smoking ruin, I told myself, looking resolutely through the side window.

There was comparatively little traffic, and in any case Amy is an excellent driver. The green hedges streamed past, sprinkled here and there with curds of white May blossom. Cows stood knee deep in lush meadows, the sunshine gleaming on their glossy coats. The heat shimmered on Salisbury Plain. The distant hills were smudges of blue in the clear atmosphere, and the sun grew hotter as we sped on.

We stopped for lunch, and again later in the afternoon to have a walk. The lane where we drew off ran deep between steep banks. Primroses were still out on the shady side, and young bracken and hart's tongue fern delighted us both. Through a gateway we saw a little stream far below us, and on a tree stump a humped bird.

'Look!' whispered Amy, and even as she grabbed my arm, the bird spread its wings and dived towards the water – a vivid flash of pink and blue.

'A kingfisher!' we cried together.

'That means good luck,' Amy told me, as we set off to the car to resume our trip.

We reached Penzance soon after tea, wandered round the town, ate an admirable dinner, and slept like tops.

The helicopter journey across to St. Mary's the next morning was exciting. Below us the farms and trees looked like the models which my children so enjoy setting out, and

between the islands the sea glinted in the sunshine, green and blue, with creamy surf lashing the rocks. I wished the journey could have lasted longer. One saw so much, at just the right height it seemed to me, and I looked forward to the return journey.

We took a boat from St. Mary's to Tresco, and were soon settled in our hotel. Hanging out of the bedroom window, I surveyed the scene.

The light was wonderful, pellucid and luminous. It reminded me of the light Amy and I had rejoiced in when we spent a holiday in Crete together some years earlier. Perhaps all islands have this peculiar quality, a reflection, maybe, of the water around them.

The sea was as vivid a blue as the kingfisher's flashing wings, and toppled lazily upon white sandy beaches which I had only seen before in holiday brochures. Gorse blazed yellow nearby, and the accumulation of dazzling colours was heady stuff indeed.

Amy entered the room as I gazed, entranced.

'I think I could settle here for ever,' I told her.

'It can be pretty windy,' she warned me. 'You've only seen its fair-weather face.'

'It can be pretty windy at Fairacre,' I retorted, 'and not half as beautiful.'

'Wait until you've seen the rest,' said Amy. 'There's plenty to fall in love with.'

As usual, she was right. Everyone told us how lucky we were with the weather, for the sun shone for every day of our short stay, and we were able to quarter the island of Tresco on foot and visit the miraculous Abbey Gardens.

Sometimes we took a boat to one of the neighbouring

islands, and Amy, who is almost as knowledgeable about birds as Henry Mawne, was thrilled to study all sorts of rare varieties at St. Agnes through her field glasses.

I was far less energetic, being quite content to soak up the wonderful sunshine and sea air, and to give admiring grunts when Amy told me about such wonders as rock thrushes and buntings and kittiwakes and divers she was observing with rapture.

The days passed all too swiftly. As our boat chugged away from Tresco and its white sands, I promised myself another visit before I was too old and decrepit to enjoy tramping round its beautiful bays.

On our long drive back I tried to tell Amy how much I had appreciated the holiday, and how perfect she was as a companion and guide.

She patted my knee.

'You do me good,' she said, and then went on to say the most surprising things.

'I envy you, you know, teaching away at Fairacre, always busy, knowing where you are going, seeing progress with those lucky children of yours. I seem to lead such a *useless* sort of life.'

'I've never heard such rubbish,' I protested. 'Why, you run that house perfectly, and look after James, and still find time for all sorts of good works, like that poetry evening, for instance. What's more, you look a dream always and are a delight to everyone's eye.'

'Well, thank you, my dear. I'm grateful, but the truth is, it's not enough. I can do all those things quite easily, I suppose, and so do thousands of other ordinary women like me, but I should like to do something which is especially *me*! I used to paint passably, but I know I shall never be much

good at it. I wondered – don't laugh at me – but do you think I could *possibly* write my autobiography?'

'I know you could. And very well too. When are you starting?'

Amy laughed, and the tension was broken. 'Lord knows! I expect I shall be one of those people who is constantly saying she is going to write a book "when she can find the time". Lucy Clayton is one of them.'

Lucy Clayton was at college when we were, and I found her insufferable. Amy sees her occasionally, while I try to avoid her.

'Lucy Clayton,' I said, 'is incapable of *speaking* the Queen's English let alone *writing* it. But you carry on, Amy. I'll see you keep at it, and I promise to buy the first copy.'

'You are very encouraging,' said Amy. 'As good as a tonic.'

'Or a holiday in the Scillies, maybe? Do you know, Amy, we shall be home in less than an hour, and for once in my life I shall have mixed feelings about being in Fairacre again.'

6 June

Of course, when it came to it, I slipped back into my usual routine within hours, and the glories of the Scillies seemed just a happy dream. A surprising number of people commented on my improved appearance.

'You was looking a bit peaky,' Mr Willet told me. 'I said to the missus a way back, "Miss Read looks proper poorly," but now, well, you looks as hearty as my old porker in his sty!'

Mrs Pringle's description was even more impressive.

'They've fattened you up a treat. You looked like a ghost before you had that holiday – real white and spiteful, if you know what I mean.'

I replied civilly that I was glad to know that I looked better. Privately I wondered what on earth I must have looked like to have been described as 'proper poorly', 'white and spiteful' and even now – after my metamorphosis – as 'a porker'. Ah well! At least vanity would not be added to my array of sins.

'See *The Caxley* since you've been back?' asked Mrs Pringle. I translated this as meaning *The Caxley Chronicle*. The phrase *The Caxley* can cover one or two objects, such as the local bus to the market town. I have heard people say, 'You'll have to catch *The Caxley* and then change.'

I admitted that I had not yet looked at the paper.

'It's got Mrs Benson's house in it this week. Nice place it

looks – bigger than it is really. Something to do with the way they tilts the camera no doubt.'

'We shall all miss her,' I said.

'The worst of it is, it don't give no price,' said Mrs Pringle gloomily. 'I do like to see how much people has the nerve to ask these days. Looks as though it's going to be auctioned. I suppose these 'ere estate agents hopes people will be carried away and offer more than it's worth. I remember my brother-in-law going crazy at one sale and buying a piece of stair carpet for three pounds.'

'That sounds quite a bargain to me.'

'Not when you had to lug away a broken fireguard, one of them exercising bicycles, a zinc bath and four chamber pots, if you'll excuse my mentioning them.'

'Not at all,' I said graciously.

'My sister fairly gave him a taste of her tongue, for all she belongs to the Plymouth Brethren. They had to pay Percy Potter another pound for bringing the stuff home on his carrier's van, and of course all the neighbours fell about laughing and making coarse remarks when the stuff came up the front path. No, my brother-in-law never heard the last of that, I can tell you!'

Mrs Pringle heaved herself from the front desk where she had been resting, and made for the stove. A dead leaf was sullying its summer perfection, and Mrs Pringle removed it with as much venom as she would have displayed if it had been a tarantula spider.

Later that day I looked up the advertisement. Holly Lodge certainly made an attractive picture, and the accommodation sounded ideal.

'Too big for us,' I told Tibby, 'and too expensive. But I hope some nice family comes to enjoy it.'

'The property includes a self-contained flat comprising a large sitting room, bedroom, bath and kitchen, on the ground floor, all in immaculate condition.'

Poor Miss Quinn, I thought! How she will hate leaving her flat, all in immaculate condition! I knew how happy she had been in Joan Benson's company. As Fairacre folk had said truly, it would not be easy for her to find such a home elsewhere.

And although I only knew Miriam Quinn slightly, I should be sorry to see her go from Fairacre. I liked her quiet contentment, the tranquil exterior which hid, I suspected, a power house of energy.

She obviously loved Fairacre, her solitude and her uninterrupted thoughts.

We had a lot in common.

During our stay in Tresco I had tried to tell Amy something of the feelings which had stirred me that afternoon alone in the schoolroom. Was it possible, I asked her, to put across such a theme in our centenary celebrations?

Amy was thoughtful for a time, and then said that she doubted if it would be possible.

'It's something purely evocative,' she said. 'I'm quite sure that lots of people in Fairacre feel the same way about their old school, but to express it, especially through the children who are the agents in this case, is well-nigh impossible, I think.

'You'll have to be content with coming down to a more earthy approach. Your idea of various happenings during the hundred years seems far more practical, and incidentally will show the continuity you are aiming at. Play for simplicity, is my advice.'

I was sure Amy was right, the more I thought about it. Anything verging on the high faluting could prove boring or sentimental.

I asked Miss Briggs to stay to tea one afternoon, and we set about tackling the programme. Not that our surroundings were conducive to heavy thought. The pinks in my border were beginning to shake out their shaggy heads, and the crimson feathers of peony petals fluttered to the baked earth beneath.

We sat in the shade of my old plum tree, tea cups in hand, and relished the peace of a June afternoon. In the distance we could hear the steady thumping of a baler. Someone had cut an early crop of hay, it seemed. A blackbird scurried among the plants in the dry border, searching for titbits for its young family, and overhead our ever-present downland larks kept up their fervent outpouring.

'Well, I suppose we'd better make a start,' I said at last. I could easily have drifted into sleep in these soporific surroundings, but it was hardly a good example to my assistant.

'Are you thinking of ten scenes, one for each decade,' asked Miss Briggs with unusual briskness, 'or a scene for each reign?'

'I hadn't really decided that point,' I admitted.

'And we shall have to have a narrator, of course. You'd better do that.'

I began to feel some awe for Miss Briggs. Who would have imagined she would be quite so efficient?

'I had dallied with the idea of one of the children doing that,' I replied.

'Oh, I think the thing needs to be held together by someone with authority,' said Miss Briggs. 'Besides, none of the

children really reads well enough, and all of them are bound to be nervous in front of an audience.'

I did not like to say that I should be nervous myself, but agreed meekly that it might be a good idea for me to do the linking. 'But not much of it,' I added. 'Just a few sentences to show what is happening in the world outside, and then a true scene straight from the log book.'

'And what about music?'

'Oh, heavens above,' I groaned. My piano playing is minimal, and Miss Briggs's non-existent. We could have records, I supposed?

'Well, we'll think about that,' said my assistant, now busily making notes on a pad. 'But some singing might go down well, if we can get an accompanist. After all, that piano of ours has been here since the school started. It ought to have a part in the performance.'

We worked for an hour or more as the teapot cooled in the grass at our feet, and a few early gnats hovered around. By that time, we had decided that the next step was to ransack the log book for suitable scenes, with not too many players in them, and to use the whole school as a chorus whenever it could be incorporated.

'Must let the mums see their offspring in the limelight,' remarked Miss Briggs sagaciously. 'It's half the battle.'

With that, we carried in our tea things and I saw the lady off, feeling more respect for my partner than ever before.

As all Fairacre had foreseen, work began on the skylight some two months later than planned, and it was quite clear that the rest of the summer term would pass to the accompaniment of loud noises above, and showers of a century's rubbish falling about us.

To give Reg Thorn his due, he certainly apologised very prettily. No doubt he got plenty of practice, was my private tart comment. He also rigged up a tarpaulin just under the skylight which was intended to catch the bits, but also blocked a great deal of light. I had not realised how much we relied on this ancient window for illumination until the tarpaulin flapped above my desk.

It was all very annoying, and of course the children's attention was more distracted than ever. Reg Thorn appeared himself for the first hour or so each day, and then left his two younger assistants to carry on.

'Got quite a lot of other jobs on hand,' he explained. 'Got some shelving for the Mawnes, and a little job at Beech Green. If I keep an eye on them it keeps you all happy.'

I should like to have pointed out that finishing one job satisfactorily and then proceeding to the next on the date given originally and staying there till *that* job was done, would make us all a great deal happier. But before I could voice these sentiments Reg Thorn had departed. Such expert slipping away could also be the result of years of experience, I thought to myself.

Later in the morning, when we were about to clear the desks ready for school dinner, Eileen Burton rushed in from the lobby in a state of panic.

'There's a funny man in the playground,' she gasped.

At once there was a rush to the door. The mob checked there and turned to me in some dismay.

'He's all dressed up in white, miss.'

'Got one of them sun 'ats on, miss.'

'He's blowing smoke, miss.'

'Looks like a man from Mars to me, miss,' said the school wag.

'Well, let me come through and then I can see,' I said. A narrow passage was made through the milling mass.

Sure enough, a white-clad figure, crowned with a topee from which white veiling fell to the shoulders, roamed apparently aimlessly round the playground. In its hand was a contraption with a nozzle which occasionally belched blue smoke. Memories of a recent television programme, which I had been too idle to switch off, came back to me.

'It's the vicar,' I told them.

'He'd never dress up all funny,' Ernest rebuked me.

'Looking for bees,' I continued. 'Now go inside, and I'll have a word with him.'

Reluctantly they moved back a few feet. I did not imagine for a moment that they would return to their desks. Curiosity was too strong for them, but at least they stayed in the safety of the lobby and watched the proceedings.

I was within touching distance of our vicar before he became aware of me, so engrossed was he in surveying the hedges and trees which border the playground.

'Oh, my dear Miss Read,' he exclaimed. 'How you startled me!'

I expressed my regret.

'I should have let you know that I was coming, but time pressed. Mr Lamb rang to say a swarm of bees was passing over – he thought they might be mine – so of course I got my things together, and ventured out.'

He compressed the bellows of the gadget in his hand and smoke issued forth.

'My smoker,' he said, with pride. 'It's still working, thank heaven. It calms the bees so that you can drop them into the skep easily.'

He nodded towards the school wall where a fine straw skep awaited the elusive swarm.

'But surely, they might be miles away,' I said. At that moment, Mrs Partridge's face peered over the wall which divides the school playground from the vicar's garden.

'Gerald! Gerald! Margaret Waters has just rung to say the bees are in her damson tree, and could you come quickly before they get into the chimney.'

'Into the chimney?' echoed the vicar in amazement. 'Why on earth should they wish to go into a *chimney* when they can enjoy the sunshine and fresh air on a damson tree?'

'I don't know the *reason*, Gerald,' said Mrs Partridge, sounding justifiably exasperated, 'I am simply repeating her message – so *hurry*!'

The vicar obediently collected his skep, threw back the veil from his perspiring countenance, and set off on his errand of mercy.

Later, Mr Willet spoke of the episode.

'D'you see the vicar in his moonship gear this morning? My word, he fair set all the village dogs barking their heads off as he went by! And young Mrs Smith's baby was outside in his pram, and hasn't stopped bawling since.'

'But did he take the swarm?' I asked.

'Oh, he took 'em all right,' said Mr Willet off-handedly. 'They're in the skep in the shade. Miss Waters said the vicar's coming to get them at dusk. But just to be on the safe side she told Mr Mawne, and he's promised to help collect 'em. He's a better man than I am, Gunga Din,' said Mr Willet, misquoting Kipling. 'I wouldn't go near a swarm of bees for all the tea in China. Did I ever tell you about my old gran's?'

'Yes,' I said, and went to pick up an infant who had fallen painfully and deservedly from the coke pile.

There was an agreeable literary sequel to this adventure. When the vicar called to bring in the hymn list at the end of the week, I naturally enquired after the bees.

'It was an extraordinary thing,' said the vicar. 'Henry and I collected the skep during the evening, and he helped me to transfer it to an old hive he lent me. But do you know, they simply would not stay in it! Luckily, I had a new hive not in use, so later we transferred them to that one, and since then we've had no trouble.'

'What was wrong with Henry's hive, do you think?'

'I think dear old Parson Woodforde put his finger on it some two hundred years ago. You know his diary, I have no doubt?'

I very nearly said it was my Bible, but remembering to whom I was speaking, hastily said it was a great favourite of mine.

'I looked up the passage, and he says something to the effect that he too had to hive a swarm twice. The first hive had evidently been kept in a barn and he suspected that mice or other small animals had used it. I liked his final comment that: "Bees are particularly Nice and Cleanly." He must have been a singularly kind and observant man, and obviously loved his bees.'

Such a warm smile illumined the cherubic countenance of our own parson, that I thought he shared many of Parson Woodforde's virtues.

The Caxley Spring Festival had netted over a thousand pounds, the local paper informed us, and more was expected as one or two extra efforts were still to be held. One of these was a flower festival involving half a dozen beautifully decked churches, St. Patrick's being one of them.

I wandered in one evening to admire the exquisite arrangements. To my mind every one was perfect, a miracle of form and fragrance. It astonished me to hear the comments of two women who were following me round the display. They were evidently keen flower arrangers and knew all the things one should be looking for.

'My dear,' said one, 'just *look* at that pedestal! One can positively see the Oasis!'

'Dreadful,' agreed her friend, with a shudder, 'and she has obviously *never heard* of the Hogarth line!'

I only hoped that the arranger was not within earshot.

When I emerged from the church into the golden evening, a woman hailed me. Her name, luckily, I remembered. She was a Mrs Austen, and once belonged to our Women's Institute. We had not seen each other for months, and we greeted each other enthusiastically.

As she had seen the flowers and had time to spare, she came back to the schoolhouse with me.

'We're at Springbourne now,' she told me. 'My husband had the chance of a job in London, but we wouldn't take it although the money was better. We've been countrymen ever since we were evacuated.'

'Tell me more,' I begged her. 'Were you at Fairacre School? You know it's our centenary this year?'

'Yes, I was, and no, I didn't know,' she replied. 'I came down right at the beginning of the war. We lived in Camberwell in south London, and pretty crowded we were in our flat. There were three of us children. I was the youngest, just six when war broke out. We'd all been to the big L.C.C. school round the corner, and a very good grounding we got there.

'Mind you, the classes were big – over fifty of us

altogether, and the teachers had to keep order pretty well or nothing would have been learnt. Looking back, we did a lot of class work the children today wouldn't like. Chanting tables, and reading round the class out of the same reader, that sort of thing. And no end of spelling tests and mental arithmetic, all done very fast, and devil take the hindmost.'

'But you got on, obviously.'

'Oh, we all got on. In those days the teachers were the best in the country, we were told. They got the highest salaries, so the committee could take the pick of the training colleges when they appointed staff. They certainly made us work. I think that's partly why I liked Fairacre so much. The pace was slower and the teachers were quieter.'

'Was that all you liked? It must have been an upheaval to be evacuated.'

She shook her head. 'I told you we were crowded at home, and at school. Mine was a very respectable family. Mother kept us all spotless, and the house was polished to the nines. But we only had one room really to live in comfortably – the front room – and that was turned into a bedroom at night for my two brothers.

'Behind that was the kitchen, and it was always so dark that we had to have the gas burning. And behind that was the only bedroom, where I slept on a little truckle-bed next to my parents.'

'Any garden?'

'Just a tiny paved yard where Mother hung her washing. If we wanted to see grass we had to be taken to the park. We weren't allowed to go on our own, because the roads were too busy.'

'So all these fields seemed wonderful?'

'Do you know, when we got out at Caxley Station and

stood in lines with our little cardboard boxes holding our gas masks, some of the children were crying. But not me! There were lovely grassy banks, and roses in flower, and the air was just beautiful. I felt I had come home.'

'And that feeling stayed?'

'It's never gone away! As we drove to Fairacre with our new foster parents I grew happier and happier. Of course, I missed my father and mother, and at night-time, if I woke, I sometimes wept a bit for them. But Fairacre was bliss to me, and the children were kind to us as well as the teachers.'

'I'm glad to hear it.'

'We all squashed up together in the desks. Two of our teachers had come with us, nice lively girls they were. It couldn't have been easy for anyone, because every scrap of space was used, and we even had a couple of classes in the village hall. But after a bit, a lot of the children drifted back to London as there weren't any raids, so things settled down very comfortably. Mr Fortescue was the headmaster, and Miss Clare was teaching here then. How is she?'

I gave her news of our old friend.

'If ever there was a saint, she's one,' said Mrs Austen. 'I suppose she's coming to the celebrations?'

'I hope she'll tell us some of her memories,' I replied. 'She knows more about Fairacre School than anyone living.'

'She helped us all to settle in,' remembered Mrs Austen. 'You know there were a lot of things that shook us about the country. Cows for one, and earth closets for another. And I was scared stiff of real darkness in a winter's lane, after lamp posts along the pavements. I think our hostesses had plenty to put up with. On the whole I like to think that we three didn't give too much trouble. We'd been brought up quite strictly, and my parents came down at least twice a

month, and made sure we behaved properly. But there were some pretty rough families, as you can guess, and all that talk about bed-wetting and head lice and impetigo and scabies and so on – well, a lot of it was true.'

'We get the odd case now,' I told her. 'Fairacre isn't unadulterated Arcady, you know.'

'I realise that, but to me as a six-year-old Fairacre *was* Arcady, and this part of England has stayed that way, to my mind, ever since.'

'I'm inclined to agree,' I said.

Mrs Pringle arrived the next morning looking full of importance, and with no trace of a limp. She had the appearance of one with a message to deliver.

It was sad news.

'Bob Willet says he won't be in today until later. His poor brother Sid has passed on, and Bob's gone over there to see his sister-in-law and fix up the funeral.'

I murmured condolences.

'Well, he's been bad for months, poor soul. Something to do with his digestion – the *lower* end of it, if you know what I mean. I never liked to ask Bob too much about it, as it was rather a *personal* complaint.'

'Aren't they all?'

'Some,' said Mrs Pringle frostily, 'is more personal than others.' And she swept away.

Mr Willet looked rather subdued when he appeared in the late afternoon, and shook his head sadly when I expressed my sorrow.

'Thank God I didn't have to see him dead,' he said. 'Never let anyone show you a corpse, specially if you've been fond of the person. My mum made me kiss my

grandma in her coffin, and I've never got over it. What's more, I can never remember my gran as she was when she was alive. The look of her dead face is the only one I can see. A pity! She was a lively old party and I loved her a lot.'

I said I'd heard about her from several of her Fairacre friends.

'She was good to us kids. There was five of us, and not much money, of course. We lived in a cottage at Springbourne and my gran lived nearby. We always called in going to and from school, and she used to put an apple or some plums in our dinner basket.

'Sid was the eldest. He was quite a scholar, used to sit there when old Hope was headmaster.' Mr Willet nodded towards a corner desk at the back. 'He could have gone to the grammar school, but with all of us to keep Dad said he'd best get out working. Old Sid never complained and he made a durn fine cabinet maker in the end, but I reckon he minded a bit about not going to Caxley Grammar.'

Mr Willet sighed, and began to make for the door. 'It's a funny thing, when someone dies, you never remember them as they were then, but always as children. I saw poor old Sid in hospital last week, but all I can see now is Sid about ten, lugging the rush basket with our school dinners up the hill here to Fairacre School. Or swinging our little sister round and round by her hands, or feeding his pet rabbit.'

He opened the schoolroom door. 'Old Sid will always be about ten for me. Funny really!'

'Perhaps that's as it should be,' I told him.

When I saw Amy next I repeated Mr Willet's remarks about viewing the dead.

'It's perfectly true,' she agreed. 'I can't say I've seen many dead people, but the two aunts whose bodies I saw simply will not come to life for me now. I always do my best *not* to see corpses for that reason. I like to remember my relatives as they were.'

'I'm remarkably short of close relatives,' I said, 'though I'm told I look more and more like my Aunt Bessie the older I grow. I'm sorry to say she was remarkably plain, but very determined.'

'I often wonder if we only see the *good* points of relatives in ourselves. You say your Aunt Bessie was *determined*. Maybe she was just pig-headed. I know I like to think I have my Aunt Maud's efficiency, but really I know she was plain *bossy*, and nearly drove poor Uncle Edward demented. She would tidy away his jigsaw puzzle and put it back in the box when he was only halfway through.'

'Strong grounds for divorce,' I said. 'Have some coffee?'

And we went into the kitchen together to make it.

7 July

Speculation about Holly Lodge grew keener as the weeks passed. The preliminary announcement of its sale by auction, 'unless sold privately beforehand', whetted all appetites.

Mrs Pringle had heard from an unspecified source, but she told me it was as true as she stood there, that nothing under fifty thousand pounds would be considered. Mr Willet observed that people must need their heads examined when it came to buying houses these days, and Reg Thorn said he could remember when Holly Lodge belonged to that miserable old faggot that drove a Liverpool phaeton. His name was on the tip of his tongue, but he reckoned it had gone for the moment. Anyway, when he had died – and no one mourned his going, that was a fact – Holly Lodge went for six hundred to a nice old party from the other side of Caxley. Six hundred, mark you!

Later in the morning, he drew aside the tarpaulin, sending a shower of dried paint and wood splinters upon us, poked his face through the gap, and said:

'Potter! That was the name! Josiah Potter, and a nasty bit of work he was too.'

He then withdrew, allowing me to send Ernest out to the lobby for the dustpan and brush, whilst I continued my interrupted discourse on mediaeval farming methods.

The sale of Holly Lodge occupied the inhabitants of

Fairacre very pleasurably. The history of the house, the quirks of its various owners and, of course, the scandalous amount of money being asked for it at the moment, were all mulled over with the greatest enjoyment.

Whether any would-be purchasers had inspected the house was difficult to say. Holly Lodge was a little distance from the centre of the village and well hidden from prying eyes by the high hedge which gave the house its name. It was one of Fairacre's more retired establishments, and as Mrs Pringle remarked wistfully: 'It's difficult to find out what goes on in there.'

It so happened that I met Miriam Quinn and Joan Benson on separate occasions within a week. I had gone into Caxley on one sunny Saturday morning to buy a pair of summer shoes, and was still reeling from the shock of the amount I had just handed over, when I bumped into Miriam Quinn.

She commiserated with me.

'I can sympathise. I've just come from inspecting cotton frocks, and have decided that my present shabby collection can do another year – if not two or three.'

I asked after Joan.

'Run off her feet at the moment, with people coming to view. She won't have any difficulty in disposing of it, I'm sure, but she does so want to see it in good hands. Half the viewers have appalling plans for turning it into flats, or a home for delinquent boys or some such.'

I said that it must be a trying time for them both.

'Well, there it is. I haven't found anything remotely suitable for myself, and I'm now at the limbo stage, telling myself I may as well wait and see, and perhaps something will turn up. Somehow one gets numb after a bit.'

'Maybe that's nature's protection,' I said, as we parted.

Joan Benson I met in the village a day or two later. She was struggling with an overloaded carrier bag which had collapsed under the strain, and only had one handle intact.

'I really should have brought the car, but I thought it would do me good to walk on such a heavenly day. In any case, I only intended to buy about four things, and now look at me!'

'Here, put some in my basket, and come back with me and I'll let you have a good tough bag. I'm going to have a cup of tea anyway, so do join me.'

The children had gone home, and I had been to the post office to send off a couple of urgent missives to the office, which would probably not be opened for days, if I knew anything about it.

Over tea, Joan told me more about the horrors of selling a home. 'I don't know which is worse – trying to find a home, or trying to get rid of one. For two pins, I'd call the whole thing off and just stay at Holly Lodge until I'm carried out feet first.'

'There would be general rejoicing if you did decide to stay,' I told her.

'Well, that's nice to hear, but I really must be sensible and look ahead. This wretched arthritis gets steadily more troublesome, and sometimes I find it quite difficult to get upstairs. And the house is far too big now that I'm alone, and costs the earth to heat. And much as I love gardening, I simply cannot cope with that great one at Holly Lodge, and help gets more and more impossible to find, and more and more expensive.'

She sighed, and shook her head at the proffered biscuit tin.

'What a misery I sound! I'm not really unhappy, I've been so kindly looked after in Fairacre I shall miss the life here horribly. But my daughter is quite right. If I can't drive, I shall be absolutely done for in Fairacre, and I'm finding it quite painful sometimes. And I'm sorry to say that I am now refusing to drive at night, or if it's foggy or icy.'

'That cuts it down quite considerably,' I agreed, and she laughed.

'But it's selling the house which is the real problem. I don't want Miriam to have to go. She's been quite wonderful to me, and is so happily ensconced in that little annexe. If only we could find a nice quiet family that would be glad to have her there, and people that Miriam could get on with, it would be perfect. But that means selling to someone we know, and so far no one in that category has emerged. And some of the viewers have fairly curdled my blood with their plans for the house!'

'They probably wouldn't get them passed anyway when it came to the point.'

'But I *love* that house,' cried Joan. 'I simply hate the idea of it being torn about. If only some nice couple who like it as it is would appear, I should sell cheerfully. As it is, I still have to find myself somewhere near Barbara. She is quite marvellous about vetting places, but with young children she is very tied, and I feel I must go and stay with her before long to have a good scout round myself.'

She began to collect her shopping.

'I've run on far too long, but you are so sympathetic. And thank you for the delicious tea, and the bag, and best of all for *listening*.'

On the doorstep she paused.

'You won't mention my concern about Miriam, will you? I should hate her to think I was turning buyers away because of her. It's not *quite* like that, as I'm sure you understand, but she is so independent . . .'

Her voice trailed away.

'Never fear,' I assured her. 'I've lived in a village long enough to know how to be discreet. Though even then, it's sometimes difficult to keep the boat up straight.'

She waved, and departed with her burden.

Mr Lamb at the post office unearthed a handful of ancient postcards from the back of a little-used drawer. He came across one of Fairacre School which he kindly gave me, and I pored over it with a magnifying glass.

This photograph must have been taken in the first decade of this century, judging by the dress of the children. They are all gathered in the lane outside the school and there is not a single piece of traffic in sight.

How instantly that picture carried me into a vanished world! The boys are grouped together on one side of the lane, and every one of them wears a cap. Some are in Norfolk breeches, some in short and some in long trousers. Quite a few have jackets too big for them, some too small, with their bony wrists hanging from tight sleeves, but almost all sport Eton collars and stout boots.

The girls, carefully separated from the boys by the width of the lane, wear black stockings and boots, white starched pinafores over their frocks, and some have hats as well. Altogether there must be around seventy children in this photograph. The staff seems to be hidden by the throng,

with the exception of one stolid-looking young man who towers above the girls.

I looked in vain for Miss Clare who must have been there at that time, but either she was absent that day or was engulfed by her charges somewhere at the rear of the party.

The school building looked exactly the same, and I recognised several trees as old friends, although considerably shorter. But a magnificent barn, end on to the road, has now gone. The rough grass still grows as thickly at the edge of the lane, and one small child holds a flower to his face, enjoying its scent forever.

With so many memories crowding upon me during this centenary year, I found this scene particularly moving, and shall always be grateful to Mr Lamb for presenting me with such an irreplaceable treasure.

With the end of term in sight I conferred with Miss Briggs about our plans. It seemed wise to let parents know in good time about our centenary affairs, especially those who might have costumes to prepare.

'After all, it is *next term*,' I pointed out, 'and Fairacre folk don't like to be hurried into things.'

'I should think that seldom happens,' replied my assistant. 'I've never met such a slow lot of parents. It's about time Fairacre moved with the times, and woke up.'

I was too taken aback by this attack to answer for a moment. Talk about the pot calling the kettle black, was my first reaction!

'And I'm beginning to wonder,' she went on, 'if I don't owe it to myself to change to a livelier job.'

I hardly liked to point out that she had had some months

of unemployment before she landed the Fairacre post. Also that she would need a glowing reference from me, which in all honesty I could not supply, to take her to another job, and in any case her probationary year had at least another term to run.

'If you do decide to try your luck,' I said at last, 'you know how much notice you must give. But if you'll take my advice I should get all the experience you can here before you think of changing.'

'Nothing seems to *happen* here!' cried my discontented assistant. 'I should think Fairacre School was exactly like this a hundred years ago! And, as far as I can see, it will be exactly the same a hundred years hence!'

Privately I hoped it would be, but I know full well that the wind of change buffets us daily, and that a school which has shrunk from that thriving community in Mr Lamb's photograph to the twenty-odd children who now comprise the school cannot hope to survive long.

'I think you must make an effort to join some activity or other which you'll enjoy in Caxley,' I said. 'What about the Operatic Society, or Caxley Dramatic Club? You like tennis, I know, and there are two good clubs in Caxley which you might enjoy. At least you would meet other young people. I know it must be pretty lonely for you here with no other young staff.'

'No one's asked me to join anything,' muttered Miss Briggs sulkily.

I began to feel my small stock of patience becoming as exhausted as Herr Hitler's.

'Well, of course, they haven't! They don't know you are *there*! Go along to a meeting, or find out the name of the secretary, and say you want to join. It's up to you. You can't

expect these organisations to search the highways and byways.'

'I don't know if I shall have time, with all this centenary fuss to arrange,' said Miss Briggs, as though the entire burden of our celebrations rested on her dandruff-sprinkled shoulders.

I took a deep breath.

'Which brings us to the point. You'd better come to tea tomorrow and we'll draft out our plan.'

'I wash my hair tomorrow after school,' she said.

Far be it from me to stop that, was my unworthy thought.

'Make it Friday,' I said shortly, and got out the register.

Amy called the following evening, and I was glad that Miss Briggs was elsewhere attending to her hair. I enquired after the progress of the autobiography.

'Well, it's uphill work, I can tell you! As you know, I always think one's childhood is the most interesting part of an autobiography. But then, where does one begin?'

'I should think: "I was born on May the Whatever in Nether Wallop or Somesuch."'

'I feel that's too bald. I think people are glad to be told something about one's parents, but I dread going back too far and having sixteen, if not thirty-two, dubious portraits of forebears on each side.'

'I rather agree.'

'On the other hand, there were some very colourful ancestors on my mother's side. Two brothers were transported to Australia for stealing sheep and cattle.' Amy spoke with considerable pride.

'Well, put 'em in,' I advised.

'It would certainly swell the volume a little. You've no idea how much writing is needed to make a page of print. It's really quite daunting. I'm thinking of throwing in a distant great-uncle too. He was defrocked sometime in the last century for conduct not befitting the clergy. Something to do with the choir boys, I gather, but it's so difficult to find any clear evidence after all this time.'

'I'd no idea you had such a disreputable background, Amy.'

'My immediate background is blameless,' she assured me. 'And very dull too. My grandparents and parents seem to have worked hard, kept out of debt, looked after their small families, and generally been worthy and respectable. The consequence is that they make pretty dull reading matter, and I wonder if it might be a good idea to start farther back. I could have a family tree in the front.'

'Does anyone ever look at them? All I find is that having pulled the thing out, it is impossible to fold it correctly again, and you have half a yard of tissue paper in your lap all the time you are reading.'

'That's true,' agreed Amy. 'But going back to your first idea of plunging straight in with one's birth – do you think readers are *really gripped* by hearing about your being bottle fed and having your adenoids out, and the way you had hysterics at the age of four when Father Christmas kissed you, reeking of whisky?'

'All those things might create a sympathetic bond,' I said. 'As these confounded educationists tell us *ad nauseam*, children should be able to identify themselves with the characters they are reading about. Though how you can identify with Sinbad the Sailor or Tom Thumb beats me.'

'Well, all I can say is that I have spent a good hour after tea

every day for the past fortnight, pushing along my reluctant ball point, and I don't suppose I have written enough to fill four pages of a real book. It's very disheartening.'

'Cheer up!' I said. 'Think how splendid it will look piled up in the book shops with queues outside fighting to get in to buy it. And you on television. Possibly on *This Is Your Life*. Just think of that!'

'I refuse to consider it,' said Amy firmly.

Mrs Partridge, the vicar's wife, called at the school the next morning, and the children sat up with smiles wreathing their faces.

They like Mrs Partridge. I like to think it is for herself alone, for she is a kind, warm-hearted person and devoted to the young, but I have the feeling that she is welcomed more for the bag of boiled sweets which she so often brings with her.

Today was no exception, except that the sweets were toffees and not fruit drops. The children's response to this largesse was ecstatic, as Patrick handed round the bag.

'Now, my dear,' said Mrs Partridge when all were busy sucking. 'I wonder if you can do me a favour.'

What answer is there to that after such generosity?

'Of course,' I said rashly.

'I'm short of collectors for my *Save The Children* flag day next week, and I wondered if you could help.'

'Where would you want me to go?' I asked, resigned to my lot.

'Well, I'm doing from The Beetle and Wedge to the crossroads, and Margaret Waters is doing the other side of the road, and Joan Benson was to have done that outlying part from her house to Tyler's Row, but she has had to hare

off to look at a couple of houses her daughter has found. It is that stretch that I hoped you might find time to do.'

I agreed to take over Joan's territory, and Mrs Partridge whipped a piece of paper from the top of the basket she was carrying, and placed a collecting tin on my desk with incredible speed.

'That's *most* kind of you, dear,' she said briskly. 'Could you let me have it back by Thursday? And here is your official badge, and the flags.'

The piece of paper had successfully hidden all these things in the basket, and I noticed yet another collecting tin and more flags, still to be allotted presumably.

'I'll do that,' I promised. Bang go the two evenings I had earmarked for making strawberry jam and bottling cherries, I thought!

She wished the children goodbye, and they replied with their diction somewhat impeded by toffee, but true love shining in their eyes.

The door had hardly closed before Eileen Burton was sick on the floor, and one of the Coggs twins began to choke on a large piece of sweet which had gone down the wrong way.

I hastily put the collecting box on the window sill before going to the rescue.

Save The Children indeed! What about the teachers?

Miss Briggs duly stayed late on Friday, and accompanied me to the school house for tea. She appeared somewhat monosyllabic and sulky, but whether she was feeling resentful at staying after school, or whether she was simply being natural – Mr Willet's 'a fair old lump of a girl' came to mind – I could not say.

However, she cheered up a little after three cups of tea, brown bread and honey followed by a large slice of Dundee cake, and we settled down with pencils and notebooks to our task.

'I think six scenes will be ample,' I said, 'which means something from the reigns of Victoria, Edward the Seventh, George the Fifth, Edward the Eighth – unless we leave him out – George the Sixth, and our present Queen.'

'Good idea,' agreed Miss Briggs, sucking a sticky finger. 'If we had a scene for every decade that would make . . . how many?'

'Ten,' I told her. 'You ought to know that – child of the metric system as you are.'

'Yes, well – if we had the scenes lasting only ten minutes that would be far too long, wouldn't it?'

'My feeling entirely. We can't expect people to sit on the school seats for more than an hour altogether, and if we have a few songs, and then tea afterwards it is as much as the human frame can take.'

'Have you found some likely stories from the log book?'

'One or two. I thought for the first scene we could use the boy Pratt putting on the school clock, and being caught by the head mistress.'

'Lovely! But how will he climb up? Would he pile up the desks?'

I repressed a shudder.

'No. We'll have Mr Willet's step ladder to hand. After all, it just *may* have been left in the schoolroom. And through all the scenes we'll use the old side desk, and the actors will be in period costume, of course. When we get to Elizabeth the Second we can push on a modern desk. The old style were in use when I first came here. I must say, they were pretty sturdy.'

'Then what?' asked my assistant, bringing me back to the work in hand.

'Well, for Edward the Seventh, I thought it would be marvellous if I could say something like: "It was in this reign that a new pupil teacher took up her duties", and in walks Miss Clare!'

'Perfect!'

'Then she could tell us about her experiences of that time. I have sounded her, and she's game to do it. Frankly, I think it will be the high spot of the whole proceedings.'

'What about George the Fifth?'

'I think it will have to have something to do with the Great War.'

I told her about Miss Clare's memories of the babies fraying pieces of cotton material to make field dressings. We could enlarge on helping-the-war effort theme, without dwelling unduly on the horrors which many of the older people in the audience would remember all too well. I wondered if one of the parents who went as a child from Fairacre School to the Wembley Exhibition might give an enthusiastic first-hand account of a country child's memories of that memorable charabanc ride to London in the twenties. Mr Lamb perhaps? Or Mrs Willet? I promised to follow up the idea.

The more we thought about Edward the Eighth's brief reign the stronger became our resolve to leave out a scene, and simply let the narrator comment on that passage of time. Apart from the Abdication, which really had very little impact on the children of the school, there was little to mark the reign's fleeting impression on the village.

The 1939–45 war, which followed within three years, had much more effect, of course, and we resolved to show the

crowded desks, with the gas mask boxes lodged thereupon, and one or two wartime posters pinned up – as evidently there had been in Mr Fortescue's session as headmaster at that time. Luckily, Mr Willet still had two precious relics, one showing the results of careless talk and the other of wasting food. There were one or two incidents in the log book which could form the basis of a scene, and perhaps Mrs Austen of Springbourne might be prevailed upon to give her impressions of Fairacre School from an evacuee's point of view.

As for our last, and present-day, scene, what could be better than drawing the audience's attention to the children's exhibition of work in both rooms, singing by the whole school, and the narrator pointing out such facts as the vanishing of those over eleven to the local comprehensive school and cutting down the numbers of Fairacre School drastically after the 1944 Act?

Finally, I had asked the vicar if he would appear at the end and remind us all that the church had always played an important part in the hundred years of Fairacre School. He was willing to do this, and to end our proceedings with a prayer for blessings received in the past, and our hopes for the future.

'That should take us up to tea very nicely,' said Miss Briggs kindly.

'We'll all need it by then,' I assured her. 'And now let's rough out which children would be best as the actors.'

It took us until nearly seven o'clock, but we felt it had been worth it. Certainly, Miss Briggs departed looking very much more cheerful than when she arrived, and had been surprisingly helpful.

* * *

The weather had been perfect, at least in my eyes, for the last few weeks of term. The sun had shone from a cloudless sky, every playtime had found the schoolroom deserted and the playground crowded with good-tempered children playing with unusual placidity. But I was surprised, nevertheless, to hear that an official drought had been declared, and we were all being exhorted to save water.

It always beats me how, in the temperate climate we are supposed to enjoy, panic sets in as soon as any mild and foreseen variations from the normal weather conditions prevail. If three inches of snow fall in January, the headlines scream about disrupted rail services, motorway chaos, children marooned in school buses and lambs dying in drifts. The country, they say dramatically, has been brought to a standstill. They seem to cope pretty well in Canada, or America and Switzerland, it seems to me, with about thirty times the amount of precipitation.

And why, as in the present circumstances, have we to watch each precious drop of water? Way back in February, we were sloshing about knee-deep in the stuff, as the swollen rivers overflowed, and Mr Roberts was out rescuing lambs at Springbourne.

In any event, we were all blissfully happy in the scorching sun, and I scuffed through the dust at the edge of the road on my way to the grocer's after school, glorying in the heat. It was beginning to look like the end of summer, with the grass drying prematurely and even some yellow leaves appearing on the fruit trees. Miss Waters's privet hedge was in flower, the small white pyramids of blossom giving out that faint sickly smell which is the essence of summer.

White convolvulus plants scrambled along the wire fence which borders the post office garden, the purity of their

trumpets sadly tarnished with dust and heat. Below them, a root of scarlet poppies flamed, giving out their hot peppery fragrance as the dry wind shook them.

I met the vicar as I returned. He greeted me cheerfully and told me that his bees were extremely active.

'No more swarms?'

'Not yet, but this is the sort of weather that might set them off,' he told me. 'The swarm I collected from Margaret Waters has settled in beautifully. Very attractive bees – rather paler than my first, and so busy! Really they are an example to one in this heat. I must confess I find it most trying, and shall welcome the rain when it comes.'

Mr Willet hailed me from the churchyard when I was nearly home, and I walked across to see him. It was cool in the shade of the massive yew tree where I stood. Mr Willet was busy cutting long grass from some of the ancient burial mounds with a bill-hook.

'Hot work,' I commented.

'Suits me,' said my caretaker, mopping his glistening face. He came and stood beside me, and together we surveyed the sleeping place of the Fairacre dead. It was all very peaceful. Some midges drifted in clouds near the hedge, and a peacock butterfly opened and shut its beautiful wings upon the warm stone slab commemorating some village worthy.

With the centenary always to the front of my mind these days, I wondered how many of those resting here had attended the little school hard by, and what they had thought of it. As if reading my thoughts, Mr Willet said that there was a mort of folk these days as preferred to go up in smoke, and he wondered if it was right.

'We certainly miss all those lovely inscriptions,' I said.

'Personally, I enjoy a potter round this churchyard reading about virtuous wives and devoted mothers mourned by their fourteen sorrowing children. I've even got a soft spot for that terrible marble angel in memory of Mr Parr who died in 1870, "Benefactor and Brother To All".'

'Nice bit of work,' agreed Mr Willet. 'I likes a bit of white marble myself. Can't take to that polished pink granite. Might just as well have a bit of cold brawn on top of you, from the looks of it.'

'Well, I must go home,' I said reluctantly. 'Tibby expects a meal.'

'You spoils that cat. It'll get fatty heart the way you feeds it.'

'He's got a large frame,' I protested.

'Not surprising, the amount he packs away,' replied Mr Willet. 'I'd better get on too. There's plenty of old Fairacre pupils wants tidying up by the south wall. You ever thought of that? You'll maybe get some ghosts at them celebrations of yours.'

'I rather hope we shall,' I said, stepping round the grave-stone of one Sally Gray who died in 1890 in her 63rd year. She would have been fifty-three when Fairacre School was newly built, I thought, making my way home through the heat.

How the history of this little village pressed around one!

Obedient to Mrs Partridge's behest, I set off on my collect-ing stint one hot evening.

For once, clouds covered the sky. They were ominously dark, but made no appreciable difference to the heat. It was about to break, and I only hoped that I should get my job done before that happened.

People were generous with their donations, and my tin was soon quite heavy, and chiefly with silver, not copper coins. I had left Joan Benson's house until last, as it was the furthest from home, and I could then have an uninterrupted walk back to feed my overweight cat at the right time.

A few drops of rain began to patter against the holly hedge round the garden as I opened the gate. All the windows were shut, including those in Miriam Quinn's annexe at the side, and there was that indefinable feeling of blankness that always seems to emanate from a deserted house. However, I decided to try my luck. I remembered that Joan had been going to look at a house near her daughter's, but hoped that she would have returned.

I was unlucky. No one answered the bell, and the rain began to fall in torrents. I was well sheltered in the deep porch, and sat down on a sturdy bench which ran along one side to watch the downpour.

It was wonderful to see the plants reviving in the heavy shower. The dusty drive was soon pock-marked with large raindrops, and then with tiny rivulets that snaked their way downhill to the gate. The holly hedge began to glisten with drops, and the thirsty flowers in the parched border seemed to lift their heads in response to this benison of refreshing rain.

Drops began to stream from the porch, until I began to feel that I was surveying the garden through a curtain of glass beads. The smell of water on hot stone rose all around me, and I began to realise how desperately the earth had been waiting for the rain.

It was obvious that Miriam Quinn had not returned yet from the office in Caxley. It was quite likely that there would be flooding there, I surmised, for the river Cax

overflows very readily, and the low-lying parts of the town, particularly the area known as 'The Marsh' floods with depressing regularity, despite the efforts of drainage experts to control this nuisance.

But my spirits rose when I heard a car scrunching up the back drive on the wet gravel. Here, no doubt, was Miriam returning. But I was wrong. The car did not stop at the annexe, but swept up to the porch where I was sitting, and pulled up with a squealing of brakes.

Out of the car leapt Henry Mawne, head down through the blinding rain, and met me face to face.

'Good Lord! Have you rung?'

'Yes, but there's no one at home. I was waiting for the worst of the rain to go.'

Henry looked agitated. He jingled some coins in his pocket, and bounced up and down on his toes, gazing at the watery scene.

'Oh dear! Oh dear! Now I wonder when she will be back. Any idea?'

'None at all, I'm afraid.'

I told him about Joan's departure for her house hunting.

'Well, let me give you a lift back. You might be stuck here for hours. It looks as though it has set in for the night.'

I was very grateful, and we drove back through the glistening lanes, with the rain drumming on the roof of the car, and the windscreen wipers working away like maniacs.

'Come in,' I said, when we drew up at my front door, but he refused.

'It's about Joan's house,' he began, rather explosively. 'Is it still on the market, do you know?'

I said I thought it was.

'We've been in Ireland for the past three weeks, looking

up relatives there, and I missed *The Caxley Chronicle*'s
advertisement. You see, I was wondering if it would suit
David and Irene.'

'Do they know about it?'

'No, that's the point. I thought Joan might let me have a
look, and if I thought it a possibility I would tell them on the
telephone, and they could come down at once to view. It
seems to me that you have to work at the speed of light these
days, if you want to buy a house. What's she asking for it?'

Again I had to confess ignorance. I really wanted to get
into my own abode, but Henry seemed to want to un-
burden himself.

'I do wish you'd come in,' I urged him, but he was
adamant. He sat staring straight ahead through the rain-
beaded windscreen, his fingers drumming on the wheel,
and a little nerve twitching in his cheek.

'It's all very difficult. I know they hope to move from the
London house, and get further out. Better for Simon too, in
the holidays. Better for all of them when you think of what
David and the boy went through there when poor Teresa
lost her sanity.'

I murmured sympathetically. I knew only too well how
strung up that young boy had been when he had been one of
my pupils for a few summer weeks.

'On the other hand, I don't want to interfere. A second
marriage can always be a bit dicey, I think, and they may
loathe the idea of being near us, or any relatives, for that
matter. But this place looks about the right size for them.
Three bedrooms, I believe?'

'And the annexe,' I said.

'But surely Miriam Quinn's in that?'

'She is at the moment.'

'Nice woman. I shouldn't think Irene and David would want her to go.'

There was silence for a time. The rain continued to throb relentlessly above and around us. A few blackbirds scrabbled joyfully under the bushes, enjoying the softened soil after the hard surface of the past weeks.

'He has regular trips these days to Holland, Belgium and Norway, so Irene would be glad of Miriam next door, I should imagine. And it's only an hour's drive to Heathrow. It took him pretty well that time to get across London.'

I could see that he was thinking aloud, putting the pros and cons to himself, and really attempting to make a decision.

'I should simply ring David and let him think it over,' I said, stating the obvious.

To my surprise, he seized my hands in his and shook them warmly. 'An excellent notion!' he exclaimed. 'After all, it's his decision, isn't it?'

He leant across to open the door for me, beaming the while.

'Yes, I'll do that immediately. What a help you've been!'

He sped off, cutting short my thanks, and I entered to be greeted by my starving Tibby.

While she wolfed down raw liver I sipped a drink and thought, for the umpteenth time, about this business of buying a house.

For years I have meant to do it. After all, the time flies by, and when I reached retirement age I should have to have somewhere to live. Now that Fairacre School's numbers had sunk perilously low, I might well find myself homeless if the school were closed.

I felt reasonably sure that I would not be turned out into

the snow like some Victorian heroine. I might even be offered the house first, if it were to be sold, as no doubt it would be eventually. In any case, I should get plenty of notice to quit, if it came to that. But the thing was, where should I go? Somewhere nearby would be ideal.

And secondly, what should I use for money? My meagre savings might rise to a deposit on the house, but would a building society give me a mortgage at my age?

I had been a fool not to buy when prices were less astronomic, as Amy pointed out when she called one afternoon.

'I've told you time and time again,' she said severely. 'And you've done nothing all these years.'

'I know,' I said meekly. 'Well, I've just lived from day to day. And jolly nice it's been,' I added defiantly.

Amy laughed. 'Well, my dear old silly, you know you can always have a bed at Bent, if the worse comes to the worst.' She looked at me speculatively. 'How much could you raise if you saw something you liked?'

I told her.

'It would hardly buy the bathroom,' she said. 'Would you let me lend you some money?'

'No, indeed!' I said.

'I've got quite a nice little nest egg, and you might just as well have some of it. Think it over, anyway.'

'You are sweet to think of it, but honestly I couldn't possibly accept.'

'Well, the offer will stand, darling,' said Amy, getting up to go.

'Besides, if I bought now, I should have to let it while I'm still teaching, and you know how impossible it is to get tenants out if they dig in their heels. No, I think I must

just soldier on as I am. Lord knows I'm happy enough this way.'

'Bless you, so you are! And as the old song says: "You die if you worry, You die if you don't, So why worry at all?"'

And on this cheering note Amy departed.

'Nice drop of rain,' commented Mrs Pringle, with unwonted affability the next morning. 'My lettuces have picked up wonderful, and the water butt's full again.'

I said it seemed to have done a lot of good everywhere except for the aperture where the skylight once had pride of place. A fine puddle had cascaded on to the tarpaulin and thence to the floor. Luckily, I had been prudent enough to shift my desk during these protracted building operations, or we should have had more serious damage.

Mrs Pringle's countenance assumed its usual gloom as she surveyed the mess. 'I'll have a straight word with Reg Thorn when I see him,' she boomed.

I felt a pang of sympathy for the poor wretch, maddening though he was. He would meet his match in Mrs Pringle.

The delays and confusion which had accompanied the removal of the skylight and the replacement by a simple dormer window had to be seen to be believed. It seemed to me that Reg Thorn was constantly driving to the builder's merchant, or the timber yard, in Caxley, to acquire or replace new pieces of window equipment which surely should have been bought at the beginning and assembled in his own workshop. What he spent in petrol alone must have made a hole in the taxpayers' pockets, but I suppose none of his fuming customers could get at him whilst in transit, so that from his point of view he was leading a comparatively peaceful life.

Mrs Pringle began to mop up, muttering to herself the while and clanging the bucket. I looked up a hymn for morning prayers before getting Ernest to ring the school bell to alert any strugglers still in the lanes or fields of Fairacre.

These last few days of term are always busy. This time, the last week seemed fuller than ever, for I wanted to visit the parents of the principal actors to see their reaction to making costumes for the favoured few.

Linda Moffat was to be one of the stars as Miss Richards, the first headmistress of Fairacre School. It was she who caned John Pratt in July 1882, and we had cast Patrick, who is small but with a good loud voice, as the youthful sinner. Mrs Moffat is a skilful dressmaker, and I felt sure that she would not only make Linda's costume superbly, but would be generous enough to lend a hand with the others if need be.

I also rang Mrs Austen to sound her out about her contribution of an evacuee's memories to our performance. To my joy, she was most enthusiastic and promised to prepare a script which we could discuss.

Altogether it was a satisfactory ending to the school year. There was a chance of another family coming to live in the village, as Mr Roberts had engaged a new shepherd who had three children. This was encouraging as it would mean an increase next term in my dangerously low numbers. The sun appeared again after the storm and, apart from the annoyance of the skylight non-activity, all appeared hopeful in my little world.

The vicar called to wish the children a happy holiday, and added his usual rider about helping their mothers. This was followed by the ritual: 'The same to you, sir!' which is always considered the height of humour by my pupils.

They dispersed boisterously into the summer sunshine, and as their voices died away down the lane, I wandered across to the school house, rejoicing in the long weeks of blissful freedom ahead.

8 August

My holiday plans were simple. The first few days had been spent in coping with neglected jobs such as weeding the border and washing the kitchen paintwork.

I had made arrangements to spend a fortnight in Norfolk with an old friend, and meanwhile Miss Clare had accepted an invitation from me to spend a few days at Fairacre at the beginning of the month.

The spare room lay in an unusual state of pristine splendour. The furniture gleamed from Mrs Pringle's ministrations. The feather bed was beautifully puffed up beneath a fresh chintz bedspread. On the table at the bedside was a posy of all the sweetest-smelling flowers I had been able to pick in the garden. Lavender, roses, pinks and a sprig or two of night-scented stock made a handsome nosegay in a little lustre jug which had once been my mother's.

I had been invited to tea at Miss Clare's, and went over to fetch her with a buoyant heart. I always enjoy visiting that neat cottage, thatched by Dolly Clare's father when the family first went to live there. It had two downstairs rooms, both of good size, and two bedrooms above. A little bathroom had been added when main water had come, at long last, to Beech Green some years ago.

The garden was large for a cottage. Miss Clare still kept the front one tidy and gay with flowers, but the larger part at the back was used as a vegetable plot by a young man in

the village who was glad to have the produce for his large family. He kept Dolly supplied with all that she needed, so that it was an ideal arrangement.

The best white cloth had been spread in my honour, and the thin ancient teaspoons of silver gleamed brightly. The best tea set, with a pretty pattern of pansies, was in evidence, and the usual plate of wafer-thin bread and butter and a splendid sponge cake, which I knew would be as light as a feather, showed that the mistress of the house had been busy.

Beyond the lattice windowpane the downs shimmered in a blue heat haze. It was a tranquil spot and Dolly Clare had lived there from the age of six, first with her family, and then alone for a number of years. To her great joy, her lifelong friend Emily Davis had joined her for several years, and the two old ladies had lived in perfect harmony until Emily's death a few years earlier.

Much had happened under this old thatched roof. The joys and griefs of a family, the sharing of a nation's wars, and always the relentless pressure of poverty. But it was a happy house; one felt it as soon as one crossed the threshold. Here was a haven, a quiet backwater where one could rest tranquilly away from the turbulent mainstream of life. This blessed peace, I well knew, stemmed mainly from the quiet spirit who lived there, but even without her presence one was conscious of a home which had been loved by many generations.

'I have been given some nerine bulbs,' said Miss Clare, entering with the tea pot. 'Do you know anything about them?'

'They say that if they like you they grow like weeds. If not, you'll never be able to rear them.'

'We'll live in hope then. George Annett says they need lots of manure, but Bob Willet says the exact opposite! Lots of sandy soil at the foot of a south-facing wall, was his advice.'

'Why not do that, and bung on lots of manure in the autumn? That way you are hedging your bets, I should think.'

'I remember seeing them years ago in Devon, when a friend took me away for a few days at the October half-term. So many of the gardens had great clumps of these beautiful rose-pink heads. I've never felt I could afford to buy them, but now I've been given some I should grieve if I mistreated them.'

I promised that we would look up the care of nerines in my new gardening book the minute we were home, and our conversation turned to her contribution to the centenary celebrations.

'I am quite looking forward to it,' said Dolly, carefully folding a thin slice of bread and butter. 'I suppose I ought to feel nervous, but I'm not, you know. After all, most of those present will be old pupils of mine. And that particular period, in King Edward's time, was a very happy one for me. I was a pupil teacher for several years then at Fairacre School, and dear Emily was my constant companion. We were so lucky to have Mr Wardle as our headmaster. He was a cheerful soul, and always out to help us both.'

'And you and Emily stayed together?'

'Well, no. She found a post south of Caxley, and I can't tell you how I missed her. We met when we could and caught up with our news, and exchanged our views on teaching. And if we met in Caxley, we went window shop-ping. That's all we could afford.'

Miss Clare laughed. 'We were very short of money. Everybody was. I don't suppose there was a single child at Fairacre School in those days who wasn't dressed in secondhand clothes. They were handed down from one child to the next, and gratefully received from any of the more well-to-do families. As for jumble sales, they were serious shopping expeditions then, not just an afternoon's spree in the village. I had a tweed cape cut down from a full-sized one of poor Miss Lilian's, which I wore for years.'

Poor Miss Lilian, I remembered, had been the feeble-minded daughter of one of the leading families in Beech Green. It was a never-to-be-forgotten tragedy that she and her mother perished on the Titanic in 1912 as they crossed the Atlantic to consult an eminent American brain surgeon in the hope of effecting Lilian's recovery.

'I think shortage of money was the chief worry then. There wasn't so much concern with health. As long as you could keep going and earn a bit, you tended to ignore minor aches and pains, and perhaps it was a good thing, although people often struggled on when really they should have gone to the doctor. But he needed paying, you see. It was all an uphill struggle, and I know many of the children came hungry to school. The older people could remember the rebellion of some of the agricultural workers when they smashed machinery, and shouted for bread. When I see the bonny children of today, and remember some of those in my early classes, I feel thankful that times have changed.'

'You'll talk about this, I hope, when you give us your memories?'

'Indeed I will,' said Miss Clare with spirit, 'for now I think too much is taken for granted, and thankfulness is

becoming as dead as perseverance and truthfulness and a great many other fine old-fashioned virtues.'

She sat back from the table and looked through the window at the tall hollyhocks outside. From her pensive expression I knew that her thoughts were years away.

She took a deep breath, and gave me her sweet smile.

'Well, shall we be going?'

We cleared away, and Dolly went slowly round the house, closing windows and locking doors.

Within half an hour we were travelling along the familiar lane which Dolly had traversed daily for many years, in fair weather and foul, until St. Patrick's church spire pierced the skyline, and we were back in Fairacre again and looking up 'Nerines' in my latest gardening book.

Mr Willet turned up the next morning, balancing a pair of shears on the bars of his bicycle.

'Promised I'd do that box edging,' he shouted through the kitchen window. 'All right to tackle it now? Got a wedding this afternoon.'

'Hello, Bob,' said Miss Clare, appearing in the doorway.

'Well, I'm blowed!' said Mr Willet beaming. 'And how be you keeping, Dolly? You looks younger than ever. Got some magic secret, have you?'

Dolly Clare laughed. 'I don't say much about my aches and pains, Bob. Doesn't do any good, and bores people stiff.'

'I tells everyone if I've got a finger ache,' replied Mr Willet robustly. 'Makes me feel a durn sight better when I've unloaded all my woes on to someone else.'

She followed her old friend into the sunshine, and I watched them talking animatedly as Bob Willet surveyed

the job to be tackled. They would have plenty of gossip to exchange, I guessed.

Reg Thorn's business was closed for a fortnight's holiday, so that we were spared the racket of banging tools, the boys' transistor and their vigorous exchange of opinions over football and cricket matters.

When I carried out the coffee cups some time later, the sun was so hot that we dragged my ancient deckchairs into the shade of the apple tree.

'Funny how you can drink hot coffee winter and summer,' commented Mr Willet, drying his moustache on the back of his hand, 'and still it do you a power of good.'

'They're a fine pair of shears,' observed Dolly, eyeing the shining blades resting on the grass by Bob's feet.

'Yes, well, I likes my own tools. Miss Read here do have a pair of shears – so-called – but they does more harm than good, twizzling up the sappy bits and wrenching away at the twiggy bits like a host of rats 'ad been at work.'

'Thanks,' I said.

'No need to be sarky,' said Mr Willet amiably. 'Some knows how to look after tools, and some don't, that's all I'm saying.'

He struggled from the deck chair.

'I suppose I'd best get on. You women would keep me here all morning with your gossiping.'

'Well—!' I began.

'By the way, I see that young Simon in the village as I come up here. He staying with the Mawnes d'you know?'

'I hadn't heard. How does he look?'

'Much the same as ever – a long streak of nothin', and lookin' as though butter wouldn't melt in his mouth, the

young varmint. When I think of our Snowy as he did in, I could give that boy a leathering and enjoy it!'

Mr Willet's face grew puce at the remembrance of Simon's part in the death of Fairacre's albino robin not so long ago. I decided to change the subject.

'Any chance of seeing you here tomorrow?'

'Ah! I might manage that if I'm spared. This edging of yours will need a few hours on it, the state it's got into.'

I picked up the tray, and left Dolly to watch her old friend at work.

In the kitchen, putting the cups to soak, I wondered if Simon's parents had come to Fairacre to have a look at Joan Benson's house. I did not propose to mention this possibility to anyone, as I did not want to spread any rumours. However, no matter how prudently I held my tongue, there was no doubt in my mind that whatever was decided under the Mawnes' or the Bensons' roofs would very soon be common knowledge in our little community.

Miss Clare was with me for a week, and the weather stayed sunny for all that time. We took picnic lunches up on the Downs, or down by the little brook at Springbourne, as it purled along beneath drooping willows on its way to join the Cax before the river flowed through Caxley. Everywhere we went held memories for Dolly and, like all old people, her early years were clearer in her mind than more recent ones.

I found her recollections fascinating, and only wished I had a recording machine with me all the time. It certainly made me decide to get one ready for the centenary day when I could record her talk for future generations. Dolly's lifetime spanned the age-old rural life of hard work geared

to the pace of man and horse, and modern life geared to the pace of cars, lorries and aircraft. Children of Dolly's generation were lucky to have travelled twenty miles from home. Many of them had never seen the sea, some sixty or seventy miles distant, nor travelled in a train, nor visited a town any larger than Caxley.

Their grandchildren thought nothing of flying anywhere across the globe, of talking to relatives in New Zealand as they sat by their own firesides, and of buying the produce of the world set out temptingly at the village shop. Once Dolly and her contemporaries had gone, the way of life which had been known and expressed in poetry, prose and pictures for centuries would vanish. It was a sobering thought.

But it was the small personal memories that I cherished as we took our drives around the countryside which Dolly knew so well.

'That was where old Mrs Johns lived,' she said as we passed a tumbledown cottage with a collapsed roof of thatch. 'She wore a bustle, you know, till the end of her life. A funny little soul, who kept that place spotless.'

'Ernie White was killed in that field,' she commented. 'A tractor tipped over and pinned the poor soul there for hours. People said it was a judgement for doing away with the horses.'

She sighed.

'And that's where Emily's Edgar lived. She should have been there by rights, but he married his nurse, you know, and my dear Emily never got over it, brave face though she showed to the world.'

She showed me where she and Emily tobogganned as children, where she took her pupils to collect hazel nuts and

frogspawn, and then holly to decorate St. Patrick's church
at Christmas time. It was borne in upon me how closely the
seasons were woven into the fabric of the country child's
life in those days. They were out so much more than today's
children. They walked everywhere. No school buses
whisked them past beds of violets, wild strawberries, sprays
of luscious blackberries, all known and treasured by their
grandparents.

One afternoon, I invited Mrs Austen to tea and it was a
rare treat for me to listen to the war-time reminiscences of
evacuee and teacher at Fairacre School in the early forties.

'Everything was so different from our home and school
at New Cross in south London,' said Mrs Austen. 'For one
thing, I was used to an enormous three-storey building with
infants on the ground floor, big girls on the next, and boys
at the top. It was lovely to be mixed up together, such *a few*
of us it seemed, in a dear little school like Fairacre's.'

'You certainly settled down wonderfully,' commented
Miss Clare.

'I think I found the biggest differences, though, at Mrs
Pratt's, where we were billeted. She couldn't have been
kinder, and I kept in touch with her until she died, but there
were some things which shook me as a child. No flush
lavatory for one. And lighting lamps and candles, instead of
switching on the electric light. I dreaded having to go down
the garden to the privy in the dark. Mrs Pratt used to light a
hurricane lamp for me, but it cast such shadows I was even
more terrified.'

'Was there no commode in your bedroom?' enquired
Miss Clare with concern.

'Well, yes – but I hated using it. It seemed so *wrong* to me.
I'd never met such a thing, you see. And another thing that

appalled me was the number of flies everywhere, and all taken for granted. At home, in London, my mother bustled a stray fly away as if it were poisonous – which it was, I always thought – but Mrs Pratt even had a paper ball hung up near the ceiling and called it the flies' playground.'

'We had one too, I remember,' said Miss Clare.

'There was another ball on the mantelpiece made of silver paper. We all collected every scrap of tin foil and it was carefully wrapped round the ball. It was an enormous weight. I can't think what happened to it eventually.'

'It went to the hospital in Caxley,' Miss Clare told her. 'Still does, I believe, but now they like it flat.'

'I was very fond of Mrs Pratt,' said Mrs Austen, 'but frightened of her old mother who lived down the road. Do you remember that little boy – I forget his name – who lived with her?'

'I do indeed,' said Dolly. 'He was called Stephen, a foster-child, and really old Mrs Hall had no business to have him. She was far too frail and suffered from tuberculosis, and in any case much too ancient to take care of a young child. But it was difficult to find homes for those orphans, and I suppose the local authority thought it was suitable. In any case, the Halls needed the maintenance money, but I was glad when that child was moved elsewhere.'

'So was I! I used to collect him to bring him along to school, and the smell in that house was ghastly. And the poor old thing was always coughing. She used to crouch on the rag rug in front of the fire with the ash pan pulled out, and spit horribly into the hot ashes. Sometimes she had no breath to speak to me, but just gazed at me with those watery blue eyes and motioned me to take Stephen out of the way. I did too, as quickly as I could.'

'He went into the army eventually,' Dolly told her, 'and did very well. I still hear from him at Christmas, dear boy.'

Her voice was warm with affection. Were there any of her pupils, I wondered, who failed to kindle a spark of remembered happiness in their old teacher? Even the malefactors, dealt with sternly in their youth, were now seen through the rosy haze of time. And why not?

I took Dolly back to her cottage with the greatest reluctance, I had enjoyed her serene company so much. But she insisted that she had a number of little household jobs to do, and some bottles of fruit to prepare for the store cupboard, so that I left her looking happy in her shining kitchen with the cat for company.

I went on to Bent to lunch with Amy. I found her house as welcoming and beautiful as Dolly Clare's, although three times the size, of course.

'How do you manage to keep it so immaculate?' I cried. 'I've never seen a speck of dust or one dead flower in this place, all the years I've visited here.'

'Elementary organisation,' said Amy. 'You too could have an immaculate house if you planned your routine.'

'You remind me of those advertisements, Amy. "You too can have a beautiful bust".'

'I liked the one about piano-playing in our youth. "You too can be a concert pianist", or something like that.'

'Better than that! "My friends used to laugh when I sat down at the piano". Remember?'

'Mine still do,' said Amy. 'It must be lovely to have a talent of some sort.'

'How's the autobiography?'

'Oh dear, oh dear! I was afraid you'd ask! I'm stuck at

myself aged eight, and all I can remember are idiotic things like tying reef knots as a Brownie, and my father cranking up our first family car, and having to help him fix canvas and mica side curtains to it when it rained. I don't think it's very stirring stuff, not a bit like some of these successful memoirs where the authors remember all sorts of psychological hook-ups and traumatic experiences when they found the cat having kittens in the laundry basket. I wonder why they can do it, and I can't?'

'Probably because you have a much more normal mind,' I assured her. 'And anyway, who's to know they didn't make it all up?'

'I never thought of that!'

'Frankly, I should shelve it for a week or two, and go back to it when you feel like it. Anyway, the weather's too good to stick about indoors pushing the pen.'

'I believe you're right. I've hardly been into Caxley at all since starting the book. Incidentally, I saw your young teacher there the last time I was shopping.'

'Our Miss Briggs? I wonder what she was doing in Caxley? I thought she was at home, in one of those spas – Droitwich or Buxton or somewhere up north. Malvern perhaps.'

'Malvern's *west*, dear. She was with a young man, and they appeared to be very affectionate.'

'Well, I'm blowed! Perhaps she came back to collect something, and brought her young man with her from Harrogate or whatever. It was during the holidays, I take it, that you saw her?'

'Yes, the beginning of last week.'

'Well, I'm glad to hear she's found an interest at last. It may liven her up. Mr Willet calls her "a fair old lump

of a girl", and I don't think one can better that description.'

'Poor thing!' said Amy. 'Anyway, she looked quite animated and pretty in the High Street.'

'Ah! The transformation wrought by love! I must try it some time.'

'I wish you would,' said Amy forcefully, returning to a well-worn theme, 'but aren't you leaving it rather late?'

Trust old friends to tell you the unpalatable truth!

Mrs Pringle arrived 'to bottom' me as she elegantly terms performing the house cleaning. Sometimes she only has time 'to put me to rights,' and that is bad enough. 'To be bottomed' involves taking down curtains and pictures, pulling out a heavy Welsh dresser and generally creating mayhem. I try and make myself scarce when threatened with bottoming, but on this occasion there was no escape as I was expecting the lawn mower to be returned from the repairer's and wanted to pay him.

Halfway through the dire proceedings I was allowed to pick my way through displaced furniture piled in the kitchen to put on the kettle for a restorative cup of tea.

Mrs Pringle, militant in a flowered overall with the sleeves rolled up to expose wrestler's forearms, had a fanatical look in her eyes.

'You seen the top of that dresser of yours?' she asked.

'No. What's wrong with it?'

'*Wrong with it?*' echoed Mrs Pringle triumphantly. 'It's got two inches of dust on it as you could grow potatoes in.'

'Oh, come . . .' I began weakly.

'And what's more, down the back, was a letter unopened and dated months ago.'

'Good heavens! Where is it?'

Mrs Pringle handed me an envelope. The address was handwritten, and I recognised it as Lucy Clayton's writing. She had been at college with Amy and me, and I cordially detested her.

'No one that matters,' I said with some relief, and made the tea.

We took it into the garden. The sight of my house I found upsetting.

'Well, I must say it's a treat to breathe a bit of clean air after all that dust and filth,' announced Mrs Pringle, stirring her tea. 'You heard about Mrs Partridge?'

'No. What's happened?'

'She had to go to hospital, poor soul.'

I was genuinely shocked. I am devoted to our vicar's wife, and the thought of her in hospital was even more upsetting than the chaos in my house.

'When did she go?'

'Last Saturday.'

'And it's Wednesday today! I am sorry. What is it, do you know?'

'Bees. The vicar's bees.'

'But she wouldn't need to be three, I mean four, days in hospital with a bee sting, surely?'

'Who said she was?'

'What?'

'In hospital for four days. All I said was that she went in Saturday. She come out Saturday too.'

Mrs Pringle took a long draught of tea and looked com-

placent. She has brought irritating her listeners to a fine art, I'll give her that.

'Well, go on. Tell me it all from the beginning.'

'Mrs Partridge told me herself as she was simply up the garden picking some nice sprigs of parsley to make parsley sauce for a nice bit of fresh haddock she'd got from that nice fishmonger in Caxley . . .'

Who probably had a nice shop, I thought impatiently.

'*Miles* away from the hive, she said, when one of the nasty things came and bit her by the eye, and she swelled up awful. Couldn't see out of that eye in a quarter of an hour, and the other not much better, and the vicar looking every-where for his glasses to read how big a dose of some bee medicine you had to take if bitten – as she had been, of course – and worried to death all the time, in case it was fatal. It can be, you know. My old uncle was never right after being set on by bees, and he died soon after.'

'Really? How dreadful!'

'Mind you, he was ninety-four,' Mrs Pringle admitted, 'but we all said as it was the bee stings as hastened his end. I told the vicar about it.'

Job's comforter, as ever, was my private comment.

'Anyway, she took these tablets, and the vicar got out the car and took her into Caxley Cottage Hospital, and her head was fair swimming by the time she got there. She reckoned it was the medicine. The doctor said it could have been, and give her something to help, and some ointment. She come straight back and went to bed, poor thing, and you can still see where its fangs went into her.'

She heaved herself to her feet.

'Well, I'd best get on. No rest for the wicked, my mother used to say.'

She surveyed my reclining form with a sour expression.

'Though that don't always seem to fit the case, come to think of it.'

After she had returned to the fray, I opened Lucy's letter. It was dated February 12th, which showed how long it had been collecting the dust at the back of the dresser.

In it Lucy informed me that Mr and Mrs Ambrose B. Edelstein and their two grown-up children were to be in England for three months. They came from – here an illegible place name, possibly Minnesota, Minever or even Minnehaha – where they took a keen interest in Education, and the Professor had several degrees in the subject. They were such a nice family – I thought of Mrs Pringle – and would be fascinated by a glimpse of Fairacre School, so she had taken the liberty of giving them my telephone number, and they would be ringing me to arrange a convenient day to visit. No need to put them up, or get them meals, as they were planning to stop in Caxley, but she was sure I would enjoy having them in school for a day just letting them have a free rein talking to the children and looking through their work.

She was ever my affectionate Lucy, and added a post-script saying that there was absolutely no need for me to feel that I must reply. I breathed a sigh of relief for mercies received, calculated that the Edelsteins had now been safely back in Minniewhatsit for several months, and fell into a blissful sleep.

Mrs Pringle and the lawnmower man brought me back to earth, half an hour later, and life began anew.

My Norfolk holiday was a great success. There is some-

thing about the bracing salty air of that magnificent county, with its massive skies and pellucid light, which is wonderfully restorative. In the summer, that is. I have only once experienced really wintry weather in that area, and hope never to again. Such piercing cold, straight from the steppes of Russia, it seemed, had an intensity never met with in Fairacre, even though we are always telling each other that we live in a cold spot.

On the way to stay with my old friend, and on my return journey, I spent a few hours in Cambridge, so dear to me, and renewed my delight with walks along the Backs, Parker's Piece and Midsummer Common. August is not the best month to see Cambridge, or any other place for that matter, for the trees and grass begin to look worn and shabby, the first glory of summer has gone, and the true fire and radiance of autumn has not begun. But to my devoted eye, there was beauty enough and to spare, and I hung over Clare Bridge and watched the scattered yellow willow leaves floating gently beneath me with the same rapture which I felt in my youth.

There is so little water in Fairacre, and I do not realise how much I miss it until I come across a river, or a lake, or even a modest garden fountain, and experience that surge of joy for this most beautiful of the elements.

But, as always, it was good to get back to my own home. Tibby greeted me with some hauteur. She looked upon my absence as dereliction of duty, and was not going to put herself out with a lot of fulsome welcoming. Later, if I did the right thing with offerings of rabbit or finely chopped pig's liver, she might condescend to accept me again.

Mrs Pringle had obviously been bottoming me in my absence, and the house shone. She had even put some sweet

peas in a vase on the mantelpiece, a gesture which, from one of her morose mood, I much appreciated.

Later, I wrote to my Norfolk friend and decided that it would do me good to walk to the post office. The evening was overcast, and it was sad to see how much shorter the days were growing. Already there were yellow leaves fluttering down from the old plum tree in the garden, and dahlias and Michaelmas daisies were opening in the border. Far too soon, autumn would be upon us and lovely though it always was at Fairacre, with its flaming beech trees and bronzed hedges, yet there was sadness too at the passing of summer and all its outdoor pleasures.

Letter in hand, I opened the front door to find Joan Benson about to thread the Parish Magazine through the letter box.

'Come in,' I cried.

'But you're just going out.'

'Not really. The post's gone anyway, and this will keep till tomorrow.'

'Then I will. I've a stone or something in my shoe, and perhaps I can sit down and investigate.'

It turned out to be a nail, and we had a few minutes of amateurish hammering to try and remedy the matter. We found the activity extremely frustrating, as there was not room enough inside the shoe to manoeuvre the hammer. However, by dint of banging energetically we effected a partial cure.

'We ought to have one of those little anvil things,' said Joan 'with three feet on them. Is it called a cobbler's last?'

I confessed ignorance. 'All I know about a cobbler's last is that he should stick to it,' I said, 'but I never really knew what it meant.'

'Like so many sayings,' agreed Joan, standing up to test her shoe. 'All my eye and Betty Martin, for instance.'

'Or right as a trivet.'

'Or being on tenterhooks. This shoe's fine now, thank you. You could set up as a cobbler, as a side line to teaching, you know.'

'I'll consider it. I might need something to do when I retire.'

'You're not thinking of that yet, surely? Incidentally, will you stay here?'

'I doubt it. By that time I rather think this house and school will be on the market. Any sensible woman would have bought a little place of her own before now, but I'm afraid I've left it a bit late.'

Joan Benson nodded understandingly. 'Well, I can sympathise. This house hunting is so *wearing*. I've had another

week with my daughter searching for a suitable home, but the more I look the less I like.'

'What exactly are you looking for?'

'You may well ask! Something with no stairs – a ground floor flat or a bungalow. But I *must* have a little bit of garden, and ideally it should have some trees, and be the sort of private place where one can sit and ruminate without too many people around. The snag is, of course, that it's virtually impossible to find such a place. Barbara is very anxious for me to have an apartment in an old people's home near her, and lovely though it is – it's an old vicarage with a cedar tree on the lawn and even an old nuttery with Kentish cob nuts – one would be among a score or so of other old people, all individually quite charming I have no doubt, but never *alone*.'

'I can understand how you feel.'

'Do you like your solitude too?'

'It's the breath of life to me,' I confessed. 'Perhaps it's because I am with a crowd all day. All I know is, that to come into this little house and to hear the clock ticking and the cat purring, is sheer bliss to me. I can truthfully say I've never felt lonely in my life.'

'Well, I can't say that,' admitted Joan. 'When you've had a husband and children, and latterly my darling mother, always about the place, then to be alone is – not exactly *frightening*, but definitely *disconcerting*. I suppose the ideal thing would be to find a flat near Barbara so that she could see me frequently, but not have me under her feet. She presses me sometimes to make my home with them, and sometimes when I get back exhausted from house hunting I almost give in. But it would never do. It wouldn't be fair to her, or to the children, or to me, to be honest.

Grandchildren are adorable for a time, but it's asking too much to have them with you constantly when you are getting on, and I'm quite sure the same thing applies in reverse.'

She picked up the basket containing the few remaining copies of the parish magazine. 'I must finish my little job. Mrs Partridge usually does it, noble soul, but she's away for a few days. You've heard, I expect, about Holly Lodge?'

'No indeed. I only came back from Norfolk a couple of hours ago, so I haven't caught up with the Fairacre news.'

'I think I've sold it. Henry Mawne asked me if his nephew David and his wife could come and have a look at it. A very nice couple. Do you know them?'

I told her the little about them that I knew.

'Well, they are now trying to sell their own place, which shouldn't be too difficult. Miriam knows them rather better than I do, and the marvellous thing is that they hope Miriam will continue to live in the annexe.'

'She must be very pleased.'

A little frown of worry puckered Joan's brow.

'It is *exactly* what I'd hoped for, and I'm sure it will work out beautifully, but at the moment Miriam is now wondering if they are only being kind, and would really want the annexe for themselves. We've all done our best to persuade her that she need not have such qualms, and as she's such a sensible person I'm sure she will realise that is the truth very soon.'

She began to make her way towards the door.

'Do you sometimes find even the most straightforward people horribly *complicated*?' she asked.

'Frequently,' I replied. 'Perhaps that's why we relish our solitude.'

Reg Thorn and his two young men were now back on the school roof. The dormer window was now recognisable, but still seemed to be giving the three of them a certain amount of trouble. In my innocence, I had imagined that the job might take about three weeks, with perhaps a few more days allowed for bad weather, or difficulty in obtaining parts for it, and so on. But here we were, months later, and still no sign of completion.

I never seemed to be able to catch Reg himself. I would see him in the distance from my kitchen window, but by the time I had walked across to speak to him he had leapt into his van and driven off in a cloud of dust. Dodging irate employers, I guessed, was second nature to him by now.

The young men were fast becoming as evasive, at least in making excuses. One was fair, with fast-receding hair; this seemed sad, as he could not have been much more than twenty-five. The other seemed to be covered in thick black hair: head, beard and chest were one luxuriant growth. Only his dark eyes seemed to be visible among this lushness, and it was he who usually answered my questions. His name was Wayne.

'Well, it's like this, miss. The timber merchant's been closed for the holidays, and when he opened last week he couldn't let us have what we wanted because he'd had a sudden order in from that new estate.'

It all sounded pretty weak to me, but there were any number of excuses, equally futile, that were trotted out in answer to my queries, and I began to give up.

Wayne was a nice young man, anyway, and I half

respected his loyalty to Reg Thorn. He told me that he had been with him for four years, and had learnt a lot.

'My dad's in the same trade,' he told me, 'and when he gives up I'll probably take over there.'

'Didn't he want you to work with him?'

'Not my dad! Said he didn't want me under his feet while he could still do a day's work, and got me fixed up with Reg. Better for us both, he said. And anyway, I've promised to carry on when he retires.'

'And will he?'

'Not before he's ninety, I don't suppose. I'll be drawing me pension, I reckon, before he gives up.'

Wayne's father, I thought, seemed worthy of respect.

Term began again in the last week of the month. The children, as always, appeared to have forgotten in six weeks everything they had ever learnt under my tuition, but looked brown and cheerful and ready for the new school year.

Miss Briggs looked equally healthy and almost vivacious. She gave me a large smile when I met her in the playground, and included the two young men on the roof in her affability. The infants welcomed her with affection when we went into school, and one of the smallest presented her with a stick of peppermint rock.

'I got it at Berrisford,' he told her. 'My dad took us there on his day off, and we've kep' it safe on the dresser ever since.'

Miss Briggs thanked him with such obvious gratitude that I thought it would be churlish to point out that it had obviously been sucked at one end.

After all, I told myself, it was the thought that counted, and what were a few germs between friends?

9 September

I always enjoy the early part of the autumn term. The new entrants soon settle down, and it is good to have fresh faces in the infants' room. This year there were four new babies and luckily all were good-natured youngsters who refrained from bawling when their mothers left them, but looked about them, bright-eyed and as inquisitive as squirrels at all these fresh interests.

For the last few years we have tried to let the newcomers visit us for a half-day a week in the preceding term, so that they become familiar with their surroundings.

This has helped enormously when they finally make a start at the beginning of the school year. It is a great strain on a young child to be thrust, not only among large numbers of bigger children, but also into a strange building where each has to find his own clothes peg, his desk, the wash basins and, most important of all, the lavatory.

Miss Briggs seemed much more settled, I thought, and certainly better tempered. No one could call her enthusiastic or charming, but her general demeanour was much more cheerful. This had a good effect on her class, and I supposed that the change in attitude resulted from the mellowing influence of the unknown young man, and also the fact that she now felt more confident in her work after two terms of teaching. She was far readier too, I was relieved to see, to remain after school when needed. Quite often she did not

go until Reg Thorn's workmen finished at four-thirty, and seemed glad to take on extra little jobs connected with the coming celebrations.

Things were going well in that direction. Mrs Moffat invited me to see Linda's Victorian dress, and I accompanied her from the butcher's where we had met one Saturday morning.

In the room set aside for her sewing, there hung her latest masterpiece. It was a perfect replica of Miss Richards's frock of the early 1880s, as dimly seen in a faded photograph I had found among the school records.

It was made of black woollen crêpe, complete with bustle, and draped over a pleated underskirt of black satin. At the neck was a ruffle of white lace, and embedded in the snowy froth was a beautiful jet brooch.

I exclaimed with admiration.

'Well, it's mostly bits and pieces,' she said modestly, though obviously pleased at my reaction.

'The black material is from an evening frock of mine. The satin was a skirt lining, and the lace I had by me. The bustle is made of foam rubber – much more comfortable than the original horse hair, I should think.'

'And that lovely brooch?'

'My grandmother's. It was the mourning brooch she bought when her father died. She also had a pretty little mourning ring made from his signet ring, but it was lost not long afterwards.'

'Well, Linda's going to be the belle of the ball on this occasion,' I said, stroking the costume.

'Don't be too sure! I think young Patrick will run her pretty close. I've been helping his mother make a serge suit with knee breeches – Norfolk style, you know – and with an

Eton collar and bow tie he's going to look absolutely splen-
did. The only difficulty is persuading Patrick that he won't
look what he terms "a proper sissy" in it.'

'I'll work on that problem,' I promised her as I took my
leave.

Mrs Pringle arrived at school one morning looking
unusually militant. I soon learnt the cause.

'That niece of mine, that Minnie, that *awful* Minnie!'

She gulped with fury, slapping viciously at a desk with
her duster.

My heart sank. Minnie Pringle, still known by that name
although she is a married woman, is the mother of several
children, most of them illegitimate. In a weak moment I
once engaged her as a second charwoman, and the havoc she
managed to wreak in my house had to be seen to be
believed. Whatever had happened to Minnie, I decided now,
nothing would persuade me to have her in my home again.

'What has she done?' I ventured to ask her irate aunt.

'She's been and left her Ern, that's what. Had some sort of
tiff last night, and up and left him with all those kids.'

'You mean she left the children with Ern?'

'No, no, no! I wish she had! She's brought 'em all up to
our place, and I've left her grizzling over the corn flakes. I've
told her straight she's to go back to Ern as soon as she's got
breakfast down 'em.'

'What went wrong, do you think?'

'Well, you know our Min as well as I do. She's come
across that chap Bert again, as she was sweet on once.'

I remembered that Bert was the man who had taken up
his abode in their house at Springbourne. Rather naturally
Ern had resented it, and there had been ructions.

'But surely Bert got a job elsewhere?'

'Only laying gas pipes. He soon got done with that and made a pretty penny too at it. Now he's having a rest on the Social Security, and you know what they says about Satan finding work for idle hands to do? Well, he's found some with our Min, and Ern's cutting up rough.'

At this moment Eileen Burton rushed in to ask if she could pull the school bell 'as it wasn't fair the boys always done it'.

I was too surprised by this passionate plea on behalf of equality for women to correct her grammar, and agreed to her request.

Meanwhile Mrs Pringle, limping heavily, had taken herself into the infants' room to continue her onslaught on the furniture, and I shelved Minnie Pringle's problems to face my own.

We were having a spell of unsettled weather. Two days would be calm and golden and the farmers would be wreathed in smiles as they fetched home the last of the harvest, or busily baled the golden straw. Then two or three days of rain would follow, drenching the straw awaiting collection, and filling our playground with extensive puddles which positively challenged the naughtier children to play 'Splashem' in defiance of my veto on the game.

I had just dashed across the playground through a shower at the end of afternoon school, when the telephone rang. Elizabeth Mawne was calling.

'I'm begging a favour,' she began.

'Fire away.'

'Well, I know you often go to Caxley on a Saturday morning, and I wondered if you could give me a lift. I'm

going to Jenner's to pick up a christening mug – the christening is the next day and Jenner's have kept me in suspense all this time. Our car's out of order, or I wouldn't bother you.'

I said that I should be delighted, particularly as I had a clock which had been waiting to be mended for quite six months, and I too would visit Jenner's with her.

By half-past ten on Saturday we were on our way, splashing through the streaming lanes on one of the wettest days of our changeable spell.

'It really is annoying,' said Mrs Mawne. 'All my roses are turning brown with the rain, and I am doing the church flowers this Sunday and was relying on roses for my arrangements. The most reliable flowers in the garden at the moment are marigolds. Perhaps not quite right for church decoration.'

'Why not? Everyone likes them, and they always look so cheerful. I'd plump for the marigolds every time.'

'Perhaps I will,' agreed Mrs Mawne, but she sounded doubtful. There is no gainsaying, I thought, that the ladies who take their flower-arranging seriously store up a mint of trouble for themselves one way or another.

'You've heard that David hopes to move into Holly Lodge?'

I said that I had.

'Henry was so grateful to you for advising him. He gets into rather a tizzy over things like that.'

'But I did nothing,' I protested.

'You let him *bumble on* to you,' said his wife. 'It helped. He rang David straightaway, and he and Irene think it is exactly what they want. David can go to town by train quite easily, or on the motorway. He'll have to get a second car,

but there we are. It will be good to have them at hand, and it will be so much healthier for them all, particularly for Simon. He's a frail child.'

I thought of the strength which had gone into the hurling of that quoit which had killed our dear albino robin, but said nothing.

'Of course, Joan Benson has to find somewhere, and David is still advertising his place, but we hope the move can be made well before Christmas. At a pinch, they can move in with us temporarily, but we hope it won't come to that. It wouldn't please *any* of us, and between ourselves, I think poor Henry would go mad.'

I jammed on the brakes to avoid a suicidal pheasant who strutted with great dignity and deliberation across the road in front of us.

'Of course,' continued Elizabeth, when we drove on, 'you are so lucky having a place of your own. I imagine you will stay on there when you retire?'

I explained my position.

'So what will you do? I hadn't realised that the school-house was virtually a tied cottage.'

'Oh, something will turn up,' I said with a cheerfulness I did not feel. 'Well, here we are, and miracles will never cease! There's actually a parking place.'

Jenner's is an old-fashioned shop, run in earlier times by the widow of the original jeweller, Edward Jenner. Although she is now bedridden, her two sons who run the business consult her over every transaction in the shop, which is somewhat trying if you are in a hurry.

Sometimes a good bellow up the stairs suffices. A faint reply is vaguely heard by the customer, and one of the sons returns to cope with the matter, fortified by mother's help.

But today, Mrs Mawne and I had to wait while John Jenner pounded up the stairs holding two christening mugs.

Time passed. We shifted from one foot to the other, and studied barometers, clocks, wrist watches, dress rings, engagement rings, babies' spoons and pushers, rose bowls, and innumerable candlesticks.

It was obvious that Elizabeth was growing even more impatient than I was. She has not had to put up with waiting for others, and is extremely forthright in her speech when crossed. I wondered what sort of welcome John Jenner would get on his return. Elizabeth's foot was tapping dangerously when he appeared at last.

'Your mother, Mr Jenner,' she said severely, 'reminds me of the Almighty. Invisible and omnipotent.'

'She's all of that,' agreed John Jenner.

Determined though I was not to get mixed up in Minnie Pringle's matrimonial squalls, yet nevertheless I found myself unwillingly involved.

She arrived one day in the following week with three of her brood to see if they could attend Fairacre School while she was 'with auntie'. There was not much I could do about it, and so I agreed with as much grace as I could muster.

I handed the three into the charge of Linda Moffat, who is a kind motherly child with plenty of sense. She undertook to show them where to hang their coats, and so on.

Meanwhile, Minnie showed no desire to leave my presence. The children were still out in the playground as it was only twenty to nine. Miss Briggs had not yet arrived, and so had no inkling of two new infants to be added – temporarily, I trusted – to her roll. The eldest child would be with me.

Minnie looked as much like a scarecrow as she had always done. Her ankle-length frock must once have been an evening dress. Over it she wore a thick ribbed pullover which had half a dozen grimy badges tacked on to it. Her bare feet were thrust into broken peep-toe sandals of scarlet plastic material, and her red hair was as unkempt as a well-used floor mop.

A young baby was asleep under the hood of the battered pram in the lobby, and a toddler with a repellently runny nose sat at the other end. With five children under nine one

could not help but feel sorry for poor silly Minnie, but I steeled myself to withstand any offers of renewed house-work. I had suffered enough in the past.

'You heard about my Ern?' she enquired.

I said guardedly that Mrs Pringle had said that he had left home.

'Ah! But did she tell you where he'd gone?'

'No.'

'Back to that Mrs Fowler in Caxley!'

Minnie spoke triumphantly, as though she had scored a point. Frankly, I was flummoxed. An earlier union between the renowned Mrs Fowler and Minnie's Ern had ended in such acrimony that I should have thought that they would never see each other again.

'She's been at him for months to go back as a lodger. Misses the money, see? Well, now he's gone.'

'Just like that? He must have had a reason.'

Minnie hesitated, running her dirty fingernails through her equally dirty locks. She seemed to be struggling with a desire to tell me all.

It won.

'I don't mind you knowing, but Ern got a bit nasty about Bert popping in, and he took his belt to me. Then Bert got wild and clocked him one, so Ern cleared off, and the language what he used I wouldn't tell a lady like you. Real *rude*, it was! Animals and that!'

'But where will you live? I believe the house is in your name, isn't it?'

'That's right. But I'm feared of sleeping there alone in case Ern comes back.'

'I should certainly move back as soon as you can,' I advised her, thinking of myself as much as Minnie, I don't

mind admitting. 'The council won't want the place empty, and I gather your aunt can't have you there.'

'She don't seem very pleased about it,' agreed Minnie, taking a grubby handkerchief to the toddler's nose, and not before time. 'I'll be all right. I'm going to get Bert to sleep in until Ern comes back.'

She gave me her wide demented smile and pushed the pram out of the lobby.

'I'll be all right,' echoed in my brain for most of the day. Inconsistent, crazy, immoral, come to think of it, there was no doubt that Minnie would emerge from this little battle quite unscathed. It would be the non-belligerents, encountered on the way, who would be scarred.

Amy called to see me one blustery afternoon. She had brought me the latest collection of Flora Thompson's writings as a present, and as a lover of *Lark Rise to Candleford* I could hardly wait to begin *A Country Calendar*.

'You spoil me', I told her.

'I know. You can give me a cup of tea in exchange.'

'And where have you been?' I asked, as I warmed the teapot.

'Oxford. Bumbling round Blackwell's in a happy daze, and spending far too much money. I tell myself I am getting Christmas presents, but I known damn well I shan't be able to part with any of them.'

'Never mind. Think how it boosts trade.'

'Mind you, I did get a splendid eiderdown for the spare room, but can you guess what it's called?'

'Not a clue.'

'Well, wait for it. On the label it says: *Morsnugga*!'

'I don't believe it.'

'I'd show you if I could be bothered to unwrap it, you doubting Thomas! For two pins, I would have given it back, but it was the only one which was the right colour, and I only hope my visitors will sleep too soundly to want to read eiderdown labels. But I ask you – *Morsnugga*! It really is the end, isn't it?'

'It could have been something with "cosy" in it, spelt with a "K".'

'That's true. This is a first-class cup of tea. I can well do with it. Shopping creases me these days, and I used to enjoy it.'

'How's the book getting on?'

'It isn't. I'm still aged eight, and I honestly don't think I can go on. It seems a pity. I've done about eight thousand words, and the thought of doing another fifty or sixty, which is what is needed, I gather, for a book's length, is too daunting for words.'

'Can't you do something with the bit you've done? Make a magazine article, say, or a talk for the radio?'

Amy looked thoughtful. 'That's an idea. I could make something of being a Brownie half a century ago, and there's quite a nice episode about my mother opening a flower show when the marquee collapsed.'

'It all sounds good clean fun to me,' I told her, refilling her tea cup. 'You have a bash. You can't waste all that effort.'

'I agree. Do you know, I sometimes think you are more intelligent than you look.'

'Thank you, Amy,' I said. 'I shall treasure that remark.'

The wind was more violent than ever when Amy departed. Branches clashed overhead, plants shuddered in the on-

slaught, and a weird hooting came from the television aerial as the wind whistled around it.

Tibby rushed in through the front door as I waved farewell to Amy. She looked startled and affronted. I had little sympathy for her as she can get into shelter through the cat flap on the back door, but this is beneath her dignity if anyone is about to open a proper door for the lady.

It was good to get indoors again. I cleared away our tea things, put aside a pile of exercise books due to be corrected, and settled down gleefully with my lovely new book. After twenty minutes' bliss, a strange sound became evident. It was difficult to pin-point just what and just where it was in the confusion of noises outside, but to my horror it sounded remarkably like heavy breathing.

A burglar, with bronchitis? But he would hardly be at his work in such a condition. An escaped lunatic? But our nearest asylum was some twenty miles away. Some poor traveller taken ill and needing my assistance? If my conjecture was correct, he would need a doctor and oxygen tent immediately.

It was all very unnerving. The longer I listened, the more sure I became that it really was breathing that I could hear. What on earth should I do? It is on occasions like this that I realise how useful a husband could be. How lovely to be able to say: 'I think someone is breaking in, dear,' and to settle back while a masculine hand raises the poker.

However, spinsters learn to cope alone, and I decided that I must go and investigate. Tibby remained quite unmoved by the noise, which was unusual. Anything strange often causes her to growl, and to bristle with fright or fury, which only adds to one's misgivings.

I took the poker in hand, and went to the front door,

switching on lights as I went. Outside, grazing peacefully
among my herbaceous plants was a fine Guernsey cow,
one of Mr Roberts's herd, I guessed. By the light from the
hall I caught sight of my lawn, heavily indented by
hoofs, and wondered what Mr Willet would have to say
about his newly mown grass when he turned up next
morning.

The cow gazed benignly at me, some choice penstemon
flowers dangling from her rotating jaw. She seemed pleased
to see me, and made a gentle lowing noise through her
mouthful of light supper.

Much relieved – for who would not prefer a kindly, if
hungry cow to an escaped madman? – I rang Mr Roberts's
number and awaited rescue.

As I had guessed, Mr Willet was most indignant when he
saw the state of my lawn the next morning.

'Never saw such a muck-up in all my borns,' he said,
blowing out his moustache with disgust. 'You wants to sue
old Roberts. That animal's done pounds' worth of damage.'

'I can't do that,' I protested. 'It's one of the hazards of
living in the country. Cows do get out sometimes.'

'Not if the fences is kept proper,' replied Mr Willet
sternly. 'Well, if you won't do nothing, you won't, of
course, but I shall tell him what I think when I comes across
him next.'

'Oh, don't make trouble!' I begged him. 'If I don't mind
why should you?'

'Because I shall have the rolling and flattening of this lot, I
can see, that's why!'

Against such straight reasoning I could say nothing, but
made my way to school.

Here more trouble awaited me. Water had blown through the half-finished dormer window and made a pool on the floor. Joseph Coggs was doing his best to mop it up, but in his zeal was using Mrs Pringle's new duster and I foresaw some ructions.

'Let me have that, Joseph,' I said snatching it from him, 'and get the old floor cloth from the lobby.'

I was wondering if I could tear home, and put the duster to dry out of Mrs Pringle's sight, when the lady arrived, and caught me duster-handed.

'And who,' she boomed, 'done that?'

'It was used in error,' I said placatingly. 'One of the children was mopping up and didn't realise—'

At this moment, Joseph appeared with the floor cloth and Mrs Pringle rounded on him before I could intervene.

'You use my dusters once more, young Joe, and you'll get my hand round your ear-hole! Understand?'

Poor Joe turned pale. Mrs Pringle has hands like hams, and it was no idle threat.

'You can leave the cloth with me, Joseph,' I said hastily, 'and go into the playground until the bell goes.'

I mustered all the dignity I could manage whilst dangling a wet rag in each hand.

'I will see to this,' I said coldly, 'and please don't bully the children.'

Mrs Pringle grabbed the duster and shook it violently. 'You can do what you like with that floor cloth,' she shouted, 'but I'm not trusting you with my nice new duster.'

With that she thrust the damp duster into her black oilcloth bag, presumably to be taken home for its correct treatment, and I was left to mop the floor and curse Mrs

Pringle, dormer windows, the wind, and Reg Thorn with equal intensity.

Miss Briggs arrived half an hour late with laryngitis. She had had a puncture, luckily in Beech Green, she whispered painfully, and two of Mr Annett's big boys had changed the wheel for her.

I went into the infants' room with her to supply their wants, and to tell them of their teacher's affliction and the necessity for exemplary behaviour. It was going to be one of those days, I thought grimly, as Wayne switched on his transistor set overhead and filled the air with discord.

As it happened, with Miss Briggs's normally stentorian tones now hushed, it was the quietest day at Fairacre school since her arrival.

The rough weather had done some damage in our area. A tarpaulin had blown from a newly built stack of straw and caught itself in a neighbouring plum tree, bringing down several laden branches.

A branch had crashed on Henry Mawne's greenhouse, and rumour had it that the vicar had gone in his pyjamas to make sure that his beehives were safe.

In my own garden, the cow had done more damage than the weather, but the television aerial was sloping at an extraordinary angle.

'I can fix that, miss,' Wayne assured me. 'Just got to straighten one of the window catches, and then I'll be there.'

The dormer window, so Reg Thorn said, when I was successful in catching him one morning, would be finished in a fortnight.

'Just a final coat of paint, and we won't be bothering you no more,' he told me with pride. 'How d'you think it looks?'

'Fine,' I said, gazing at the new structure. To be honest, I was not sure about it. It looked heavy and awkward, jutting out from the old roof, but I was so used to the unobtrusive line of the old skylight that anything different was bound to strike me as peculiar. Mr Willet's derogatory remarks too may have influenced me. In any case, the new window must surely be an improvement on the former one which had plagued all the inhabitants of Fairacre school for generations.

Wayne put my aerial to rights as he promised and I thanked him at playtime.

'Don't you mind heights?' I asked him.

'Enjoy 'em,' he said beaming. 'My uncle was a steeplejack. Used to scramble up factory chimneys and walk round the rim at the top.'

To hear about it made me feel queasy.

'No good being a builder unless you've got the stomach for heights,' said Wayne, carrying Reg Thorn's ladder back to its proper place.

The children came out of school to play, and I was thankful that sunshine had followed the stormy weather. Miss Briggs emerged too to take up her playground duty, and Wayne hurried over to talk to her. It was good to see her so friendly and animated, I thought. She would miss the young company when our dormer window was done at last.

The Pringle children were still with us and much as I wanted to know what Minnie's plans were – if any – I was anxious not to appear too curious by asking Mrs Pringle about conditions at her home. However, she appeared one morning with a nasty scratch down one cheek and a large lump on her forehead.

'Good lord, Mrs Pringle,' I exclaimed, 'have you had a fall?'

'No. But someone else has,' she told me with enormous satisfaction.

She settled herself on the front desk, her usual perch when about to give me all the news. I glanced anxiously at the clock. No need to ring the school bell yet, and although I had still to look out the morning hymn and open the windows, it seemed far more important to me to hear the story behind Mrs Pringle's injuries.

'Well, it's like this. That Minnie wouldn't do nothing about getting Ern back as long as Bert was around and she could see him. I threatened to put her and the kids out in the road, but you know our Min. Water off a duck's back it was, and me going half-barmy with that lot under my feet.'

'But I thought Ern worked at Springbourne Manor. Didn't the Potters wonder where he was when he didn't turn up?'

'That's just it! He *did* turn up! Come on the bus from Caxley each morning, so the Potters never twigged anything was wrong for some time. But, of course, someone tittle-tattled to Mr Potter, and he waylaid Bert, as he sacked for pinching the vegetables if you remember, and got the truth out of him about Minnie and Ern.'

'What happened?'

'He ticked off Bert, and told him not to come between husband and wife, and to keep out of Springbourne or he'd set the police on him. Then he come up our place the other day and had a good talking to Minnie. He told her that Ern would lose his job if she didn't persuade him to go back to live in Springbourne.'

'And did she?'

'Not Minnie! She's a proper soft one! Said Ern might hit her and she was scared, though if he promised to treat her right she might go back. I said to her: "If you won't persuade Ern, then I will, my girl! I've had enough of you and your brats eating me out of house and home, and using my sheets and towels, day in and day out!" So yesterday evening I went to Caxley, and sorted things out.'

She fingered the bump on her head with pride. I was mightily impressed at the thought of even such a doughty fighter as Mrs Pringle facing the formidable Mrs Fowler. She once lived in Fairacre, and was a tough shrewish woman who frightened the life out of me just to look at her.

'You went to Mrs Fowler's?'

'I did indeed. She started shouting before I'd hardly got the words out of my mouth about Ern. "You let me in and we can talk this over nicely," I said to her, but what she said in return I wouldn't sully my lips by repeating. She made a run at me and that's when I got this scratch, the spiteful cat.'

'Did you retaliate?'

'If you mean did I give her as good as I got, I certainly did. Two handfuls of her hair I tore out, and I blacked her eye.'

Mrs Pringle spoke with quiet satisfaction. It must have been a real battle of the dinosaurs, I thought, and I wondered if the neighbours had enjoyed it.

'She said Ern wasn't there, but down The Barleycorn, and what's more he spent all his time there. Then she slammed the door in my face. I was about to go off to the pub to see if she was telling the truth, when she opened a top window and chucked a suitcase at me, with Ern's things in evidently. Anyway, that's what caused this bump – not that woman.'

At this juncture, Joseph Coggs put his head round the

door to say was it time for the bell, and could he ring it?

'Not just yet, Joe. Mrs Pringle and I are having a little talk. I'll call you in a few minutes.'

Joseph vanished.

'Go on! Was he there?'

'He was. I picked up the case and went round the corner and found him in the bar. We just had time to get the last bus back.'

'He came without any trouble?' I asked mystified.

'I *took him*,' said Mrs Pringle.

I gazed at her with respect.

Outside I could hear the sound of children's voices. Were my latest pupils among them? I asked my cleaner.

'They're all going back to Springbourne tonight. Mr Potter's lending Ern the van to fetch the lot, and told him straight that he's out on his ear if he don't treat our Minnie right.'

'And you think he will behave now?'

'If he don't,' said Mrs Pringle rising majestically, 'he knows there's *two* of us can settle him.'

She made her way into the lobby, and I called Joseph in to ring the bell, some five minutes after time.

Meanwhile, I looked out the morning hymn, and settled for *Fight the Good Fight*, as an appropriate choice in the circumstances.

10 October

Oddly enough, I heard more about the clashing of the monsters from Amy when she visited me a few days later. Her window cleaner lives next door to Mrs Fowler in Caxley, and he evidently gave her a lively description of the scene.

'He and his wife went upstairs to get a better view from the bedroom window,' Amy told me. 'And whatever Mrs P. may say to the contrary, her language was quite as lurid as Mrs Fowler's. He said their money was on Mrs Pringle right from the start. "She'd got the *motive* and the *spirit* and the *weight!*" was how he put it.'

'Very neatly put too. They must have made an unholy noise. It's a wonder the neighbours didn't call the police.'

'They were enjoying it so much I don't think they wanted to break it up. According to him, it was pretty plain that Ern was getting fed up at Mrs Fowler's anyway. She used to expect him to do all the odd jobs around the house when he got back from Springbourne, and the food was rather sparse, I gather.'

'I can well believe that! Mrs Fowler had the reputation of being the stingiest woman in Fairacre when she lived here.'

'So it looks as though Ern was ripe for the picking, and Mrs P. plucked him at the right moment.'

'Well, heaven bless the old harridan,' I said. 'Now we've seen the last of Minnie and her brood.'

'For a time, anyway,' Amy said. 'I've no doubt they'll turn up in your life again before long.'

'Heaven forbid! Tell me, how's the dismemberment of the book going?'

Amy looked quite animated. 'I sent two short episodes to *Woman's Hour* and they've taken one. I'm going up to broadcast it, probably early next year.'

'Marvellous! We'll have it on at school in the afternoon. Tell me more.'

'Well, I'm writing an account of our sick room at school.'

'It sounds somewhat morbid.'

'Not really. It's supposed to be rather funny. You've no idea how dreadfully depressing that place was. It's doing me good to write it out of my system.'

'What was wrong with it?'

'Everything! For one thing, it was a symphony in green, of all colours.'

'Very restful, they say.'

'Not when you're bilious, as most of the inmates were. And the greens didn't harmonise, to make it worse. And the only decoration was a past pupil's lettering exercise in the most excruciating calligraphy, quite impossible to read from one's sick bed, but it was evidently that passage from Chaucer about the poor scholar who had twenty books clad in black and red. What with the writing and the spelling, one could feel one's mind giving way.'

'You should have closed your eyes.'

'Even so you were assailed by the most nauseating smell of something the mistress who had attended you burnt on an enamel plate on the floor. It was called Persian tape, if I remember rightly, and if you weren't sick when you arrived you pretty soon were once the Persian tape got going.'

'Were you allowed visitors?'

'Only the odd relative. Anyway, this ghastly place was at the very top of a high building, and most people jibbed at all the stairs. Patients were always in a state of collapse when they finally arrived, with their knees like jelly.'

'Well, I hope you can do justice to it,' I said. 'It sounds as though you have plenty of material.'

'It should do something for my suppressed emotions anyway,' said Amy, with evident satisfaction. 'Now tell me your news. How's the centenary programme going?'

'I'm having Linda and Patrick over here after school tomorrow to try them out with their lines. Miss Clare, bless her, needs no rehearsing, nor Mrs Austen, and Mr Lamb from the post office has promised to tell us something about the famous trip to Wembley in the 1920s. It's not going to be such a formidable job as I first thought, and Miss Briggs is being unusually helpful with the singing.'

'Do you think she'll stay?'

'I'm beginning to hope so. She's much more cheerful since she found that young man, and she's gradually forgetting a lot of the high-falutin' rubbish she was stuffed with at college, thank heaven.'

'Well, good luck with it all,' said Amy, collecting her things. 'By the way, James and I are having a short break in Wales next week to make up for his missing Tresco in the summer, so I shan't see you for a time.'

'Do you know, I thought I might go again next summer to Tresco. I loved it so much.'

'Then book up early,' advised Amy. 'We're going again, but in May, when you'll be hard at work, of course, and we've already staked our claim.'

'It seems rather soon,' I said, 'to book for August.'

'*You do it now*!' replied Amy sternly. 'What a terrible procrastinator you are! I wonder anything *ever* gets done in this establishment. Now mind! Sit down and write to that hotel this evening.'

'Yes, Amy,' I said meekly.

I had written the simplest possible dialogue for Linda as Miss Richards, and for Patrick as the bad boy John Pratt, but even so they seemed to find it difficult to memorise.

'Don't worry if it's not exactly the same,' I implored them. 'As long as you get the meaning across, that's all that matters.'

If anything, this confused them even more. We had a break, and I produced lemonade and biscuits. Tibby entered and received a great deal of admiration from the two, and then we resumed. After two or three attempts, things went more smoothly. Linda seemed to be less self-conscious than Patrick and with practice I thought the little scene should go well.

'We'll try it with the other children one day this week,' I promised them, 'and by that time you'll know your lines so well, it will be much easier to concentrate on the movements.'

They looked doubtful, and I must confess that if these two comparatively bright pupils made such heavy weather of their parts, it did not look too hopeful for the rest of my cast. Again I felt thankful that most of the performances would be in the more capable hands of three or more adults.

They departed clutching their two-page scripts with them, their young brows furrowed with anxiety. Perhaps I was expecting too much from them, I thought, as I waved them goodbye? Fairacre children are shy by nature, and

perhaps the idea of displaying their modest talents in front of parents and, even worse, their schoolfellows, was going to prove too much for their nerves.

We could only wait and see.

As so often happens in October, the weather was balmy, the skies cloudless, and that clear light peculiar to a fine autumn bathed Fairacre in end-of-summer beauty.

The hedges were bright with glossy berries. The trees were beginning to blaze in all shades of yellow, bronze and crimson, and the cottage gardens, so far untouched by frost, were still gay with asters, Michaelmas daisies, chrysanthemums and dahlias.

I relish these sparkling autumn days, all the more keenly because one knows that there cannot be many of them before waking one morning to a hoary scene and the knowledge that winter has arrived. I took the children out for plenty of exhilarating walks on the downs, and after tea each day walked again on my own before the sun set. By six o'clock it was beginning to grow chilly, and I enjoyed lighting a fire and congratulating myself on having the best of both worlds while the fine spell lasted.

On one of my solitary walks, through a little copse at the foot of the downs, I came across Miriam Quinn who was enjoying the fresh air as much as I was, to judge by her pink cheeks and bright eyes. We walked along together in great content.

'This is the breath of life to me,' she said, 'after the office. I look forward to it all day. Caxley's all very well for working, but I simply couldn't go back there to live after Fairacre.'

'You're not proposing to, are you?' I asked.

She looked thoughtful, bending down to remove a briar which had caught her skirt.

'No. I'm staying, and I hope I'm doing the right thing. You know the young Mawnes are taking over?'

I said that Joan had told me.

'Well, I still have slight doubts about whether they truly want me living under the same roof. They've been terribly kind, and pressed me to stay, and as I honestly can't find a thing worth considering elsewhere, I have agreed. In any case, I love it here, as you know, and it would be a dreadful wrench to have to leave.'

'I'm sure they really do want you to stay. Henry Mawne was relieved to know you would be there when David was away on his business trips. I remember him saying how comforting it would be for Irene to have company in the house at night.'

'Really?' Miriam sounded pleased but slightly incredulous. 'I hadn't thought of that. I must say, it's nice to be useful. I have already offered to sit with young Simon in the holidays if they want to go out in the evening. Irene seemed pleased about that, which delighted me.'

'It would help them enormously, I'm sure.'

We walked along in silence for a short time, until we emerged into one of Mr Roberts's fields, and turned towards the village. Miriam seemed to be turning over my remarks in her mind.

'You know,' she said at last, 'one of the difficulties of being single is that there is no one to discuss these little problems with. It's so easy to see just one's own point of view. I'm glad you told me about Henry Mawne's comment. Of course, he's quite right. I'm afraid I've been far too self-centred over all this business – anxious not to intrude,

anxious about finding somewhere else, in fact, thoroughly steamed up and not really thinking of Irene and David's side of the problem. That must be one of the bonuses of married life, I imagine – being able to share one's troubles.'

'Except that you've got two people's troubles then,' I pointed out. 'Think how relatively uncomplicated our spinsterhood is!'

Miriam stopped in her tracks and laughed aloud. It was good to see her usually pensive expression replaced by joyous animation. She ought to laugh more often, I thought.

'Perhaps you're right. Anyway, I'm glad we met in the wood. I'm going home in a much more cheerful state of mind. What about coming back to Holly Lodge for a drink?'

'I'd love to,' I said, and we stepped out briskly together.

The vicar called in to school one gloriously sunny afternoon, and we enthused about the weather. He is as devoted to the sun as I am, and when the rest of the villagers are collapsing with heat, he and I gloat together on perfect conditions for sun-worshippers.

He bore a jar of his own honey, and presented it to me with considerable pride. I thanked him sincerely, and enquired after the bees.

'They've really done splendidly. I collected about sixty pounds of honey. It's so rewarding to see it pouring out of the extractor in a beautiful golden stream. To think that those dear bees have made thousands and thousands of trips, all through the summer, to collect the delicious stuff from all our beautiful Fairacre flowers!'

Obviously, our vicar was enraptured.

'Are they still about?'

'Yes, indeed! As busy as ever. I think they are collecting from the bramble flowers and willow herb now. I don't propose to take any more. What they fetch in now will help them through the winter.'

'Is there much for you to do to prepare them for the cold weather?'

'A *great deal*,' said he earnestly. 'They will need some sugar syrup, and I intend to put up the mouse guards at the entrances. They creep in, you know, for shelter, and possibly the honey. Quite alarming for the bees. I shall certainly take steps to protect them from marauders.'

He took a slip of paper from his pocket and consulted it.

'A quarter of mushrooms, half of tomatoes, a dozen large eggs – no, that isn't it.'

He turned over the paper.

'Ah! Here we are, on the back of my wife's shopping list, you see. First of all, how is the new window?'

'So far, so good,' I told him.

'That's fine. Really, the old skylight was a sore trial when the weather was rough. We should have a snug winter with this new one.'

I said I hoped so.

'Then the next thing I have here is to fix a date for the centenary service.'

He lowered the paper and looked unhappy. 'I rather think I shall have to combine it with a Sunday service in December. My diary has suddenly become horribly full for that month. What do you think? I thought perhaps the Sunday before Christmas might be suitable. It would be the last Sunday of term, and we could have prayers and hymns suitable to the occasion at morning service, and my sermon would be on the subject of our heritage here in the village.'

'It sounds ideal,' I said, 'and the church would be looking festive too by that stage.'

'Certainly,' said the vicar looking mightily relieved at my amiability. What did he expect, I wondered? That I might fling myself to the floor, screaming and drumming my heels?

'The crib would certainly be in place, and no doubt some of the Christmas greenery. Perhaps we could arrange for the children to do some of the decorations, as they do for Harvest Festival?'

'That's a nice idea,' I said, but had private reservations

about how the flower ladies would react to juvenile assistance at Christmas time.

'Good, good!' said Mr Partridge, making for the door. 'I really ought to have a bonfire, I've so much garden stuff to burn, but I intend to wait until dusk. Nothing is going to detract from this beautiful sunshine if I can help it.'

'A case of "Gather ye rosebuds while ye may",' I quoted.

'Absolutely, Miss Read. Absolutely!'

He looked at the children with his usual benevolence.

'I should take them for a walk this afternoon,' he whispered confidentially.

'Don't worry,' I told him. 'It's at the head of the agenda.'

11 November

It was a relief to be without Minnie Pringle's three children. Not that they were naughty or rumbustious. In fact, they were just the opposite, and sat immobile in their desks contributing nothing and, as far as one could see, taking in nothing.

They were all mouth-breathers, which was hardly surprising considering the revolting state of their nasal passages, and no amount of advice, persuasion or example succeeded in showing them how to blow their noses. They were like their mother in being almost unteachable, but without her demented energy. What they would do when it came to earning a living I shuddered to think. No doubt an indulgent welfare state would give them far more for doing nothing than they were capable of earning anyway.

But if I were relieved to see the back of Minnie's brood, I was really sorry to say farewell to the shepherd's children. Perhaps he had found a better job than his new one with Mr Roberts?

Mr Willet enlightened me.

'Bin pinchin'. Not just the odd egg or swede and that. He done in one of Mr Roberts's sheep, and sold it to that back-street butcher in Caxley. Ought to be deported, the pair of 'em, but I don't suppose they'll get more than probation when the case comes up.'

'Well, they certainly won't get deported,' I assured Mr Willet. 'Anyway, who'd want them?'

'We don't, that's for sure! And Mr Roberts is hopping mad. Now he's got to start all over again getting some new chap. Can't trust a soul these days, Miss Read. They'd take your teeth off of the table if you was fool enough to leave 'em there.'

'At the moment,' I told him, 'my teeth – what are left of them – don't take out.'

Mr Willet looked sympathetic.

'Then you've a mort of trouble ahead of you. I'm thankful to say all mine are national gnashers now, and it's a great comfort to be able to take 'em out now and again to give me gums a nice airing.'

He set out across the playground, and then turned.

'Bring the numbers down a bit though, won't it? Them Pringle kids and shepherd's lot? Bet you'll be hearing from the office.'

'Oh, shut up,' I begged him.

For the horrid fact was much in my mind too.

Another cause for relief was the absence of Reg Thorn's men. I had grown quite fond of them both, and found Wayne particularly sensible and friendly. Nevertheless, it was wonderful to be free of that everlasting cacophony from their transistor radio, and from the bangs and thumps as they worked overhead.

Mr Willet still looked askance at the finished product, but as I pointed out, no rain had come through now that it was completed, and we certainly seemed to have more light.

'Hasn't had a fair test yet,' Mr Willet warned me. 'You wait till that old wind gets up!'

Unfortunately, we did not have to wait long. The halcyon October weather broke early in November with lashing rain and a high wind.

I was relieved to see that no water came through, as it certainly would have done in the old days, but there was an annoying drumming sound as the wind caught the jutting framework. I was not too happy about this vibration, and rang Reg Thorn during the dinner hour. For once he was at home.

'I've got to come over to Springbourne this afternoon,' he told me. 'I'll pop in on my way.'

As one might expect, the wind had dropped considerably by the time he arrived, and the drumming was hardly in evidence. Nevertheless, he clambered up to the window and seemed to make a fairly exhaustive study of the structure.

'Right as a trivet,' he assured me when he descended. 'Good bit of work that! You don't need to worry about a thing. Them boys of mine know what they're up to. By the way, have you heard about Ted Richards?'

I looked blank. 'Do I know him?'

'Young Wayne's dad. He's had a stroke. The boy's off work for a few days, helping out.'

'I'm sorry to hear that. How's the old man getting on?'

'Pretty well. His speech is back, and the doctor says his arm is coming round. Shook the old boy though. I reckon I'll be losing Wayne, and I'll be sorry. He's a good worker, and a bit more up top than some I could mention. Still, his dad comes first, I can see that.'

He stepped back to take a last satisfied look at his creation, and then departed.

I woke in the night to the howling of a terrific gale. I could

hear a door banging downstairs, and got out of bed to go and shut it. As I did so a horrific rumbling sounded over-head, and I guessed that a tile had blown loose and was bumping down the roof.

The larder door was ajar and banging every time the gusts came through the small window. I closed both, and returned through the roaring to my bed.

But sleep was impossible. We get these frighteningly strong winds up here on the Downs, and a great deal of damage is done to our houses and farm buildings, not to mention trees and gardens. Usually I comfort myself with the thought that I have survived plenty of these rough nights, but this one seemed peculiarly vicious. One thing, it would test Reg Thorn's new window, I thought.

I dropped off again about six, the storm still raging, so that I overslept and had to hurry around to get over to school in time. To my dismay there was rain water on the floor beneath the window. On looking up, I could see that the whole structure seemed to be slanting, but that the water appeared to be dripping to the right of it.

I went outside and bumped into Mr Willet, and pointed out the damage. He surveyed it in silence for a full minute.

'It's the roof timbers, I reckon, not so much the window. It's no good patching old with new and expecting 'em both to thrive. Best get old Reg again, I suppose.'

He came inside with me and surveyed the puddle. Drips from above enlarged it steadily.

'Quite like old times, ain't it?' said Mr Willet, with evident satisfaction.

I rang Reg and left a message with his wife as he was out, of course. Mrs Pringle was mopping up when I returned.

She was wearing a new cretonne overall and an expression of extreme martyrdom.

'This is something I could have done without,' she said sourly. 'My leg's proper blazing this morning. I didn't hardly know how to get up the street.'

'I'll get one of the children to do it,' I said. Mrs Pringle wrung out the floor cloth, and shuffled to her feet.

'Too late! It's done now. And I hope you'll tell Reg Thorn what you think of him when he deigns to turn up.'

I told her that I had telephoned.

'Well, I shall have a word with him whatever you decide to do. Shoddy workmanship, that's what that is.'

'What a very pretty overall,' I replied, trying to pour oil on troubled waters. The old harridan looked slightly less gloomy.

'Minnie give it to me when she left. That's one blessing, I must say, to have the house to myself at last. But for how long, I wonder? That girl's still hankering after that Bert, you know. It's as though she can't help herself. Nothing but a prawn of fate, if you take my meaning.'

I said that I thought I did.

'Well, Ern's come round, and seems to be working regular – if work you can call it, leaning on a spade up Springbourne Manor and having cups of tea at all hours in the greenhouse. He don't know yet about Bert, and I've threatened to tell him, to try and get our Min to come to her senses. Sometimes I wonder if she's right in her head, Miss Read, I do straight.'

I agreed warmly. Mrs Pringle picked up her pail and limped to the lobby.

Later, Miss Briggs and I surveyed the damaged window more closely, as we awaited the arrival of Reg Thorn.

'It seems such a shame after all that hard work,' said my assistant.

'It does. By the way, did you know that the dark young man's name was Richards?'

'Yes.'

'Reg Thorn tells me that his father has had a stroke, poor fellow.'

'I know.'

'I wonder if it means that Wayne will have to leave Reg Thorn? He seemed to think so. It is bad luck.'

'Not for Wayne, I shouldn't think,' observed Miss Briggs, and the conversation ended abruptly as the youngest Coggs child approached bearing a dead, and very smelly, starling.

Afterwards it occurred to me that Miss Briggs seemed to know far more about the Richards than I did. Hardly surprising, I told myself, as she talked to the two boys far more than I did, and may well have bumped into them in Caxley recently.

Reg Thorn did not arrive until school ended. It was still blowing, still cold, and still depressing. I went indoors for my tea, leaving him to discover the worst. Twenty minutes later, having thawed out, I repented, and took him out a mug of tea.

But he had gone.

Rehearsals continued, and I was glad to see that the children seemed much less self-conscious as they began to be familiar with their lines and their movements about the stage – or rather, the schoolroom floor.

The costumes were practically finished, thanks largely I knew to Mrs Moffat's generosity with her time and skill.

Nothing second-rate ever came from that lady's needle, and I was confident that our cast would be beautifully dressed.

We ran through the whole programme to time it one afternoon, and were pleasantly surprised to find that the whole thing took about an hour and a quarter. As we were following this with our tea party, we should have two full and happy afternoons, the first for the infants' parents and friends, and the repeat performance the next day for the juniors and the rest of those wanting to come.

The vicar called in one day to give me the good news that the managers were providing our birthday cake, and that Mrs Willet had offered to bake it – or rather two of them, one for each afternoon.

'It's very generous of them,' I said. 'And if Mrs Willet's in charge of the cooking, we know everything will be absolutely superb.'

'It was Henry's idea really. He thought Mrs Willet, as an old Fairacre pupil, might be agreeable, and she just jumped at the chance. She said it would have been a disgrace to ask some Caxley baker to make Fairacre's centenary cake. She's working out the cost, which we're delighted to meet as our small contribution to the fun.'

It was marvellous to see how enthusiastic the whole village was about our celebrations. There was no doubt about it, Fairacre School was the heart of our village, and memories of their own schooldays quickened the adults' response to this tribute to its hundred years. Its influence could never be estimated. I only hoped that it would be able to continue to serve the village as it had always done.

Our numbers were smaller than ever before, and I did my

best to push that unpleasant fact, and its even more un-
pleasant consequences, into the back of my mind.

But I was not always successful.

Joan Benson rang one evening to invite me to a small party
for farewell drinks.

'I'd love to come,' I said, 'but "farewell" sounds so sad.'

'Oh, I think I shall pop back from time to time,' she said
cheerfully. 'Miriam insists, and so do Irene and David. I
must say that now it's arrived, I feel much happier about
going than I have all these months.'

'So you've found something in Sussex?'

'I think so. Nothing really fixed yet, but David and Irene
have sold their flat, and their buyers want to move in almost
immediately. The Mawnes were very sweet and did not
want to hurry me – in fact they'd made plans to stay in
Caxley, or with Henry and Elizabeth – but it's far better for
everyone if they move in here at once, and in any case, I can
stay with my daughter until my new abode is ready.'

'We shall all miss you. Particularly Miriam.'

'It's kind of you to say so. Actually Miriam seems much
more settled about the move now. I think she's suddenly
realised that the Mawnes genuinely want her to stay, and
now that she feels she can be useful to them, her attitude has
changed entirely. I must say, I feel much happier about
deserting her. She so loves Fairacre, it would have been
tragic if she had had to uproot herself after such a short stay.'

I wished her luck with her plans, and said that I would
look forward to the party on December the first.

Two days later Reg Thorn arrived with three men who,
from their somewhat formal attire, were probably from the

building department of the county education office. They all gazed at the poor dormer window, still hopelessly askew, and a good deal of head-shaking went on and grave looks were exchanged. From my strategic lookout post by the classroom window it seemed that Reg Thorn grew increasingly unhappy during the conference, but of course I could not hear what was being said.

After about half an hour, when we had settled down to arithmetic, one of the three strangers knocked at the door and asked if he could have a word with me. Reg Thorn and the other two men seemed to have disappeared.

'I'm afraid that this is going to be a bigger job than we thought,' he said. 'Mr Thorn will be dismantling the present structure immediately, as it is not too safe.'

I must have looked alarmed, for he went on hastily.

'Nothing too daunting! You and the children will be quite all right. But for the time being we propose to put a large piece of perspex over the aperture to keep out the weather while we investigate the roof timbers again.'

Trust our Mr Willet to have been right from the word 'Go', was my private comment, but naturally I kept mum.

'And when will Reg Thorn start the dismantling?' I asked.

'This afternoon,' replied the man. He sounded rather grim, I thought. 'And the sooner the better,' he added.

I was in entire agreement.

Mrs Willet called in during the evening to return a cookery book which I had lent her some time ago, and I took the opportunity of saying how pleased we all were to hear that she was making the birthday cake.

'*Cakes*,' she corrected me. 'It wouldn't be seemly to have half a cake at the second tea party. It's just as simple to make two nice cakes as the one.' She hesitated for a moment. 'Which brings me to the candles,' she continued.

'How do you mean?'

'Well, I reckon we ought to have a hundred candles – those weeny little cake ones, you know – and now I'll need *two* hundred for the two cakes.'

It seemed what her husband would call 'a mort of candles' to me, but I supposed she knew best.

'I've got it all planned out, you see. I'm doing two big square cakes, because it's easier to cut them fairly that way. And if I put ten candles to a row, and have ten rows, it will work out lovely.'

I expressed genuine admiration.

'Oh, it's nothing,' said Mrs Willet modestly. 'I've been baking big cakes in Fairacre for all my married life – W.I. dos and Sunday School treats and that, but I want these two cakes to be the best I've ever done – a sort of "Thank you" to the school. Anyway, I enjoy a good baking day.'

'I bet Mr Willet does too,' I said.

'Oh, he's a splendid eater!' said his wife enthusiastically. 'Always was. We always said the Willet boys had enough in their dinner basket to feed the whole school.'

I remembered Mr Willet's remark about his recently dead brother who had carried the rush basket to school, and the largesse from Grandma which topped up the original victuals.

'I remember Miss Clare saying once that as long as a person could eat, then there couldn't be much wrong with him. She used to give us lessons about hygiene as we got to the top of the school. Very useful too in later life. Some-

times I used to think poor Mr Hope might not have taken to drink if he had had a better appetite. Hardly ate anything, you know. Mrs Hope used to worry about it. But there, he was a poet, poor soul, as no doubt you know, Miss Read, and poets don't seem to need food, do they?'

I thought of Timothy Ferdinand wolfing down Amy's delicious provender at her dinner party, and asking for the veal patties to take home.

'Some don't, I imagine, Mrs Willet,' I said diplomatically, 'but there are undoubtedly some poets who do.'

'Maybe, but what I was going to ask you, Miss Read, was could you possibly buy the candles for me when you go to Caxley on Saturday? I'd like to have them in good time, and I've no plans to go into town just yet.'

I said I would be very pleased to do it.

'And you will get a receipt, won't you?' she begged. 'The managers want to pay every penny, and have told me to make a note of *everything*.'

I promised that I would do so, and she departed looking relieved.

The job of dismantling the offending dormer window went along at a spanking pace. I thought ruefully that it was obviously much quicker to demolish than to build, remembering the months we had endured noise and the ingress of the weather.

To my surprise, Wayne Richards reappeared as well as his former companion. I asked after his father.

'Getting on fine, that's why I'm here for the rest of the week. Reg is in a bit of a taking over this business, and Dad said it would be best to help him out, as the job's got to be done quickly.'

I did not like to ask about his own plans for the future, but he volunteered the information.

'I'm starting in with Dad on a business footing at the beginning of December. Suits us both very well, and there's plenty of work about. He's not one to get in a panic about his health, but I think this last attack rocked him, and he won't do as much as he always has done. About time he eased off a bit, and I'll be glad to take over more of the work. There's only me to carry it on, so I'd better learn the ropes pretty quickly.'

He gave me a flashing smile through the black beard, and mounted the ladder again.

Amy arrived one afternoon in the same week just as the children were going home. She had asked me to look through the article about the sick room and to give her my opinion on it.

The two young men were up on the roof manhandling the large piece of perspex into place.

'Shan't see you tomorrow,' shouted Wayne. 'We'll have this fixed tonight in case we get some rain.'

'Well, thanks for all you've done,' I called back.

Amy and I walked across the playground to my house where Tibby, ever ravenous, gave us a rapturous welcome.

'What's his name?' enquired Amy, slipping off her coat.

'Who?'

'The bearded fellow. Miss Briggs's young man.'

'Miss Briggs's young man?' I echoed. 'That's Reg Thorn's young man! He's called Wayne Richards. His father's a builder too.'

'He's also Miss Briggs's young man,' said Amy patiently.

'At least, he's the one she was with way back in the summer. The one I told you about.'

'You didn't tell me it was *Wayne*,' I said accusingly.

'I didn't know it was Wayne until two seconds ago,' said Amy reasonably. 'But that's certainly the same fellow. I couldn't forget a beard of that magnitude.'

'Well, I'm blowed!' I said, turning over this interesting piece of knowledge. 'I had no idea this was going on, but it explains quite a lot.'

'How do you mean?'

'Well, the improvement in temper, and the willingness to stay after school – at least, until the boy finishes work. I wonder I didn't twig before, with all this happening before my very eyes, as they say.'

'Why should you? They weren't likely to be particularly demonstrative before you and all those knowing pupils. As two sensible young people they hoped to keep their affairs to themselves, as far as you can in a village.'

'Well, I must say I'm delighted with the news. He's a good fellow, and going to have a steady job with his father. I would have thought he could have done better than our Miss Briggs, though.'

'No doubt she has hidden charms,' said Amy.

'Obviously.' I continued to think about this interesting disclosure.

'One thing,' I told Amy. 'She'll probably stay here teaching. It will be nice to know that I shan't have to start advertising for another infants' teacher yet.'

'Aren't you rushing ahead a trifle?' enquired Amy. 'Give the poor things time to sort out their romance.'

'Who started all this anyway?' I retorted.

12 December

Our temporary skylight was a great success. For one thing, it was considerably wider than the original one, as the aperture had been made larger to take the ill-fated dormer window, and so allowed much more light to come through.

As it lay snug and flat against the roof there was no dreadful drumming noise, and from outside, I must say, the line of the roof looked better to my eyes than the somewhat clumsy dormer window. I was beginning to wonder if the powers that be would finally decide to replace the old skylight with another of more up-to-date construction.

The men who had come with Reg Thorn to inspect the damage after the gale, came again after school one day and spent a long session inside and outside the old building.

Their decision was conveyed to me later by a letter from the office telling me that work on the roof timbers would be put in hand as soon as school broke up. The new window would be finished before the children returned in January, and they were sorry for the inconvenience. They added, rather decently I thought, that unusually severe weather had jeopardised Mr Thorn's work, and that further consultations would be needed to settle the design of the new lights, under the circumstances.

'Mark my words,' said Mr Willet, when I mentioned this

to him. 'Reg Thorn will be putting in another skylight. And a durn good thing too. That dormer was wrong from the start, for our old roof. I told you, didn't I, they must have gone into all that pretty thorough when the old place was built in 1880? And they built to last then too.'

Mrs Pringle, who had entered during this conversation, added her mite.

'One thing, it should make Reg Thorn get a move on for once. I take it he won't get paid till the job's done, and he must have lost a packet already. It's an ill wind as blows nobody any good.'

Joan Benson's sitting room was crowded when I arrived on the evening of the party.

It was a pleasant surprise to see David and Irene Mawne among the guests, and Joan was busy introducing the new owners of Holly Lodge to the one or two people whom they had not met before. Irene's brother, Horace Umbleditch, who teaches at a prep school not far from Amy at Bent, was also there, and it was good to see him again.

The room was looking very festive with a ceiling-high Christmas tree already in place.

'Too early, I know,' said Joan, to the admirers, 'but I intended to enjoy my last Christmas here, and to have all the trimmings.'

I found myself by Henry Mawne and asked when his nephew hoped to move in.

'Just before Christmas, I think, though one can never be certain of these things. The removal people seem to think about the 20th December, and Joan has been absolutely adamant that she will be out by then. We are full of admiration for the way she is coping. She's definitely having the

house she went to see a week or so ago, and luckily, those people are off on the twelfth.'

'Can she be sure?'

'He's in the army and being posted to the Middle East. That's one thing about the services, once you've got your marching orders, you know where you are. A great relief all round. David's buyers fiddled about until he and Irene were nearly demented, but now that's satisfactorily tied up.'

Miriam Quinn approached and Henry drifted away to talk to the vicar. I asked her if she were going away for Christmas.

'Yes, I'm off to Norfolk to my brother's. I thought it would be more fun for David and Irene to have their first Christmas here on their own. Of course, young Simon will be here, and I believe Henry and Elizabeth have been invited to Christmas dinner. Quite a family affair, and I shall enjoy being with my own folk too, of course. What are you going to do?'

I told her that I had in mind to invite Dolly Clare to spend Christmas and Boxing Day with me. She would be with me overnight for the centenary celebrations earlier in the month, but if she were willing to come later as well, it would be an added joy.

'Do you know, I've never met her, and would love to.'

'Then we'll fix up a meeting in the New Year,' I promised. 'But we're being called to order.'

Sure enough, the vicar called for silence, and made a graceful little speech, wishing Joan well and welcoming the young Mawnes. We raised our glasses, and drank their healths.

I thought, yet again, how lucky we are in Fairacre to have

so many good people united in friendship within our parish bounds.

As our two-day celebrations drew near, excitement began to run high. As well as the entertainment, it was my duty, as always, to provide the annual village tea party. This is paid for from our school funds, raised during the year by such things as jumble sales and bazaars, and I do the ordering.

This time it was obvious that we should need twice as much food, although Mrs Willet's masterpieces should certainly fill up appreciative stomachs. We are lucky enough still to have a baker in Fairacre. He also keeps the village shop, so that I went up one evening to discuss with him such things as scones, buns, lardy cake, and what he calls 'confections' – that is such mouth-watering and fattening things as almond slices, macaroons and madeleines.

Usually I order sliced loaves as well, and spend hours making sandwiches in my kitchen. But this year, with so much else to occupy my time, I decided to give them a miss.

By the time we had finished poring over the order, it was plain to me that we should have to have some more money-raising efforts early in the New Year, as the existing school kitty would be seriously depleted.

And why not, I asked myself? It's not every year that one celebrates one's hundredth birthday! Fairacre School was going to do its friends proud – and enjoy every minute of it.

The two performances and tea parties were to take place on the last Thursday and Friday of term.

Mrs Annett from Beech Green (who as Miss Gray was once my infants' teacher until the neighbouring headmaster snatched her from me into matrimony) brought Miss Clare

with her, as our old friend was to stay the night so that she did not get over-tired. I was to return her to her own cottage on Friday evening.

At half-past two parents and friends came flooding into the ancient schoolroom. We had pushed back the dividing partition, and the action was to take place at the infants' end of the room. The quaking actors and actresses were huddled into the lobby. Miss Clare, serene as ever, did her best to calm their nerves while I greeted our guests, and told them a little of what they would be seeing – with reasonable luck.

I had never seen our little school so packed, and this, of course, was only half our audience. I found it intensely moving to see so many old people, some of whom had been pupils before the first world war and would remember Miss Clare as a young pupil teacher. It was good too to see so many friends, some comparative newcomers to Fairacre, like the Mawnes, who had come to do us honour and to join in this home-spun tribute to our school.

I read the entry from the original log book, and Linda and Patrick took the stage. There was warm applause as they entered, due largely, I think, to the superb costumes which Mrs Moffat had created.

After looking somewhat scared at this unexpected welcome, the two became quite confident, and went through their little scene. The caning went down extremely well, and a baby in the front row brought the house down by shouting: 'Give 'im some more!' in the most bloodthirsty manner. Obviously, I should have to keep an eye on this juvenile sadist when he came under my care in two or three years' time.

'In King Edward the Seventh's reign,' I said loudly, for

hidden Dolly Clare's benefit, 'Fairacre School had a new young pupil teacher.'

Here Dolly entered, smiling, and the applause grew deafening. We had placed the old high chair, in which she had sat for so many years, in front of the audience, and with just one page of notes Dolly began her reminiscences.

Her listeners gave her rapt attention. She confined her memories to the early years of her teaching at the school, and mentioned many children – many now dead, or killed in the 1914–1918 war – remembered clearly by the older ones present.

She touched on the clothes worn, the lunches brought, the great distances trudged in all weathers, and the universal poverty which dogged almost all. She also dwelt on the happiness found in simple things: the occasional treat, the annual outing, harvest home, a visit from the bishop, as well as the ineffable joy of country things such as the first primroses, the cuckoo's call and the return of the swallows.

There was no doubt about it. As I had suspected, Miss Clare's contribution, made incidentally without any recourse to her notes, was the highlight of the afternoon, although the following scene, showing the school's part in the war of George the Fifth's reign, obviously moved many of those who could remember those sad times.

Mr Lamb's recollections of the trip to Wembley from the school gave us all a chance to laugh. Some of his contemporaries interrupted his narrative with downright contradictions, but it was all done with such enthusiasm and merriment that his contribution was a resounding success.

Mrs Austen's vivid account of an evacuee's view of Fairacre was warmly received, and probably because she

was a woman, she was not open to the same outspoken comments which had punctuated Mr Lamb's account.

Then it was my turn to give an idea of the school in the reign of our present Queen Elizabeth the Second. I had tried to make it a brief survey and as interesting as possible, but feared it might be something of a comedown after the earlier contributions.

It was a kind audience, however, and genuinely interested, I felt, in the changes which had taken place since the Act of 1944 when the children over eleven went off to Beech Green or Caxley Grammar School, and Fairacre was left as a junior school. The repercussions of the ancient grammar school being obliged to become a comprehensive school were also mentioned, for this fact touched many of the families present.

The children's work was on display round the walls and at one end of the room, and I invited the audience to inspect everything and to see how methods of work had altered over the hundred years. The whole school then clustered on to our temporary stage and sang two songs very sweetly.

Finally, the vicar rose and made a fine speech about the great part this old school had played in village life, and complimented everyone on the work done, not only on the stage this afternoon, but behind the scenes for many, many years. He then asked us all to join in a prayer of thanksgiving for mercies received in the past, and to call a blessing on Fairacre School's future.

While this was being done and heads were bent, I could hear the welcome sound of Mrs Pringle and her band of helpers, dealing with the tea things in the other lobby. Festivity was about to follow reverence.

It was astonishing to see how quickly the mounds of

provender vanished. Appetites are keen in our sharp down-land air, and I was kept busy filling cups from the tea urn borrowed from the Woman's Institute for the two occa-sions.

But at last the great moment came when the vicar called for silence, the door opened and Mrs Willet came staggering in, bearing the magnificent cake ablaze with one hundred candles. A great cheer went up and the ancient floorboards quaked under the stamping of stout country boots.

We had asked Miss Clare, as the oldest pupil present, and the youngest child from the infants' room to cut the cake together. My bread knife only just proved equal to severing the beautifully dark, rich mixture, but the two won through eventually and a slice was delivered to everyone present.

It was dark by the time the last of our visitors had gone. The fragrance of the fruit cake still lingered about the empty schoolroom, and far too many crumbs lay upon the floor.

'It all went beautifully,' I said to Miss Clare before we walked across the playground to my home. 'But I don't know what Mrs Pringle will say when she sees the mess.'

'What Mrs Pringle says,' Miss Clare told me, 'can have very little meaning in face of a hundred years of our school's history.'

And with this comforting thought we strolled home to take our ease. There was a sharp nip in the air, and our breath was visible in the dusk.

'A frost tonight,' said Miss Clare. 'The first real one of the winter.'

Sure enough, when I took her breakfast tray into my spare room the next morning, the trees and grass were white with

hoar frost. It was a lovely sight, but a pointer to things to come.

Miss Clare protested about being waited on, but I was adamant that she stayed in bed for an hour or two longer. We had a repeat performance to go through in the afternoon, and I knew that there would be a great many friends who would want to talk to her.

As it was the last day of term, too, I should be busy clearing up and trying to remind the children of the date of our return in January, as well as keeping them relatively calm and prepared for their final performance. I found that it was no easy task. Success had quite gone to their heads, and I had never known them quite so excited and noisy. I pushed them out early to play in the frosty playground and to run off some of their excess energy.

Miss Briggs, whose class was suffering from the same *joie de vivre*, joined me in the playground, and we gave them all a further ten minutes of strenuous exercise. If anything, these tactics seemed to rouse them even more, but we ushered the breathless mob indoors, and I suggested that a story might calm them down.

'We have to expect this sort of thing on the last day of term,' I said indulgently. 'And then, of course, there's Christmas looming ahead. Are you going home?'

'Yes,' said my assistant.

'Tonight? Will you want to get off early?'

I wished I could remember if it were Droitwich or Harrogate. Somewhere a good distance away, I knew.

'No. It seemed better to go tomorrow in the light, and anyway Wayne doesn't finish until tomorrow morning.'

I must have looked blank.

'I'm driving home to Leamington and taking him with me.'

Leamington. I must remember *Leamington.*

'That will be nice for you both,' I said, anxious not to appear too pressing, but Miss Briggs was well launched.

'My parents know about him, of course, but haven't met him yet. I expect we'll announce our engagement at Christmas.'

I said, quite truthfully, that I was delighted to hear the news, and that Wayne was a fine young man.

Miss Briggs gave me the biggest smile I had yet seen upon her countenance, and we returned to the noisy rabble within.

Our second afternoon was even more successful than the first. For one thing, all those taking part were more relaxed, and the audience was even larger than the day before. How they all managed to squeeze in I shall never fathom.

Mrs Willet's second cake was as rapturously received as the first, and almost all the school's offerings went too. The few cakes that remained, I put into a paper bag to give surreptitiously to the Coggs family later.

Miss Clare was surrounded by friends, among them Elizabeth Mawne who had not met her before. Their conversation was animated, and I was glad to see my old friend Dolly so lively. I began to realise, more sharply than ever before, that she normally lacked company, and I was glad that I was about to invite her to spend Christmas with me.

Even Mrs Pringle seemed to have mellowed with our festivities, and said nothing about the floor strewn with crumbs.

'I'll see to that tea urn,' she said. 'The W.I. can turn a bit funny if it's not returned pronto, and *clean*.'

At last we said goodbye to our guests, reiterated the phrase: 'Term begins on January the sixth' to those willing to listen, who were few among the general pandemonium, and left the schoolroom to the ministrations of Mrs Pringle and Mr and Mrs Willet, who insisted on putting all to rights.

'Well,' I said to Miss Clare, when we sank exhausted one each side of my sitting-room fire. 'I'm whacked! Someone else will have to cope with the next centenary.'

'But it's really been *memorable*!' replied Dolly. 'How glad I am to have seen it – and to have taken part!'

'Have a glass of sherry,' I said, struggling to my feet. 'We need a pick-me-up after all that.'

'Here's to Fairacre School,' said Dolly, raising her glass, and we drank thankfully.

'Have you any plans for Christmas?' I asked, after the first rejuvenating mouthful.

'None. Except that I expect the kind Annetts will invite me there for Christmas Day.'

I said how much I should like her to come to Fairacre for the two days, or longer if she could manage it.

'There's nothing I should enjoy more,' she told me. And so it was happily settled.

'I can honestly say I never feel truly lonely,' she went on, 'but now that I'm such a great age I've no one of my own left. Ada's children lost touch years ago, even before my sister died. Of course, dear Emily meant more to me than anyone in the world, but when she went there was really no one left, except good friends like you. I believe you are in the same boat?'

'I suppose so. No really close relations, though I have a dear aunt, and some jolly cousins, but they are all as busy as I am, and we don't keep in touch as we should. No, I'm like you, very glad of good friends who live near enough to see frequently, like you and the Annetts and dear old Amy at Bent, who wants to meet you incidentally.'

'That will be nice,' said Dolly. She sounded a trifle abstracted, and I wondered if she were over-tired, which would not be surprising. She took another sip from her glass, and then put it carefully on the side table.

'I think I ought to tell you something which perhaps I should have told you before. When I was talking to that nice Mrs Mawne this afternoon, I realised for the first time that you might be worrying about what might happen to you if this school ever had to close.'

'Well, that's been a possibility for years, of course,' I said, puzzled.

'You see, my dear, having no relatives to speak of, I left everything to dear Emily as she had nowhere of her own to live, and only a tiny pension. Not that I had much more, of course, but I did have the cottage to shelter us. When she had gone, I went one day to Caxley to see young Mr Lovejoy and to alter my will.'

Young Mr Lovejoy, I knew, was about to retire as he was now in his sixties. But to Miss Clare, whose family had dealt with the old-established solicitors for two or three generations, young Mr Lovejoy must seem a mere boy.

'He was as charming as ever,' said Dolly, 'and we made out a nice simple little will, leaving some money to the church at Beech Green and the same to Fairacre. My few trinkets I've left to Isobel Annett. Nothing much of value there, I'm afraid, but some are quite pretty.'

'She'll treasure them, I'm sure,' I said.

Miss Clare picked up her glass again. 'And the house I've left to you.'

I felt my jaw drop. I gazed at her, speechless with shock.

'Do you mind?' asked Dolly very gently.

'Mind?' I croaked. 'I don't know what to say!'

'I wanted it to be a surprise for you when I'd gone. I knew you hadn't made any arrangements to buy a place, and I thought you could find a home there while you looked round, if you wanted something better.'

'There is nothing better!' I whispered. My voice seemed to have collapsed completely, and my heart was jumping about like a frog.

'Well, of course, I'd always hoped that you would want to live in it, and be as happy as I have there. I ought to have realised though that you might be worrying about the future. It wasn't until this afternoon, when Mrs Mawne mentioned it, that I saw that I had really been rather self-indulgent in trying to keep my plans secret.'

'Dolly,' I began, trying to control my wavering voice, 'I don't know how to thank you. I'm absolutely over-whelmed, and don't deserve such generosity. I'll try to tell you soon how I feel – but I'm too overjoyed for words just now.'

'Good!' said Dolly comfortably. 'Well, that's settled. Now to more practical matters. What would you like for a Christmas present?'

I went over to kiss her.

'You've just given me one,' I told her.

Later that evening, I took Dolly home, and saw her safely into bed with her hot water bottle and a warm drink. By

that time, I had recovered enough to tell her how I felt about her wonderful gesture. It made the future quite different for me, and I was still too dazed to comprehend fully just what it would mean.

I locked the cottage door as directed, and put the key back through the letter box. I still could not believe that one day – long distant, I sincerely prayed – this lovely house might be mine.

'I shall never sleep a wink,' I said to myself, as I drove back through the frosty night.

But I fell into bed within ten minutes of reaching home, and slept like a log until seven.

I resolved to say nothing about my proposed legacy to any one. Dolly wanted to keep it a secret, and I should respect that wish.

But buoyed up with my wonderful news, I set about all the Christmas tasks I had neglected during our celebrations.

Christmas cards were arriving thick and fast. Trees, flowers, robins, skating parties, and every imaginable winter activity glowed from the tributes on my mantel-piece, and I must get down to sending off some of my own.

The card I cherished most was a photograph of a baby seal sent to me by the kind people at the Tresco hotel. The seal had been born on the beach nearby, and no other Christmas card could touch it for its delightful appeal. It took pride of place among the others.

It also galvanised me into doing something which Amy had urged me to do long ago. The first letter of the holidays was to that same hotel, booking a room for a fortnight in August. How Amy would approve!

The frost continued. The ground was iron hard and every

morning found the grass and trees covered with hoar frost. Ice was everywhere, and the roads treacherous.

Miss Clare sent a message to say that she had decided against coming to the school service at St. Patrick's the next Sunday, because of the weather, but would look forward to seeing me on Christmas Eve for tea at her house. We should miss her at the service, but I was relieved to know that she was not venturing out in this bitter weather. I hoped that by the following Wednesday the thaw would have set in.

Attendance at morning service on Sunday must have delighted Gerald Partridge's heart. Parents, pupils, managers and other friends of Fairacre School turned up in full force, and there were very few empty pews.

The singing was hearty, and I had found time to coach the children in the two hymns chosen particularly for this occasion, so that they added to the joyful noise considerably. The vicar's sermon was a model of sincerity, brevity and gratitude, and Mr Annett had chosen some stirring music for the service. The final voluntary was Mozart's *Turkish March*, and I wondered, yet again, how anyone, Turks or otherwise, could march in step to that dancing rhythm.

But it was a joyous and uplifting ending to our centenary celebrations.

By Wednesday, the murky cold weather had lifted slightly. It was still bitterly cold, but the roads had thawed, and for two or three hours at midday a feeble sun dispersed the clouds.

I drove over to Beech Green and walked up the short path to Dolly Clare's cottage with the most unusual feelings. Pleasure at being there was now mingled with something like awe. That this, one day, might be mine! I could still not

fully realise my good fortune, and felt very humble in the
face of Dolly's superb generosity. Of one thing I could be
certain. The cottage would be cherished as dearly as before,
and if ever her gentle ghost reappeared it would be given
honour and a warm welcome.

We were at St. Patrick's the next morning, admiring the
Christmas roses, the holly, the ivy and the mistletoe. Mr
Partridge's suggestion that the children might help had not
been followed up, and certainly the flower-arranging ladies
had made a superb job of their labour of love without
juvenile aid.

We walked back through the thin winter sunshine to find
that the chicken I had left roasting was done to a turn, and
the small pudding was bubbling cheerfully on the stove.

After our modest Christmas dinner we indulged in a glass
of port and both slipped off into slumber, awaking just in
time to listen to the Queen's message.

We spent the rest of Christmas Day and Boxing Day very
quietly and lazily, going for short walks round the familiar
lanes of Fairacre when the sun came through in the early
afternoon. But it was always good to return to the fireside
and to pick up our knitting, or attempt to solve the cross-
word puzzle, or sometimes simply to doze. To tell the truth,
I was dog-tired at the end of term, and this one had been
particularly arduous. Not that I would have missed any of
our jollifications for a minute, but I began to realise just how
exhausted I was when I could relax at home. Dolly Clare
was the perfect companion for this pace of life, serene,
undemanding and unfailingly happy.

I managed to persuade her to stay until the Saturday
morning, but no longer. She was anxious not to put her
good neighbour to any unnecessary trouble.

'She is looking after the cat,' she said, 'and getting in my milk and bread. And no doubt she will light a fire, and generally cosset the house, so I must get back to look after myself.'

We drove over in the morning, and sure enough a fire blazed in the grate. We settled down to enjoy a cup of coffee before I returned.

'I've lived here for six reigns now,' said Miss Clare, looking about her. 'I thought when I was telling our friends about my time as a pupil teacher at Fairacre, that I must have closed the door of this cottage some thousands of times and set off on my bicycle along the lane to that dear old school. I've seen the trees and fields breaking into leaf, shading the road later, turning into the gold of autumn and then bitter nakedness, for more years than I care to remember. But always this cottage has been the beginning and end of every journey. The thought that you will do the same after me gives me infinite pleasure. I don't know when I've felt quite so happy.'

'I can echo that,' I told her.

No snow came to our downland country during the remaining days of December, but the skies were ominously grey and the iron cold made one feel that this respite might be short-lived. On New Year's Eve I was invited to the Mawnes for the evening. I walked through the village in the frosty air to the sound of the bells ringing a practice peal at St. Patrick's.

Well, the Old Year had been good to me, I thought. I had seen Fairacre School celebrating a hundred years of useful work, and my personal life had been enriched by friends old and new. And Dolly Clare's incredible kindness had put the

final seal upon a memorable year. I had a great deal to be thankful for.

So what would the New Year bring, I wondered, opening the gate of the Mawnes's house? Lights gleamed in the windows. A lantern by the door lit up the welcoming holly wreath dangling its scarlet ribbons against the white paint.

'Come in, come in!' called Henry, opening the door, 'and a Happy New Year to you, and all Fairacre!'

SUMMER AT FAIRACRE

To
Dotti
With love

CONTENTS

1	The First Day of Spring	233
2	Minor Irritations	246
3	Henry Mawne Needs Company	257
4	The Coggs Are in Distress	269
5	Easter Holidays	281
6	Public Duties	293
7	More Worries for the Coggs Family	307
8	Strange Behaviour of Amy	319
9	Troubles Never Come Singly	331
10	Mrs Pringle Deserts Us	343
11	Amy's Party	355
12	Minnie Pringle Lends a Hand	367
13	Mr Willet to the Rescue	377
14	Rain and Romance	390
15	Summer's Bounty	401
16	Sunshine and Sports	414
17	Off to the Wedding	426
18	Away From it All	437
19	Mrs Pringle on the War Path	448
20	The End of Summer	460

1 The First Day of Spring

'WHAT the Hanover d'you make of this, Miss Read?'

Mr Willet took the cap from his head and shook the snow from it, spattering the schoolroom floor with dark spots.

'Twenty-first of March,' he went on. 'First day of spring, and I reckon there's a good inch of snow all over.'

'Well, it can't last,' I replied. 'It's melting already in the playground.'

A clashing of pails from the lobby told of the presence of Mrs Pringle, our school cleaner. Both she and Bob Willet, the caretaker, come soon after eight each morning to see that Fairacre School is in good trim to start the day.

'And how's Madam Sunshine today?' asked Mr Willet, nodding towards the source of noise. He was prudent enough, I noticed, to lower his voice.

As village schoolmistress, Mrs Pringle is one of the crosses I have to bear. Mrs Pringle enjoys the gloomier side of life, and is never so happy as when she is discussing distressing ailments, other people's peccadilloes, impending disasters or a really slap-up funeral, preferably with inner knowledge of how much money was left by the deceased and to whom it is going.

Square, sturdy and sixtyish, Mrs Pringle is as tough as an old boot, but she has 'a Bad Leg' which dominates our lives at Fairacre. If Mrs Pringle decides that she is over-worked, and this happens quite often, the afflicted limb is liable to rapid deterioration, and gives its owner a pronounced limp. One can

always tell, from the severity of Mrs Pringle's hobbling, what sort of mood the lady is in. There is no love lost between Mr Willet and our cleaner, and I have to be very circumspect in dealing with both.

This is not always an easy task, as both parties can be over-sensitive to the reaction of the other. I have to tread as warily as Agag, and then, more often than not, I find that one of them has taken umbrage.

Usually, of course, it is Mrs Pringle, who is always on the look-out for the odd insult. One need only comment, in a perfunctory way, about the amount of grime children can collect on their hands, and Mrs Pringle begins to bridle and to point out, with unnecessary acrimony, that there is always a plentiful supply of soap put out in the lobby. Moreover, that very soap has been put there with her own two over-worked hands, and the basins have been cleaned so thoroughly – again by those same hands – that it would be possible to eat your dinner in them, should you feel so disposed.

When I first came to Fairacre as the village schoolmistress I used to try to stem this flow of umbrage-taking by making ineffectual apologies and explanations. I know better now. It is far more satisfactory to let Mrs Pringle have her head, and to allow the torrent to flow over one. She thoroughly enjoys it, and I have now become so hardened that it makes very little impression. Over the years we have shaken down together pretty well, and the occasional clash of wills does neither of us serious harm.

On this particular morning we all three had cause for dismay. A particularly cold winter was being followed by an equally unpleasant early spring. The tortoise stoves were still needed to warm the school, and the children continued to wear their winter clothing. My own tweed skirts and thick cardigans had been in use for months now, and we all longed for sunshine, flowers and lighter clothing.

'When I was a boy,' said Mr Willet, 'I reckoned to go birds' nesting this time of year, and there was primroses and violets in the hedge bottoms. And my old dad's rhubarb was sprouting real steady. Look at it these days! We don't get no spring worth spitting on, and nothing don't start stirring till May. There was some chap on the telly t'other night as said the seasons are just the same as ever was. He don't know the half.'

'I agree,' I assured him.

'And this other bloke he said as the earth's axle – or some such word – has tilted off true a bit, so the weather's changed. I reckon that's more like it.'

He pulled an old-fashioned red and white spotted handkerchief from his corduroys' pocket, and blew his nose with impressive trumpeting.

'Never got rid of me Christmas cold neither,' he informed me, stuffing the handkerchief away. 'Ah! I near forgot! Could you do with a morsel of winter savoy? Good thing to have a bit of fresh greens this weather. That frozen stuff's all very well for second best, but you can't beat the real thing.'

'I'd love some,' I said.

At that moment, the door burst open, and Joseph Coggs and four more boys rushed in bearing a furious cat.

'It's a stray, miss,' they chorused. 'It was under Mr Roberts' hedge, miss. It's *starving*, miss.'

The cat was struggling frenziedly in Joseph's tight clasp. It was certainly cross, but did not appear emaciated to my eye.

Mr Willet scrutinised it closely.

'That's one of Mr Roberts' farm cats,' he pronounced. 'I know it very well. It's like its ma, with one white leg. You take it back, boy, or you'll be in trouble.'

Five pairs of eyes turned anxiously in my direction.

'You'd better do as Mr Willet says,' I told them. 'At playtime you can go back to the place where you found him, and if he's still there you can take down some bread and milk.'

Mollified by this compromise, the deputation and its victim departed.

Mr Willet looked at me and shook his head.

'You're too soft with 'em by half,' he told me. 'In my day, Mr Hope would have given 'em all a clip round the ear for trying on a trick like that.'

'Teachers are not allowed to strike children these days,' I said.

'More's the pity,' replied Mr Willet, making for the door.

His way was barred by the formidable bulk of Mrs Pringle who was advancing with an outstretched hand.

Upon it were balanced a few fragments of a small paint brush.

'What's all this 'ere, may I ask?' she boomed.

Mr Willet and I surveyed her wet palm and the debris.

'Don't need much eyesight to see it's been a paint brush in its time,' replied Mr Willet with withering sarcasm.

'Then what's it doing down the plug hole of the wash basin?' demanded Mrs Pringle, fixing me with a stern glance.

'Someone's been trying to hide evidence,' I said. 'Put it on my desk and I'll sort it out.'

Mrs Pringle deposited her burden, and a number of soapy drops, dangerously near the register, and turned to face me, arms akimbo.

'What them children need,' she announced, 'is a bit of old-fashioned discipline.'

'I've been telling her that,' said Mr Willet.

And the two departed, in rare unity, as I went to ring the bell.

By playtime, almost all the snow had vanished. There was still some whiteness under the school hedge, and the tiles on the north-facing roof were edged with shallow snow.

The children were disappointed.

It only needs a flurry of snowflakes to set them agog with anticipation. Making snowmen, complete with pipe, hat and pebbles for eyes, tobogganing down the hill near Beech Green, scoring off old enemies with well-thrown snowballs – all these delights seem within reach, but usually melt away as swiftly as the snow itself.

Joseph Coggs and his rescue party prompted my memory, and were allowed to dash down the lane to see if the cat was still languishing under the hedge. As expected, they returned somewhat crestfallen.

'Mr Roberts was up the yard,' Patrick said, 'and we told him about that poor old stray, and he said it wasn't no stray, but one of his'n –'

'His,' I corrected automatically.

'That's right, miss. His'n. So we just come back.'

'Came back.'

'Like I said,' agreed Patrick. I let the matter rest.

Village schoolmistresses, and no doubt those who teach in town schools too, recognise the utter futility of trying to correct certain phrases. Fairacre's intractable examples include:

'Miss, the nib of my pencil's bin and broke.'

'Miss, could you threadle my needle?'

And, of course, 'I never done it.'

As for the correct usage of the verbs 'to lend' and 'to borrow', I despair of ever getting this particular piece of grammar across.

'Can I have a lend of your duster, miss?' This is the usual phrase. Sometimes it is 'a borrow of'. If I had as many five-pound notes as the number of times I have carefully rephrased these requests I should have retired from teaching long ago with a comfortable income.

Now that the affair of the cat was settled, a lesson on fractions was undertaken until the dinner van arrived. Sliced cold lamb, beetroot and coleslaw, followed by bottled plums and pink blancmange is not my idea of a cheering lunch on a bleak March day, but the children tackled it with their usual gusto, and rushed out to play afterwards with their spirits as boisterous as the wind which buffeted them from the downs above.

That evening, sitting by a log fire as though it were December instead of the first day of spring, I had a surprise visit from my old friend Amy.

We were at college together many years ago. She is now married to a businessman who seems to earn a great deal of money. This busy life involves much travelling, and Amy is often left alone while he is away either here or abroad.

James is a charmer, and devoted to the opposite sex. Personally, I am sure that he adores Amy, but whether he is wholly faithful to her, I have my doubts. Although Amy is far too

loyal to voice her suspicions, she is pretty shrewd, and I think she knows quite well that some of these so-called business trips include other interests.

'A fire! How marvellous!' she said, holding out her beautifully manicured hands to the blaze. 'Nothing like the first day of spring for making one appreciate a log fire.'

'Coffee or sherry?'

'What sort of sherry? You are't still offering that stuff you won at the last raffle?'

When you have known Amy as long as I have you do not take umbrage at this sort of remark.

'That was jolly nice sherry. Good and fruity. The vicar and I finished it off last week.'

'Coffee, I think after all.'

'Instant,' I said, 'and you're lucky to get that!'

Amy chuckled, and fished in her elegant Italian handbag for a cigarette. She followed me into the kitchen.

'I often wonder why you don't get matching kitchen units,' she said, surveying my equipment.

'No money to pay for them,' I told her, spooning out the coffee. 'Top of the milk, or hot milk?'

'Top, please.'

'Good. It saves messing up a saucepan. No point in making work.'

'If you organised this kitchen you could cut down the work. For one thing, all your working tops would be the same height.'

'But I don't want them all the same height,' I protested. 'If I'm mincing I use the table. If I'm washing lettuce, I need the sink which is deeper. The draining board's just the right height for chopping cabbage –'

'Very well, very well! You needn't go on! Obviously, you've become quite accustomed to these primitive surroundings and don't intend to change now.'

'That's right,' I said amicably. 'Would you like a ginger nut?'

'I should love one. I haven't had a ginger nut for years, but I warn you, I'll have to dunk it. I've got a filling that's cracked across.'

'I think we've both got to the stage where it's permissible to dunk ginger nuts. Won't be long before we're mumbling our gruel with our gums.'

'Speak for yourself,' said Amy.

We settled ourselves by the fire.

'I've brought the Caxley Festival programme with me. I thought we might go to a few of the events.'

'What's on offer?'

'A concert in the Parish Church. Modern music mainly. Lots of Bartok.'

'Count me out, Amy dear. Those pews nearly crippled me at the carol service, and at least we stood up now and again. Besides, I can't take Bartok.'

'The trouble with you,' said Amy severely, 'is that you close your mind to progress. Well, what about this exhibition of modern sculpture?'

'Where's that?'

'It's all hefty outdoor stuff, I gather. They've roped off part of the common.'

'It sounds nice and peaceful. But what happens if it rains?'

'As the Duke of Norfolk said, with admirable brevity, when asked the same question about the Coronation: "*We get wet!*" '

'Carry on.'

'Your Henry Mawne appears to be giving a couple of lectures on British birds.'

'He's not my Henry Mawne, I'm thankful to say, but I expect I've heard those lectures several times in our village hall.'

'Eighteenth-century silver in the museum? Demonstration

of hand-weaving? Three mid-European plays about the rise of the peasant classes?'

'The silver sounds agreeable,' I said cautiously.

'You do live dangerously, don't you?' said Amy. 'Tell you what, I'll leave the programme here and you can look it through and let me know. Frankly, I'm game for anything. James will be away for most of that time.'

'Where is he going?'

'Holland first, I believe. Something to do with diamond merchants. Not that James will see much of the diamonds, but the money gets put into other things.'

'The Dutch are very clever at trading, I believe.'

'So I gather. Didn't they own the East Indies at one time? All those spices and jewels?'

'My knowledge is pretty hazy. I only know they were jolly good sailors and had the cheek to sail up the Thames, or perhaps it was the Medway, and had to be chased off by someone who had a broom on the mast.'

'I don't believe it! Why on the *mast* anyway?'

'Amy, I really know nothing about the Dutch except that Holland gets flooded very easily, and the housewives are exceptionally clean. I should ask James about them when he gets back. After all, he will have first-hand knowledge.'

'Not of the housewives, I hope,' said Amy, with unusual tartness. She stubbed out her cigarette viciously. 'If that's the time, I'd better be off. James makes an early start for Edinburgh tomorrow.'

'He certainly keeps busy,' I said accompanying her to the door.

'Too busy at times,' replied Amy, getting into her glossy car. 'I've told him not to be surprised if I take a leaf out of his book and have a break myself one day.'

It was said lightly, but there was an underlying grimness which disconcerted me.

She blew me a kiss and drove off, and I returned to the fireside with food for thought.

The chilly weather continued for the rest of March. A few hardy primroses had braved the elements in the garden, and knotted bluebell flowers crouched in their glossy leaves, obviously unwilling to do more until the weather grew warmer.

The leaves were still tightly furled on the trees. The winter silhouettes of the beeches and limes still showed up starkly black against the grey sky.

At night, I was glad of my comforting fire, and still put a hot water bottle in my bed halfway through the evening. The frosts were severe, and it would be many weary weeks before the geranium cuttings on my window sill could be put out in the garden.

I remembered Mr Willet's words about the Marchs of old, and I knew that he was right. Somehow, nowadays we seemed to get no real spring, none of those balmy tender days when one could walk in the woods admiring the rosettes of primroses, noting the glutinous stalk of a trampled bluebell, with the whole vista lit by a spangle of young leaves.

The children coughed and sniffed as they had done all the winter, yet would still attempt to go out into the bleak playground without their coats until bullied into them by their elders. Winter ills were rife in the village at large, and the March meeting of the Women's Institute, a hardy collection of souls, was cancelled as the village hall stove had gone on strike, and no one could brave the arctic conditions there with the windows glazed, both inside and out, with thin ice.

One frosty evening when I was settled by the fire marking essays, and getting rather tired of correcting 'brids' and 'grils', someone rang the front door bell.

As I crossed the little hall I remembered all the warnings

about opening doors to strangers, particularly if one was alone in the house. I am always advising people to go upstairs and find out who the caller is from an upstairs window, but naturally I never do this myself, as I don't remember such things until the door is wide open.

Luckily, tonight's visitor was only Henry Mawne with some draw tickets to sell, and he seemed glad to come in.

'I shouldn't really,' he said, wiping his perfectly clean shoes vigorously on the mat, 'but to tell the truth, it's a good deal colder than I bargained for when I set out, and I shan't call anywhere else.'

I nobly stumped up fifty pence for a book of tickets to support some wild bird project dear to Henry's ornithological heart, and offered him a drink which he refused.

He stretched his legs out to the blaze, and looked settled for the evening.

I stacked the exercise books away and fetched a block of mint sweet.

'Well, indulge yourself with this,' I said, breaking it with some difficulty. 'It says it is as supplied to *successful* polar expeditions. I suppose the *unsuccessful* ones were foolish enough to forget to pack the stuff.'

'Ah! My favourite sweet,' said he, taking the largest fragment. 'Where do you get it?'

'Mr Lamb at the Post Office keeps it.'

'I never knew that!' He crunched happily, and I wondered if he proposed to stay for some time. I had two telephone calls to make, and had planned to wash my hair, but obviously a host's duties came before these things.

Why is it, I wondered, surveying my guest's relaxed attitude, that people generally imagine that a single woman is dying for company? After all, a woman living alone has just as many chores to do as her married counterpart. In fact, she is probably busier, as she has to do them all herself.

When I return from the school I still face my household tasks, correspondence – far too much of it – and the ever-present washing, ironing and mending. Gardening, shopping and modest entertaining have also to be fitted in, and I do what I can to help in various village activities, even if it only involves minding the Hat and Shoe stall at the W.I. jumble sale while the chief stall-holder slips off for a tea break. I am also fair game for anyone collecting contributions to various bazaars, and keep a supply of home-made jam and marmalade for instant largesse to these worthy causes.

It is not that I am an unsocial person, but having spent the best part of the day with a host of demanding children, my fellow-teacher, not to mention Mrs Pringle, Mr Willet and various callers of educational complexion, I am really very content to gain the blissful solitude of the school house, and a few hours of peace.

'How's Elizabeth?' I asked politely. Mrs Mawne is an energetic member of the Fairacre community, and keeps her husband up to his duties as the vicar's right hand, as well as his numerous commitments as an authority on birds.

'Oh, she's in Ireland,' said Henry. 'Gone to see an old aunt of hers. The poor thing has always been difficult, and has gone through companion after companion since her husband Roderick died.'

'You make her sound somewhat cannibalistic,' I replied.

'She is, my dear, she is!' Henry sat up, scattering a few fragments of mint sweet on the hearth rug. I was amused to watch him collecting them carefully on a licked finger and transferring them to his mouth.

'Elizabeth's gone over to see if she can persuade her into a nursing home. Fat chance of that, as far as I can see. Nothing short of dynamite will get her out of that barn of a place she lives in.'

'Has she always lived there?'

'Ever since she married some sixty years ago. It's one of those mouldering old Victorian castles, all pepper-pot turrets and cross-draughts, and the most peculiar fungi growing in the attic bedrooms. Still, it does give shelter to some rare owls and bats, and for that reason I should be sorry to see the place pulled down.'

'Is that likely to happen?'

'Very likely, I should think, if she can be persuaded to sell. My chief concern is that Elizabeth doesn't bring her back to stay with us. The position would be quite impossible. We really have enough to do looking after ourselves these days, and I can't think how we'd manage with dear old aunt Thora in our midst.'

'How old is she?'

'Ninety-three, and good for another ten years.'

He sighed heavily, and put two logs thoughtfully on my fire. I watched him in amused silence.

'And when do you expect Elizabeth to come back?'

'God knows,' he said morosely. 'The house is deathly quiet without her. It's one of the reasons I came out tonight, to see a bit of company.'

He rose suddenly from the chair.

'Nice of you to have me in like this,' he said, struggling into his coat. 'I'll pop in again, if I may. You always cheer me up and I'm sure you are as lonely as I am.'

I smiled politely as I took him to the door.

'Bang goes my hair wash,' I said to Tibby on my return.

2 Minor Irritations

MUCH to my annoyance, I found that I could not sleep after Mr Mawne's visit.

I had forgotten to put my hot water bottle in the bed, disturbed from my comfortable routine by my guest, and this may have been the reason for my unusual wakefulness.

After tossing and turning for two or three hours, I realised that I was ravenously hungry, and decided to go downstairs for sustenance. While some milk was heating on the stove, I collected an assortment of goodies on a tray. What, I thought, would a dietician make of a banana, a digestive biscuit and a spoonful of stewed plums? It should keep me going until breakfast-time anyway.

It was unusually quiet in the kitchen at one o'clock in the morning. Moonlight had been flooding in when I entered it, silvering the plates in the rack over the sink, and throwing squares of light over the brick floor. In the distance I could hear the wavering cry of an owl, and I stood relishing this rare night-time beauty before switching on the electric light and turning all to prosaic normality.

For years, Fairacre had been without the boon of electricity. When finally it was brought into the school house I welcomed it rapturously, and never cease to marvel at the transformation it has made to my everyday living.

Nevertheless, it is good to be reminded now and again, as in those few silent moonlit minutes, of how things were when I first came to live here, and how they had been for generations of Fairacre folk before me.

I carried my bounty back to bed and enjoyed it whilst reading my ever-present bedside book, *The Diary of a Country Parson*. This good man of the eighteenth century never fails to amuse, teach and enchant me. I felt quite abstemious about my modest trayful as I read that for dinner on November 24, 1795, Parson Woodforde enjoyed 'Hashed-Calf's Head, a boiled Chicken and some bacon, a Leg of Mutton rosted, and a Norfolk batter-Pudding and drippings, after that we had a Duck rosted, Maccaroni and Tarts. By way of Desert, we had white Currants, Pears and Apples, and Filberts.'

In February of the next year he gave 'to an old decayed Fisherman O.I.O.' (This was one shilling.) He goes on to remark:

'He was the Man that brought me once some very indifferent Spratts.'

This last entry made me laugh so much that I finished my snack, switched off my ever-blessed bedside lamp, and was asleep in ten minutes.

Before school the next morning, I was alarmed to see that Mrs Pringle's limp was much in evidence. What could have happened? Had I inadvertently spilt something vicious such as red ink on her immaculate floor boards? Had the sink overflowed, the plug stopped up with that cursed ubiquitous bubble gum beloved of Fairacre's children? Had the stove gone out? All these hazards flashed before me like the drowning man's swift summary of his life, or so we are told.

Luckily, for once it was not my fault that Mrs Pringle's leg had seen fit 'to flare-up'. As had happened many times before, the cause of her discomfort was her niece, Minnie Pringle.

Minnie's I.Q. is extremely low. She cannot read, has difficulty in signing her name and is virtually incapable of doing the simplest work, as I know to my cost. In a weak moment once, I let her help in my house, and it would need a stronger

pen than mine, and far more time than I could spare, to catalogue the appalling list of damages she managed to inflict. I will give just two instances. She thought that a cushion cover looked grubby, and put it to soak, complete with its contents, into neat bleach in the sink. I must say, in all fairness, that the sink had never looked so pristine, although the smell in the kitchen was enough to choke one.

Her second effort was to dismantle the electric cooker in order to give it 'a good going-over'. Fortunately Mrs Pringle arrived in time to switch off the current at the main, or doubtless I should have found Minnie electrocuted on the kitchen floor amidst the debris. It took Mr Willet and me all the evening to put the thing together again, and I have never heard so many whispered curses, from that upright churchman, on any other occasion.

This time, it appeared, Minnie had been obliged to take one of her children to hospital, and had deposited the rest with Mrs Pringle at a moment's notice.

'Called in as bold as brass with them four little varmints, just as I was getting down to give the kitchen floor a nice wash-over with some suds I had left from rinsing out the tea-cloths.'

'What had happened to the fifth?'

Minnie's children are by a variety of fathers. True, she is married, not all that long ago, but that is to an elderly man, called Ern, with children of his own. The marriage is a stormy one, which is hardly surprising, and Bert, an earlier paramour, always seems to be bobbing up and distracting Minnie's scatter-brained attention from her wifely duties.

'Well, Ern went up to the Potters' to see if the lawn mower was in good nick for the summer, and he took young Basil with him. Why, don't ask me!'

I had no intention of asking, especially as it was almost time to let in the children, and Miss Briggs, my assistant, was hovering around as if waiting for something.

'Anyway, Ern left the thing running while he went for the oil can and that little faggot put his hand in. Took the tops off of three fingers.'

'Oh no!'

'Oh yes! And that stupid Ern and Minnie hadn't got the plain common sense to take the tops with 'em to the hospital to be sewn on again.'

Miss Briggs emitted a small yelp. I sat down quickly in my chair and concentrated my attention on a rather wispy late hyacinth growing over water. I cannot take gory details, and Mrs Pringle spares one absolutely nothing.

'I think it's time for the bell,' I said cravenly to Miss Briggs. She hurried away.

'And don't tell me any more,' I begged Mrs Pringle. 'Not about the injuries, I mean. I'm very sorry for the child. Is he staying in hospital long?'

'No, more's the pity. Minnie gets him this afternoon and I've said they can all have tea with me, and she can take 'em home straight to bed.'

'Well, that's very good of you,' I said. 'You must be a tower of strength to that little familyy.'

A horrid thought struck me.

'You're not thinking of keeping any of the school-age ones with you?' This has happened in the past, and of course they attend my school temporarily and a sore trial they are.

'Not likely,' said my cleaner succintly.

She rose from the front desk and made her way to the lobby. I think my tribute to her had pleased her.

Her limp had vanished.

At playtime, while the children swarmed happily outside, Miss Briggs broached the subject which she had been trying to bring to my notice, without success, as Mrs Pringle's horrendous account of young Basil's mishap was then in spate.

She has been engaged to a cheerful young builder called Wayne for some time now. He was working for Reg Thorn, a local builder, when he replaced our leaking skylight – not altogether successfully, as it is becoming apparent – and that is how the two young people first met.

The wedding is planned for the summer, soon after the end of the school year, and Miss Briggs' urgent problem was the fitting of her wedding dress. Could she *possibly*, she implored me, go half an hour earlier tomorrow to go to the dressmaker in Caxley who had just heard that she must go into hospital and wanted to make a start on the dress before she took to her hospital bed?

'That's no problem,' I assured her. 'The whole school can play Fox and Geese and Grandmother's Steps and I Sent a Letter to my Love. We don't get enough games altogether.'

'It might rain,' said she anxiously.

'I can still read,' I told her.

She returned to her class much relieved, and I remembered her early days with me when I had been obliged to point out to her that it was her duty to remain until all the infants were accounted for at the end of the afternoon, and that the fact that the clock said three-thirty was not the signal for instant departure. She had improved considerably, whether mellowed by love or simply by discovering that she could do her job quite well, was a matter for conjecture.

Mr Willet's summing up had been that she was 'a fair old lump of a girl' when she first arrived at Fairacre. It had been difficult to talk to her, and I had found her downright surly at times. However, we now hit it off very well, and I thought that Wayne's influence had been all to the good. She proposed to continue teaching after her marriage, and for this I was grateful. New appointments are always hazardous, and in a two-teacher school such as ours it is absolutely essential that the pair can work happily together.

Of course, I pondered, there might be babies coming along, but she could always have maternity leave and then come back if she wanted to.

It then occurred to me that, as usual, I was allowing my mind to run well ahead. After all, we had not had the wedding dress fitted yet. It was rather early to be counting chicks.

Furthermore, through the lofty windows I could see a row of moving heads. Obviously, a procession of children was running along the coke pile, and it was high time that that little caper was stopped.

Seizing the hand bell, I made my way into the playground.

That afternoon the first mild breeze began to blow. The weathervane on St Patrick's steeple had veered to the south-west, the clouds scudded along at a merry rate, and here and there the sunshine broke through, gilding the bare branches and raising our spirits. Could spring be here at last?

The children sniffed the air as appreciatively as eager dogs out on a walk, and I let them go to play five minutes earlier than usual, although with stern threats about the consequences of going *near*, let alone *on*, the coke pile.

When I went to call them in I saw that Gerald Partridge, our much-loved vicar, was among the crowd, his venerable cape, green with age, billowing from his shoulders in the breeze.

'My dear Miss Read,' he said, clasping my hands in his. The leopard-skin gloves of winter were not in evidence today, a sure sign that the weather was warmer.

'Come into school,' I said.

'No, no! It's so lovely to welcome a mild breeze. Let us enjoy the air out here. I've brought a letter from my wife. No need to answer it immediately. You may want to consider your reply. That's why she decided not to telephone you.'

'What's it about?' I asked, alarm raising its ugly head.

Was another pot of marmalade needed for some good cause?

Was I being invited to one of Mrs Partridge's cheese and wine parties to meet some eminent divine? If so, a simple telephone call had always been considered fitting, so what hidden complications were inside the envelope?

'Look at it in the peace of your own home,' advised the vicar. Perhaps my consternation was writ large upon my face. In any case, Gerald Partridge, though vague in many ways, is remarkably sensitive to other people's feelings. I stuffed it into my jacket pocket.

'I always think,' said the vicar, changing the subject with aplomb, 'that you have one of the finest views in Fairacre.' He gazed across Mr Roberts' young corn to the massive bulk of the downs on the sky-line.

'So do I,' I told him.

' "*I will lift up my eyes unto the hills: from whence cometh my*

help," ' quoted Mr Partridge. 'You know I find them as much comfort as the psalmist did. They put our own petty affairs into perspective.'

'Absolutely,' I agreed. 'Like ducks.'

'Ducks?'

' "*From troubles of the world*
I turn to ducks,
Beautiful, comical things, sleeping
or curled . . ." The rest escapes me but I'll look it up for you.'

'I should appreciate that,' said the vicar gravely. 'Ducks or downs, we all need to gather comfort where we can, and I find a great deal in remembered fragments of writing.'

A breathless five-year-old rushed up to us.

'Miss, one of them Coggs kids has been to the lavatory on the lobby floor.'

'That,' I told her, 'is what is known as a contradiction of terms, but I'll come at once.'

'In that case,' said the vicar, 'I must let you return to your duties.'

He departed, I thought, with unnecessary haste, and I went to find the floor cloth.

What with one thing and another, I had forgotten Mrs Partridge's missive until I was rummaging for a handkerchief in my jacket pocket, whilst waiting for the kettle to boil in my peaceful kitchen. Out fell the envelope and up surged my misgivings again.

I read it while I sipped my tea. After suitable greetings the letter continued:

'My dear friend Hazel Smith is trying to raise some money for the Save The Children Fund in Caxley, and is organising an evening meeting which is going to be billed as "Our Children".

'She is asking several speakers to say a few words and then to

answer questions from the floor. I know she has a local magistrate who will talk about the juvenile court, and a most eminent educationalist, as well as a local doctor who specialises in children's ailments – a *paediatrician*, I believe is the correct word unless I am confusing it with something to do with *feet*, or even *worse* – but a very nice man indeed who once was on TV in one of those upsetting medical series.

'I took the liberty of mentioning your name to her and she may get in touch to see if you would be a member of the panel. Perhaps you could talk on young children in school? Or children's literature? Anyway, I do so hope you don't mind my mentioning you to her. You would be *so good*, and I know you would love Hazel.

'There would be a cold buffet and wine after the meeting, and a chance to get to know a great many people who are *really caring* about the young, just as you are.'

She was mine affectionately after three pages.

'Oh lor', Tibby,' I said to the cat. 'Now what do I do?'

But that unfeeling animal continued to wash his face vigorously, callous to the sufferings of his mistress.

With this awful prospect before me I spent the evening in a fine state of dithering. My first instinct was to turn down the proposal with a flat refusal. I had no wish to turn out for an evening in Caxley, and a downright antipathy to my unknown panel members.

They were probably all as charming as Mrs Partridge's old friend Hazel. They certainly appeared to be much more public-spirited, unless of course they had been coerced into it and were feeling quite as reluctant as I was myself. But I see far too much of people 'who care for the young' and on the whole I find them exhaustingly earnest. I know I care for the young – look at the floor cloth interlude only that afternoon, and you can't get much nearer the bone of caring than that! Neverthe-

less, the thought of answering a lot of solemn questions about possible damage done to the young child's ego by thwarting it of some simple pleasure such as flooding the bathroom or jumping on the cat, filled me with horror.

Besides what should I talk about? Even ten minutes' speaking takes the devil of a lot of writing, and I know my limits. No, I should have to decline.

Having decided this, I then remembered the many kindnesses that Mrs Partridge has shown to me and the school, and began to feel a mean-spirited wretch. Would it hurt me to give up one evening? (*Yes*, squeaked my baser self.) Mrs Partridge must consider me capable of the job or I shouldn't have been asked. (Probably the seventeenth person on her list, all the others having sensibly made plans to go abroad, have visitors, contract shingles, and so on.) It would be letting down dear Mrs Partridge if I fobbed off Hazel Thingummy with some weak excuse.

At that moment, the telephone bell rang, and I jumped as though I had been shot. This must be it! Well, better answer it and be guarded. Ask if I might ring her tomorrow when I've thought it over.

I gave my number in a cracked voice. To my enormous relief it was Amy.

'Have you got a cold?' she asked solicitously.

I babbled out my present problems, and Amy forbore to laugh, at least out loud.

'What a funny old thing you are,' she commented, in such a loving voice that I very nearly burst into tears. 'You give the impression of being in command of every situation –'

'Surely not!'

'And yet you go all to pieces over a simple little matter like this.'

'But it isn't a simple little matter, Amy,' I wailed. 'It scares me stiff, the whole idea, and yet I'm so fond of Mrs Partridge, I

really don't want to hurt her by appearing disobliging. And, of course, it's a very good cause. Saving the children, I mean. Why, come to think of it, I spend my whole life saving children!'

I told her that sad tale of the floor cloth.

'I should think that is evading Mrs Pringle's wrath rather than saving children,' commented Amy shrewdly. 'But do you know what I'd do?'

'No, tell me quickly,' I urged.

'Forget it for this evening. Go to bed early with a nice juicy book to read. Ten chances to one you'll know your own mind in the morning.'

'Thank you, Amy,' I said humbly and put down the receiver.

Within a minute the telephone rang again. It was Amy.

'Don't be so swift putting the phone back,' she said. 'I didn't have a chance to tell you why I was ringing.'

I apologised.

'I just wondered if you'd decided on any of the Caxley Festival items. I ought to start booking, I think.'

'Amy,' I began, 'I'm afraid I haven't got round to –'

'Never mind, never mind! Just tuck it away in your subconscious with Mrs Partridge's proposition, and you can deal with both tomorrow.'

It was her turn to replace the receiver. Her tone had been kindly and forgiving, and I returned to my fireside thanking the gods for the good friends whom I hardly seemed to deserve.

3 Henry Mawne Needs Company

AFTER a night of solid sleep I felt robust enough to accede to Mrs Partridge's proposal, and decided to telephone after school that day to say how delighted I should be if her friend Hazel needed my services on the panel. Really, civilisation has a lot to answer for! What would happen if we all spoke the unvarnished truth?

As my egg boiled that morning, I turned March over on the wall calendar and read the new motto. It said:

> *A man's reach should exceed his grasp,*
> *Or what's a Heaven for?*

Could this refer to my brave decision? Should I find myself the most knowledgeable member of the panel on that fateful night? Would *The Caxley Chronicle* have a paragraph about the brilliance of repartee, breadth of knowledge, personal charm and, of course, the innate modesty of the head teacher of Fairacre School? Fame could go no higher.

While I dallied with this day dream, I noticed two things. This was April Fool's Day, so I must be on my guard in school this morning, and my egg had cracked and was fizzing all over the stove.

When I came to eat it, I found, predictably enough, that it was hard-boiled. Not that I minded. To me, an egg is an egg however it turns up, but I am always amused to hear people say scathingly that they know someone 'who couldn't boil an egg', as though this act of cookery is the simplest thing imaginable.

Strangely enough, it is jolly difficult to get an egg with a firm white and a delectably moist yolk. It all depends on size, freshness, thickness of shell, and naturally, on the accuracy of the egg-timer or clock. Being called to the telephone does not help either, as I know to my cost.

Well, now, I wondered as I spooned mine down, what little tricks would my naughty children have been up to? One April Fool's Day I had managed to stop them from tying a rope just above floor level at the lobby door. Their victim then would have been Mrs Pringle, without doubt, and the consequences not in the least humorous, as I pointed out to them. A little clean fun was one thing. Injury to people was another. They were suitably chastened, and since then have found minor ways of celebrating the day.

At first sight, all seemed as usual in the school room. I opened my desk, alert to find a mammoth spider or even a grass snake, but there was nothing of that nature there. My chair had no drawing pin or blob of glue on it. The piano keys were clean, the hymn book unsullied. Their little jokes are usually perpetrated in the first half-hour at school. Could they have forgotten? After twelve o'clock the magic was supposed to have vanished, and any larking about was reckoned invalid by ancient tradition.

We ploughed gently on through arithmetic and reading. Playtime passed without incident, and I had quite forgotten to be on my guard, as no doubt my wily flock had intended.

At twenty to twelve, before the dinner lady arrived, I set them to copy Robert Bridges' adorable poem 'Spring Goeth All In White' from the blackboard. This was to be a combined exercise in learning a poem and engaging their skills in handwriting.

It was while I was concentrating on my own fair hand, as I wrote the last two lines, that Ernest's voice rang out with horrid urgency.

'Miss! Quick! Patrick's fainted!'

This has happened before, so that I dropped the chalk, and was at Patrick's side in one second flat. The child had his head on the desk, and as I bent to attend to him the roar of delight nearly raised the roof.

'April Fool, miss! You're April Fool!'

Patrick sat up, rosy with health and mirth, and I joined in the general hilarity.

It seemed to me, remembering the rope in the lobby, the odd spider and stickiness, that I had got off lightly this year.

That evening, full of noble thoughts, I rang Mrs Partridge to say that I should be willing, if needed by her friend, to take my place on the panel.

'How lovely!' boomed Mrs Partridge. 'I've no doubt Hazel

will be as delighted as I am, and I'm sure she will be in touch very soon.'

I replied suitably, and rang off, wondering if a well-deserved bolt from the blue would descend upon me for downright untruthfulness. It is to such passes, I thought gloomily, that Doing One's Duty, commits a frail body.

Far too often, it seems to me, I am prevailed upon, as in this instance, to undertake some task which I abhor. Why do I do it? And how best can one minimise these occurrences?

I suppose that one could give up belonging to certain clubs or activities that engender these minor irritations. For instance, if I were not a member of the Women's Institute I suppose I should not be roped in for providing something for teas, or for manning a stall, or for entering some competition for which I have no natural aptitude but give in weakly, to such strong characters as Mrs Partridge, because they have not enough entries.

On the other hand, should one retreat and become a self-imposed hermit, simply to avoid trouble? After all, I like living in Fairacre, and I am a quite important member of its little community, I suppose, although Mrs Pringle would no doubt think otherwise. Consequently, I must take on my share of the burdens.

I remember an aunt of mine saying once: 'Now that I've turned seventy, I'm not going to join anything which has *meetings*!'

It must be a family failing, I think.

Later that evening I was somewhat taken aback to find Henry Mawne on my doorstep again. He was carrying a fine bunch of daffodils, and came indoors with a beaming smile.

'Thought you'd enjoy these. They're always early in that dell of ours, and everyone likes daffodils.'

'They do indeed,' I said. 'The most cheering flowers of the

spring, I always think. Mine are nowhere near ready. I often wonder what variety Shakespeare's were that took "the winds of March with beauty". Pretty early, I suspect.'

'Poetic licence. After all, he couldn't have had "winds of April". It would've put out the rhythm,' said Henry, sitting down heavily. 'Are you busy? Things are a bit quiet at home without Elizabeth, and I felt in the need of company.'

I could hardly say that he was a confounded nuisance, I certainly was busy, and how soon would he be off, when I was holding a bunch of the daffodils he had so kindly given me. Here was civilised behaviour rearing its ugly head again!

'Would you like a drink?'

'No thanks, I don't tipple much these days. Tends to repeat, like radishes.'

'Or cucumber. Excuse me for a moment. I'll go and put these in water.'

I have a nice Coalport vase shaped like a trumpet which is invaluable for a non-arranger of flowers like me. Drop a bunch into it and the flowers obligingly fall comfortably into place. I carried it back to my sitting room with real pride.

'Good lord,' said my guest. 'That was quick! Elizabeth takes half an hour to arrange a vase of flowers.'

'She does the thing properly,' I told him, 'and gives everyone a great deal of pleasure too. My arrangements are of the Fairacre Primitive school.'

'And none the worse for that,' he said kindly. I began to warm to the man.

'I'm giving a couple of lectures during the Caxley Festival,' he went on, 'and I wondered if you would care to come.'

'It sounds lovely,' I said. 'Which dates would they be?' I added, playing for time.

'I haven't brought the programme, but I think it is on a Thursday. One in the first week, and one in the second week of May.'

'Well, thank you very much. May I let you know?'

'Of course. Elizabeth ought to be back before then, but it's not at all sure. Aunt Thora is giving her the deuce of a time. No nearer getting her into a nursing home, I gather, from what Elizabeth said on the phone.'

'Old people like their own way.'

'That's putting it mildly. As long as she doesn't arrive in Fairacre with Elizabeth, that's all I ask.'

He settled in for another half-hour, but stirred himself when the clock struck nine.

'I'd better be going. Nice to have your company.'

'Well, I'm sure Elizabeth will be home again soon.'

'It's rather doubtful. That's why it would be particularly pleasant if you could attend my lectures. I get in rather a bother about them. Lose my spectacles, or muddle up the pages of my talk. Elizabeth looks after me very well on these occasions.'

I accompanied him to the door and waved him goodbye.

In my early days at Fairacre, Henry Mawne had been thought a bachelor on his arrival in the village. Elizabeth had then been on one of her protracted visits to relations in Ireland, and the local inhabitants, including Mrs Partridge, I recalled, had done their level best 'to bring us together', envisaging an elderly bridal couple tottering from St Patrick's between a guard of honour formed by my pupils and, possibly, some of Henry's bird-lovers' club.

It had been a most embarrassing situation, and I was quite determined not to get embroiled with Henry Mawne while his wife was away. As for accepting his invitation to the bird lectures, that was now completely out. I should just have to find a water-tight excuse for both occasions, or I could imagine the tongues wagging all the way from Fairacre to Caxley.

The Mawnes and I have grown quite close over the years. His great-nephew, Simon, attended my school for a short

time, and incurred the wrath of the whole village by slaying an albino robin which we all adored.

He was still seen here in the school holidays, as his father David had remarried after the tragic death of Simon's mother, and he had bought a house in the village. David was away quite a lot, but his wife Irene did a certain amount of entertaining at Holly Lodge, and I was often lucky enough to be invited to family occasions. Nevertheless, I did not want Henry Mawne's attentions in his present circumstances. I did not flatter myself that my *beaux yeux* were the attraction, but knew quite well that he was lonely at the moment, and simply wanted some company.

Unfortunately, one's affairs are under constant scrutiny in a village, and as a headmistress I must appear to be above reproach. I alone know how many and varied are my failings, but I hope that flirting is not among them, particularly with an elderly and happily married man like silly old Henry.

Before school the next morning Mrs Pringle greeted me with an unaccustomed smile.

'A little bird told me you had a visitor last night. And a nice bunch of daffs,' she added archly.

I forbore to reply.

For a blissful few days in early April we had warm and sunny weather, and the children and I took full advantage of it.

We even had one or two lessons outside, sitting in the playground in the shelter of the old school walls. The elder bushes were sprouting young leaves, and a few celandines turned shiny, yellow faces to the sun at the edge of Mr Roberts' field.

Already some of his lambs frisked in the field near his farmhouse, and their bleating carried to us on the warm spring breeze.

A pair of blackbirds was hard at work gathering nesting

material, and as far as I could see the nest was being built low down in an ancient lauristinus bush in my garden. This shrub, much loved by the Victorians, is rather scorned by Fairacre gardeners today, but I treasure it because of its glossy evergreen leaves and its heartening way of producing pink and white blossom all through the darkest days of winter.

'Scatter-brained animals, them blackbirds,' is Mr Willet's dictum, and he does not waste any pity on them, as I do, when Tibby or any other marauder attacks the young ones. Rarely a spring passes without my trying to screen an obvious black-bird's nest from Tibby's view. It is impossible to keep an eye on the cat while I am at school, and what horrors go on in my absence I shudder to think.

'Well, it's only nature,' says Mr Willet. 'Them blackbirds gobble up worms but you don't wipe your eye about that, now do you? So what's wrong with your Tibby helping himself to a snack now and again?'

The copse at the foot of the downs was also busy with birds, as we discovered on one of our numerous nature walks during the fine spell.

A few early primroses were opening, and the wild honey-suckle had put forth small strong leaves. It was all heady stuff after a long and miserable winter. The wood smelt of moss and damp earth. Every aspect of spring assailed our senses, the warmth, the fragrance, the welcome flowers and leaves. Even the first, bright, fringed leaves of the stinging nettles received our blessing.

Easter Day was only a week or so away. Soon Fairacre school would be on holiday. What better way to spend the last few days of term than relishing this forerunner of joys to come?

During the last week of term, two things happened which gave me much food for thought.

In the first place, I had a very kind letter from Mrs Partridge's old friend giving me details of the dreaded evening when I had rashly offered my services on the panel.

After profuse thanks, the letter continued:

'The other members of the panel include Doctor Eric Biddle who specialises in children's complaints and has very advanced ideas on children's diet. I expect you have met him, as his practice is just south of Caxley. He once appeared in a television programme, so of course we are extremely lucky to get such a notable figure for our little evening.

'The other man is Councillor James Ellis who is a magistrate on the Caxley bench and chairman of the Juvenile Court panel. He is a charming man, and has taken a degree in Child Psychology in the Open University. He has a very sympathetic way with young offenders, as you may have noticed from reports in our local paper.

'The lady who will keep you company is an outstanding educationalist who has set up her own school near the teachers' training college where she is a much respected lecturer. We are very fortunate to get her to come on the panel, as she is in great demand as a speaker, and has an international reputation. Her name is Miss Crabbe.'

Good grief! That wicked old hag? I put the letter down, and took a large gulp of my breakfast coffee to get over the shock.

So our paths were destined to cross again! Miss Crabbe had taught one of my assistants, by name Hilary Jackson, some years ago.

Miss Jackson was an opinionated young woman who had imbibed her lecturer's psychology theories hook, line and sinker. She also had, what was termed in my schooldays, 'a crush' on the redoubtable Miss Crabbe, and everything that the older woman did or said was considered absolutely perfect.

One dreadful weekend I had been obliged to put up this

paragon, and to endure the most awful pseudo-psychological jargon whilst Hilary hung on her every word.

At that time, the girl was going through a highly emotional phase. She had become infatuated with a local gamekeeper who was old enough to know better than to encourage the foolish girl. I was at my wits' end to know how to cope with this crisis, and agitated calls to her parents, and from them to me, aged me considerably.

Miss Crabbe's visit proved in fact to be a heavily disguised blessing, for she soon got wind of the affair, and flung off in a fit of jealous pique.

Things had been most uncomfortable at Fairacre School, and I had privately thought, and not for the first time, what a confounded nuisance love could be. How right of E. M. Delafield to put it far below good teeth and a sound bank balance, in order of merit!

After a few months, Miss Crabbe offered the olive branch and, as the gamekeeper had found another love, Hilary Jackson accepted with alacrity, and the last I heard of the pair was that they were both interested in the progressive school mentioned in Hazel Smith's letter.

Well, well! It would be fun to see if Miss Crabbe was still as formidable as when we last met. Then, I recalled, she had told me she was not a flesh-eater, and a hard time I had had of it trying to find enough non-meat sustenance that weekend. I only hoped that there would be plenty of cheese offered after our ordeal.

The second surprise came one balmy evening when I was dawdling through the village on my way to post a letter.

Hurrying in the opposite direction was Miriam Quinn. She seemed to be in some agitation.

'You're in a hurry,' I quipped.

'I'm a fugitive,' she explained, with a smile.

'From what?'

'From whom, is the right question. As a matter of fact, Henry Mawne.'

Miriam lives in the attractive annexe to Holly Lodge where now David and Irene Mawne live. It is some little way from the centre of Fairacre, a charming house tucked away behind a high holly hedge which gives the place its name.

'He's been coming down some evenings to have a meal with David and Irene while Elizabeth is away. That suits everyone, of course, but once he's had it he will gravitate to my end of the establishment, and I'm really getting rather cheesed off.'

'I can sympathise.'

'So tonight I told a white lie and said I was paying a visit to someone in the village, and here I am on the run.'

'Pay a visit to me,' I said, 'I'd love it.'

'Truly?'

'Truly,' I assured her.

We posted the letter, and wandered back to the school house.

'He's paid me two surprise visits,' I told her when we were comfortably settled in our armchairs. 'He seems to need company pretty badly.'

'Between ourselves,' said Miriam, 'I'm inclined to think that Elizabeth is to blame. Irene was telling me that there have been several periods in her married life when she has just pushed off. Sometimes for months.'

I remembered Henry's first year at Fairacre, with no wife in evidence.

'You don't think this is another protracted absence?' I asked, with some alarm. The thought of choking off Henry's attentions with tact, kindness and firmness, was a daunting one.

'Who knows? The snag is that we're all fond of the dear old boy, but this popping in to see us maiden ladies certainly sets the village tongues wagging, and I don't want Elizabeth to be upset when she does return.'

I told her about Mrs Pringle's coy remark about my bouquet of daffodils.

'I'm going to see how things go for a few days,' said Miriam. 'With any luck we'll hear that she is on her way home, and our troubles will be at an end.'

'But if nothing happens?'

'I've decided to tell Irene how I feel –'

'Me too,' I begged. 'Put in a word for a beleaguered school-marm.'

'And ask her to speak to him about it. It's just thoughtless-ness on his part, I'm sure. He's too nice a fellow to want to embarrass us. Leave it to me.'

'I shall be only too delighted,' I assured her. 'And now, as you are paying me an official visit, what about scrambled eggs on toast? You can always upgrade them to an omelette if you are questioned about the meal you had.'

'An excellent idea,' agreed Miriam, following me into the kitchen.

4 The Coggs Are in Distress

OUR local paper, *The Caxley Chronicle*, is much esteemed in Fairacre. I suppose that the headlines on the front page are the first to be read, closely followed by Births, Marriages and Deaths, and accounts of cases dealt with by the Caxley magistrates coming in third.

Among the latter, during the last week of term, the name Coggs caught my eye. Arthur Coggs, father of Joseph, girl twins and one or two other offspring, is an incorrigible rogue, and Fairacre has no time for him.

He is out of work more often than in, which is hardly surprising. Any money which he does earn goes mainly on drink, and his poor wife sees very little of it.

He is a very weak character, and easily led by his drinking companions, many of whom are habitual offenders and well known to the local magistrates. Arthur is the fellow that they get to keep a look-out while they are engaged in such pastimes as breaking into shops and offices at night, or stripping lead from the roofs of ancient buildings.

It is Arthur who is persuaded to drive a van to a hide-out in the country, or to deliver stolen goods from one malefactor to another in the chain. Left alone, I think that Arthur might be quite content to do a little poaching, or local petty thieving, but he is helpless to withstand the pressure put upon him by his wilier companions who use him without a qualm.

Of course, he gets payment, but a very small share of the total sum, I imagine, and it is a befuddled mixture of feelings which keeps him on the fringe of this collection of petty

criminals. He is proud to belong to these desperadoes, and flattered by their attention. If he is called 'chicken', he will bluster, and then do anything required of him. There is a certain amount of fear mixed up in his general reaction. One or two of his companions are not above menacing him, and there have been occasional injuries, such as a suspicious cut at the throat and a broken finger, which were never satisfactorily explained, although Doctor Martin, who has known the family for years, guesses the cause and has no hesitation in giving Arthur some trenchant advice which, of course, is not taken. Poor old Arthur, we all agree, is past redemption.

This week's *Caxley Chronicle* gave a short account of the proceedings of the case in which Arthur was involved. It ended with the chairman's comment that in view of the seriousness of the crime, and his deplorable record, he would be sentenced to six months' imprisonment.

'Seen the Caxley?' asked Mrs Pringle the next morning. 'The Caxley' can refer to the local paper or to the bus which very infrequently used to serve the village. This time I knew Mrs Pringle referred to the paper, and to Arthur Coggs' tribulations in particular.

'What's six months?' she demanded. 'That means four, I suppose. They takes off a bit for good conduct, though why they should, you may well ask.'

'It will keep him out of the way for the summer in any case,' I pointed out.

'He'll start all over again when he does get out,' said Mrs Pringle, with some truth. 'When I think that Arthur Coggs signed the pledge the same year as I did, it fair makes me grieve! He didn't keep that vow long did he? I mind his sister Ethel took the pledge the same day. As nice a girl as you could wish to meet, with long black hair as she could sit on. When it was down, I mean.'

I had a brief mental picture of a brunette attempting to sit

on her hair when it was pinned up. Mrs Pringle continued unabated.

'All dressed in white she was. It was her old confirmation dress, I recall, and very nice too with a crochet collar. Ethel and Arthur's old ma was a great one for crochet. Yards of it she did. Bedspreads, table clorths, nothing was too much for her, and Ethel's drawers, if you will pardon the word, was always edged with crochet work.'

'Mrs Pringle,' I began, glancing at the clock, but one might just as well try to stop the Niagara Falls as our cleaner in full spate.

'She went into the Caxley Co-op when she left school. The bacon counter. She married Charlie Tibble whose uncle used to sweep the High Street, if you remember, a funny old party with a waxed moustache like the Kaiser.'

'No, I don't think I ever saw him. And now, Mrs Pringle –'

'I was always fond of Ethel,' she continued. 'Never deserved to have a rapscallion like that Arthur for a brother. Mind you, she's not the good looker she was. Got rather fat, but she'd had two boys and they was both nine-pounders which don't do a woman much good, especially is she's narrow in the hips. They've been in trouble too, so I hear.'

'What sort of trouble?'

'Fighting, and that, in pubs.'

'So they didn't take after Ethel?'

'Doesn't look like it. Both on probation, I was told.'

She gave a massive sigh, and picked up the dustpan.

'Ah well! Bad blood will out, I always say, and I can't stand here gossiping with you all day.'

There was general sympathy in the village for Arthur's wife, although it was agreed that by this time she must be inured to any discomfort caused by her husband's absences from home.

Mr Willet was more forthright.

'She's far better off without that good-for-nothing round the house. He's not above giving her a walloping when he's the worse for drink, and I reckon it's a dog's life when he's about.'

'I suppose she'll be worse off financially though,' I suggested.

Mr Willet snorted.

'She gets the same hand-out as anyone else, plus the children's allowances which ain't to be sneezed at in that Coggs family. And she's got a little cleaning at the vicarage, and I know for a fact she brings home some pretty tasty bits of left-overs what the Partridges give her. She had a basin of beef drippin' last Thursday as fair made my mouth water. Lovely that'd be on toast with a sprinkle of salt. I told her so, and she said she'd try it on the kids. Now, wouldn't you have thought she'd 'ave known that anyway? A poor feckless body, she is! My Alice tries to give her a few tips like getting bones and simmering them with a few root veg, but she still goes on buying them great packets of cornflakes for three times the price.'

I sympathised with good kind-hearted Mrs Willet. I too am constantly casting my pearls before swine. How many of the poems I offer my children carry any weight beside the comics they devour? I like to think that an occasional felicitous phrase will stick, and one day give them pleasure to recall. One must live in hope, as a teacher, or go under for ever.

Although Mrs Coggs' plight was a familiar one, I somehow could not put the little family out of my mind after these two conversations.

Joseph and his younger twin sisters seemed unmoved by this latest disaster, and as they were the only children of school age I had little idea of how the younger ones were faring. There were two toddlers, and a weakly-looking baby which seemed to spend its time in a battered pram which smelled overpoweringly of ammonia and disintegrating plastic fabric.

In many ways, poor, apathetic Mrs Coggs had much in

common with Mrs Pringle's crazy niece Minnie. Both had a tribe of neglected children. Both lived in a state of dirt and muddle. Both had trouble with their menfolk, and neither seemed to have any idea of managing money, as Mrs Willet had discovered.

If anything, Minnie was less to be pitied. Despite her turbulent domestic life, she seemed to enjoy the excitement of two men competing for her favours at the same time. Her bevy of noisy wet-nosed children did not seem to ruffle her. The wide mad grin stayed permanently on her freckled face. She could not read, nor tell the time, relying on the chimes of St Patrick's church to give her a rough idea of the passage of the hours or the arrival of the Caxley bus, when the village was fortunate enough to have such a service. But she always seemed to find life utterly absorbing and pleasurable, living as she did in the present. With her limited intelligence, the past was soon forgotten, and what lay in the future was beyond her comprehension. In some ways, one could almost envy Minnie's dotty euphoria. She seemed immune to remorse or apprehension.

Mrs Coggs was only marginally more intelligent, but was much more pathetic. She certainly remembered the past, and lived in fear of her husband's violence, knowing only too well, from experience, what terror and damage he could cause when drunk. Lack of money, and utter hopelessness, contributed to her neglect of the children, and any attempts to help her met with overpowering apathy, as the local probation officer could testify. Mrs Coggs had once been discovered shoplifting, and the time she had spent under supervision from the probation service had certainly given some help and direction to the family. But once that had gone, the same slip-shod ways returned. Perhaps, as Mr Willet had said, the departure of Arthur to the care of Her Majesty's prison might give his pathetic wife some relief. Time alone would tell.

★ ★ ★

Elizabeth Mawne was still away from home, and no one seemed to have any news of her.

Henry spoke of her quite cheerfully, and with no hint of there being anything untoward in the circumstances. Perhaps he was accustomed to his wife's absences, as Miriam had told me.

He had called again, so Mr Willet informed me, but luckily I had gone to see Amy who lives some miles south of Caxley in the village of Bent, so that I missed him.

'He'd got a great roll of books with him,' Mr Willet informed me. 'Books', I took it, meant magazines. It is the common term here for anything printed. I was just congratulating myself on my timely absence from home on that particular evening when my caretaker sent my hopes plummeting.

'I was oiling that dratted lock on the lobby door, and I says should I take the books for you, but Mr Mawne said he'd come again another time.'

'He could have left them in the porch.'

'Well, he never, did 'e? Strikes me he wanted an excuse to pay you another visit. Seems he's a bit lost without his missus.'

Confound the fellow, I thought! However, no point in making a fuss about it, and certainly no need to let Mr Willet see how annoyed I was. It would be all over the village in no time.

I gave Mr Willet what I imagined was a carefree smile.

'Nice to see the hedges beginning to show green,' I observed, casually changing the subject.

'I wouldn't encourage him, if I was you,' said Mr Willet.

He was gone before I could reply. Perhaps it was as well.

But the slight irritation caused by Henry Mawne was overwhelmed in the bliss of breaking up.

All teachers are glad to welcome the end of term, and particularly the end of the winter term when the weather is at its most bitter, playtimes have to be spent indoors, pupils and staff are suffering from coughs, colds and worse afflictions, and tempers are short.

To add to our general happiness, the sun shone warmly, the little birds fluttered about their nest-building and egg-hatching, and a few early tulips ventured into flower. What could be more hopeful?

We set about tidying up the classroom in the afternoon. Desks were relieved of mountains of used paper, the flower vases were emptied and washed, pencils and pens collected, text books and exercise books stacked in the cupboards, so that the time soon came when the children had nothing to occupy them, and we were back to simple games such as I Spy and Left and Right. This invaluable aid to teachers consists of hiding a piece of chalk in one or the other hand, then holding out the two fists, naming a child and then displaying one's open palms. If the child chosen has guessed correctly it is his turn to come to the front and continue. That such an unsophisticated game should give so much pleasure does one's heart good these days.

At half past three we heard the scraping of chairs as the babies, beyond the partition between our two rooms, pre-pared to depart. Excited voices were upraised in grace, Miss Briggs' stentorian tones preceded a general exodus towards their lobby, and silence fell.

The massive wall clock ticked ponderously. Outside, a robin chattered, scolding the infants no doubt. Patrick stood, fists outstretched trying to decide who should have the honour of guessing 'left or right'.

'Eileen,' he said at last, breaking the spell.

'Right,' she said, and it was.

'Last turn,' I said, one eye on the clock.

The usual groans of dismay assailed me.

'But, miss, I ain't 'ad no turn yet!'

'Eileen Burton's bin twice!'

'It's not fair! The girls have had more'n us boys.'

'Does anyone want to stay in after school?' I enquired politely.

Silence fell. Eileen fiddled with the chalk behind her back. After a lengthy pause, she held out her two fists.

'Joseph,' she said.

'Left,' croaked Joseph in his hoarse little voice.

'Well done,' I said. 'Now you remember, Joseph, next time we play that it's your turn to start.'

'It'll be next term, miss,' he pointed out. It was a joyous thought.

'All stand. Hands together, eyes closed.'

We sang grace, somewhat discordantly, and rather faster than usual.

But we were truly thankful, every one of us.

Later that evening I pottered about happily in my house and garden, savouring the joy of the first few hours of the Easter holidays.

Now I need not watch the clock. I could have my breakfast later than usual. I could dally in the bath. Who knows? I might even get round to washing the curtains.

Mrs Pringle, no doubt, would soon be badgering me about spring cleaning on her weekly visit to the schoolhouse. The fever hits her early. I am fast becoming immune to it as the years pass, and have pointed out frequently to my tyrant that if the house is cleaned regularly, and occasionally 'bottomed', as she puts it, which means a ghastly upheaval, then surely spring cleaning is not necessary.

I lose this battle every time, of course, as I know I shall from the outset. The day will come when I return from school to

find the shabbily comfortable chairs stripped of their chintz covers, and Mrs Pringle confronting me with handfuls of debris she has collected from the cracks, such as peanuts, pencils, knitting needles, and once a lipstick of Amy's, which thankfully had not shed its lid.

But so far nothing had been said about our annual upheaval, and in my present buoyant mood I was hopeful. Perhaps she had forgotten? Perhaps the renowned bad leg was in one of its combustible moods, and when this afflicted limb 'flares up', as its owner puts it, any activity is severely restricted. It can work to my advantage occasionally, as in this case.

I woke the next morning to blue skies and a wonderful sense of freedom. Lying back on my pillows watching the unfurling pink tiny leaves of the copper beech fluttering in the morning breeze, I made plans for my first day of the holidays. I should cook myself bacon as well as an egg. Usually, a boiled egg is the standard schoolday breakfast. While it boils, I can rush about watering pot plants, emptying the tidy bin, putting tea towels to soak and generally getting ahead with essential daily chores.

Today I should stand at my ease turning bacon in a leisurely fashion and enjoying its aroma. Tibby should have bacon rinds – a particular treat – and we would both celebrate.

Then I should settle down with the crossword puzzle. It is surely the height of luxury to do the crossword puzzle early in the day. It seems so delightfully decadent when normally one is at work.

I should take my time over a little flower arranging. I might clean the upstairs windows. I might ring Amy and invite her to tea. In fact, the day spread before me full of enchanting small ploys which I might or might not do. No timetable threatened me. No inspectors would call. No children would disturb me. Oh, thrice-blessed holidays!

As might be expected, I was not allowed to live on these

dizzy heights for long. Life always manages to pull the rug from under one's feet and bring one to earth with a bump.

I certainly enjoyed my bacon and egg, and I was happily settled with the crossword at nine-fifteen, when the postman delivered an electricity bill of horrifying size, a pamphlet from an animal rescue society with a distressing photograph of an emaciated dog which I knew would haunt me for nights to come, and a postcard from Henry Mawne requesting the pleasure of my company at a sherry party. He had added: 'Do come. Love, Henry' which I thought quite unnecessary and particularly thoughtless, for he must have known, as well as I did, that Mr Lamb at the Post Office, as well as the postman, would have read it with extreme delight. What an irritating fellow he was! I should certainly decline, and without love.

But these were minor pin pricks. Worse was to come. I was enjoying a rest in the garden. There is a sheltered spot at the back of the house where the sun warms one comfortably and there is no wind. My peace was disturbed by the arrival of Mrs Pringle and her niece Minnie, with a retinue of grubby children.

For one awful minute I envisaged the dreaded spring cleaning, but Mrs Pringle soon put me right.

'Minnie's Basil's got to go up to the hospital in May.' She indicated a minute boy with his mother's tousled red hair, freckles, and a much-bandaged hand.

'She was wondering if the school ones could come for the day, as I've offered to look after the lot while she's up there. Never know what time you'll get back from those places, do you? I mean everyone's appointment turns out to be for ten o'clock, so you might be hanging about till midnight.'

I agreed hastily. May seemed a long way off, and in any case if Mrs Pringle was being so noble as to have that little tribe for the day, it was very small beer on my part to accommodate the older children in school.

'Ain't you lucky?' cried Minnie to her offspring, who simply nodded owlishly without speaking.

'And how is Basil's hand?' I was foolish enough to ask.

Minnie grabbed it, and was about to unwrap the grubby bandage.

'Like to see it? Coming on nice it is!'

'No, no!' I squeaked. I have no stomach for such horrors, and people like nurses who have to cope daily with such matters have my sincere respect.

Minnie looked disappointed. Obviously, she considered it was a privilege to be shown Basil's mutilated fingers.

'I'm sure it's best to keep the wounds covered,' I said weakly. 'Germs and things, you know.'

'Quite right,' said Mrs Pringle with approval. 'Well, that's all right then, Minnie. We'll be getting back for our tea, now you've got things fixed up.'

I accompanied them to the gate.

'By the way,' said my cleaner, 'about time we did a bit of spring cleaning.'

5 Easter Holidays

EARLY in the holidays Amy spent an evening with me. She arrived bearing a beautiful monogrammed suitcase containing contributions to our W.I. Jumble Sale.

Only Amy, I thought, would pack jumble with so much tissue paper and in such an elegant container. Most of the stuff in the hall had been thrust into carrier bags, or was wrapped in all-embracing old tablecloths or motheaten blankets tied up by the corners. A few choice specimens were on wire hangers, and dangled from the curtain rods over the windows. Sorting out was to take place the next afternoon and Amy's things would certainly be quickly snapped up, I could foresee, by the helpers, if Mrs Partridge did not keep a sharp eye on things.

I suppose this craving to have first pick is universal, and it certainly is at its strongest during preparations for bazaars, jumble sales and the like. I often think it is a marvel that anything gets left to put out on the stalls, and I frequently see a handbag of mine in the village, that went directly from my house to a helper in the hall by-passing the jumble sale altogether.

Mrs Partridge, as a vicar's wife, is quite aware of human frailty and has made a sensible and practical rule. Helpers are allowed to buy one article – and one only – before the sale. That is their reward for the time and energy they put into the job. After that they must muck in with the rest of us, milling about from stall to stall. I must say, Mrs Partridge's rule works well. Perhaps my handbag was the sole choice of its present owner as a helper's bonus – a charitable thought.

'We'd better transfer it all to another case,' I said, 'then you can take yours home with you.'

'Oh, don't bother, my dear. Leave it as it is and I'll collect the case another time.'

'But supposing it gets nicked?' I protested. 'The vicar's coat was sold once, and Mrs Lamb's shopping basket. I couldn't bear to see this beauty rattling off in someone's van.'

'Don't be so pessimistic. Of course, nothing will happen to it. You should have more trust in your fellows.'

'Well, if I have to tell you that it vanished when my back was turned, I hope you won't forget the gipsy's warning.'

'I promise not to blame you. There's quite enough to worry about, I find, without fussing about a suitcase.'

For one moment, I feared that Amy was about to unburden her problems concerning James's absences from home, and my heart sank. I very much dislike being the recipient of secrets, particularly marital ones, but I need not have worried.

'Do you find,' asked Amy, settling back on the sofa, 'that things prey on your mind more heavily as you grow older? I always imagined that it was only the young that suffered agonies, over spots on the face, or unrequited love, but really I seem to do nothing but plan against all sorts of horrors that may never occur.'

'How d'you mean? Illness, or accidents?'

'Partly. I mean that I never take the car out without wondering if it will break down in some lonely spot. Then I rehearse what I should do if a convict on the run came up and threatened me. Should I give him my handbag without a struggle? Should I attempt to take the axe away from him? That sort of thing.'

'If he had an axe, I should give him anything he required,' I answered.

'More likely, of course,' went on Amy, fitting a cigarette into a long elegant holder, 'is the business of finding oneself in a strange town with the car locked, and one's keys and

handbag still inside. Not to mention one's mac, and it's pouring cats and dogs. I often think of that one.'

'What a masochist you are! I had no idea you led such a lurid mental life.'

'I don't enjoy it,' confessed Amy, 'but I can't seem to control all this planning for trouble. Take this awful man, for instance.'

'Which awful man?'

'The one *The Caxley Chronicle* is full of these last few weeks. He's a positive nut-case. One of these wretched fellows who rings door bells, and then throws open his raincoat to the person who opens the door. Of course, he has nothing on, and very annoying it must be to be confronted like that when you are expecting the fish man.'

'Well, you would shut the door and ring the police, surely?'

'My dear girl, that's been done dozens of times, but they simply can't catch him. Actually, I've thought of an excellent plan if he comes to Bent. I'd better tell you, as this is just the sort of house he'd visit, and one really should be prepared.'

'Thanks,' I said. 'Very reassuring, I must say.'

'I propose to keep a small jar of dye on the window sill by the front door, and if there's any nonsense like that I shall throw it all over him.'

'How will that help?'

'At least the police will be able to recognise him. I should only use *vegetable* dye – in fact I've a little pot of green which will do beautifully. Nothing to harm the poor fellow, as he's obviously *non compos mentis*, and will probably go straight from the magistrates' court to a looney bin. But I do advise you to do the same. Two lots of dye are better than one, and we should really be doing a public service.'

She took a long pull at her beautiful cigarette holder, and blew two perfect smoke rings. Then she looked at me sharply.

'Are you laughing?'

A great painful gale, which I had been trying to suppress, broke forth, and Amy joined me in a prolonged bout of refreshing giggles.

'Amy,' I said, wiping my eyes, 'you'll be the death of me.'

'More likely the awful man will be. I wonder what sets them off on this sort of caper?'

'Frustrated passion perhaps?'

'But there are far more obvious ways of expressing frustrated passion. Suicide, for instance, or poetry. After all, some of the most telling poems have dealt with unrequited love. Do you remember those two rather nice young men we met at Cambridge years ago?'

'Which ones? And did they suffer from frustrated passion? Over us, I hope.'

'No, no, no! They just discussed poems about it. We all got rather cross, I remember. We were picnicking at Grantchester, and they were both at Trinity. Can't recall their names now, but there were in the Madrigal Society. Spotty, rather, but nice boys.'

'They've completely vanished in the mists of time for me,' I confessed. 'But which poems did they recommend for sheer desperate longing of the beloved?'

'One plumped for that little sixteenth-century verse:

> *Western wind, when wilt thou blow,*
> *The small rain down can rain?*
> *Christ, if my love were in my arms*
> *And I in my bed again!*

It is harrowing, isn't it?'

'Hits the nail on the head,' I agreed. 'But what did the other one suggest?'

'He was all for "Night and Day" by Cole Porter, and after we'd played it on their portable gramophone about ten times that afternoon we were inclined to agree.'

She tapped ash from her cigarette and rose.

'Well, I must be off. Don't forget about the dye, darling, and good luck with the jumble sale. I must say, a few hours with you does me a world of good. I haven't giggled till my ribs ached since before I was married.'

'I expect marriage brought you to your senses,' I said lightly, and then wished that I had not spoken.

'I'm afraid it didn't do that,' said Amy soberly.

At the front door she kissed me, a rare occurrence between us, and I felt overcome with pity for her as I waved her farewell.

Damn James! He must give her even more trouble than the awful man, poor Amy!

Early April was at its best that year, with far more sunshine than showers.

I spent happy hours in the garden. The hawthorn hedge had put forth small leaves, on crimson stalks, and the polyanthus plants glowed red and yellow in the border. Arabis and aubretia added mats of white and purple, and already the air was beginning to grow heady with the scent of flowers and new grass.

What can beat a warm English spring? Perhaps we cherish it more because it is so rare these days, I thought, picking a minute white violet from under the hedge, and inhaling its fragrance. I remembered Mr Willet's theory that the earth had tilted, which resulted in the chilly weather we had been enduring. When the sun shone so tenderly upon us it was hard to remember those bitter days of only a week or two earlier. I lived blissfully in the present, and drove over to visit Miss Clare at Beech Green.

Dolly Clare must be the best loved person for miles around. For years she taught at Fairacre School, and I was fortunate enough to find her in serene charge of the infants' class when I became headmistress of the school. Ill health forced her to

retire to the little thatched cottage at Beech Green, some two or three miles away. She had been a young child of six when she first went to live there with her parents and sister Ada. Always the little house seems welcoming. The furniture gleams, in winter a bright fire cheers the room and always, whatever the season, there are flowers. In the darkest days of January Dolly Clare still manages to find some sprigs of yellow winter jasmine or a bowl of indoor bulbs to delight herself and her visitors.

I have always loved the cottage, and not so long ago Dolly staggered me by telling me that she had left it to me in her will. What such generosity means to me, I cannot express adequately. All I know is, that I was moved to tears – a rare occurrence for me – and I am still overwhelmed by my undeserved good fortune.

On this fine spring afternoon, I took with me a posy of polyanthus and a pot of freshly-made lemon curd. There was a scent of spring in the air, and the lane between Fairacre and Thrush Green wound between hedges hazy with young leaf. With still over a week of holiday before me, I sang as blithely as the lark above me, if not quite as tunefully.

Miss Clare looked as pretty as ever. Despite her great age, her eyes were bright and her skin clear. To my delight, I found a fine black cat sitting in an armchair.

'And who is this?'

'Well, my dear, he's been living rough around here for some months, and during the winter I put out a little straw bed in a wooden box the greengrocer gave me. I put it in the woodshed and left the window open, and he used it every night, you know.'

'I bet he did. And I suppose he found a good supper there too?'

Dolly Clare laughed.

'Of course he did! And top and bottom of it is, he moved in

here a week or two ago, and he's such a dear, I really must take him on.'

He certainly was a handsome animal, and graciously allowed me to stroke him.

'He's found a good spot,' I observed. 'What will you do if you go away?'

'I'm not likely to go far at my age,' said Dolly. 'And I've some kind neighbours. Luckily, he eats anything.'

'More than I can say for my pernickety Tibby.'

'Now sit down, and tell me all the Fairacre news.'

I embarked on the ever-enthralling village concerns, such as Mrs Partridge's plot to get me on the panel game, Mr Willet's garden, Mrs Mawne's continued absence in Ireland, a jumble sale threatened for next week, Mr Annett, the choirmaster's, tribulations with the Easter anthem, Miss Briggs' approaching marriage and, finally, poor Mrs Coggs' trials with Arthur in prison.

'Best place for him,' said Dolly calmly. 'But I don't know that she'll be any better off without him, except that she should be less afraid. That poor soul will never be able to cope with life.'

'Bob Willet seemed to think she'd be better off financially, anyway, without Arthur taking his earnings, such as they are, to the pub nightly.'

Dolly shook her head.

'I doubt it. She has no idea of management. Years ago, when the family was arriving thick and fast, Alice Willet and I had a talk with her about cheap nourishing food to buy, and how best to manage the little bit of money she had weekly. We even offered to mind some of it for her to keep it out of Arthur's clutches, but it was quite hopeless. We used to give her clothes too – things she could cut down for the children. Dear Alice even taught her to knit and gave her wool and needles to make simple things like mittens for the children and scarves, but it

was all beyond her. In the end, we faced the fact that nothing practical could be done to help her. We just gave a hand when a crisis occurred. But those pathetic children! They're the ones I grieve for.'

'Me too,' I said, 'particularly Joseph.'

'Perhaps she simply lacked early training,' continued Dolly. 'I know our family was quite as poor when we were young. As you know, my father never earned much at his job as a thatcher, and when he had his accident, things were pretty desperate. But somehow, my mother managed. We were always clean and tidy, and there was something in the pot for dinner, usually a rabbit given to us by a kind neighbour, or some good soup made from bones with lots of vegetables from the garden. We never went hungry, and we learned to be happy with very little. I honestly never remember being sorry for myself. My sister Ada and I thought we had a lovely home, and so we did.'

She rose and went into the kitchen to put on the kettle. I followed her and looked appreciatively at the sunny room which would one day – far, far ahead, I sincerely hoped – be my own.

From the rafters near the window hung some drying herbs and a string bag with last season's onions.

A row of blue and white striped china pots stood on the shelf near the stove, labelled currants, sugar, tea, coffee and salt. A fat brown tea pot stood beside the kettle waiting to be warmed, and on the brick floor there was a generous helping of milk, in an enamel pie dish, for Dolly's new companion.

'I simply love this house,' I said impulsively.

'That's why I'm so glad you are going to have it,' said Dolly, pouring a silver stream into the tea pot.

That evening I pondered on Mrs Coggs as seen through Dolly Clare's eyes. My old friend and Alice Willet were both warm-

hearted realists. They must have spent many hours and much
energy in trying to train Joseph Coggs' mother into more
methodical ways. I liked the calm way in which Dolly had told
me that they soon realised that their efforts were fruitless.
There was no recrimination against their poor pupil, and no
self-pity about the time wasted on her. There was simply this
sensible acceptance of a hopeless case, but an awareness too of
their own neighbourly duty to the family should any crisis
occur. I could not help thinking that Mrs Coggs must have
been heartened by the kindness and support of those two good
women, even if her home and family still appeared as slovenly
and neglected as ever.

I felt pretty sure too that Dolly Clare and Alice Willet must
have helped Mrs Coggs with an occasional gift of money, as
well as the more usual presents of garden produce which we
are all proud to offer to our neighbours.

Teachers are not rich people, and Dolly would never have

earned much compared with college-trained and certificated colleagues, for she was of the old pupil-teacher category. Nevertheless, she was always neatly dressed, never in debt, and managed to find something to give to those less fortunate like Mrs Coggs.

Her example made me feel a positive spendthrift. It was true that I was never seriously in debt, that my wardrobe was respectable, though nowhere near as extensive and elegant as dear Amy's, and that my home was reasonably furnished. But I should never be the careful manager of money that Dolly Clare was. I suppose, I thought ruefully, I fall somewhere between Dolly and Mrs Coggs for financial efficiency.

There are feckless bodies in all walks of life, of course, and I was reminded of a passage in one of William Howard Russell's letters to his wife. He was writing from the Crimea in 1856, in one of his rare free moments from following the campaign for *The Times*. Obviously, his wife Mary was adding to his anxieties by her imprudent spending, and I like the diplomatic way he expresses his concern.

'Riches,' he writes, 'are not happiness indeed, but there is great difficulty in living happy without them.'

A universal truth indeed, and one which poor Mrs Coggs would undoubtedly endorse.

I was beginning to count the few remaining precious days of the Easter holiday with as much concentration as a miser with his gold.

Half the things I had intended to do remained undone, but I had cleaned all the windows, defrosted the refrigerator, made four pots of lemon curd, and parted with the more disreputable of my garments for the benefit of the approaching jumble sale.

My chief accomplishment was the partial routing of Mrs Pringle intent upon the dreaded spring cleaning. I made the jumble sale a useful excuse.

'Just the sitting room,' I implored her. 'I've so much sorting out to do on the dining room table, and I promised to write the labels this time, so that I shall be in your way if we try to do too much.'

I feared that this feeble defence would fall before Mrs Pringle's implacable front, but to my surprise she agreed.

'Give me a chance to get to grips with it in there any-way,' she conceded. 'I don't suppose you've ever given the woodwork on them chairs a nice rub over with vinegar and water.'

'Well, no,' I admitted.

'Then that's what it'll get now,' she said flatly, making for the sink.

'I'll start the overall bottoming when you're back in school,' she continued. 'The top of them pelmets of yours would grow potatoes, I don't doubt, up there in your bedroom. Good thing you're not aspergic to Dust and Dirt. You'd be a hospital case in no time.'

Reprieved from the complete chaos of spring cleaning, I meekly said nothing in my defence, and tried to turn a deaf ear to the horrific bangings which emanated from the sitting-room.

I escaped into the garden, and revelled in the spring weather. No doubt, as soon as term started, we should get a return to the arctic conditions we had endured in March, but meanwhile it was bliss to hear the lambs bleating in the distance, and to watch the rooks building their ramshackle nests near the church spire. Did they recognise the gilded weathercock near-by as an inanimate kinsman, I wondered?

Mr Willet spent an afternoon with me and we planted a row of new potatoes, with some Celtic name, such as Aran Pilot or Ulster Chieftain, which Mr Willet assured me were the only really tasty ones to be grown in our soil.

We also planted peas and carrots and I had visions of modest

dinner parties with the vegetable dishes overflowing with my own produce.

But the greatest thrill of all came three days before term started. As I shook out my tablecloth after breakfast, there was the unmistakable twittering of swallows, and there on the electricity wire were two little beauties.

For the rest of the day they flashed around the house, arrows of blue-black satin plumage, and before nightfall they had re-discovered last year's nest in the front porch, and were busy putting it to rights for this year's brood.

What did it matter if the doorstep would be plastered with droppings, much to Mrs Pringle's wrath? What did it matter if I had to hustle Tibby away during their rearing activities?

The swallows were back, and now summer had really arrived.

6 Public Duties

THE W.I. jumble sale took place in the village hall on Saturday afternoon. Fortunately, I was not required to man one of the stalls this time, as evidently a bevy of new helpers had volunteered for this hazardous job.

One of them I saw was Miriam Quinn who was in charge of the children's clothes' stall. She smiled across the room at me as I struggled with my own offerings for the produce stall. I had managed to find some pots of marmalade, one of my precious lemon curd – a real sacrifice, this – two cabbages, and a batch of flapjacks which I prayed had survived their journey intact, and not ended up in shame-making crumbs.

Mrs Partridge was in charge of the produce and accepted my contributions enthusiastically.

'Oh, how lovely! Marmalade is always a best seller, and what superb cabbages! Just look, Mrs James, aren't they splendid? May I sell you one for Sunday dinner?'

Mrs James looked at my offerings disparagingly.

'Got better'n them up home,' she announced, passing on to the next stall.

Mrs Partridge, accustomed to this sort of thing after many years as a vicar's wife, remained undismayed.

'Well, well, well! Someone else is going to be lucky, I can see.'

It is no wonder that our vicar's wife is unanimously chosen as president of so many village affairs. She has tact, resilience, and can rise with good humour to any emergency. I am one of her devoted admirers.

Mrs Pringle was in sole charge of the Shoe and Hat stall. This has been her prerogative for all the years I can remember, and she presides over it with implacable authority. Woe betide anyone foolish enough to try to bargain with Mrs Pringle! If a pair of size four grey suede evening shoes with Louis heels, dating from the twenties, has a chalked price of fifty pence on the soles, then that is what any would-be purchaser must be prepared to pay. I once saw a stranger offer her half the marked price for a pair of wellingtons. After Mrs Pringle had finished with him he made straight for the door, poor fellow.

'How's it going?' I enquired of her. She rattled her pudding basin with some satisfaction.

'Doing quite nicely, although there don't seem to be much call for hats these days.'

'People just don't wear them,' I commiserated, eyeing the yellowing panamas, a small feather pill-box with a veil, four identical picture hats in mauve silk with pleated brims, presumable once the get-up of four unfortunate bridesmaids, and several floral confections, among which I recognised a rather fetching one of my own, and was hurt to see it priced at five pence. Why, I'd paid guineas for it ten years ago for somebody's wedding!

'There's a nice one here,' said Mrs Pringle, burrowing under the pile, and surfacing with a battered object which she held out for my inspection.

'Crushed velvet,' she said. 'Suit you nicely, I reckon.'

Crushed all right, I thought, and as it was a particularly dreadful beetroot colour, I turned it down flat. Mrs Pringle began to draw in her breath, ready for some verbal assault, and I fled to Miriam's stall to escape.

Poor Miriam was in the clutches of a middle-aged newcomer to the village who had arrived late with her contributions to Miriam's stall, and was busy shaking out children's garments and suggesting prices.

'These two skirts shouldn't go at anything less than a pound apiece,' she informed Miriam. 'And I'd put a reserve of seventy-five pence on these blouses. I made them myself, from best quality Viyella for my grand-daughters, and they're hardly worn, as you can see. These little track suits too are in perfect condition. A pity to part with them, but they are too small now.'

Miriam cast an agonised look at me. The lady was busy rummaging in another of her many carrier bags, and was now producing children's shoes of all shapes and sizes.

Some customers were beginning to get impatient, and were besieging Miriam with upheld garments and money. I decided to come to the rescue.

'Shoes,' I said firmly, 'have to go to Mrs Pringle next door.'

She looked up with some dislike.

'But these are *children's* shoes!'

'Nevertheless, all shoes have to go to Mrs Pringle. Shall I take you to meet her?'

'No indeed. I know Mrs Pringle quite well, and can deal with her myself.'

She bustled off, and Miriam finished dealing with the batch of importunate customers.

'That was kind of you,' she said with relief. 'Really, I'd no idea of the hazards of holding a stall when I took it on. As for people's exaggerated idea of the worth of the jumble they're delivering, you begin to wonder why they're parting with it!'

'T'was ever thus,' I quoted to her, and went to buy a cake.

As usual, I was far too late to find the sort I like. It is common knowledge that the cake stall, on these occasions, is the first to sell out. The number of fine fruit cakes and toothsome sponges, which are secreted in the shade under the table, tell all too clearly of those wise people who have dropped a discreet word to the stall holders beforehand and have 'Reserved' put on these goodies.

By the time I arrived, there were a few rock cakes with burnt currants in evidence, some home-made crumbly biscuits and one large cake which I eyed doubtfully.

'Madeira?' I asked Mrs Lamb.

'No, dear. It's caraway seed cake. I can't think why it hasn't been snapped up. It's one of Alice Willet's too.'

'If I liked seed cake, I'd have it like a shot,' I assured her, and passed on sadly.

Joseph Coggs was standing by the bran tub, watching several of his schoolfellows diving for treasure. He looked wistful.

'Here on your own?' I asked him.

'Mum's gettin' shoes,' he answered, nodding towards Mrs Pringle, and sure enough, there was Mrs Coggs trying to fit the twins' feet into some of the shoes which, I suspected, had just been delivered by Miriam's tormentor. I only hoped Mrs Coggs would be successful, and I knew that Mrs Pringle would be sympathetic beneath her grim exterior.

I fished in my purse and gave a tenpenny piece to Joseph.

'Have a go, Joseph,' I said.

'But they's only threepence a go,' said he.

'Well then, have three goes.'

'But then there's a penny I owes you.'

'Keep it for luck,' I said.

'Thanks, miss,' he replied, and the smile he gave me was reward enough.

'Time I was off,' I told him making for the door.

I was pleased to have given him pleasure. I was even more pleased to think how well his arithmetic was coming on. Once a schoolteacher, always a schoolteacher, I told myself, on the way home.

The first day of term dawned hazily, foretelling a fine day to come.

Although, as usual, half my plans for the holidays had not materialised, I felt a certain sense of accomplishment. At least part of the house had been bottomed by Mrs Pringle. I had written to a number of neglected correspondents. The cupboards were tidy. I had worked hard in the garden, and done my duty at the jumble sale.

Now these activities would have to take second place to my teaching duties, and I prepared to go across the playground to start the day.

With Amy's warning in mind, I carefully closed the downstairs windows of the school house and locked back and front doors. Of course, it was doubtful if the sort of mentally-disturbed fellow whom Amy had described would be interested in entering my house to steal any valuables. Come to think of it, what would he find? A small silver sauce boat and a couple of silver napkin rings comprised my silver collection. Aunt Clara's seed pearl necklace was hidden in a handkerchief sachet in the drawer of my dressing table, and the only other object of value was a nice Chippendale carver chair which I had fallen for at a local auction some years earlier.

Hardly the sort of piece to be secreted by an opportunist sneak-thief, particularly one who evidently wore nothing but a raincoat.

However, the police had begged us to secure our property as best we could, and I felt a most virtuous glow as I walked across to school with the door key in my pocket.

Mrs Pringle, dustpan in hand, greeted me dourly.

'You promised to let me have that pudding basin back as I lent you last week with the bird food in it. I needs it for dinner today.'

'Damn!' I said, loudly enough to give joy to a knot of attentive children who nudged each other, happy at my lapse.

I turned to retrace my footsteps, unlocked the front door, retrieved the pudding basin, and returned to school.

'There you are,' I said to Mrs Pringle, who accepted it graciously. 'And many thanks for the bits and pieces.'

My cleaner leant towards me, her voice unusually low and confidential.

'There wasn't no call to swear in front of the children. They gets quite enough of that from the telly.'

I took the rebuke with good grace. It was deserved.

Halfway through prayers I remembered that I had omitted to lock the front door.

Ah well!

The swallows were hard at work putting the finishing touches to their nest. I watched them tugging at moss on the gravel path, fluttering clumsily at their task. It was strange to see how awkward they were. In the air, their natural element, they were such miracles of aerobatic movement that it made the contrast even more remarkable.

Within a day or two, the nest was as they wanted it, and the female settled to her egg-laying. She took no notice of the comings and goings at the front door below her. The male was attentive, swooping in and out with food for her, and ignoring any human activity. I wondered how many babies we should have this year. Last year there had been five, and a good squash there had been in the nest, not to mention the mess on the tiles of the floor below.

One year Mr Willet, scandalised at the state of my porch, had hung a plywood tray of his own making just below the nest. The swallows were furious, and chattered away on a nearby wire, refusing to have anything to do with the nest. Meekly, I took it down.

'They'd soon find some other daft body as'd let 'em nest in their place,' said Mr Willet flatly, 'if you was to stand your ground and leave that there board in place.'

'But I want the swallows!' I protested.

'Then you has to have the mess as well,' Mr Willet told me.

'I really don't mind. Visitors must just go to the back door. Most of them do anyway.'

'Well, don't let Ma Pringle see this porch,' he warned me, and made off before I could reply.

The dreaded evening in aid of the Save The Children Fund came round all too soon.

Alas! My usual hopes that an infectious illness would incapacitate me, that an unsuspected volcano had erupted in Caxley, or that Judgement Day had happily intervened, were dashed yet again, and I found myself dressing for the occasion in deepest gloom.

Should I wear my new patent leather court shoes that hurt, or my scuffed grey suede ones with the scratched left heel – a legacy from letting in the clutch – which were comfortable?

The choice of dress was simpler, either my patterned navy-blue silk, or a white lace blouse with a black velvet skirt. I had spent several evenings studying the ladies' attire in television panel games but with little satisfaction. For one thing, I did not own an off-the-shoulder creation in satin trimmed with either sequins or marabou feathers. Neither did I have anything with a neckline which plunged to the nether regions. Nor did I favour the other extreme of fashion which made use of a crumpled blouse of grubby cheesecloth and a medallion swinging on a long chain.

I had felt that perhaps I should rush into Caxley and buy an entirely new outfit for the occasion, but natural lethargy, combined with my usual shortage of funds, soon persuaded me that my present wardrobe would supply something suitable.

In the end, I set off in the navy-blue silk, the painful shoes, and Aunt Clara's seed pearls. I could do no more. My best

patent leather handbag contained my few pathetic notes on children's books, a subject about which I thought I knew a little, but now felt positive that I knew nothing at all.

The meeting was held in a Caxley hall some distance from the market square. This meant that the car had to be parked at some way away from the building, and I limped through the streets to my doom.

A kind middle-aged lady was fluttering about the entrance lobby, and came towards me.

'Miss Crabbe?' she asked.

'No!' I replied, rather more forcefully than the query needed. 'No, my name is Read. I'm from Fairacre. Are you Mrs Smith?'

'Oh no!' she said, sounding shocked. 'Mrs Smith is terribly busy inside with the platform arrangements. I've just been told to greet the panel people and take them into the side room for sherry.'

I followed her down the side of the hall, which was already alarmingly full of people, and into a little room which seemed even fuller.

Mrs Partridge's friend, Hazel Smith, hurried towards me with outstretched hands.

'Now let me introduce you,' she said, leading me around the room. 'You are the first to arrive. Dr Biddle has just telephoned to say he will be a trifle late, and Mr Ellis has only just left court, but I'm sure he won't be long. Miss Crabbe has some distance to come, of course.'

I met some three dozen people whose names I did not catch, and whose faces I should not remember, and expressed my delight at meeting them, and accepted a sherry dry enough to wither the tongue. I should really have liked a long drink of water, but realised that this would have looked eccentric, so twiddled my glass and listened to the rising crescendo of noise about me.

At long last my three companions arrived. Dr Biddle I knew slightly. He was a heavily-built man, with dark hair and a careworn expression which was hardly surprising, I thought, if he dealt daily with children in poor health. I was careworn enough, in all conscience, dealing daily with children in good health. He had my sympathy.

James Ellis, a Caxley councillor and chairman of the juvenile bench at the local court, was also known to me through his spate of letters to *The Caxley Chronicle*. The subject was usually child behaviour, and as he was a bachelor he naturally had very strong views about the way in which one should deal with the young, particularly those who appeared before him at court.

Most of the readers of that eminent weekly, including myself, thought that Mr Ellis's attitude to young offenders was gentle to the point of being deferential. Whilst not actually congratulating young thugs on their success in robbing old ladies of their possessions, his sympathy with their reasons for doing so – broken homes, lack of love, low intelligence, uncaring parents and all the usual stuff – was so eloquently expressed and quoted at such length in the paper that some susceptible readers' withers were wrung.

The majority, however, with their feet still firmly on the ground, found their spokesman in Mr Willet.

'My old dad,' said he, 'would have dealt with 'em in half the time, and with no expense. I bet he'd have stopped their capers!'

Mr Ellis greeted me kindly, and wore a beautiful dove-grey suit which I much admired.

He was followed by Miss Crabbe who held my hand and said what a pleasure it was to find that I was still at my old post and doing such sterling work, she had no doubt, which made me feel lazy, unambitious and a failure, which I am sure was intended.

She herself, I thought cattily, had not improved with the years. Her scanty hair was drawn back to a bun, and her face was much lined. She wore a tight frock of an unbecoming burgundy colour, and one of the buttons on the front of the bodice was missing. I felt smugly well-dressed after noticing this.

She was passed into Mr Ellis's care, and I could see that their minds were as one from their earnest expressions and wise noddings of heads. I was happily embroiled with a young reporter from *The Caxley Chronicle* who made notes with an indelible pencil, which one rarely sees these days. Between jottings he sucked the pencil, and I was fascinated to watch his tongue turn from lilac to a rich purple. It would have done credit to a prize chow.

All too soon we were summoned to the door by Mrs Smith. Dr Biddle was to speak first, then it was my turn, then Mr Ellis's, and finally Miss Crabbe would conclude the proceed-

ings, rather on the lines of keeping the best wine until last, I supposed.

The sea of faces was decidely disconcerting, but at least I would have time to compose myself, and have a quick glance at my poor notes, as Dr Biddle did his stint.

He was greeted with warm applause. He is popular in the area, and the fact that he once appeared on our television screens has added greatly to the awed esteem in which he is held.

He gave a brisk little talk about children's ailments, the importance of inculcating sensible dietary habits, and spoke reassuringly about infectious diseases, everyday accidents and the inestimable worth of our local casualty department. All in all, it was just what the audience needed, and the questions came thick and fast.

The good doctor coped brilliantly, even fielding some awkward ones from a dedicated herbalist in the front row who asked his opinion of woundwort for open sores, and the advantages of sage leaves in cleaning teeth.

All too soon he sat down, and I rose, trembling, to my feet. My feeble talk came to life when I gave a few suggestions for general reading, when there was a great scuffling in handbags for pencils and paper, and people scribbled busily. It was just like being in school again.

'Do you think children should read anything they like?'

'Aren't they better off watching telly?'

'Is my five-year-old too young for a dictionary?'

'How can I wean my son from horror comics?'

These were a few of the questions hurled at me, which I did my best to answer truthfully, but with nothing like the dexterity of my predecessor.

Luckily, I was saved by the chairman's bell, and settled back thankfully to listen to Mr Ellis. His discourse was, predictably, on the vulnerability and sensitivity of young things, and the

absolute necessity of letting them find themselves in their own way and time.

'Think of a tender young plant,' he exhorted us. 'It grows by throwing out delicate tendrils to climb upward to the sky. If we try to bend those tendrils, if we handle them too harshly, the plant is damaged beyond repair. All we can do, as parents, as teachers or as any one with the care of young people, is to provide a warm and loving atmosphere, and to encourage the upward trend towards light and knowledge.'

There was a good deal more in the same vein, and a certain amount of muttering when he sat down.

A few questions, which might well have been formed by Mr Willet, were asked about discipline, learning right from wrong, parental responsibility, and plain old-fashioned respect for authority, and these drew forth some kindly generalisations from Mr Ellis which made nobody any the wiser. The applause was luke-warm.

Miss Crabbe was much as I remembered her on the terrible weekend she had spent under my roof. She ploughed along with her lecture, in a slightly nasal monotonous drone, complimenting Mr Ellis on his acute understanding of the Child Mind, and enlarging on the need to make use of the wonders of modern psychology when any difficulties in child behaviour became apparent.

I had a pretty shrewd idea that this was one of the lectures she gave regularly to her students, watered down a little for the present audience.

Everyone was amazingly polite, and the questions, though few, were to the point. Time had run on, and we were all conscious of the chinking of wine glasses and the welcome clatter of plates at the back of the hall, where the helpers were preparing to revive us.

The applause when at last Miss Crabbe sat down was deafening. The lady flushed with pleasure, as we all clapped

heartily. I felt that our enthusiasm was caused probably more by relief than rapture, but at least the evening had been successful, and the ordeal was now over.

We raised our glasses and our cheese straws to each other, four disparate individuals, bound together for one brief hour by common suffering.

7 More Worries for the Coggs Family

MAY arrived in a flurry of blustery showers. In school the windows rattled, the doors thumped, and the replaced skylight let in almost as fierce a draught as the old one.

The weather had turned chilly enough to warrant lighting the stoves, but now that officially it was summer time, and Mrs Pringle would be at her most militant if the idea were mooted, we did our best by donning winter cardigans again, and hoping for the best.

Every now and again, black clouds brought hailstones to dance in the playground, and to dash the tender spring flowers to the ground. It was sad to see the first blooms of the cherry and plum trees scattered like confetti on the ground after these periodic onslaughts. The early bees, which had been active during the halcyon holiday spell, were nowhere to be seen. It seemed as if winter had struck again.

Tibby, who had spent all his days, and nights too, as far as I could judge, curled up in a clump of catmint, was now content to find indoor haunts, preferably on my bed or on the sitting room sofa. One evening of particularly cold showers I lit my fire, and rejoiced. And so did Tibby. Luckily, Mrs Pringle was not about to chide us.

It was on one of these cold mornings that I went across about eight o'clock to unlock the school in readiness for Mrs Pringle's ministrations.

Squatting against the door, his arms wrapped round him for warmth, was Joseph Coggs.

'You're early,' I said lightly.

He nodded.

I looked at him more closely. His bare legs were cold with goose flesh, his shabby sandals were soaking wet, and I suspected that he had been weeping.

'What's happened?' I asked more gently.

He shook his head without replying.

I unlocked the door, and left things ready for the school cleaner.

Bending down, I hauled the little boy to his feet.

'Come and have some breakfast with me,' I offered. He put a cold hand in mine, and we went across to the school house.

After a cup of milky coffee and some scrambled egg on toast, he looked more cheerful. I forbore to question him. It would all come out before long, I guessed. Probably he had broken something and Mrs Coggs had cuffed him. He was devoted to his poor slatternly mother, and could not bear to have her cross with him. Sudden flight from such a situation

would be his natural reaction, and the fact that he was so ravenous meant that he had not had the doorstep of bread and margarine, which I knew was his usual first meal of the day.

I went into the sitting room to collect a pile of exercise books and some new wall charts, and when I returned to the kitchen he was putting the breakfast china very carefully into the sink.

'Shall us wash it?' he enquired. They were his first words. Already he looked better.

'No, forget them, Joe. Let them soak.'

He turned on the tap, and watched the crockery being submerged.

'You'd better pop up to the bathroom and wash your hands and face,' I directed. He knew my home very well, as he often came to help in the garden, and had once or twice given me a hand in moving bits and pieces upstairs.

He vanished for five minutes while I put away the food. When he reappeared, I looked at him without speaking.

He took a deep breath.

'My mum's bad,' he said at last.

'In bed?'

'In hospital. The amb'lance come.'

'Were you alone all night?'

'No. Auntie come and took the girls. I went next door with baby.'

'To Mrs George?'

He nodded. The tears looked very near again. I decided not to question him too closely. No doubt Mrs Pringle would give me all the details, with horrific embellishments, when we met in a few minutes. But I had to know one thing.

'Does Mrs George know where you are?'

'I shouted as what I was coming up here when I left. What's more, I ain't goin' back.'

I had never seen him look so stubborn. The silence in the kitchen was suddenly broken by the sound of the school bell.

'Come on, Joe. We're going to be late,' I said, making for the door. 'You carry the charts, then I can lock up.'

We crossed the playground, dodging games of marbles, twirling skipping ropes, and flying children, and entered the lobby.

Mrs Pringle, arms akimbo, was waiting, heavy with news.

'You got 'im then,' were her first words, as she eyed Joseph with strong disapproval.

'Run along, Joe, and give out the hymn books,' I said. It was plain that there was plenty to be said, and I did not intend the boy to hear.

Mrs Pringle shuffled a little closer.

'His ma was took bad sudden. Appendix or something. Fair screeching in pain she was, so Bella George told me, until the doctor give her a shot of something. No one knows what, of course, but it's to be hoped he knows his business.'

'But what about the children? When did this happen?'

'Sometime after midnight. She banged on the bedroom wall and yelled out of the window to Bella and Jack next door. Lucky they sleeps light. It was Jack called the doctor from the phone box. Bit of luck it hadn't been verminised this week.'

'Vandalised,' I said automatically, ever the teacher. 'And has anyone heard when she will be back?'

Mrs Pringle's mouth turned down lugubriously.

'Who's to say? I mean, once you gets into a hospital there's no knowing, is there? Half the time you're thrown out as soon as you're sewn up, and the other half you lays there being observed for weeks.'

'But the children?'

'Well now,' began my cleaner, settling her bulk upon a wash basin much too frail, in my opinion, to carry such weight. She looked as though her story could continue for hours, and I began to feel anxious about my delayed school assembly.

'Ethel Tibble, Arthur's sister as I was telling you about the other day, she and Charlie come out in the van and took the little girls back to Caxley with 'em. And Bella and Jack took in Joe and the baby for the night. But young Joe never slept a wink, so Bella said, and sheered off when her back was turned cutting Jack's sandwiches.'

'I'd better go and see her at playtime,' I said. 'She may know more about Mrs Coggs by then. But now I must get on. We're all behind this morning.'

'I wouldn't mind betting,' replied Mrs Pringle bridling, 'as Bella knows a lot less than I do.'

I would not mind betting on it either, I thought, hastening to my duties.

I left the school in Miss Briggs' charge at playtime, and drove swiftly to the other end of Fairacre where the council houses stand.

I received some interested glances as I went through the village, and guessed that my dereliction of duty would soon be common knowledge in the community. What would be the conjectures, I wondered? A sudden brainstorm? An assignation with Henry Mawne – still, unfortunately, a grass widower? A dash to the station en route for a train to my distant home, where accident or sudden death had occurred? There was no end to the dramas which could be imagined.

Bella George was a comfortable middle-aged body, whose husband was a long-distance lorry-driver.

She ushered me into her sitting room, and came at once to the point.

'You've got our Joe safe, I reckon?'

'That's true. What's the position?'

'Well, I said I'd take him and the baby, and Ethel Tibble's got the little girls. As you know, they've got a corner shop in Caxley, mainly sweets and tobacco, and they don't have much

room upstairs, so they could only manage to fit in the girls. But they'll be all right with Ethel. It's Joe's the trouble.'

'Is it any help if I have him? He's used to me.'

Her face lit up.

'Would you, Miss Read? He don't seem to settle here, though dear knows why not. He sees enough of us. The baby's no trouble. Nice to have him in the house.'

'Any news of Mrs Coggs?'

'None yet.'

'I'll ring the hospital during the day and let you know. And I'd better let Mrs Tibble know what's happening too.'

A thought struck me.

'I suppose I'd better take Joseph's nightclothes if he's settling with me.'

Bella's jolly laugh set the ornaments on the mantelpiece ringing.

'Lord bless you, Miss Read, there's not a scrap of night

clothing among the lot of 'em! Those kids sleep in their vests, if they've got 'em, and if not it's their birthday suits!'

'I should have known,' I said. 'Well, I must get back to the school, and I'll call again when I know more.'

I drove soberly back to school. Were we still the two nations that Disraeli spoke of? It looked very much like it.

Later that evening, when Joseph had been bathed and was tucked up in the spare bed wearing an old singlet of mine, I rang the hospital.

Mrs Coggs, I was told, was round from the operation, and doing nicely. It was too early to say when she would be fit to come home.

Well, I thought, at least I had been spared that irritating word 'comfortable'. I recalled W. W. Jacob's account of one Bob Pretty who was 'what the doctor called comfortable', and what the narrator of the incident said: 'He would not soil his lips by repeating.'

My other call to Ethel Tibble, Arthur Coggs' sister, was equally satisfactory. She said she would pass on my message to Bella George as she was just setting off for Fairacre to collect some of the children's clothes, and it would save me a trip. We agreed to keep in touch, and she said if she could find anything of Joe's she would drop it in.

'Not that I expect much,' she said. 'You know that household as well as I do. I can't say I'm very proud of my brother. That place is a disgrace.'

I made non-committal noises, and rang off, but I pondered on her remarks as I ate my modest supper of soup and cheese and biscuits. The place certainly was a disgrace, partly due to Mrs Coggs' inability to cope with its running and her fear of Arthur's violence, but there must surely be this other cause – the driblets of money which came so spasmodically that regular budgeting was impossible.

I was fortunate. A cheque was paid into my bank account at the end of each month. I was no financial wizard, and often hard-pressed in the week before I was paid, but my store cupboard could provide for me in lean times and, thanks to Mr Willet, my garden produced fresh fruit and vegetables. I need never go hungry.

The Caxley Building Society took care of my modest savings, and I had some sixty or seventy pounds in my cherished Post Office savings' account. Friends in the profession managed far better than I did, raising families, buying houses, taking trips abroad, and still contriving to save regularly. Compared with them, I was a poor manager. But then, I comforted myself, compared with Joseph's mother, I was a paragon of efficiency. It was all relative.

I washed up, and set the breakfast for two in the kitchen. Boiled eggs tomorrow. It would be good to have Joseph's company for a few days.

By nine o'clock, I realised how tired I was, and was about to go to bed when the front door bell rang.

It was Ethel with a carrier bag of Joe's garments.

'No, I won't come in,' she said, in answer to my invitation. 'It's a proper job lot in there,' she added, nodding at the bag. 'And none too clean. I'd burn a few of them things, if I was you.'

She departed into the dusk.

I left the bag in the hall for tomorrow's attention, and went wearily to bed.

Joseph fitted into the household with no bother at all. I found him helpful with the daily chores, keen to wash up, to fetch and carry, and he straightened his bed each morning without being told. For a child with his chaotic upbringing, he was remarkably practical and obviously liked order in his surroundings.

He even straightened piles of exercise books in the process of being marked, and set my pens and pencils in order in my pen tray. The only thing he found daunting was the setting of a table, but after a few demonstrations he soon mastered that art as well.

As I had suspected, young Joseph Coggs was a quick learner, and as he grew older his progress was becoming more assured. I had great hopes for my young friend's future.

He was much more alert than I was to the doings of the birds in my garden. He inspected the sitting swallow at a discreet distance, and it was he who pointed out the sparrowhawk who hunted along the hedges bordering the school playground and the fields beyond.

'He watches out for them little birds,' he told me, 'and catches 'em when they flutters away frightened. I bet he had that hen blackbird as brought off a brood in your lilac.'

'What makes you think that?'

'Her ol' man keeps all on singing for another mate. Been at it all the week. He was the only one feeding them young 'uns, didn't you see?'

I had not, but obviously Joseph was keenly aware of the tragedy. Perhaps he had a fellow feeling for motherless young.

Mr Willet confirmed Joe's findings. He also told me that he had a whitethroat nesting in his garden, and promised to take the boy to see it. I was glad that the child was so happy in his new surroundings. It looked as though his mother would be in the hospital rather longer than we had thought. The trouble seemed to be diverticulitis, and it was plain that her general poor health would retard her recovery. We could only hope that enforced rest and proper diet would be of benefit to her eventually. Bella George, Ethel Tibble and I had all visited her and given her news of the children. It seemed to me that she was hardly aware of any domestic problems left behind at Fairacre, and although she thanked all of us in a vague way, I

suspect that she was in such a debilitated state that anxiety was beyond her powers. It was better so.

One evening I was helping Joseph with a mammoth jigsaw puzzle, to the neglect of a pile of ironing, when the door bell rang and Henry Mawne appeared beaming on the doorstep.

Now what, I thought, ushering him in.

'Ah! A young visitor!' he cried, espying Joseph perched on his chair at the table.

'Yes, he's staying here for a little while,' I told him.

Henry began to rummage in his pockets, and finally produced two dog-eared tickets.

'For my two lectures,' he explained. 'I'll pick you up in good time, and perhaps you would look after my notes for me?'

I was taken aback.

'But I thought I had explained that I shouldn't be able to come,' I cried. Obviously, this wretched fellow was not going to take 'No' for an answer. Joseph's eyes went from one to the other of us with intense interest.

'Well, I hadn't taken that in, I must say. Surely you can arrange things so that you can look after me? I'm really relying on you.'

'It's quite impossible,' I said firmly. 'Won't Elizabeth be back by then?'

'Very doubtful. Very doubtful indeed.'

He looked at me speculatively.

'What are you doing on those two evenings anyway?'

'My friend Amy has plans for me,' I said. It was half true, anyway. I decided to carry the war into the enemy's camp.

'Why not find someone who is free? There must be several keen bird people at your meetings who would be far more competent than I am to help you.'

'Perhaps Miriam Quinn would enjoy my lectures,' he hazarded.

'She's very busy, I know,' I said hastily, supporting my unsuspecting friend.

'I think I'll trot round there while I'm out, and just see if she will be free,' he said, picking up the tickets. 'I'm so dis- appointed that you can't come. I really feel quite let down.'

I made no reply, but accompanied him to the door.

As soon as he had shut the gate I rushed to the telephone and rang Miriam.

'Well, many thanks for the warning,' she said cheerfully. 'I shall pay a hasty visit to the wood and pick primroses until the coast's clear.'

'Why don't you like that man?' asked Joseph when I re- turned.

I did not propose to answer this direct question with a direct lie, nor, for that matter, with a direct truth.

'Here,' I said, bending over the table, 'let's fish out all the blue bits and get the sky done before bed-time.'

When we went over to the school the next morning, I found three children, whom I did not at first recognise, sitting in a row in the front desk.

Mrs Pringle, immense in a flowered overall, emerged from the infants' room, dustpan in hand.

'Minnie's lot,' she said. 'Just for the day, like you said. She's up home, giving Basil a good clean-up. Left him hollering something awful, didn't us?'

The three little Pringles nodded silently. I was relieved to see that their noses were not running. It made a pleasant change. No doubt Mrs Pringle had recently attended to this item of personal hygiene.

'Minnie says as she ought to be back about two or three,' went on my cleaner, 'but you knows hospitals. Time stands still, as they say. Anyway, I've left a pound of sausages at the ready, and I only hope she don't burn the pan.'

'Well, we'll look after these three for the day,' I told her. 'Miss Briggs can have the smallest, and these two can stay with me.'

Mrs Pringle advanced upon the trio, holding out her hand to the youngest. Without warning, all three threw back their heads and began to emit ear-splitting yells.

'Leave them! Leave them!' I begged Mrs Pringle. 'I'll see to it later. They can stay as they are for prayers.'

Obviously, the Pringle brigade was going to be a somewhat disruptive element in our normal routine.

Joseph, standing by my desk, broke his silence.

'I reckons they could do with a sweet,' he remarked conversationally. He made for the cupboard which holds the boiled-sweet tin.

'Not a bad idea,' I said, as he undid the lid. Expectancy was in the air. The room was blissfully quiet. Even Mrs Pringle stood transfixed, watching the boy.

'And take one for yourself, Joe,' I said to my ally.

8 Strange Behaviour of Amy

TWO days later, Amy arrived to take me to a piano recital in the Corn Exchange, one of the highlights of the Caxley Festival.

Kind Alice Willet had offered to sit-in with young Joseph, and arrived laden with enough knitting to keep her hands occupied for three weeks, let alone three hours. I went off with an easy conscience.

Amy was unusually subdued, I thought, as we drove to Caxley.

'I've had a slight headache for the last two days,' she admitted. 'Nothing much. I'm only glad we haven't got to sit through Wagner played by a full orchestra. A nice tinkly bit of Mozart on the piano is just about right.'

'Are you sure you are up to it? I'm quite happy to give it a miss, you know.'

'No, indeed. It's a good programme – light and melodious, thank God. I'm looking forward to it.'

We drove in silence until we approached Caxley.

'There is just one thing,' she said at last. 'I don't think I'll be able to go with you to the outdoor sculpture exhibition. If I gave you the tickets, could you find a companion?'

I explained about Joseph. Could she find two other people?

'Of course,' she replied. She sounded rather relieved. 'I believe it's going to be a permanent display eventually, so perhaps we can go later in the summer.'

And so the matter was left. I told her about Henry Mawne's lectures and my own prevarication, and a good thing it was

that I had done so, for Henry was sitting only two rows from us, in the company of a young fluffy-haired girl who seemed somewhat in awe of him.

We met in the interval when introductions were made.

'Eileen Bonamy, one of our most devoted bird-watchers,' said Henry, gazing fondly at his companion. 'She is going to help me during my lectures.'

'I'm so glad,' I said, with absolute truth.

'Miss Read was already engaged with you, I believe,' said Henry turning to Amy.

'Yes indeed,' said that stalwart friend. 'As you know, she is always in great demand.'

We were saved by the bell, summoning us back to our places.

'Thank you, Amy,' I said, 'for coming to my rescue.'

'No doubt you'd do the same for me,' replied Amy.

We settled back to enjoy an elegant little piece by Schubert.

Later, when we parted at my gate, Amy gave me a good-night kiss.

'I may not see you for a bit,' she said, 'so look after yourself. By the way, have you looked out that dye for the awful man?'

'I'd forgotten all about him.'

'As far as I can see,' said Amy severely, 'you'll be one of his easiest victims.'

She drove off with a cheerful hooting, and I went indoors feeling that Amy was herself again.

The unseasonable and chilly weather suddenly changed, and May became 'the loveliest month' which the poets praise.

Sunlight flooded the ancient schoolroom, and chalk dust danced in the slanting rays. The massive brass inkstand on my desk gleamed like gold, and little rainbows glanced from the glass over the photograph of our Queen, centrally placed on the rear wall, in the most honoured position.

The nature table was bright with specimens of coltsfoot, primrose, dandelion, an early wild daffodil and a cowslip. Why, I wondered yet again, are so many of our early wild flowers yellow? No one seems to know.

The cherry tree in the Post Office garden dangled white flowers, and everywhere, it seemed, the fruit trees were breaking into a froth of blossom and tender green leaf. The lilac bush in the most sheltered corner of my garden was in full bloom, and the heady scent floated up to my bedroom window in the warm nights. This old-fashioned pale mauve variety was always ahead of its more sophisticated companions, the white and the dark purple. It meant that the school house garden was fragrant for several weeks, for by the time the first blooms had turned rusty the others followed with their own scent. Later still the double white philadelphus, or mock orange blossom, as the Fairacre folk call it, would continue to delight our noses. It grows by my compost heap, and obviously enjoys its nourishment from that less pleasantly odorous source.

I had planted double dwarf tulips in the urn in front of the

house. It is hopeless to grow the stately tall variety in this windswept quarter. I have seen a splendid row of scarlet beauties, tall and straight as guardsmen, flattened in ten minutes by a sudden onslaught of mighty wind from the downs. I learnt my lesson early here, and this year the short rosy tulips held their own against the elements and delighted all who saw them. Even Mr Willet admired them, calling my urn 'a brave show'.

We all thrived in the sunshine. Tibby basked in the shelter of a hedge. Even the little birds, now finding enough chalky dust for a bath, were ignored, as they performed their toilet.

One of the most welcome visitors to the school during this halcyon period was my pupil Ernest's pet tortoise. This hardy reptile survives even our cold Fairacre winters and always comes to school for a spring visit after he has emerged from his hibernation in a box of straw under the stairs of Ernest's cottage. He lumbers around the room, thumping his shell against the legs of the desks, accepting a morsel of fruit or a young leaf now and again, and generally adding his tribute to the coming of fair weather.

I was reminded of Gilbert White's tortoise which he observed so lovingly at a village near Lewes. He noted that: 'The tortoise, like other reptiles, has an arbitrary stomach; and can refrain from eating as well as breathing for a great part of the year.'

We do not see Ernest's tortoise regularly enough to test Gilbert White's assertion that it makes 'an excellent weather-glass'. He goes on to say that 'as sure as it walks elate, and as it were on tip-toe, feeding with great earnestness in a morning, so sure will it rain before night.'

Sometimes I think it would be a good idea to have a permanent tortoise on the strength. Certainly Ernest's is much loved at Fairacre school and his visit is a highlight of early summer.

It was during this warm spell that Mrs Coggs was discharged from hospital, and Joseph went back to his own home.

I missed his company in the house, and his cheerful presence at the breakfast table.

The baby went back to its own home too, but Ethel Tibble had volunteered to keep the little girls for another week to give her sister-in-law time to recover.

Bella George was a stalwart neighbour and the district nurse was calling regularly. It looked as though Mrs Coggs would have plenty of support in the first days of her home-coming.

One evening Miriam Quinn called to ask if I could collect for the Red Cross at the school end of the village. She had undertaken the Holly Lodge part, and Alice Willet, ever willing, had nobly taken on the main street of the village.

'In fact,' said Miriam, 'she's doing two-thirds of the job, but she says she can easily fit it in with her other work, and it's handy if she has to go a second time. It's only when you go collecting these days that you realise how many houses are empty during working hours.'

'Nice pickings for the opportunist thief,' I commented.

'It seems to me that they operate even if people are in,' replied Miriam. 'Joan Benson had her week's groceries lifted, basket and all, while she was upstairs taking off her coat.'

Joan Benson had once owned Holly Lodge where Miriam lived in the annexe. She had sold it to David and Irene Mawne, who now lived there, and had gone to live near her daughter in Sussex after her husband's death.

We all missed her in the village, and I was pleased when Miriam told me that she was coming to stay with her for a few days.

'Do bring her round one evening,' I said.

'I'd love to.' She hesitated for a moment and then went on. 'It would be an enormous help to me if she could call after school one day, perhaps?'

'Of course. Any day she likes. I'm here at four.'

'The thing is I'm going to be unexpectedly busy during that week, preparing for a business conference. Joan understands, but I feel I'm being somewhat neglectful.'

I assured her truthfully that Joan Benson would be welcome at any time. Miriam looked relieved.

'Another thing. Elizabeth Mawne is coming home.'

'Now that is good news! I've had three telephone calls from Henry this week, and my excuses are getting thinner every time. Did Irene speak to him? Or to Elizabeth?'

'Luckily there was no need. You know the fluffy little thing who was hanging on his words at the lecture? Eileen Something?'

'Bonamy.'

'That's right. Well, apparently after that she pursued Henry doggedly, and after the first flush of flattery had faded, Henry began to feel that he was being hunted. One or two friends in Caxley and Fairacre had added their mite by saying he was making himself ridiculous by encouraging an innocent girl young enough to be his daughter. You know the kind remarks people make in such a situation!'

'Indeed I do!'

'Well, Henry began to get desperate – so desperate in fact, that he rang Elizabeth and asked when she proposed to return.'

'And what was the answer to that?'

'Immediately! The ancient aunt had completely changed her tune, and instead of vowing to end up in her own bed with nothing altered in that great barn of a place she lives in, she told Elizabeth tearfully that she needed looking after, that nobody cared for her, the house was too big, too cold and too expensive to run, and she had decided that life in a comfortable nursing home was what she wanted.'

'I should think Elizabeth was flabbergasted.'

'Not too flabbergasted to act at once, and to fix up her admission immediately to the nursing home she'd had in mind for months.'

'So that's settled.'

'Well, she's not there yet, but with any luck she will be within a week. Elizabeth has put the house on the market already, striking while the iron was hot, as they say.'

She rose to go, and I went with her to the gate. The air was balmy, and a newly-emerged bat flitted between the trees.

'What a relief all round,' I said.

'Except for poor Eileen Bonamy. I hear she's considering applying for a post overseas.'

'I hope Henry gives her a very nice farewell present. She deserves it, poor girl.'

It was a week later that Joan Benson came to tea with me after school.

Her hair was a little greyer, but her figure was as trim and her eyes as bright as ever. How was she enjoying life in Sussex, I asked her?

'Well, I feel very much the grandmother with the children so much with me, but I like that. People are very friendly, I'm already on the W.I. Committee —'

'That was inevitable,' I broke in.

'I suppose so,' she replied, laughing. 'All village newcomers get roped in, don't they? Yes, there's lots to do, and it's good to have the family at hand, but it was marvellous to come back to Fairacre. Here, you see, I really ran my own life.'

I must have looked surprised, for she went on.

'I mean, I was still a wife. And a daughter too, as my mother was living with us, you remember.'

I did indeed. Mrs Penwood had been a charming old lady though very frail when she first accompanied Ambrose and Joan Benson to Holly Lodge. She had died within a few

months of Ambrose, and it was soon after that that Miriam had gone to live in the annexe, as Joan's lodger.

'I was very much my own person,' continued Joan. 'I felt needed, valuable, appreciated, both by my mother and my husband. I always faced the knowledge that my mother would go very soon after we moved here, and I missed her sorely, but Ambrose's death really shattered me.'

'I can well understand that, although I'm not likely to experience such a loss.'

'I don't know which is worse, the awful feeling that a shared life is broken, or the fact that everything seems so pointless when one is alone. It hardly seems worth the bother of cooking, for instance, or buying new clothes. For the first few weeks I lived on tins of soup, cups of coffee and biscuits, until my daughter made me see reason. What really pulled me together was her good sense. "I've just lost a father, and I don't want to lose a mother too," she said one day. It was blunt speaking, but after that I buckled to, and went shopping again, and faced all the financial affairs I had been shelving, and generally took up living again.'

'You're a brave woman,' I told her.

'Not really, but looking back I realise I was lucky in the way things happened to me then. For one thing, I had the house virtually to myself while I was getting over the shock. Miriam was there at night, but by day I was alone, and it helped me. So many of my friends in the same position have found company absolutely essential, but others, like me, want time alone to adjust to the idea of widowhood. I had that, and then just when I was beginning to get to the recluse stage, my daughter pulled me back into the world, and I bless her for it.'

I refilled her tea cup.

'And that's enough of my affairs,' she said briskly. 'Now tell me how things have been going with Fairacre. Any hatches, matches or dispatches?'

I told her several of each, and brought her up to date with Fairacre and Caxley news.

After tea we inspected the garden in warm sunlight, and then I wrote a note to Miriam, accepting her invitation to supper at the end of the week, for Joan to carry back with her.

'Any hope of you ever coming back here to live?' I asked as she said her farewells.

'When I see it like this, all flowers and sunlight, I'm sorely tempted, but I remember the winters here, and believe me, Sussex is a good deal kinder to my old bones when the cold weather comes!'

'You have to be tough to withstand the winds of Fairacre,' I agreed. 'I've already started knitting a hefty cardigan in double-knitting wool ready for next winter.'

Mrs Pringle regaled me with a blow-by-blow account of how Basil Pringle's fingers had to be dressed, and very upsetting I found it first thing the next morning. As usual it was impossible to quell the flow.

'And how are the others getting on?' I enquired hastily, hoping to lead her to pleasanter topics. The little Pringles' one day with me had been distinctly exhausting, and I must confess I was thankful that they were not my responsibility permanently.

'Much as usual,' replied Mrs Pringle shortly. 'Now, I meant to let you know the latest about Mrs Coggs.'

'She's progressing well, I gather.'

'And who told you that, may I ask? She looks as near death's door as a great many as are now in the churchyard, to my knowledge. What's more she showed me her operation scar –'

'Well, don't tell me!' I cried. But one might as well try to stop the Nile in flood.

'All of nine inches long and double punch holes like boot

eyelets. An 'orrible sight!' said Mrs Pringle with relish. 'I thought my poor old ma's was bad enough, but this was more inflamed, if you follow me. I told her so.'

Trust Mrs Pringle to be pessimistic! I could bear no more, and walked swiftly into the infants' room on the pretext of speaking to Miss Briggs. I might have known that she would pursue me.

'And if I may say so,' she boomed behind me, 'you look a bit peaky yourself.'

'That,' I said firmly, 'is hardly surprising in the circumstances.'

And I shut the door smartly in her face.

Later, I was to rue this lapse on my part. Looking back, I see now, that this was the beginning of a rapid decline in Mrs Pringle's comparative patience and good temper.

I think if I could have foreseen the consequences, I would have made a superhuman effort to control my feelings – heaven alone knows I get plenty of practice in my dealings with Mrs Pringle! But I had been sorely goaded, and retaliated with the slammed door, sad to say.

Other matters cropped up about that time which distracted my attention from Mrs Pringle's pronounced limp, always in evidence when she has taken umbrage.

An evening or two later, James, Amy's husband, telephoned. He sounded unusually agitated, and dispensed with his habitual opening compliments which I found surprising.

'I'm ringing about Amy. Is she with you by any chance?'

'No,' I said, somewhat bewildered.

'Well, it's the oddest thing, but she's not here, and some of her clothes have gone, and her cheque book and so on, and not a word left for me. No note. Nothing. I can't make it out.'

'Come to think of it,' I said, 'she mentioned something

about being away for a time. Naturally, I assumed that you knew.'

'That I don't!' James sounded thoroughly cross.

'Are you sure that her note hasn't slipped down somewhere and got hidden?' I enquired.

'Of course I'm sure!' snapped James. 'I've searched everywhere. There's not a clue as to where she can be, and it's jolly upsetting.'

'Have you rung anyone else?'

'No. You were the first. I thought she might have driven over to you, and stayed the night, I got home yesterday about seven, expecting her to arrive during the evening. In fact, I rang you about nine or ten, and there was no answer.'

He sounded aggrieved. I explained that I had spent the evening with Miriam Quinn and Joan Benson.

'She'll probably ring you any time now,' I said, trying to comfort him.

'Well, if she doesn't do so before dark, I shall inform the police. For all I know, she may be lying murdered in a lay-by.'

Why a *lay-by*, I wondered? But it was no moment to discuss this interesting side-line. Obviously, the poor chap was becoming more distraught every minute, and I was hard put to it to know how best to help him.

'If you think she might have been involved in an accident,' I began carefully, 'perhaps you should ring the local hospitals.'

'Oh, for pity's sake!' shouted the exasperated man, 'don't make things worse! What a ghoul you are, suggesting she might be lying injured in hospital!'

It was hardly the time to remind him that he had imagined his poor wife lying murdered in a lay-by, which was far more ghoulish than my modest and reasonable suggestion.

'If I hear anything at all to help you, I'll ring immediately,' I promised him, and put down the receiver.

'Now I wonder,' I said to Tibby, 'is Amy really in trouble, or is she just enjoying her freedom somewhere, with thoughts of what's sauce for the gander holds true for the goose?'

9 Troubles Never Come Singly

THE mystery of Amy's disappearance had to be shelved in the pressure of day to day school problems, but I intended to get in touch with James to find out if he had heard from her. Knowing James, I thought it would be unlikely if he rang me, whatever the news.

In the midst of halcyon weather, I struggled with a spate of problems. Miss Briggs fell ill with some sort of stomach trouble, and so was absent from school. My anguished pleas to the education office were met with some sympathy but little practical help. Supply teachers, it seemed, were like gold dust in our area.

I put down the telephone and racked my brain. In the old days, Miss Clare used to step into the breach. Sometimes Amy, a first-class teacher, had come to our aid. Old helpers like Mrs Bonner and Mrs Finch-Edwards had now moved away, and the outlook appeared bleak.

I struggled all through the first day of Miss Briggs' absence with the dividing door open, and by making sorties between the two rooms, a certain amount of work was kept going, but this state of things was far from satisfactory.

In the evening I rang Miss Briggs' landlady in Caxley to enquire how my assistant was progressing. I must confess that I hoped she was soon going to be fit to return, as much for my own sake as hers.

'Still in bed,' was the depressing response to my enquiry. 'To my mind, it's just nerves, Miss Read. Getting upset about

the coming wedding. Girls do get these funny ideas, as no doubt you know.'

I had to admit that pre-marital qualms had never been experienced by me.

'Oh, it's quite common,' she assured me. 'You wonder if you're doing the right thing, you know. And then all the arrangements are a dreadful worry. Should you ask everybody, or nobody? I well remember how suicidal I got before my own wedding. I took such a dislike to my wedding dress, I threatened to go in my mackintosh. My mother couldn't do anything with me!'

She sounded rather proud of the fact, I thought, and privately congratulated myself on having escaped such traumas. There are many occasions when I thank my stars that I am single. This was one of them.

Getting back to the point, I asked if Miss Briggs seemed likely to be back within a few days.

'Oh, I doubt it,' she replied cheerfully. 'The doctor came this morning and I've just fetched the tablets he prescribed, and she says they make her feel awful, so what with the germs she's got and the cure the doctor's given her, I should say she'll be laid low for at least a week!'

A real Job's comforter here, obviously.

'Well, give her my love and I hope she will soon feel better,' I replied civilly.

And I went to prepare my modest supper for a little comfort.

I awoke about four o'clock the next morning with a stupendous idea. Why not ask Isobel Annett if she could come as a supply teacher in the infants' room in Miss Briggs' place? As Miss Gray, many years before, she had been one of my most successful assistants, until whipped from under my very nose by Mr Annett, the headmaster of our next village school, to become his wife.

It has been a happy marriage, for which I am doubly grateful, for his first wife was tragically killed, and when our paths first crossed he was a most unhappy and irritable fellow. Isobel has been the means of turning him into a cheerful family man. They are both musical and energetic, and much in demand at local concerts and musical festivals. Would she consider dropping her hobbies and household duties to hold sway in the infants' room she knew so well? I intended to ask her.

She sounded somewhat taken aback on the telephone.

'But it's years since I stood in front of a class,' she began. I burst in to tell her that, like riding a bicycle, one never quite lost the knack of teaching.

'And I half-promised to play for community singing at the concert for the blind in Caxley next Tuesday.'

I said that surely someone else could do that?

'How long would you need me?' she asked. This sounded much more hopeful, and I said that with any luck a week, or perhaps ten days, would see us through.

I could almost hear her brain working at the other end of the line, and began to plead my extreme necessity.

'I simply can't manage without help, and honestly I have tried. The office is a dead loss, and Miss Clare is past it, of course. As for Amy, she seems to have disappeared –'

'*Disappeared*! How do you mean?'

I hastily back-tracked.

'Well, she's away at the moment, so that's another person unavailable.' Better not to let rumours fly unnecessarily, I told myself. The village would have Amy eloping before one could turn round.

'So you see,' I added pathetically, 'I am in a terrible quandary, and would be so very grateful, Isobel, if you could manage to help us.'

'I'll have a word with John, and ring you back,' she

promised. 'One thing, if the weather's like this I could cycle.'

'And if it's wet I can fetch you,' I said enthusiastically. 'Don't let the travelling worry you. I'll see to that, and if you want to get away early to get a meal ready I can easily manage both classes for the last period in the afternoon.'

'Well, I won't be long making up my mind. Will you be in all the evening?'

'Yes, yes,' I cried.

And with my hand ready to snatch up the telephone, I thought, and with high hopes.

For the next hour or so I hovered about the house within earshot of the telephone bell. I wanted to get in touch with James to hear if he had any news of Amy, but I knew that Isobel would undoubtedly try to ring me at the very same moment, and so I resisted temptation.

My mind turned to another of my present problems. Mrs Pringle's limp seemed to have worsened in the last day or two, and her manner was distinctly frosty. It stemmed, I guessed, from my shortness of temper after enduring her ghastly descriptions of Basil Pringle's and Mrs Coggs' afflictions. However, I had no intention of apologising, and we had had far worse tiffs before this one. No doubt she would come round in time, but that morning's conversation had certainly been heavily ominous.

'How's Minnie getting on?' I had enquired. 'Not giving you any trouble?'

'No more than others I could name,' said the lady blackly.

'Good!' I replied, with false cheerfulness. 'So things are going smoothly?'

'I wouldn't say that.' (I bet you wouldn't, I thought.) 'With all there is to do in this place, I've more than enough on my plate. And all taken for granted! Not a word of praise from one week's end to the other.'

'Oh, come now, Mrs Pringle! You know your work's appreciated, but you can't expect praise all the time. Why, dammit, I don't ask you to admire our work when it's done, do I? I mean, that nature table is exceptionally splendid at the moment, but I don't expect you or anyone else to gush over it.'

'I don't feel like gushing, as you call it, when I've got to bend down to sweep up the mess it makes. It's more work for me, and just when I could well do without it, with my leg.'

Mr Willet had arrived at this moment, and the conversation ended with Mrs Pringle limping heavily into the lobby. Obviously, something more than her usual grievances was worrying her, but Mrs Pringle's martyred moods appear so frequently that it is impossible to waste much time on them.

But still, I told myself, the poor old dear was getting on, and perhaps I should make the effort and be gentler with her in the future.

And with this rare charitable thought, I went to cut up raw liver for Tibby's supper.

As was only to be expected, the telephone rang whilst I was in the midst of this gory operation with hands that rivalled Lady Macbeth's.

It was Isobel, and yes, she could come tomorrow, and it would be absolutely splendid to be back, but what about The Office?

I said I would see to that. I told her that she was an angel, I should sleep easily in my bed that night, and it would be marvellous to see her again in her own infants' room.

And now for James, I thought, when I had replaced the receiver.

The bell rang for such a long time that I decided that Amy's house must be empty, and was about to ring off when James answered.

He sounded breathless.

'Oh, it's you!' he panted. 'Sorry I was so long answering. The bacon was spluttering, and I think I've burnt the frying pan. Hell of a lot of smoke in the kitchen. What temperature do you use when you're frying?'

I said I had no idea. I turned the heat down if the pan smoked, and up if it didn't. It seemed to work.

'Any news of Amy?' I asked. 'I've been worrying about her.'

'Not half as much as I have! The police know she's missing, and I've had to give a minute description of her. As though I know how tall she is, or how much she weighs! As for what she was wearing "on the day of her disappearance", as they keep saying, I simply don't know.'

I expressed my sympathy.

'I suppose you haven't any idea where she could be?' He sounded suspicious. 'I mean, you two are pretty thick, She might have dropped a hint, or even told you outright, and then sworn you to secrecy.'

'I don't know any more than you do,' I said indignantly. 'You ought to know I wouldn't be such a rat as to let you worry like this!'

'Oh, sorry, sorry!' he cried hastily. 'It's just such a problem! How on earth do you begin to look for a wife who has vanished?'

'Well, I imagine you do exactly what you have done – told the police, rung up friends, had a word with the neighbours. I suppose you could put an advertisement in the Personal Column,' I ended doubtfully.

'You don't happen to know,' said James, sounding carefully casual, 'of any men friends she has been seeing lately? I know I have to be away a lot, and I believe Horace Umbleditch has been calling.'

'*Horace Umbleditch?*' My voice emerged as a startled yelp. Horace Umbleditch is a blameless bachelor who teaches at a

local prep school. The very idea of his pursuing any married lady – or a single one, for that matter – was quite unthinkable.

I rose to Horace's defence.

'I'm horrified to hear that you are even suspecting dear old Horace of such behaviour! And of course Amy would never countenance such conduct anyway. I advise you to keep a check on your jealousy, James, for that's what this is.'

I could have gone on much longer, so incensed was I, but James burst in.

'Oh, don't be such an old schoolmarm! Here I am beside myself with worry, the house is a shambles, and I can hardly see across the kitchen for smoke! Do you reckon the frying pan's too hot for sausages?'

'How should I know?' I replied crossly, and slammed down the receiver.

Thank God I didn't have a husband!

Mr Annett dropped his wife at Fairacre School at half past eight the next morning.

'No, I won't come in,' he said in reply to my invitation. 'Must get back to my own chores.'

'I promise to look after her well,' I said, waving him off.

Isobel looked remarkably cheerful for one thrown into an arduous job with such suddenness.

We went together into the school. Mrs Pringle was brandishing a duster.

'Here's an old friend come to help us out,' I cried.

'Good morning,' grunted Mrs Pringle.

'I'm quite looking forward to a few days in my old classroom,' said Isobel pleasantly, ignoring my cleaner's hostility.

'Daresay it'll be left a good bit tidier than usual,' conceded Mrs Pringle. 'But no one can hold a candle to Miss Clare. The place was always left like a new pin. She thought of others. Not like some.'

'I don't think any of us can come up to Miss Clare's standards,' agreed Isobel, and went on her way with a smile.

'What's the matter with her?' she whispered when we were in the infants' room. 'She's worse than ever!'

'I think I've upset her. It'll blow over. You know our Mrs P.'

Isobel began to unpack her basket. It contained a pink and white checked gingham overall, I saw with approval, as well as other things.

'I daresay infant fingers are as messy as ever,' she commented. 'And I'm bound to be clumsy with poster paint and clay and all the other paraphernalia. I only hope I don't fall foul of Mrs Pringle with my activities.'

'And what are those?'

'Templates of cats in different positions. I found them on holiday and couldn't resist them. I'm going to read them *Tom*

Kitten some time, and thought they could draw round these and then paint them. Perhaps make a frieze if Miss Briggs wouldn't mind. What do you think?'

'They'll love it, and I'm sure our Miss Briggs will approve. In any case, she can always take them down later if she wants to. Honestly, Isobel, you certainly haven't lost your touch, and I can't begin to tell you how marvellous it is to have you here again.'

Ernest bustled in importantly to tell me that one of them new little 'uns what lived up street next to Eileen Burton's gran was took bad his mum said, and wouldn't be acoming.

I thanked him, decided that any grammatical correction of this statement must wait till later, and invited him to ring the bell.

'Well,' I said turning to my assistant, 'the day's begun.'

A blessed period of peace now enveloped Fairacre School. Isobel slipped back into her former quiet and efficient ways, the infants seemed to relish her efforts and I was delighted to have a tranquil infants' room after Miss Briggs' somewhat hectoring manner which tended to make her charges noisy.

Mrs Pringle continued to wear a martyred look, and the leg, always of an inflammable nature in times of stress, appeared to be in a steady state of combustion judging by the lady's limp.

I was not surprised, therefore, when she informed me that she would have to 'give that place of yours a miss this week.'

'A rest will do you good,' I said. 'I hope it will be better next week.'

'I may not come next week either,' said Mrs Pringle, her mouth turning down grimly. I began to feel some alarm, not on my account, but the school's.

'Do you want a few days off all your duties?' I enquired. 'Have you seen the doctor? I'm sure we could manage somehow if you have to be laid up.'

Mrs Pringle gave a snort of disgust.

'I saw that young whipper-snapper that Doctor Martin's got to help him. A fat lot that boy knows! Gave me a prescription for some ointment, and told me to keep it up, and wear an elastic stocking.'

'Sounds sensible to me,' I was rash enough to comment.

'Except that's what I've been trying to do for the last twenty years!' snapped the lady. 'What chance have I got to put my leg up?'

'Well, I've just been telling you – have a few days off – a week, say – and see how you get on.'

'And what good will a week do? There's times when I reckon I'll just have to give in my notice.'

There was a menacing note in Mrs Pringle's voice which has become familiar over the years. I used to try and placate the old virago. Now I am hardened. One can cry 'Wolf!' once too often.

'Only you can decide that,' I told her. 'Meanwhile, I quite understand that you won't be coming to my house until you feel up to the work. But if you do decide to give up the school cleaning, do try and give me plenty of notice so that we can advertise the job.'

'And that,' said Mrs Pringle venomously, 'is all the thanks one gets for Faithful Service!'

Her limp was more severe than ever as she retreated.

Mrs Pringle's threat of leaving, although depressingly familiar, gave me some secret disquiet that evening.

Infuriating though she is, at least she does her work conscientiously, and is proud of the way she keeps the school. I have had periods without her assistance, and I know how quickly our ancient building and its furnishings lose their surface sheen when the lady is absent.

Getting someone in her place was not going to be easy. I

feared that her crazy niece Minnie Pringle might apply for the post. Worse still, she might be the only applicant! Anyone, I decided, would be better than Minnie about the place. I had suffered much from her administrations in the past, and would be alert if she made any approaches. Apart from her complete incompetence, the tangle of Minnie's love life in which one soon became reluctantly involved, was too horrific to contemplate.

It was while these thoughts were tumbling about in my head that I first noticed a pain in my right eye. There was also a blur when I read, or watched the television screen.

Rushing to the mirror, I surveyed my eye. It looked absolutely normal. I covered it and read and watched with my left eye. That was fine, but the right one was definitely defective.

Like any other robust person, the slightest deviation from perfect health throws me into a panic. First thing in the morning, I told myself, I must ring the optician for an appointment. With any luck, my left eye would still work, otherwise it might be as well to memorise the position of the holes in the dialling plate of the telephone. Would it take me long to learn Braille, I wondered? And how quickly would one get used to a guide dog?

Pondering gloomily on these things, I turned out my medicine chest and found an ancient eye shade, which reeked, for some reason, of camphor. This fragrant article I adjusted over a pad of lint over my afflicted eye, and then wondered how quickly the left one would give out with double work to do.

'At this rate,' I told Tibby, 'I shall be out of a job, like Mrs Pringle. We'll be hard put to it to find a crust for me and a quarter of liver for you.'

Why, I thought, I can't even play a mouth organ in the gutter! When it comes to it I'm completely useless, I decided hopelessly.

Perhaps the optician could think of something – not in the

way of future employment, of course – to give me a little hope. Everyone said how marvellous Moorfields Eye Hospital was, come to think of it, and as long as one did not have to have the retina stuck on again with those awful laser beams, which presumably did a sort of stapling job like clipping papers together, one could cope with ordinary treatment, although that, perhaps mercifully, was at present unknown.

John Milton had managed quite well, I told myself, though his daughter had a tough time copying down his poems as he dictated them, as far as I remembered from accounts of the poet's home life read years ago in the pages of Arthur Mee's *My Magazine*. And I had met several active and cheerful blind people who seemed to enjoy life. Should I ever be as brave?

I made my way to bed enveloped in a cloud of apprehension and camphor, and counted the stairs earnestly on my way up.

It is as well to be prepared.

10 Mrs Pringle Deserts Us

I WOKE to bright sunshine and the blessed relief of finding that both eyes were in first-rate working order.

Nevertheless, I told myself, it would be as well to make an appointment with the optician. Why bother him, asked my craven half? He has probably more than enough to do with genuine sufferers, and could well do without panic-stricken hypochondriacs.

My craven half usually wins on these occasions, but I decided to be firm this time. So far, I had not needed spectacles, even for fine work, but no doubt I was now at the stage of life which demanded some help. At playtime I bravely made my appointment, and promised to be at the optician's the next Saturday morning.

Now and again, during the day, I toyed with the thought of the best design to suit me. I rather fancied half-glasses. They looked decidedly efficient, and a little intimidating, which is always useful for a school teacher.

On the other hand, the more modern owlish variety were definitely fashionable. Several ladies in the village favour upswept shapes, and Mrs Finch-Edwards, a somewhat flamboyant lady who acted as a supply teacher here, actually had a pair shaped rather like butterflies, with a flashing jewel in the upper wing tip. Frankly, I could not imagine myself in such dashing numbers.

When Mrs Pringle appeared, as haughty as ever, I decided not to let her manner put me off. Fairacre folk who are

proposing a trip to Caxley usually offer a lift now that we have no buses to take us to the market town.

'I'm off to the optician on Saturday morning, Mrs Pringle,' I said. 'May I give you a lift?'

'No, thank you,' said she, pulling in her three chins, and looking grumpier than ever. 'Got to have glasses at last, have you? I've never felt right about them since my Uncle George fell off his bike on Coronation Day, and the splinters of glass was rammed something cruel into his eyes. He was never the same!'

She swept off into the lobby without the hint of a limp.

To my delight, Amy rang me at half past five that evening.

She sounded calm and cheerful, and in answer to my query about where she had been, said airily: 'Oh, here and there, you know. I'm ringing now from Vanessa's.'

Vanessa, her niece, lives in a castle in Scotland, and my frugal soul was shocked at the thought of such an expensive telephone call.

'But you should have waited until after six,' I protested. 'It's so much cheaper then.'

'Well, never mind that, you old miser! I'll manage, no doubt. The thing is I'm coming home, probably tomorrow, and am arranging a little party for June the first. It's a Saturday, as you probably know. About eight or ten of us. Can you come?'

'I'd love to.'

'Good, then I'll try and get Horace Umbleditch, and the young Mawnes. Horace will balance you nicely, and I'm very fond of him.'

Remembering my last conversation with her husband James, I wondered whether I should warn her not to get too fond of the unsuspecting Horace because of James's jealousy, but even a friendship as long and sturdy as Amy's and mine would probably not stand up to such bluntness.

'Have you rung James?' I said.

'Oh lord, yes! What an old fuss-pot he is, to be sure! Now, I'm relying on you then for June the first. About seven, shall we say? I'm going to ring the others now, and get things organised from here while I have the leisure. Vanessa's feeding the baby, but sends her love.'

The line went dead, and I put down the receiver, mightily relieved to know that Amy was alive and well, and obviously in excellent spirits.

But just what had she been up to?

The school house had not received any of Mrs Pringle's attentions now for two weeks, and frankly it began to look like it.

Dusting and vacuum cleaning I did fairly regularly, but the kitchen floor really needed a good scrubbing, and the cooker was approaching the stage where it should be dismantled, immersed in soda water, and generally forced to endure the stringent measures which Mrs Pringle regularly undertook.

There was no doubt about it, if the lady was determined to leave me then I must try and get a substitute.

Matters came to a head one morning when we both arrived at the school door to find that a tap had been left on, and the wash basin having been plugged with some unknown substance, the floor was awash.

Mrs Pringle drew in her breath sharply. Her face grew redder than ever, and I began to wonder how one coped with a sudden attack of apoplexy.

'That's the last straw!' she gasped. 'That's it then! You can take my notice now. I've had enough.'

'Mrs Pringle,' I begged, 'please don't desert me now! Think things over, do!'

But she turned away, dewlap quivering with rage, and her black oilcloth bag swinging dangerously on her arm.

She stumped off towards the school gate, and one or two early arrivals hastened to get out of her way, like refugees hurrying to the side of the road when a tank comes along.

I rolled up my sleeves, turned off the tap, unplugged the basin, (bubble gum yet again, I noted), and set to with the floor cloth.

Well, at least we knew where we were. I proposed to call to see the lady that evening to get her resignation in writing, or a firm promise to return to her duties with as much willingness as her nature could muster.

After that, I must work fast to find a cleaner for my house, and if need be one for Fairacre school.

I was still wringing out the floor cloth when Isobel arrived, and I told her the tale.

'You would really be far better off without her. She's been a blight on your life ever since you came here.'

'Oh, I don't know,' I protested. 'I'm quite fond of the old harridan in a perverse sort of way, and she needs the money, I know. I can't just kick her out without giving her a chance to retract.'

'Well, see how you get on this evening,' advised Isobel. 'And if she persists in going, I should count your blessings. As a matter of fact, I think I could find a young woman for you. She lives between Fairacre and Beech Green, and wants a job, I know.'

'That sounds hopeful. One thing I'm determined not to do, and that is to employ that nutty Minnie Pringle.'

And on this note we parted to go to our respective registers and the day's business.

The weather was so balmy and seductive that it was impossible to worry about Mrs Pringle, Amy, or anything else.

May was at its loveliest. It was true that the best of the daffodils awaited deheading, and the crocuses were drooping tattered heads, but the lilac was in bud, and the peonies and irises were flaunting their showy beauty.

My peonies are of the dark red common kind which flourish here and delight me with their blowsy top-heavy blossoms. Several times I have tried to grow the white and pale pink varieties, both single and double, but despite my cosseting they have faded away. The old-fashioned crimson ones flower bravely year after year, and I bless them for their hardiness.

The mats of aubretia and golden alyssum were still a cheerful sight, and the cotoneaster by the wall was spangled with pink and white flowers. The bees droned in it all day, and the birds sang with springtime fervour.

The earth was warm and friable, just right for scattering poppy and marigold and larkspur seeds to take their chance of

providing summer colour in the gaps in the border. The air from the downs was soft and soporific, so different from the usual fresh breezes that buffet us, in all seasons, in this area.

I had my tea in the garden, relishing all these delights, and watching Tibby rolling on the gravel nearby. If only one could have more of this blessed solitude, I pondered, just enjoying the simple joys about one, when 'every prospect pleases', how good and loving and noble one would be!

But the hymn continues:

'And only man is vile', I recalled, which reminded me that I must tear myself away from my miniature Eden, and go to visit Mrs Pringle, my personal serpent, and get the interview over.

The lady opened the door a matter of two inches, and from what I could see of her stern visage, I fully expected her to slam the door in my face.

However, she pulled it open and invited me to step inside. I felt like Daniel entering the lions' den, but tried to appear calm.

'Best sit down, now you've got here,' said Mrs Pringle grudgingly, and we both sat one each side of her empty fireplace. Every metal surface gleamed, every tile shone, not a crumb or cotton end showed on the carpet, and the windows were crystal clear. I was glad Mrs Pringle could not see my own home at the moment.

As if she could read my thoughts, she said: 'I'm not up to coming back to your place, you know. There's work and work, and some's *back-breaking* work, like your kitchen floor. So it's out of the question.'

'I quite understand that,' I said, 'but my chief concern is the school cleaning. I know we have had our little upsets in the past, but I wouldn't like you to give up entirely, and I came to see whether you would change your mind.'

The lady's expression changed. One could not, in all truth-

fulness, describe it as *softening*, but the down-turned mouth was perhaps a little less severe, and the eyes a trifle less flinty. My hopes grew.

'I'm not one to change my mind, as you well know, Miss Read, and I feel I owe it to myself to have a break. I'm up and down the street to that place, day in and day out, and my leg is not what it should be. Doctor said as it needed rest, and I ought to do as he says, though I doubt whether he knows much about it, nor cares, for that matter.'

She surveyed me belligerently, evidently waiting for my comment, but I stayed silent. Mrs Pringle is a wily fish, and has to be played with care.

'Well, let's put it like this,' she continued. 'I'll have a week off and see how things go. Then I will let you know, one way or the other.'

'Right,' I said, rising. 'You rest your leg, and think things over, and have another word with the doctor. But I really must know after a week. Meanwhile, we'll do our best to manage while you're laid up.'

She showed me to the door limping heavily, and wincing every now and again.

There were some splendid madonna lilies in bud in the shelter of the cottage wall, and a line of early pinks smelling divine along the path. There was not a weed in sight.·

I complimented her upon the show of flowers.

'Not got without hard work,' was the reply. 'But nothing is in this wicked world!'

A serpent all right, I thought, smiling over the gate at my old enemy.

I drove alone into Caxley on Saturday morning, dodging a number of fledglings who sat bemusedly in the middle of the road and nearly gave me heart failure.

The hedges were beginning to turn green, and some copper

beech trees on the outskirts of Caxley were hazily pink with
tiny leaves. What a morning! What a blessed time of year! Even
the thought of my coming ordeal could not quench my spirits
on such a glorious day of early summer.

The optician was a spruce young fellow smelling deliciously
of eau-de-Cologne after-shave. He shone a bright light into
my eyes, making strange little grunts as he did so. I earnestly
hoped that they were grunts of approval and not horror at his
findings. Perhaps I should be rushed to Caxley Cottage Hos-
pital immediately, I thought, panic returning, or there would
be an urgent call to Moorfields to stand by.

After this ordeal, I submitted to the usual tests with each eye,
trying to read as far down as I could so that my new spectacles,
if needed eventually, would last as long as possible.

I can't say I cared for the lenses being dropped one after the
other before my eyes while I attempted to say if the red light
was brighter than the green. After a bit, one really cannot be
sure, just as the last pair of shoes after a fitting always feels
worse than the one before, until a superbly comfortable pair is
greeted with cries of relief, bought and borne home, only to
find that it is miles too big.

'Yes,' said my nice-smelling optician. 'You definitely need
reading glasses. I will write a prescription, and then my
assistant will show you the different frames available. Actu-
ally, I should advise you to have half-glasses. At the moment
your long sight is perfect.'

I was ushered into another room and there spent a most
agreeable twenty minutes selecting suitable frames, ending up
with some rather sedate gold-rimmed affairs which gave me a
granny-like appearance which I rather liked.

'Perhaps I ought to have chosen something more dashing,' I
said doubtfully to the young man who had taken such pains.
'Those scarlet ones look gorgeous, and those thick black ones
might make me look studious.'

'Oh, I'm sure you don't want to look *studious*,' he said rather primly, as though such a condition was rather shameful. 'And the scarlet ones are really for the young. I think you will find the half-glasses very flattering to your own, er, quieter expression.'

All the way home, I wondered if a 'quieter expression' meant plain dowdiness, and had a horrid feeling that it did.

It was an enormous thrill to see Amy's car waiting by my door when I came out of school a day or two later.

My old friend was sitting on the garden seat, her face tilted towards the sun, and her eyes closed. She looked blissfully happy and ten years' younger than when I saw her last.

'Amy!' I cried. 'What a marvellous surprise! Come and tell me all about your disappearance. You had us all rattled, I can tell you, and James rang me in the most awful lather.'

'I'm delighted to hear it,' said Amy, giving me a kiss. 'It was one of the objects of the exercise, but not the *chief* one, let me say.'

'And what was the chief one?'

Amy bent down to pull a long piece of grass and began to nibble it before replying.

'I suppose you could say it was to catch up with myself. You see, for years now, like most married women, I've always had James in mind. Would he like this frock I've just bought? Would he like a holiday in Italy, or would he prefer to go to Frinton as usual? Even down to: "I'd better not put bananas in this fruit salad because James doesn't care for them." Of course, women with children must find it even worse, I do realise that, and must be torn in several directions at once when trying to come to a decision, but it suddenly struck me that I hardly ever did *exactly* as I wanted, *when* I wanted, and it seemed a good idea to try it.'

'And did it work?'

'Perfectly. I decided just to go off without a word to anyone. The whole point was to be alone without agitated friends and relations harassing me. I remember you saying once that the days one enjoys most are those one spends alone. I know it doesn't hold good for everyone. Some people are lonely anyway, but for you, among folk all day, I can quite see the need for a breathing space.'

'But, Amy,' I protested, 'you live alone a great deal. Why the sudden flight?'

'Believe it or not, I am hardly ever alone, and it's largely my fault. Dear old Mrs Hopkins comes in three times a week to char. Bert does the garden on Tuesdays and Thursdays. I play bridge twice a week, and go to innumerable committees and good works, more fool me, I suppose. Do you think I was wrong to go?'

She sounded anxious, and quite unlike her usual confident self.

'No, I don't,' I assured her. 'I know exactly how you were feeling, and I think you were right to recognise that you must take the plunge to keep your own personality. But, tell me, where did you go?'

Amy gave a chuckle.

'Well, I drove to a health farm a few miles south of Cambridge, and stayed there for a few days being massaged and creamed and bathed – and starved, incidentally – and generally being cossetted. It was marvellously therapeutic, and I lost five pounds too, which was a bonus. And they had the best hairdresser I've ever come across. I must say, I prefer a man to do my hair, do you?'

'I think you're right. They don't seem to slice your ears off with long sharp talons as the girls do, and they don't rub your hair into tangles so viciously.'

'After that I went on to dear old Cambridge for a couple of nights, and simply drifted about the Backs, and up and down

Trumpington Street, and round the Fitzwilliam and the Botanical Gardens. It was so peaceful, and Cambridge was looking lovely, and really warm for a change. It did me a power of good.'

'I wish I'd been with you.'

'So did I, now and again, but that would have defeated my aim. I must say I began to feel more balanced with every day that passed.'

'Then what?'

'I rang Vanessa and asked if I could come up for a few days, and she was wildly welcoming. So I took two days ambling northward through some of the most spectacular country, and spent the rest of my time with Vanessa and the children.'

She threw away the chewed grass and sighed happily. 'Of course I was *slightly* guilty about James worrying, but after all he keeps me guessing often enough, and I think it's given him food for thought. I was sorry he'd bothered the police though. The poor things have quite enough to do trying to catch house-breakers and muggers and murderers, without badgering them with a perfectly happy truant wife. But what about you? Did you worry?'

'A bit,' I admitted, 'but I had the comfortable feeling you were in full control of the situation, and you see I was right. Like a cup of tea?'

'Lead me to it,' said Amy.

While the kettle boiled, she told me more about the proposed party.

'Well, Horace is free, and so are Irene and David Mawne, and I came across that nice Gerard Baker again. He called at Vanessa's on his way to some Highland village with a name like a sneeze. He's coming too. Do you remember he wrote about a poet called Aloysius Something who used to live in Fairacre?'

'Indeed I do. He called with Vanessa one morning when he

was finding out about our Loyshus, and I directed him to Mr Willet.'

'Well, he's got mixed up with a television programme about Aloysius and I think they may do some filming in the village soon.'

'What excitement! I must ask him all about it when we meet at your house.'

After tea, we walked in the garden and I picked Amy a real country bunch of mixed flowers, irises, columbine, sweet rocket, some late narcissi, and a few early roses.

She sniffed them appreciatively as she made her way to the car.

'I must get back to poor old James,' she said smiling. 'He's all of a fidget now, in case I take off again.'

'So you've still got a conscience,' I quipped.

'It's well under control,' she assured me, and drove off with a flippant tootle on the horn.

11 Amy's Party

I WAS sad to see the last of May despite the problems it had brought me. Would June ever be as glorious, as fragrant, as tender with new blossoms everywhere? Fairacre delights me in all seasons, but May is the crown of the year for me, and when exceptionally early warmth is added to its blessings, then everything is perfect in this upland village.

However, the weather forecaster, on the last evening of May, promised us a continuation of the balmy conditions, and the weather map was nicely sprinkled with high pressure areas, and isobars widely apart foretelling very light winds.

And it looked as though he would be right.

I woke on the Saturday morning to a cloudless sky, and spent a few luxurious minutes relishing the fact that I need not get up at my usual early hour. A robin was singing in the plum tree, and there were occasional chirrupings from foraging blackbirds. But the rapturous dawn chorus of some weeks earlier was fading now that the young birds were hatching and fledglings needed feeding. A sudden furious chattering and scolding fetched me from my bed and, as I had guessed, Tibby was looking up at an irate blackbird a few feet above him in the lilac bush.

As I soaked in my bath a few minutes later, I thought how lucky I was to have a bathroom to myself, and hot water at the turn of a tap.

It was not always so. I recalled the effort of dragging the zinc bath from its nail on the side of the woodshed, the boiling of rainwater in the old copper and the sloshing of buckets into the

bath. It had been hard work, but the water, brownish and silky, had left one's skin as smooth as satin, and the soap had lathered in half the time it took with the water from the mains.

Nevertheless, I told myself as I stepped out, I would not want to return to the primitive sanitary conditions of my early years at Fairacre, and I praised the Lord for mercies received.

That evening I was due at Amy's party and I donned my new pale green silk frock with some trepidation. Amy has an eagle eye for the cut and colour of garments, and although I flattered myself that the colour suited me, I was not too sure about the sleeves. They seemed rather tight at the top to me. No doubt Amy would tell me if anything were drastically wrong when we were alone together.

The sun was still quite high as I drove to Bent, slanting rays through the young foliage and dappling the road surface with sunlight and shade.

Within a mile of Amy's house, I recognised the car in front of me as David and Irene Mawnes', and saw that Horace Umbleditch, Irene's brother, was also with them. They did not see me.

I slowed down to let them get ahead. It was quite a change to realise that I was not first as usual. Amy tells me that it looks as though I don't get enough to eat and have rushed ahead to get my trotters in the trough first. I thought these porcine allusions were very rude, and I told her so.

'Well, I apologise,' she had replied, 'but it doesn't alter the fact that as soon as you enter the hall you raise your head and sniff the air ravenously like a Bisto Kid!'

'I wonder I get invited at all,' I answered. 'Anyway, it's because there are usually such luscious smells drifting about that I automatically respond.'

This time, I told myself, watching the Mawnes' car draw

ahead, I must remember my manners and try not to sniff.

James let me in. He looked as debonair as ever, but I thought he seemed a little more subdued than usual. However, he kissed me on both cheeks gallantly and led me towards the party.

I was pleased to find several people already gathered together in Amy's splendid drawing room. The French windows were open, and some of the guests, glasses in hand, were watching a little bevy of chaffinches splashing in the bird bath. Roses seemed to be everywhere, inside and out, and their perfume was marvellous.

Most of the people were old friends, but I was glad to meet Amy's new young vicar and his wife. They had only recently moved to Bent from a parish in north London, and were enthusiastic about country life.

There was also an elderly cousin of Amy's, recently widowed, who was staying for a week. Luckily I remembered that she was a fairly well-known writer of detective novels and we had plenty to talk about when we found ourselves on the same sofa.

'Do you know Basil Bradley?' I asked her. 'He writes historical novels, and lives near here.'

'We share the same publisher. Now, he really is an enormous success! I believe they print ten thousand copies at first go.'

She spoke with awe.

'I once tried to analyse his great hold on the public, but I came to the conclusion that it could not be true literary worth. That may sound catty, but I don't mean to be. His style is rather florid, I think.'

'I think he gives his readers exactly what they want,' I replied. 'They only have to look at the book jacket, and see one of his heroines, all ringlets and a high-waisted muslin gown, to know that she is going to have wild romances every ten pages,

and lots of wicked villains hoping to deflower her, and prob-
ably a cruel guardian into the bargain, and a few ghosts in the
background, and it's all going to be the mixture as before, and
very nice too.'

'I don't grudge him his popularity, for a moment,' said she
bravely, 'but it would be nice to know its secret. Have you met
him?'

'Frequently. He's a perfect dear, and we all love him. He
opens bazaars, and empties jars of coins in pubs at Christmas,
and generally pulls his weight most satisfactorily. What's
more, he's as modest as they come.'

'Really? Well, it's nice to know that he is as popular in
private as in public.' She sounded rather wistful, and I won-
dered if she had hoped for some terrible secret vices to be
disclosed, but I was unable to gratify her. Basil Bradley is
exactly as I described him, and although the men locally tend
to make disparaging remarks about his pink shirts and bow
ties, and his rather too-gorgeous silk suits in pastel shades, we
women uphold him loyally, always ending with:

'And he's so very kind to his mother!' On the whole, this
tends to be the last word on our dear Basil Bradley, and what's
wrong with that?

At this moment, Gerard Baker was ushered in by James, and
after introductions around the room he arrived at the sofa. Mrs
Hare, Amy's cousin, had been collected by the vicar and his
wife to go and inspect the garden, and so he sat by me, and I
enquired about Aloysius, our local Victorian poet.

'It's really rather exciting,' said Gerard. 'We shall be coming
out to Fairacre pretty soon to film Tyler's Row where he
lived.'

'Do the Hales know?'

'Oh, I expect so,' he said, somewhat vaguely. 'The producer
is a very conscientious young fellow.'

'Will they keep pretty closely to your script?'

'I'm not doing that!' He sounded taken aback. 'There are three, maybe four, chaps doing the writing. You need a large team for a half-hour on the telly, you know.'

It sounded extravagant to me, especially as I had read Gerard's excellent and masterly account of Aloysius's life and work. I should have thought anyone could have knocked a script into shape with some of Aloysius's regrettably flowery poems interspersed to make up the time.

'I suppose it makes work,' was the best I could do by way of comment.

We strolled out into the garden with the others. The sun was going down fast behind a clump of beeches in the distance.

Against a south-facing wall there were already some scarlet flowers on the japonica, glowing even more brilliantly in the rays of the setting sun.

Horace Umbleditch appeared at our side.

'My sister Irene makes the most marvellous japonica jelly,' he said to Gerard. 'We have it with cold meat. Delicious!'

'Japonica Jelly!' exclaimed Gerard. 'Now that sounds exactly suitable for the name of a film star, don't you think?'

'Or the title of one of Aloysius's poems perhaps?'

'Far too obvious,' observed Gerard. 'Aloysius liked such titles as "The Winnowed Seed" and "The Bashful Maiden". But look, Amy is calling us to heel.'

The vicar was on Amy's right and I was next to him. On my right was Horace whom I always enjoy meeting. He teaches at a local prep school, and his first words at the dinner table were surprising.

'I thought you were an excellent speaker at that children's do a month or so ago.'

'Good heavens! Were you there? I didn't see you. Come to think of it, I really saw *nobody*, I was so terrified. Just a pinkish splodge of mixed faces. A horrifying sight.'

'Well, we enjoyed it. I brought along our new school secretary, Eve Masters. You must meet her sometime.'

I said that I should like that and wondered privately why Horace should choose such a dreary outing for the poor woman.

As if he knew my thoughts Horace said:

'Her uncle is a big noise in the Save The Children business. It was her idea to go to the Caxley evening. To be honest, I wanted to go to the Marx Brothers' revival.'

'I wish I'd seen you. Did you linger after the show and have some refreshments?'

'We had to get away fairly early as one of the chaps on the staff was standing in for me until ten o'clock, and I didn't want to be too late back. But we heard Miss Crabbe.'

'Oh good!' I said politely.

'What a misguided old fathead she is!' observed Horace, turning over the delicious chicken in a creamy sauce which was our main course. 'She'd have been burnt as a witch two hundred years ago!'

I found myself feeling fonder of Horace than ever. What a wonderfully perceptive fellow he was, to be sure!

'Well, she was warmly applauded,' I replied, trying to be fair.

'That was only general rejoicing at the cessation of the lady's voice,' Horace assured me, and turned to talk to Amy's cousin beside him.

'I have met Gerald Partridge of Fairacre this week,' said the vicar. 'What a charming fellow! Tell me, does he let the children address him by his Christian name?'

'Good heavens, no!' I exclaimed. 'I shouldn't allow it for one thing, and I don't think it is respectful, do you?'

'*Respectful*,' repeated the young man doubtfully. 'I was not so much thinking of *respect* as of *friendliness*. I wondered if the children of Bent would like to call me "Cyril".'

'Well, that's your affair,' I answered, trying not to sound too shocked. 'I only know I should never dream of letting them use my Christian name. They don't seem to suffer any terrible traumas by having to address me as "Miss Read". What did you do about the problem in your last parish?'

'I'm afraid the children there were rather impudent, and some of them took advantage of my goodwill.'

I suddenly felt sorry for him.

'Well, if you'll take an old schoolmarm's advice, I'd say, remember that children on the whole *are* impudent, and *will* take advantage of gentleness. Time enough to indulge them when you know you can control them, but they soon get the upper hand if you are not firm from the beginning.'

'You are probably right,' he said, looking downcast.

'This is fresh fruit salad,' announced Amy, lifting the lid top from a beautiful scooped-out canteloupe melon. 'Or James will give you chocolate mousse, if you prefer it.'

The vicar cheered up at once, I was relieved to see. Food is a great comfort in times of stress.

As we were going to our cars at the end of the evening, James caught me alone as I was about to drive off.

'I'm sorry I was so brusque with you on the telephone the other evening. I was worried to death, as I'm sure you knew.'

'Of course, James. I was feeling just the same. I think Amy's little break has done her good, don't you?'

'Funny affair, really. After all, she has everything she can want here. It seemed so odd to push off into the blue like that. I can only think it was a slight mental breakdown.'

I felt a twinge of irritation. Was he really so obtuse or was he trying to square his conscience?

'She told me,' I said, 'that she simply wanted to be herself – to be her own person – with no ties of any sort. I can understand it.'

James studied his fingers on the edge of the car window. He looked thoughtful. James is no fool and I was wondering how he would react.

'I do love her, you know,' he said at last, very seriously.

'I don't doubt it for a minute,' I told him truthfully. 'And she's equally devoted to you. But no matter how happily people are married, they are still *individuals*, and have to have time now and again to realise it.'

'Yes. It's a point to bear in mind.'

'Dear old Donne,' I went on, watching Amy waving to a departing car, 'stressed that no man was an island, and so on. But I think each man *is* an island, and no one knows his neighbour completely. That's what's so shattering when someone we think we know well does something horrifying like stealing or committing suicide.'

James laughed suddenly. 'Do you want me to have night terrors? No more sermons now, or I'll burst into tears!'

He gave me a kiss through the window, and ruffled my hair as though he were my big brother.

'Goodbye, James, and thank you,' I cried, moving off.

'Thank you for casting pearls,' he replied cheekily.

Trust James to have the last word.

It was quite apparent that Mrs Pringle was not going to come again to clean my house, and so I felt free to accept Isobel's kind offer to approach the lady who lived between Fairacre and Beech Green.

'Just see if she's willing,' I said, 'and I'll pop along after school one day, or at any time that suits her, to arrange things.'

Isobel was as good as her word, and two days later I found myself sitting in little Mrs John's kitchen watching her spoon custard into her youngest's mouth.

She was small and neat, with quick movements and bright dark eyes. She reminded me of a wren or a robin.

'You wouldn't mind if I brought Teresa with me, I suppose?' she asked tentatively.

I assured her that Teresa would be very welcome. If she liked, I added, she could play with some toys with the babies' class.

This seemed to clinch the matter and it was arranged that the two of them would come on Wednesday afternoons, and a satisfactory wage was negotiated. Then a thought struck me.

'You will have to push Teresa in the pram, won't you? It's a good mile and a half. Can you manage it? Suppose it rains?'

Mrs John laughed.

'I sometimes push her to Caxley,' she replied. 'Not often, I grant you, but I enjoy walking, and when I was a child in Wales we walked everywhere.'

'If the weather is really bad,' I insisted, 'you mustn't venture out. I shall understand.'

'I'll be there,' she promised, and I felt pretty sure she would be.

By the end of the week the school was looking grubby

despite all our endeavours at self-help. Curmudgeon though she was, and a sore trial at all times, Mrs Pringle was a first-class cleaner, and the school missed the touch of her heavy hand.

On the following Saturday she arrived at my house, and I invited her in.

'No, I'm not stopping,' she replied.

'At least sit with me in the garden,' I said, making for the rustic seat. 'It will rest your leg before you go back.'

She lowered herself slowly and sighed as she came to rest.

'Well, doctor says my leg's no better, and forbids me to work,' she told me, with evident relish. I was not surprised.

'That settles it then,' I said. 'I'll advertise at once for someone to take over. Does this mean you will be retiring for good?'

She drew in her breath sharply.

'Who said "*for good*"?' she demanded. 'I'm not giving in my notice and stopping "*for good*" for anyone! It's just while my leg's flared up. I told the doctor that.'

'In that case,' I said, 'we shall have to advertise for temporary help.'

'No need to waste money on advertising,' said the lady. 'My Minnie'd give a hand while I'm laid up. That house of yours could do with a bottoming by now, as well as the school, I don't doubt.'

I explained, with secret pleasure, I must admit, that Mrs John had been engaged for my work.

Mrs Pringle bridled. 'And who might she be? You'd better warn her about the weight of that spare bed of yours, and the way the bath tap comes apart if you aren't careful. Poor soul, whoever she is, she'll find plenty to do.'

I explained who she was, and mentioned young Teresa.

Mrs Pringle shook her head gloomily.

'Ten to one she'll put her fingers in the electric sockets,' she warned me, 'and play with the switches. And you'll find

fingermarks all over the place, no matter how careful this lady is. We knows children, Miss Read. You'll rue the day, I've no doubt.'

She rose to her feet.

'Well, I must struggle back, leg or no leg. Shall I tell Minnie to come up?'

Panic enveloped me. I thought of the state of the school wash basins, and the floor of the infants' room. I also thought of the time it would take for the advertisement to be answered, and wondered if hopeless Minnie might just possibly be of use for the next few days.

I took the plunge.

'Yes, ask Minnie to come and have a look at the work. Make it clear to her that it will only be for a day or two until we get someone to take your place.'

'She'll have to bring her youngest with her,' said Mrs Pringle. 'But if you're having that Teresa I suppose you won't mind a toddler under your feet.'

'Take care of your leg,' I said in farewell.

'I'm the only one that does,' she replied bleakly.

I returned to the garden seat and pondered on the future. The thought of Minnie, toddler or no toddler in tow, was daunting, but surely she could not do much damage to the basins with a tin of Vim and a dishcloth. It might be wise to supervise the scrubbing of the infants' room floor, I told myself. Minnie was quite capable of shaking Harpic into the hot water instead of soap powder, as she could not read, and any white powder would seem suitable to her.

And I'd better make sure all the cupboards were locked, I decided. On one never-to-be-forgotten occasion she had decided to wash the shelves of the stationery cupboard, and had put back all the exercise books, coloured tissue paper, gummed squares and cartridge paper on the wet shelves, with

disastrous results. As for the sacrosanct register which all teachers are supposed to guard with their lives, snatching it from any fire which may be engulfing the school, I thought it would be prudent to take it across the playground every night to my own house, while Minnie was at her mayhem.

Tibby appeared from a clump of clove pinks, a mouse dangling from his mouth.

Seeing me, he gave a triumphant mew. The mouse, having been dropped, beat a rapid retreat, pursued in vain by Tibby.

Two minutes later, he returned lamenting loudly.

'Cheer up, Tib,' I said, 'we all have our troubles.'

12 Minnie Pringle Lends a Hand

MISS Briggs was now back in the infants' room and the dividing partition shuddered every now and again from the impact of her stentorian tones. I thought wistfully of the peace we had enjoyed during Isobel's brief reign, but tried not to dwell on the change.

The girl looked rather pale and thinner than usual.

'It was a tummy bug,' she told me, 'and the first lot of pills disagreed with me, which made matters worse. The only bright thing is that I'm an inch smaller round the waist, and my wedding dress will have to be taken in.'

I complimented her on her svelte appearance.

'You should be getting your invitation this week,' she continued. 'I do hope you can come. Do you know Leamington?'

'No, but I shall look forward to the wedding very much.'

'Good. I expect Mum can put you up, although I know we've some aunts and uncles, and my father's mother coming up from Cornwall, and some cousins from Holland that have been invited, but I'm sure we can find room. We've three bedrooms.'

I said hastily that I would not dream of troubling her mother when so many of the family would need accommodation, and I would look out for a modest hotel for my overnight stay.

'Do you know, I'm quite looking forward to it,' she said, sounding surprised. I remembered her landlady's surmise that girls about to marry frequently suffered from prenuptial nerves. Obviously our Miss Briggs was made of sterner stuff, and good luck to her.

Mr Willet summed it up when he met her on her first morning back at school.

'Looks a lot better with half a stone off, don't she? I mean, she's still a fair old lump of a girl, but got a livelier look about her. That young Wayne's done her a power of good. Nothing like marriage, Miss Read, for setting you up. You wants to try it some time.'

'Chance would be a fine thing,' I told him, opening the register.

The prolonged heat, which I relished, began to take its toll of the garden and of the children's energy.

The crimson petals pattered down from the peonies on to the dry soil. The downs shimmered in a blue haze, and I had to draw the curtains in my house against the heat of the midday sun.

The rainwater butts were empty, and a loudspeaker van from Caxley toured the villages exhorting us to save water and forbade us to use sprinklers and hoses in the parched gardens.

'I turns a deaf ear to that blighted van,' Mr Willet told me. 'It's only old Ted Bates anyway, throwing his weight about, and him no better than he should be with that fancy woman of his over Bent way. I've got some seedlings just up nice, and they gets a drop of water when needed, Ted or no Ted.'

Here was another instance of sturdy country independence born of personal knowledge. What cared Mr Willet for a flashy van and the might of the local water board? Such power was soon cut down to size by knowing old Ted who was running the thing. I found it all very heartening.

The children were listless. Perhaps they are so accustomed to the exhilarating freshness of our downland breezes that a warm and langorous environment, which suits me very well, saps their energy immediately.

Our lofty windows were propped open to their fullest

extent, and the door to the lobby, as well as the outside one to
the playground, were permanently ajar. Two large flower pots
made sure that they stayed open and Tibby took to sitting on
the outside one, washing his face and occasionally looking into
the lobby and classroom, much to the children's delight.

But despite my efforts to mitigate their sufferings the chil-
dren remained lethargic. I took them outside for lessons under
the trees at the edge of the playground, but there was so much
noise we did not get on very well.

People from the towns have the fond idea that we in the
country could hear a pin drop, and that silence enfolds us.
Here, in June, Mr Roberts was busy hay-making. The baler
thumped its way round and round the fields adjoining the
school. The vicar's lawn mower, a few yards away over the
vicarage wall, seemed to be doing overtime. Various dogs in
the village enjoyed a healthy barking, and Mr Roberts' cows
added their lowing every now and again.

We also get a number of aircraft from a nearby aerodrome,

and are in the flight path from an international airport. Some
distance away, but quite audible when the wind is in the
south-west, there is a motorway, and the hum of the traffic can
become a roar in high summer. Fairacre itself is little changed,
but sometimes I wonder if it is not a place besieged by outside
pressure.

There was little activity at playtimes. Even the coke pile was
neglected as children were too idle to climb it. Mostly they sat
in the shade of the trees, rolling marbles or chewing grass in a
desultory fashion, whilst only the really industrious essayed
such feats as making daisy-chains or knocking the heads from
plantains.

Nevertheless, it was rewarding to see how tanned and well
they all appeared in their skimpy tee-shirts and cotton shorts or
skirts. Even Joseph Coggs who rarely seems to enjoy a change
of clothes, was clad in some good summer garments which I
suspect had been bought at the W.I. jumble stall so bravely
supervised by Miriam Quinn. With any luck, I told myself,
this blissful spell of sunshine should set us up for the coming
winter.

Mrs John began her ministrations much to my relief, and
although I did not see much of her as I was in school, I did nip
across at playtime to make sure she had a cup of tea.

Teresa seemed to be a model child and played or slept in her
pram in a shady part of the garden. I returned to my duties
congratulating myself on my new helper.

It was a different kettle of fish, of course, with Minnie
Pringle barging about in school. She was only engaged to
work after school had ended. The thought of facing Minnie
Pringle at the beginning as well as the end of a school day was
more than I could endure, and I said that we could easily
manage first thing.

I stayed with Minnie on her first visit, hovering protec-

tively, not on my helper's account, but to look after the school property. Fortunately, the toddler had been left with a neighbour, so I only had Minnie to direct. I let her start on the wash basins, putting out the Vim tin, drawing her attention to its size and colour, and even – such is the ardour of the true schoolmarm – pointing out that the three letters on the side spelt VIM. Minnie nodded her tousled red locks energetically, grinning madly the while, and I wondered how soon she would forget my first lesson.

I managed to dissuade her from giving the lower panes of the lobby windows a brisk drubbing with the Vim-coated dishcloth, but she attacked a mirror with such vigour while my back was turned, that I feared the resultant scratches were there for good.

She swept the floors rather well, I thought, and I initiated her into the art of filling a pail half-full rather than brimming over, and showed her where the kneeler and scrubbing brush were kept, and the carton of soap powder. The latter perplexed her.

'You just put in enough powder to make a lather,' I told her, demonstrating with the plastic beaker kept inside. 'One measure is enough for half this size bucket.'

I swished about energetically until we had a useful mixture.

'There isn't time to do much this evening, Minnie,' I told her, 'but if you could start at the other side of the infants' room, it would help. Do a little each evening, I suggest.'

'It's dirtier by the door,' she pointed out. 'I'd best begin there.'

'Start over by the windows,' I directed, 'and work gradually this way.'

'Why?'

'Well, you won't be walking on the bit you've scrubbed, and you'll be kneeling on a dry part of the floor.'

She gazed at me in mystified silence, before bursting into a cackle of laughter.

'What a head-piece you've got on you, miss! No wonder you can learn them kids right.'

She spent the last quarter of an hour of her time working hard on the further strip of the floor. I dusted both rooms, partly to help and partly to keep my eye on our property.

'Time's up,' I said at last. 'It all looks splendid, Minnie.'

I was about to tell her that when the short hand was at five and the long one at six it meant that her duties were at an end, but somehow the thought of giving a lesson to Minnie on telling the time, after a full day's teaching, became insupportable. After all, she had already been initiated into the whereabouts of her cleaning materials, and the desirability of washing the floor without treading on the clean part.

I felt it was enough for one day. If not for Minnie, certainly for me.

On Sunday morning I breakfasted in the garden. The sun was pleasantly warm. Later, it would be too hot to enjoy its direct rays, but at nine o'clock all was perfect.

The grass was still dewy, and the Albertine rose growing over the garden shed was breaking into flower. What a marvellous old rose it is! I love the dark tight buds, the glossy foliage, and the pale pink open flowers. But best of all is its sharp-sweet scent. What matter if it only flowers once in the season, and drops its petals with profligacy? It is a true herald of summer, and I think I am fonder of it than any other rose in my cottage garden.

Later I went to church. The altar had roses on it, and some madonna lilies had been arranged on a pedestal by the lectern. Their heady scent perfumed the ancient building. Outside, the sun blazed and the distant thumping of the baler could be heard. All the farmers in the neighbourhood were literally making hay while the sun shone.

Inside, the church was cool and shadowy. I closed my eyes

the better to attend to Gerald Partridge's sermon, and hoped he would not think that I had dropped off.

It was a good theme, a celebration of summer and all its blessings. He spoke of the beauty of natural things, noticed so much more sharply when one could loiter out of doors. He touched on the renewal of friendships which winter weather had discouraged, and I thought how true this was. I recalled the joys of our nature walks and my own garden, and the trips to see Miss Clare and Amy and other good friends.

He went on to point out that beauty begets beauty, quoting an incident in the woods near Beech Green where he came across members of the Caxley art group busy transferring the woodland scene before them on to their canvases. He added another instance, dear to his heart, of the happy sound of the bees collecting nectar to transform into honey. The vicar has only recently taken to bee keeping, and his charges are very dear to him.

It was a good sermon, I thought, as we scrambled to our feet at the end of it. It encouraged us to look about us, to be grateful for all we could see, and for the bounty of the earth, and to ponder on many hidden meanings in an apparently simple message as we truly celebrated summer.

I remembered to ask Miss Briggs for her wedding present list, and pored over it anxiously one evening. The children and I would get together when Miss Briggs was absent to decide on the school's offering. Judging from the list of things needed it would probably turn out to be: 'Soup Ladle, not plastic' or one of 'Trays, various sizes'.

I was pleased to see that she also wanted 'Vases, various sizes', and I decided to plump for something which I liked as my personal present to her. It is always a pleasure to buy china and good to have an excuse to indulge one's desires.

One hot afternoon, I prevailed upon Miss Briggs to take her

charges into the shade of the trees for story time. This gave me the chance to consult my fellow conspirators about the present.

Patrick was all for giving her a pair of guinea pigs, as his pets had recently had a fine litter. It seemed to me that Patrick's guinea pigs produced litters far too often, and supply out-stripped demand heavily in Fairacre.

Eileen Burton suggested a silk eiderdown and bedspread, preferably pink 'because it's always pretty', and Ernest thought a wheelbarrow would be useful.

When I could get a word in edgeways, I pointed out that all Miss Briggs' needs were listed, and I put forward the ideas possible on our modest budget. No one was to contribute more than twenty-five pence, and ten would probably be the average.

After much heart-searching, I was delegated to buy a tray.

'As big as the money goes to,' Patrick said firmly, and I meekly agreed to do my best.

Ernest, who had been allotted the job of Miss-Briggs-observer, and had been keeping an eye on the infants' movements from the lobby door, now called out:

'She's acoming, miss! She's acoming!'

At this, the children hastily took out their readers at my suggestion, and were engrossed in their pages, with unnatural fervour.

But when Miss Briggs came in to speak to me as she went to her own room, the nudges and knowing winks would have alerted anyone more observant than my assistant to the fact that Something Was Up.

Fairacre children are not very accomplished dissemblers.

As I was taking some letters to the post a day or two later, I met Peter Hale who lives at Tyler's Row. He bought the property a

few years ago, and he and his wife have turned the row of four dilapidated cottages into one fine house.

He taught for many years at Caxley Grammar School, but has now retired and takes an active part in village affairs. I asked him if there were any developments in the proposed television programme about Aloysius, an earlier dweller at Tyler's Row.

'Well, two chaps were supposed to be coming down one day last week to see if the interior of the end part where Aloysius used to live was worth filming. It's so altered that I think it's a waste of time myself.'

'What did they say?'

'They never arrived. Diana and I stayed in, putting off an old school friend of hers who was coming to tea, incidentally, but not a word and no TV chaps.'

'Too bad. Do you think there's enough material for a programme?'

'All I can discover is a pathetic collection of dreadful doggerel in the public library, and Mr Willet's recollection of our poet's personal dirt. I can't see it making a national appeal somehow, but no doubt a skilful producer could turn it into something on the lines of "The neglected poet in a hostile world".'

'Well, I hope you don't have to hang about for the telly people anyway.'

'I don't intend to. They can fit in with my plans next time. That is, if there is a next time!'

Spoken like a true schoolmaster, I thought, as I went on my way. That was the tone of voice which had sent many to detention in times past. The telly men had met their match there.

I heard a little more about the proposed programme when Gerard Baker rang up. He seemed somewhat agitated, and wanted to know if the television team could film the school.

'You see, Aloysius attended it as a boy,' he explained.

'I suppose it would be all right,' I said doubtfully. 'What do they want exactly?'

'You may well ask! I'm beginning to wish I had no hand in it at all, there's so much to-ing and fro-ing. If I were you, I would refuse to let them inside.'

'Why? They don't take all that long, do they?'

He gave what novelists call a hollow laugh.

'They took two hours flat arranging some of Aloysius's manuscripts and a candle on a suitably scruffy table. You see, they have to play about with the lighting and sound, and heaven knows what. I should advise you to limit them to taking outside shots only. If that!'

'Well, thanks for the warning.'

'I said I'd sound you out, as I knew you. Don't let yourself in for too much. I know you are not too patient at the best of times, and this could drive you barmy.'

'Thanks,' I said. I was not exactly thrilled to hear that I was obviously an impatient harridan. Still, it was good of Gerard to give me advice.

'Tell them they can have a brief spell taking one or two shots outside the school,' I said. 'But inside is out.'

'I know what you mean,' said Gerard, and rang off.

'The wonders of modern science,' I told Tibby, 'can prove very exhausting.'

13 Mr Willet to the Rescue

I MUST say I was rather pleased with my new spectacles.

I expected a few whispers among my class when I donned them first for marking the register, but an awed silence engulfed the schoolroom as I was made the object of concentrated scrutiny.

It was not until the morning was halfway through, and the sun was beginning to get to its full power on yet another cloudless day, that the first comments came.

'Do them glasses hurt you?' Patrick asked.

'Why, no!' I responded. 'I've got them to *stop* my eyes hurting.'

Somewhat emboldened, other children now joined in.

'But why ain't 'em big enough to go over your eyes?'

'Is it cheaper, miss, to have them funny little 'uns?'

'I feels frightened when you've got them on.'

I did my best to explain the difference between long and short sight, and the difficulty in focusing as one grew older, which drew a spate of comment about the spectacles used by their elderly relatives. Ernest, who is sometimes a lot brighter than he appears, began to ask quite difficult questions about lenses which were beyond my power to answer, and when he actually used the words 'concave' and 'convex', to my astonishment, I had to admit my ignorance, and direct his attention to the mobile library van whose kind librarian might be able to find a book to answer Ernest's questions.

By the time we had exhausted the topic of my new half-glasses, and I had firmly refused to let anyone *touch* them, let

alone *look* through them, as Eileen suggested, it was almost playtime. It was so blissfully sunny outside, and the birds were chirping so merrily, that it seemed like cruelty to children to keep them indoors.

We all had an early playtime.

Amy was rather less respectful about my newly-acquired aids when she called one evening.

'They tend to *age* you, my dear,' she announced, after studying me keenly for a full minute. 'Why did you pick that particular design? Terribly academic they look, I must say!'

'Well, what's wrong with that? I am academic after all.'

'Yes, dear, in a rather juvenile sort of way, I suppose you are. But those glasses make you look like someone engaged on the third volume of somebody's biography. Tacitus, say, or Cicero.'

'That's all to the good. It's nice to look learned.'

'Yes, I suppose it's quite pleasant to look *learned*, but one doesn't want to appear *eccentric*.'

I began to get alarmed.

'You are not trying to tell me, Amy, that these spectacles make me look like a nut-case?'

'Well, not exactly like a *nut-case*,' said Amy, but with a certain doubt in her tone which increased my dismay. 'No, I wouldn't say that – quite! It's just that somehow they make you look odd. If you know what I mean,' she added.

'I can't see this conversation getting us anywhere but into deep waters,' I said. 'Tell me why you've really come.'

'Gerard Baker is getting ready to help with this television nonsense, and I offered him a bed if need be while the flap's on. I just wondered if you would like to see him while he's here?'

'That's nice of you, Amy. I always enjoy seeing Gerard.'

'Oh good!' exclaimed Amy, with unnecessary elation.

'Not in the way you mean,' I said firmly. 'Just that he's good

company, and I'll be interested to hear how the programme's going. I gather from Peter Hale that they want to do a few shots in his house, Tyler's Row.'

'Well, I hope he'll be firm about it. A friend of mine spent five hours solid being badgered from pillar to post for exactly five minutes on the box itself. She said her carpets have never been the same since, and she had to have a weekend in an exceptionally quiet hotel in Sidmouth to recover from the ordeal.'

We wandered into the garden. The sun was still quite high in the sky despite the fact that it was early evening.

'Come round to the front door,' I urged, 'and have a look at the swallow babies. I think there are five, but Mr Willet swears there are only four.'

The parent birds were still swooping across the neighbour-ing fields catching insects for their young. Tiny blue-black heads projected over the rim of the nest, and a mad twittering broke out whenever one of the parents returned with a beak full of provender.

Amy surveyed my front doorstep which was heavily cov-ered in bird droppings.

'Can't you fix something to catch all this?' she asked, looking rather disgusted.

'Mr Willet has tried, but they don't like it,' I replied.

'What with that tyrant Tibby and this family of intruders,' said Amy, 'I can see you are hopelessly out-classed. What you need is a man about the place to look after things. Now Gerard, I know for a fact, is very practical underneath that rather dilettante exterior. When can you come to meet him?'

'Oh, Amy!' I wailed. 'Won't you *ever* realise that I like being single?'

She began to laugh, as we left the shameful doorstep and went to smell the early roses instead.

'I think I know how you feel,' she said at last. 'My few days

of solitary life were wonderfully refreshing, I found. And wasn't it Katherine Mansfield who said that one of the pleasures of living alone meant that if you found a hair in your honey at least you knew it was your own?'

To my dismay there had been no answer to the advertisement for a school cleaner. I guessed that Mrs Pringle would be delighted to hear such news, and I had no intention of telling her, although I had no doubt that she would soon be in possession of the knowledge, by means of village bush telegraph.

Although I was careful to say nothing to Mr Willet, he guessed, I think, that there was no particular stampede for the job. I must say, that when one read in the newspapers about the thousands of unemployed people crying out for work, it seemed strange that no one wanted to come to Fairacre school as cleaner.

'You keepin' that dratted Minnie on then?' asked Mr Willet one afternoon. We were in the playground, and the children were fast disappearing round the bend in the lane. The sound of clashing pail and broom came from the recently-vacated classroom.

'Just until we can get a permanent person,' I said guardedly.

'You want to watch her,' warned Mr Willet. 'She was letting that little 'un of hers suck the floor cloth yesterday. Saw it myself.'

'No!' I said horrified. 'Surely not! He might get some awful disease!'

Mr Willet waved his hand airily.

'It wasn't the kid I was worrying about. But it can't do the floor cloth no good to have it chewed up like that. They costs a fortune these days, Alice says. She cuts up my old pants into nice squares for jobs like that, and that saves a pretty penny I can tell you.'

'I suppose,' I said doubtfully, 'that Mrs Pringle is really under doctor's orders still? I mean, we know she has her drawbacks –'

'You can say that again,' interjected Mr Willet.

'But she is a marvellous cleaner, and I don't think Minnie is capable of carrying on much longer.'

'You could go and see the old tartar again, I suppose,' said Mr Willet, smacking his thigh and killing a fly which the swallow babies would have relished. 'But I reckon she just wants to see how long you can stick it out with Minnie. Enjoying it, I don't doubt. There's a spiteful side to Mrs P., as well you knows.'

I did indeed, but I dare not say so to Mr Willet.

I sipped my tea in the garden, pondering on this problem. It would be a waste of time to go and see my old cleaner again. She had told me, squarely enough, that she intended to return, but in her own good time. There was no point in begging the lady to return. I must simply set about finding a stand-in for her, and get rid of the deplorable Minnie before she wrecked the school premises.

At this moment there was a sudden shindy from the school. I put my cup on the garden seat, and hurried across the playground. What horrors would appear, I wondered, as I ran? Broken windows, smashed wash basins, shattered desks, all swam before my eyes. Minnie was capable of anything.

I noticed a battered van standing in the lane by the school gate, but did not recognise it in the heat of the moment.

I burst into the building to be confronted with a ferocious-looking man, Minnie screaming behind my desk, and the floor-cloth-chewing infant yelling its head off.

'What's all this?' I shouted above the uproar.

Minnie pointed an accusing finger at the intruder.

'It's Ern,' she shrieked. 'He's upset.'

This, I thought, was stating the obvious. The fellow was

grinding his teeth, and breathing heavily. His face was flushed and his fists clenched. I had never met Minnie's husband, but it hardly seemed the time to say: 'How do you do?'

'I must ask you to leave,' I began, with as much authority as I could muster. What if he started on me? I began to wish I had taken karate lessons at Caxley Technical College.

'This is school property, and Minnie is at her duties,' I went on.

He turned on me menacingly. 'You shut your mouth! She's been at her duties all right, and with that flamin' Bert of hers. She's coming home with me. I'll sort her out without your help.'

Surprisingly, I was not frightened. I suppose it was because I was so furious with this intrusion.

'Minnie will stay here until half past five,' I told him, standing my ground. 'I advise you to go home, or I shall send for the police at once. I won't have brawling in my school.'

He let out a string of interesting expletives, many of them new to me, but to my relief he made for the door.

'I'll be waiting for you,' he said ominously to the cowering Minnie, and then strode off.

The toddler was still emitting head-splitting yells, and I made for the sweet tin before coping with Minnie. A large pear drop successfully gagged the child, although it seemed a dangerous object to put into any child's mouth in the circumstances. However, better asphyxiation than pandemonium, I thought, setting an upturned bucket to rights.

'Now Minnie,' I said, 'sit down and tell me all about it.'

It appeared, from the disjointed account that the tearful Minnie embarked upon, that Bert, her old admirer, had been visiting her in Ern's absence.

'I don't get no fun,' wailed Minnie, wiping her moist nose on the back of her hand. I went again to the cupboard and supplied a handful of tissues.

Minnie looked at them wonderingly.

'Wipe your nose with them,' I directed. She obeyed in a sketchy fashion before continuing with her narration.

'Ern don't never take me out, nor give me enough to buy the kids food and that. He'd have the bit I earns here if he could find it.'

Here she gave a damp giggle, tugged at her neckline and bent down to display a couple of pound notes pinned inside a grubby vest with an enormous safety pin. It looked mightily uncomfortable, I thought, but at least it showed that Minnie had a certain resourceful cunning.

'Auntie told me to do it,' she went on, scratching her mop of red hair. I might have known it. Trust Mrs Pringle to be one jump ahead in any conflict, as I knew from experience.

'But, Minnie, you can't go on like this. He is your husband,

after all, and he's bound to be – er – upset if you carry on with other men.'

She looked at me in amazement.

'It ain't other men, only Bert. And he don't come often. I mean, only when Ern's out.'

I gave up, and turned my attention to matters other than Minnie's marital affairs. 'The point is that I can't have this sort of thing going on in the school. What if the children had been here? Ern's language alone was –'

'He didn't say nothin' real bad. Not today, he didn't. He can say a lot worse'n that,' she added boastfully.

'Well, all I can say, Minnie, is finish your work here, and then come over to the school house before you go, and we must get something settled.'

I looked down the lane as I went home, and sure enough, Ern's van was still lurking a little farther down. To ring the police or not, I wondered?

Minnie arrived, toddler in tow, twenty minutes later, and I sat her down at the kitchen table with a restorative cup of tea. While she drank it, I washed the child's face and hands with a J-cloth which went straight into the dustbin. He was not a bad looking little boy under the grime.

' 'E's still there,' said Minnie.

'I know. I'll run you home.'

' 'E'll come after me.'

'Well, it is his home too.'

Minnie began to cry again.

'You must behave yourself, Minnie, and see it from Ern's point of view.'

We set off for Springbourne as soon as Minnie had composed herself. The van had vanished, and was not parked anywhere near Minnie's council house. The coast appeared clear.

'You'd better nip in quickly,' I said, opening the door. 'And

Minnie, start looking out for another job. I think we'd better get someone else to do the school next week.'

I wondered if the tears might flow again, but she gave me a mad grin instead.

'Bert knows a lady in Caxley who'd have me,' she said. 'Cleaning out a pub.'

I watched her enter her house, turned the car round and went thankfully home. I felt as though I had been engaged in a tough wrestling match which, come to think of it, I had.

May always seems to me to be the loveliest month of the year, but a sunny June runs it very close.

Fairacre, in high summer, takes a lot of beating. The early mornings were fresh and dewy, and I sometimes took the children for a walk as soon as the register was closed at nine-thirty.

According to the timetable we should be at our arithmetic lesson, but that could be done later when the sun was too hot to be out of doors, I told myself.

The hedgerows were at their most lush, the young leaves thick and green, with sprays of cascading wild roses, pink and fragile as shells.

The lambs were getting larger daily, but were still young enough to cavort about, butting each other and their patient mothers, and chasing up and down the fields, shaking their woolly heads, and bleating loudly.

There were birds everywhere. Bemused fledglings sat in the playground, lapwings fluttered in scores over Mr Roberts' fields, and rooks and pigeons were equally numerous as they foraged for their young. The bearded barley crop in the field near the school was beginning to bleach in the heat, and the heavy ears were bending over. There were dozens of varieties of silky grasses on the verges of Fairacre's lanes, and the nature table was adorned with them.

The swallow babies were now almost as big as their parents and made short flights from the telephone wire to the television aerial on the school house. Their bubbling chatter began at four o'clock in the morning, as I knew only too well.

The many tits seemed to have vanished, and were probably in the oak and hazel wood at the northern end of Fairacre feeding their broods on the dangling maggots which fed on the young oak leaves. No doubt they would be back, clamouring for peanut kernels, within a few weeks.

The robins too were scarce in this hot weather, although the children were delighted to see one particularly tame one perched on the upturned flower pot which held open the door. His folded wings were tipped up behind him, and he looked exactly like a man with his coat tails lifted, warming his back by the fire.

These summer nights were as lovely as the day. The moon rose each night, enormous and golden, and at its height it was almost bright enough to read a book.

There were strange movements in the garden, as hedgehogs snuffled and scuffled about. A stoat yapped, and an owl gave its eerie quavering cry. The shadows of the trees lay still and black across the silvered lawn, and moonlight glimmered on the school windows and the church roof. There was a lot to be said for being sleepless on such nights of beauty too rarely seen, and I relished them accordingly.

It was at times like these that I could forget the petty problems of the daily round. It was good to have the pinpricks of Mrs Pringle and Minnie put into perspective by the unchanging values of nature.

The Caxley Chronicle, our local paper, carried a report about a man who appeared in court on charges of indecent exposure. It sounded like Amy's 'Awful Man', and he had certainly visited

quite a number of villages in the neighbourhood, although he had been arrested in Caxley itself, in one of the parks.

The Caxley magistrates were remanding him for three weeks for psychiatric reports, I read. One day, no doubt, he would end up in a hospital for the mentally disturbed, poor fellow.

I felt guilty about forgetting to prepare myself with vegetable dye as instructed by Amy. However, I could now relax presumably, and perhaps Amy would not cross-question me further.

I folded the paper and went across to the school. This morning there was a different feel about the early hours. The sun was up, but seen through a light haze, and there was an uncanny stillness about. Already it was oppressively hot, and the open windows admitted no refreshing flow of air.

'Well, that's the end of summer,' said Mr Willet flatly, when he arrived. 'Thunder before night, you mark my words. Good thing really.'

'Why? We can't have too much sunshine, surely?'

'Seen them water-butts? Empty as egg shells. I see yours is splitting already. I give mine a splash of water now and again when old Ted Bates isn't on the prowl. Them slats shrink, see, in the heat.'

'Do you mean to say, I shall lose all the rainwater, as soon as it starts to pour?'

'Quite likely, I should say,' replied Mr Willet cheerfully. 'But on the other hand you might be lucky, and the cracks close up when the wet gets to 'em. They say the devil looks after his own.'

'Thanks,' I said tartly.

Mr Willet chuckled.

'Only my joke, Miss Read. You're a bit fazed with this cleaner business, I don't doubt. But thank heavens that Minnie Pringle finishes today. She's enough to set your teeth on edge,

and no·better than she should be with them two fellows she leads on. You was right to sack her.'

I was too taken aback to comment on this, and while I was thinking, yet again, of how little I knew of bush telegraph, he made for the door.

'You might try Bella George,' he said, pausing with a gnarled finger on the latch. 'Her old man's changed shifts this week, and she's a rare hand with a floor cloth. That is, if that dratted Pringle kid has left us any.'

He gave me a wink and vanished.

Bella George! Why not try her?

Dear Mr Willet, I thought lovingly. Ever the teacher's friend!

14 Rain and Romance

AS always, Mr Willet was right about the weather.

By mid-morning the sky was overcast and the sultry heat was oppressive. There was a curious coppery colour on a bank of clouds to the west, and no bird sang. No breath of air stirred the leaves of flowers or trees. It was as if the earth waited for what might befall.

The first distant rumblings of thunder came as the children played after school dinner. Then it came nearer, and vicious lightning cracked the skies. I called the children in, just as the first spots of rain began to fall.

Within ten minutes there was a deluge. Raindrops spun like silver coins in the playground, and the chalky dust at the edge of the field was first pock-marked and then turned to silt within seconds.

Water gushed from the gutters and cascaded from the roofs. Little rivers pelted along the sides of the lane, and the church was hidden behind a curtain of silver drops.

The noise was tremendous and awe-inspiring. Thunder crashed and lightning flashed, and I could hear some wailing from the infants next door. My own class was scared, but silent, under the onslaught. I pitied anyone caught in the storm. One would be drenched to the skin in a matter of minutes.

It was very dark in the schoolroom and I switched on the electric light. There was an almighty crackle and all the lights went out, amidst groans of dismay from the children.

'Heads down,' I said, 'and have a nap.' Some hopes, I thought, in this pandemonium, but it was impossible to work anyway. They rested their heads on their desks, and I could only hope that next door's wailing was not catching.

As suddenly as it began the rain ceased. The thunder rumbled more distantly, the lightning became less vicious. I let the children stay as they were, and wondered if they had appreciated, as keenly as I had, the patter of the raindrops on summer leaves, and the steady plop-plop from a nearby gutter. The scent of wet earth was refreshing. It made one realise how desperately thirsty the plants and small animals must have been in the long drought.

Listening to the music of 'leaves drinking rain', as W. H. Davies put it, I remembered reading that the Chinese, in ancient times, purposely planted large-leaved trees like the banana for the express purpose of hearing the pattering of rain upon them. The Chinese have always been wise enough to recognise that the minutiae of natural things can enrich life. We could learn a lot from them.

The rain continued steadily, and by the time school was over it was plain that Miss Briggs and I would have to do some ferrying home. Most of the children were clad in shorts and tee shirts, or thin cotton frocks, the light clothing they had worn for the last brilliant weeks.

A few mothers arrived, umbrellas up and children's mackintoshes over their arms. Their offspring were soon on their way.

Mr Roberts' Land Rover squelched to a halt by the gate, and he shouted an invitation to any children going near the Post Office. Half a dozen excitedly swarmed into his shelter.

Miss Briggs took two children squashed together beside her, and I was left with the Coggs' family.

Minnie Pringle arrived as they climbed into my car. She was pushing the battered pram. Its inmate looked dry enough, but

Minnie was running with water, and her red hair was in wet wisps on her forehead. Her grin though, was as fanatical as ever.

This was, with any luck, the last stint of work she would do at the school, and although I felt relief at the thought, my heart smote me.

'Minnie,' I shouted from the car, 'why don't you put your wet things in my kitchen and make yourself a cup of tea before you start?'

'Oh, lovely! Ta ever so!' enthused Minnie, turning the pram and making for the school house.

It was only when I was halfway to the Coggs' house that I began to wonder how much havoc Minnie could cause in making tea in my kitchen.

Mrs Coggs' back door opened directly into the kitchen, and I hustled the three children inside. At their mother's pressing invitation I went in too.

I have visited the house on several occasions, and always left it with relief, and yet a feeling of hopelessness. It must be the slummiest place in Fairacre, and the smell of unwashed clothes and dirty dishes can be appalling.

I cannot pretend that it was a vision of order and delight on the present occasion, but there was certainly an improvement. For one thing, there was no overpowering stench. There were only a couple of used saucepans on the draining board, and they had been filled with water and were soaking.

Most of the shabby chairs had newspapers or drying clothes spread on them, but the table was clear and even had a cloth on it. Mrs Coggs herself seemed considerably cleaner and happier. No doubt the last few weeks of sunshine had added a tan to her usually pale face, and improved her appearance, but to my mind she looked stronger altogether. Arthur's absence in prison had certainly improved his wife's health,

and I suspected that kind Alice Willet's and Bella George's assistance had helped the family enormously.

At the thought of Bella George, I recalled Mr Willet's advice. Now that I was so close, I would call at once, I decided.

I said my farewells to the Coggs, and hurried to see Bella.

I found the lady in her kitchen busy rolling out pastry. She looked as cheerful as ever and invited me to sit down, as she washed her floury hands.

'No, I'll call another time,' I said. 'You are too busy now.'

But I was overborne.

'Pastry does better for standing a while,' said Bella. 'Can I help?'

'I do hope so,' I said sincerely, and told her of my difficulties.

She looked thoughtful, and my hopes rose.

'Well, I don't see why not,' she said at last. 'Jack's on this new shift for six weeks, which means he leaves here at two in the afternoon and sometimes doesn't get home at night. There's a couple of runs a week to East Anglia and he stays overnight there. I could do what Minnie's doing now easily, but I wouldn't want to face the early morning cleaning.'

I hastily explained that that could be left until the permanent cleaner was appointed.

I told her about wages and invited her to call in the next day or so to have a look at the work involved. If she kept Fairacre School even half as clean as her own immaculate establishment we should be jolly lucky, I thought.

'Any chance of Mrs Pringle coming back?' she asked, as we stood looking at the rain.

'Not yet, I think. She knows the job is hers if she wants it, but I think we shall have to rely on kind folk like you in the meantime.'

'She did say to me,' said Bella diffidently, 'as though she wasn't going back to the job at all.'

'Oh, did she?'

In that case, I thought, I should have to think again about a permanency. Maybe it was just the lady's way of rubbing salt into my wounds. Time alone would tell.

I ran through the rain to my car, and left Bella to cope with her pie-making.

As the car swished through the puddles, I felt a surge of relief at the thought of Bella taking over from dear demented Minnie.

I must break the news to her now, I decided, and then have a much-needed cup of tea. That is, if Minnie had left me a tea pot intact.

I put my foot down, and splashed home.

There was a thick white mist over the countryside the next day, but by noon it had cleared, and the sun shone again.

It was a blissful Saturday, and I was at leisure to enjoy the refreshed garden. The lawn, recently so drab, had turned green overnight. Raindrops still sparkled on the roses, and the soil steamed gently.

My water butts were brimming over, and I should have pleasure in telling Mr Willet that they were as watertight as ever when he came on Monday morning.

Minnie Pringle had accepted her wages and her notice with cheerful inconsequence, and was far more moved by my parting present of a jar of instant coffee. Amazingly, nothing had been damaged during my brief absence, and she had even spread out the teacloth to dry.

I had said goodbye to her with infinite relief, and watched her pushing the broken-down pram through the puddles in the lane, until the bend of the road hid her from sight, and I had returned indoors.

Over my supper of scrambled eggs I had pored over the

television programmes for the evening. I was offered a nice half-hour or so of open heart surgery, in glorious technicolour, no doubt, an interview with survivors from a pit disaster, a discussion by drug addicts about their problems, or another on the subject of abortions.

'Well, Tibby,' I had said, putting aside the paper, 'I think we'll play that old record of Jack Buchanan's, and get on with the P. G. Wodehouse book from the library.'

All in all, we had a splendid evening.

Miriam Quinn called one evening after school to borrow a book of knitting patterns which I had offered to lend her.

It was an ancient book of children's garments, and its value to me was that each and every pattern was absolutely simple and turned out exactly the right size – a rare virtue in patterns.

'I thought I'd start now and knit Lovell's three a good thick woolly apiece for next Christmas. You can do with all the woollies available in that Norfolk vicarage,' said Miriam.

She often spoke of Lovell, her brother, who had a living not far from Norwich. The two were very devoted, and she was an attentive and loving aunt to his three children.

While I was pointing out one or two of the patterns which I had often used and found most effective, Amy's car drew up, and she and Gerard Baker came in.

Miriam had met Amy before, and I was about to introduce Gerard when I became conscious that they were eyeing each other with somewhat perplexed interest.

'I think we know each other,' said Gerard. 'Surely I know your brother Lovell?'

'Cambridge?' hazarded Miriam.

'Yes indeed, but I have come across him several times since then. A cousin of mine lives in his parish.'

I felt it called for a celebratory drink and went to fetch the sherry while they investigated farther.

They were hard at it, recalling old memories, when I returned to the sitting room.

'I saw you first at a May Ball,' said Gerard. 'You wore a cream-coloured frock and had a camellia in your hair.'

'Good heavens!' cried Miriam. 'What an incredible memory you must have! I must confess I don't remember that occasion half as well as you do.'

'You were rather engrossed,' commented Gerard, 'with a young fellow called Martin Farrar, if I remember rightly.'

To my surprise, Miriam turned pink. I had never before seen her confused.

'Miriam is busy planning her Christmas presents already,' I said hastily, and passed the knitting book to Amy.

Outside, a blackbird scolded from a lilac bush. Tibby, no doubt, was being provocative. A light warm breeze ruffled the curtains, the air fragrant with all the scents of summer.

'Do children still wear knitted leggings?' asked Amy, studying a photograph in my ancient book. 'Or "winter bodices", as it says here?'

'Well, not in this weather,' said Gerard. 'Have you ever known a summer like it? Why, it must be warm even in Norfolk! If it stays like this we should get the outside shots of Aloysius's cottage done in two days. We start on Thursday, incidentally.'

'Come and have supper with us on Wednesday,' said Amy, 'and I hope you will come too,' she added, turning to Miriam.

'I should love to. Thank you very much.'

'Let's take our drinks into the garden,' I suggested. 'It's too good an evening to stay indoors.'

Amy drew me aside as Gerard and Miriam went to inspect my rose bed.

'Gerard seems remarkably animated and attentive,' she said,

somewhat severely. 'I had planned to let him partner you on Wednesday, but I must see if Horace is free.'

'Oh, Amy,' I cried impatiently, 'what does it matter? It's good to see them getting on so well, and being an extra woman won't worry me, I assure you.'

'I like the table *symmetrical*,' said Amy, 'but there it is. At least, James will be with us. He tries to be home these days, particularly when I'm entertaining.'

'Good,' I said. 'I could stay away, you know,' I offered nobly, 'if you really will worry about the table plan.'

'Rubbish!' said Amy. 'Of course you must come. No doubt Gerard will be himself again by then.'

There seemed little to comment upon after this remark, and after a few turns about the garden, Amy and Gerard made their farewells.

'Well,' exclaimed Miriam, when they had gone, 'what an extraordinary encounter! You know, I do remember him now. He was terribly kind to me on that occasion. I was horribly shy, and he took the trouble to look after me beautifully in the early part of the evening. Later, Martin turned up, and I fear I paid all my attention to him for the rest of the ball. Unforgivable really.'

She looked unhappily contrite.

'All young people are a bit heartless,' I comforted her. 'Here, don't forget the knitting book. You quite inspire me to start knitting for Christmas myself.'

I awoke suddenly that night to a windowful of stars. Their brilliance was unbelievable, as bright as in a clear October sky.

There was no moon to be seen, but for the first time in my life I saw the room lit with a soft light from the stars, and recalled the old skipping rhyme which the children still use:

Moonlight, starlight,
Boney won't come out tonight.

I wonder if they know who Boney was, I thought. Tomorrow I must remember to tell them.

I climbed out of bed to survey the shadowy garden. Everything was hushed, not even a hedgehog stirred, and every leaf was motionless. I stood enchanted for several minutes, thanking the stars above me for the delight of living in Fairacre, until my feet grew chilly, I reminded myself that I must get up in time for school, and so returned to bed, and an untroubled sleep.

As is so often the case, I arrived first at Amy's, but did my best not to sniff the air like the Bisto Kid Amy said I resembled.

'I'm so glad I've got you to myself for a minute or two,' she greeted me. 'The most incredible news! I rang Horace after

visiting you, and do you know what?'

'He's ill?'

'No, no! He sounded horribly robust.'

'Got a post abroad?'

'No again! Just let me tell you instead of making these wild guesses. I really am terribly upset, and on your account, I may say.'

I stayed obediently silent.

'D'you remember that secretary person, Eve Masters? He took her to that Save The Children do, I remember you telling me?'

'Of course I do.'

'Well, they are *engaged*!'

Amy suddenly became solicitous.

'Would you like to sit down? It must be a shock.'

'Not to me it isn't, Amy. But I expect it is to you. What about your table arrangements?'

'Don't give it another thought. And really you are so brave. I'm devastated. I mean, I always hoped that you and he –'

'I didn't,' I said, 'and frankly I'm delighted to hear the news. I take it they are already booked for this evening?'

'Her parents are coming down to meet him properly, and they've booked a table at The Green Man in Caxley. I only hope they don't choose duck. My helping was unalloyed rubber last time James took me there.'

She gave me a quick kiss.

'Sure you are all right? You look wonderfully calm. I would have been piping my eye in the circumstances.'

'You are not as flinty-hearted as I am, Amy,' I told her, as her other guests came to the door. 'Inveterate match-makers are bound to get their fingers burnt,' I added primly as she went to open the door, and then had a fit of laughter as the appalling pun hit me.

'My mother,' said Amy, 'would have said you've been sleeping in the knife drawer! Too sharp by half!'

Still chuckling, she opened the door to admit the rest of her party.

15 Summer's Bounty

THE golden weather continued. For week after week the sun had gilded all with glory, and it came as quite a shock to realise that July was upon us, and still the sun shone. Soon it would be end of term, with all that that involved for a schoolmistress, and soon our Miss Briggs would be married to Wayne, and I must look out my maps to find the best route for my ageing car to take to Leamington Spa for the happy occasion.

Already some of the cornfields looked ready for cutting, and scabious and knapweed were taking the place of the Queen Anne's lace, or cow parsley, which had frothed along the road verges. The heavy storm recently seemed to have accelerated the progress of natural growth, and I grieved to see a few early asters and dahlias in bud in some of the cottage gardens. I had no desire to end this blissful summer with an early autumn.

The children had never looked so bonny, tanned as they were with constant sunshine. This should set them up properly for next winter, I told myself. Colds and coughs should be cut to a minimum with all this intake of Vitamin D, or whatever it was, with which sunlight was stuffed. I too felt on top of the world, and relished wearing light clothing and shoes for such a length of time. Usually, one's cotton frocks see the light for a few days and are then returned to the cupboard, while warmer garments are thankfully donned again. This summer all was changed, and I almost believed Mr Willet when he told me that the summers of his boyhood were ever thus.

The first brood of swallows were already accomplished fliers, and now the parents were busy building a second nest. For some reason, the first one in the front porch was deemed unsuitable, and there was much chattering and twittering as they inspected other sites.

To my dismay, they chose to build their second nest on a horizontal bundle of draining rods, which were lodged on brackets near the roof in the back porch.

'Knock it down,' advised Mr Willet. 'You get your drains blocked, and you'll be scuppered. Shall I bash it down for you?'

'No, please! Not after all their hard work. We can't do that.'

'I could,' said Mr Willet sturdily. 'You're too soft by half. I suppose if you gets trouble with your dratted drains, I'll be the fool that pushes my rods up here on my bike to see to 'em.'

'It may not happen.'

'It'd better not! Well, if that's how you want it, let's leave the little perishers. And if I gets a hernia I hopes as how you'll visit me in hospital.'

But he smiled as he said it.

Within a day or two of Amy's party a van and a car duly arrived outside Tyler's Row.

Four men, and a great quantity of paraphernalia were unloaded, including miles and miles of cable, and a number of interesting lights on stands.

The inhabitants of Fairacre tended to pause by the gateway of the Hales' place, as they went ostensibly about their business of shopping, posting letters, or simply taking their daily constitutionals.

Speculation ran rife about the true nature of their activities.

'Mr Hale ain't having 'em anywhere indoors,' said Mr Willet. 'And I don't blame him. They look a proper lot of down and outs. Not a tie between 'em!'

'They do say they might need extras. Wouldn't it be lovely to be on the telly?' said his wife.

'Mr Hale wouldn't let them cut off a branch of his apple tree what was in the way of the cameras. He can be awkward, you know. Him being a schoolmaster, I suppose. Does seem to spoil your nature,' went on Mr Willet.

'Thanks,' I said.

Mr Willet appeared unmoved by my sarcasm.

'That chap Baker what takes an interest in Loyshus, he's about.'

'I know,' I said.

'Is he hanging his hat up to Miss Quinn, would you know?'

'Not that I know of,' I said frostily, inwardly marvelling, yet again, at the village's uncanny interest in other people's private lives.

'Well, I only asks because he's been at Holly Lodge once or twice.'

'He and Miss Quinn knew each other years ago,' I admitted. 'He was at college with her brother.'

I always work on the principle that it is as well to let others know a limited amount. It keeps their minds occupied with the little that one is prepared to be known publicly. With any luck – a forlorn hope usually – the nub of the matter will remain hidden.

I pondered on this little snippet of information as I sat in the garden that evening. Mr Lamb, of the Post Office, had brought me a basket large enough to have been a baker's, and filled to the brim with gooseberries.

I set about topping and tailing them with my best nail scissors. They seemed to be the only sharp pair in the house.

It was very pleasant sitting there, with Tibby rolling about at my feet. A starling had taken up a most peculiar position at the far end of the lawn, either sunning itself, with wings

outstretched, or engaged in that odd activity called 'anting'. I was too ignorant to know exactly.

There was a distant crackling from the vicar's bonfire next door, where he was busy burning hedge cuttings. Occasionally, a wisp of blue smoke drifted across my garden towards Mr Roberts' corn. I knew the vicar himself would be in charge of this operation. He has a horror of setting fire to things, and with everything tinder-dry it would have been easy to set alight not only the corn, but the brittle hedges and trees, and even a neighbour's thatch. We have seen these tragedies in Fairacre when other people, not as careful as Mr Partridge and Mr Roberts, have burnt their stubble when the wind has been high.

How on earth, I wondered, was I going to store all these gooseberries? I supposed that I could make some jam and jelly. Gooseberry jelly is delicious with cold meats of every sort. But there is a limit to the amount of such preserves that a lone spinster can get through.

I decided to bottle some and to freeze some, but there would still be a vast quantity left. Mrs Coggs sprang to mind. She should be presented with jam and some of the bottles. Homemade gooseberry jam should go down well with all those hungry mouths to feed, and if the fruit were bottled in a good syrup then Mrs Coggs' desserts would need the minimum of cooking attention. The only difficulty would be smuggling it to Mrs Coggs without Mr Lamb knowing.

Thus settled, I turned my mind again to Mr Willet's speculation. Would Miriam ever consider giving up her happy solitude at Holly Lodge? Certainly, she seemed very animated in Gerard's company, and Amy herself had remarked on her vivacity and Gerard's attentiveness. Mind you, I reminded myself, Amy was no fair judge of the situation, biased as she was towards my own single state which she was constantly hoping to rectify. The behaviour of poor Horace Umbleditch,

who had rushed into an engagement with the school secretary, had much offended Amy, who had ear-marked him for me.

As I had pointed out gently, Horace was now approaching forty, and presumably knew what he was doing. Personally, I wished him well, and the little I had seen of Eve Masters pleased me. They should make a success of marriage.

Somehow I could not imagine Miriam taking Gerard seriously. She seemed dedicated to her career, worked harder than anyone else I knew, and relished her little abode behind the holly hedge. Irene and David Mawne were ideal landlords, ready to help if need be, but respecting Miriam's strong desire for privacy.

No, on the whole, I decided, as I snipped the last top and tail and shook the fruit level in the basket, Miriam would remain as she was. She liked her own company as dearly as I did.

I staggered into the house and put the basket on the cool bricks of the larder floor. Tomorrow would be time enough to tackle them.

There was a knock at the back door. There, on the doorstep, stood Mrs Pringle. She was carrying a basket in each hand.

They contained gooseberries.

'Come in, come in,' I invited, trying to look enthusiastic about the gifts she was bearing.

The lady smiled graciously and stepped in, putting the baskets on the kitchen table. I must be careful, I thought, not to open the larder door in her presence.

'I knows you likes a few gooseberries,' said Mrs Pringle. 'And it seems to have been a bumper crop this year.'

'It does indeed,' I agreed. 'Now come and sit down, to rest your leg, and tell me how things are going.'

Mrs Pringle seemed in a remarkably amiable mood, and I wondered if, by any chance, she had made up her mind to return.

Much as I wanted it, I refused to ask her outright. Let her make the running, I thought.

We spoke of things in general, skirting the main topic which was in our minds. That dear old standby, the weather, occupied our polite exchanges for a few minutes, while I was conscious of Mrs Pringle's beady gaze upon the furniture which was normally in her care, and which, I guessed, she hoped to see in an advanced state of dilapidation.

'And how are things at your end of the village?' I enquired.

'Well, now, I expect you know as much as I do, but let's see. Mr Mawne seems to be more settled now his wife's back. To my mind, he's a man who needs a woman to keep him company, but then what man don't?'

I took this to be a rhetorical question, and refrained from comment.

'Same as that Wayne,' went on Mrs Pringle, leaping from her end of the village to mine. 'He's proper soppy about his Miss Briggs. It's *love*, you see. Makes the world go round, as they say.'

A look of maudlin sympathy appeared on Mrs Pringle's face. I was too taken aback by this rare display of tenderness to respond.

'I take it you'll be going to the wedding?'

'Yes, I am,' I managed to reply.

'I loves a wedding myself. No matter if it's doomed from the start, I still enjoy it, though I don't hold with these pregnant girls wearing white. Minnie did, you know. I told her it was a scandal, but she would have it so.'

'How is Mrs Coggs?' I asked, anxious to steer the subject to safer ground.

'Doing nicely without Arthur. Though she's been to see him, of course.'

This was news to me.

'Yes, Mr Partridge has been up there twice, and taken her

with him. She don't say much about how Arthur is, but after all, she must feel sorry for him, and she must love him to stick by him all these years.'

Privately, I thought that poor Mrs Coggs had little alternative but to stay with her unsatisfactory husband with the tribe of children she had depending on her, but such astringent comment would have passed over Mrs Pringle's head in her present romantic mood.

And how typical of our good-hearted vicar to visit one of his most notorious back-sliders in prison! He put us to shame with his practical Christianity.

'I see that nice Mr Baker is helping the telly men,' went on Mrs Pringle. Ah, I thought! Are we now approaching the heart of the matter? Will Miriam Quinn's name crop up?

It did.

'I do hear as how he used to know Miss Quinn years ago.'

'That's right,' I agreed.

'Well, they seem to enjoy each other's company. My cousin in Caxley saw them in The Green Man one evening.'

'Really?' I said coldly.

'My cousin is barmaid there, and having a terrible time trying to slim. She's a convulsive eater, the doctor says, and with all them peanuts and crisps laying about it's a rare temptation.'

Was Mrs Pringle skating away from thin ice, I wondered? She was getting no more information from me, I vowed secretly.

'Well, there it is,' said the lady, rising majestically. 'It's the same for high and low, isn't it? Mrs Coggs, Mr Mawne, Miss Briggs and Miss Quinn, all Touched by Love, as you might say.'

I followed her into the kitchen. There was no trace of a limp, I noticed.

'Let me empty your baskets,' I said, lifting out the bowl from the sink to take her largesse.

I accompanied her across the playground to the school gate. She glanced across at the school porch.

'I take it Bella is still doing her best?'

'Yes indeed. She's doing a splendid job.'

A slightly malevolent expression crept over my old adversary's face. It gave me a feeling of relief. This was the Mrs Pringle I knew!

I walked a few yards down the lane with her. The sun still shone, and there was dust at the side of the road. Pink and white striped bindweed crept along the dusty verge, as pretty as marshmallows.

'Well, thank you again,' I said warmly. 'I shall enjoy those lovely gooseberries.'

Should I ask her outright if she proposed to return? It was on the tip of my tongue to do so, but something held me back.

Pride perhaps? Or the remembrance of that wise old adage: 'Least said, soonest mended'?

We said goodbye, and each went on her way.

While I was marking the register the next morning, there came a knock at the door, and a young man put his head round.

'I wondered if we could take a shot or two of the outside of your building?'

He had a winning manner and seemed clean enough, although Mr Willet was quite right about his lack of a tie.

Memories of the tale of the person whose carpets had suffered from five hours of programme-making assailed me.

'When do you want to come?'

'Say three o'clock?'

'That would be convenient.'

He came farther into the room. The children stood up politely, and I nodded to them.

'Good morning, sir,' they chorused.

'Oh, ah! Good morning to you too.'

He seemed somewhat startled by this everyday civility. Perhaps he was not used to being called 'Sir'. Probably just Nigel or Basil, I imagined.

'This might make rather an interesting sequence,' he said, gazing round appreciatively. 'I believe Aloysius sat at one of these desks.'

'Hardly,' I said. 'They were new in the fifties.'

'I suppose we could make a mock-up of an earlier desk,' he went on dreamily.

'I'm afraid it would be most inconvenient for you to film in here,' I said firmly. 'And anyway, I'm sure my governors would not want the children's work to be interrupted.'

'I could have a word with them,' he offered.

'I wouldn't dream of troubling you. By all means film

outside, but this interior is so much altered since Aloysius's
time –'

I broke off.

'By the way,' I added. 'What was Aloysius's surname? I've
never heard him called anything but Loyshus in Fairacre.'

He began to laugh. He was quite a nice young man, I
thought, even if he did not wear a tie.

'Lloyd! Loyshus Lloyd! How's that?'

'First-class,' I said, as he waved goodbye.

The children, of course, were wildly excited at the thought of
'being on the telly', although I did my best to explain that their
presence would be unwelcome.

'Your clothes would be all wrong, for one thing,' I pointed
out.

'We could dress up.'

'We've got them things –'

' "Those things".'

'That's right. Them things as we had for that show we done
when us was a hundred.'

I gave up trying to correct this last sentence, forbade further
discussion, and threatened them with no-story-this-afternoon
if they continued to waste time.

The day wore on. The sun blazed away, and obviously the
school would look splendid in this wonderful light when the
cameras began to turn.

Three o'clock came and went. Apart from some chirruping
from a few sparrows, and a ring dove rippling throatily from
the school roof, all was quiet as the grave.

Nothing happened throughout the reading of *Treasure
Island*, although I sensed that the children were alert for
the sound of approaching vehicles.

At a quarter to four we said grace, wished each other 'Good
afternoon', and I accompanied my flock to the school gate.

'And don't loiter,' I adjured them. 'Go straight home. I expect the filming will happen tomorrow.'

They went off reluctantly. They were bitterly disappointed, poor things.

At a quarter past six, four young men arrived, including Nigel – or possibly, Basil – and they began to wander about the playground, discussing the best vantage points.

I carried out a pot of tea, four mugs, milk, sugar and biscuits and left them to it.

I must say they were extremely grateful for their sustenance, and all the biscuits had been eaten when I went to fetch the tray an hour later.

I spent the evening making jam and bottling the first lot of gooseberries. Whilst waiting for the bottles to get done, I began to tackle Mrs Pringle's offering with my hard-pressed nail scissors.

It was while I was so engaged that Amy arrived.

'Heavens, I'm so glad to see you!' I cried. 'I'm awash with gooseberries.'

I ushered her into the kitchen. Eight pots of ruby red jam gleamed from the draining board. A rich fruity smell emanated from the oven.

'Lucky you!' said Amy. 'It smells marvellous in here.'

She gazed with wonder at the bowl awaiting my nail scissors' attention.

'Do you want some?' I asked. 'Please say you do. I'm getting to loathe the sight of a goosegog.'

'Can you really spare a few? I adore them. I like all the nice cheap fruits like rhubarb and gooseberries that other people look down on. I think they are blissful.'

I began to tip a few pounds of Mrs Pringle's gooseberries into a bag, expressing my pleasure and relief at the same time.

'Seen anything of Gerard?' asked Amy when at last we were resting in the sitting room.

'No. Well, I can't say I expected to. He's probably busy.'

'He's not too busy to visit Fairacre daily,' said Amy, somewhat severely. 'It's my belief he calls to see Miriam each evening. He only seems to use our house to sleep in.'

'He probably doesn't want to take up your time,' I said.

Amy blew three perfect smoke rings, one of her many accomplishments.

'That's as maybe,' she said eventually. 'Personally, I think that Miriam is a charming girl, and far too good for Gerard. You would have been much more suitable.'

'How do I take that?'

'You know what I mean. You have quite a lot in common with dear Gerard. Now Miriam would find a lot of things about him which she would want altered. I know James had some tiresome ways when I first knew him.'

'And is he now a reformed character?'

'I hope not. Despite the few tiresome ways just mentioned, I liked him as he was. And still do.'

'That's good. I think James is a dear. I should have snapped him up myself, if you hadn't got in first.'

Amy looked gratified.

'Yes, I'm glad I did get in first, taking it all in all. You know, it amazes me how many women think that if they marry a man they will be able to mould him to their own requirements.'

'Do they think that?'

'Indeed they do! The times I've heard a girl say: "He'll be different when he's married"! It's not only colossal cheek, I think, but such a ghastly waste of time. After all, if you don't like a man as he is, then why marry him?'

A sizzling sound from the kitchen ended our conversation. I was about to tell Amy of Mrs Pringle's sudden absorption in love, but bottled gooseberries came first.

I saw her to the car, and helped to prop the bag of gooseberries safely.

'A thousand thanks for them, my sweet,' she said, as she let in the clutch.

I returned to my fragrant kitchen. There were still gooseberries waiting in a bowl to be topped and tailed. Six bottles were now standing beside the jam jars.

The telephone rang. Mrs Mawne was at the other end. Could I do with some gooseberries? They had a bumper crop this year.

I expressed my gratitude, but explained that I really had rather more than I could cope with at the moment.

In more ways than one, I thought, when I replaced the receiver, what with end of term, Miss Briggs' wedding, Mrs Pringle's continued absence from duty, television crews and tales of Gerard into the bargain.

Too tired to cook a proper supper, I spread a hunk of bread with still-warm gooseberry jam, and washed it down with a glass of milk.

I must say, it was jolly good.

16 Sunshine and Sports

DURING the last week of term I drove to Beech Green to have tea with Miss Clare.

Despite the brilliant light and scorching heat outside, the interior of the little cottage, which would one day be my own – to my everlasting amazement – was dim and cool. Thatch is a wonderful insulator, and despite its drawbacks of attracting birds to nest in it and needing a good deal of skilled maintenance, it is good to see this natural roofing blending so beautifully into the countryside.

Her garden was as trim as ever. The borders on each side of the brick path were bright with pansies, pinks and early asters.

The vegetable plot was a miracle of tidiness. Miss Clare was now past gardening herself, but a young neighbour with a growing family was glad to have the garden, and kept Miss Clare supplied in return for her generosity. Thus everyone was pleased.

'He's almost as good as Mr Willet,' I said, surveying the rows of shallots ready for lifting, the swelling bronze onions, the peas thick on the sticks. The tops of the pea sticks, I noticed, were all cut neatly to the same level. It all looked most efficient.

'He was always a tidy boy,' said Dolly Clare indulgently, when I commented on his handiwork. 'He was at Fairacre just before your time. Very neat with his hands, and could use a ruler even as an infant.'

I rubbed a leaf of sun-warmed mint between my fingers, and inhaled the sharp scent.

'The only trouble is we are short of parsley,' went on Dolly. 'But you know what they say. It goes seven times to the devil before it germinates. I'm afraid ours never came back at all this year.'

I promised to bring her a root of mine, and we went indoors to put on the kettle.

The round table in the window had already been set. The best china, sprigged with violets, the silver teaspoons, thin with age, and bread and butter cut wafer-thin awaited us, with a splendid sponge cake of Miss Clare's own making.

One always sat up to table at Dolly's house. Only the odd cup of coffee was partaken of in an armchair, and even when she was alone the mistress of the house set the solitary place and dined, as if she had friends present, with simple dignity.

I spread some of our vicar's honey on my bread and butter,

and thought how marvellous it was that Dolly Clare, despite her age and physical frailty, had never lowered her standards. My own casual meal arrangements seemed positively slatternly in comparison.

I said as much to Dolly. She looked somewhat surprised.

'I suppose early training has something to do with it,' she said. 'My mother was a stickler for having things just so. And then, when you are as old as I am, you wonder if you might be taken suddenly, and it would be so dreadful if you were found in squalor, wouldn't it?'

'I hadn't thought of that.'

'You see, I now look upon each day as a bonus. When I wake in the morning I think how lucky I am to have yet another day to spend.'

'Even if your arthritis is painful?'

'Even then.' Dolly laughed. 'After all, some part of one's body must play up when one is over eighty. I'm luckier than some, and I still love living.'

When we had washed up, we took a turn along the field track which borders Hundred Acre Field behind Dolly's house.

The blackberry flowers were thick in the hedges, and great creamy plates of elderflowers still nodded on the northern side of the hedge.

'I tie a head in a muslin bag,' said Dolly, 'and steep it in my gooseberry jelly. It gives the most marvellous tang to it.'

I told her about my gooseberries, and my own less elegant means of coping with them.

'And look at my hands,' I said, holding out my stained fingers.

Dolly held out her own fragile hands, and I was surprised to see that they were even more stained than my own.

'Broad beans, and then blackcurrants,' she said, surveying them calmly. 'I know one should wear gloves, but the feel of

fresh young things is so pleasant that I would sooner have stained fingers. It's a small price to pay for pleasure.'

I drove home feeling all the better for an hour or two of Dolly's company. In a feverish world she is like a cool drink.

The birds were still foraging although dusk was beginning to fall, and I narrowly missed a cock pheasant, gleaming bronze in the westering sunlight, as he strolled haughtily across the lane.

The sheep had been sheared recently and they looked almost like white goats moving leisurely across the meadows. All creatures, it seemed, were flourishing in this glorious summer, and I felt lucky to count myself among them.

It had not dawned on me, until I had the wretched things, how remarkably elusive a pair of spectacles can be. If I am at school the children help me to locate them with an eager chorus of:

'On the piano, miss!'

'On the window sill, miss!'

'You're still wearing 'em, miss!' This last, of course, accompanied by much hilarity.

But in the house, it is not so easy. If I am downstairs I have left the things upstairs, and vice versa. I reckon that I take far more exercise these days simply tracking down my glasses.

Gradually, I am learning to look first by the telephone, where I need them for studying the small print of the book, then by my fireside book shelf, and thirdly by any newspaper lying about.

What happens when advancing age compels me to have two pairs, one for reading and one for long distance, is too horrific to contemplate, and bifocals, so Mrs Pringle told me once, send one headlong down any flight of stairs.

I think I shall have to get a fetching chain affair to lash them to my person, like the spectacled half of Hinge and Bracket.

The television crew remained in the village for three days, and were soon accepted as a welcome addition to Fairacre's amenities.

Peter Hale, who had evidently been very much on his guard when first approached, now seemed quite sorry that the excitement was over, and that the van and car had gone for good.

I met him on one of my evening strolls.

'D'you know, I was at school with the father of one of those chaps? The oldest one incidentally. Makes you realise your age.'

'I'm constantly meeting old pupils in Caxley,' I told him, 'and I am not only incapable of remembering their names, but also if they left three or thirteen years ago.'

'Well, that's some comfort. It was quite interesting to watch them at work. One wonders, of course, if it really takes half a day to take a few shots, and I'm jolly glad they decided against coming indoors.'

I told him that I too had banned interior filming.

'They are making a set, I gather, of a Victorian schoolroom, all hanging oil lamps and slates, and the cane well in evidence.'

'When is it going to be shown?'

'Sometime next month. They said they would let me know. I'll give you a ring as soon as I know anything.'

'Many thanks. I'm looking forward to seeing Aloysius Lloyd.'

'Was that his surname? First I knew of it! By the way, are you all right for gooseberries?'

I assured him that I was, and added: 'It seems to have been a bumper crop this year.'

After all, if I had not said it, then he would have done.

The highlight of the summer term at Fairacre School is our Sports Day. Mr Roberts, the farmer, lets us have one of his meadows for the occasion, and obligingly turns out sheep or cattle, a day or two beforehand, so that Mr Willet can rope off the course from the spectators.

It is also Mr Willet's unenviable task to clear the course of the more obvious of the cow pats, and to flatten any molehills. In this job he has the enthusiastic support of three or four of the bigger boys. I have no difficulty in maintaining order in the classroom as Sports Day approaches. The hope of being chosen as one of Mr Willet's course-clearing team makes for a very well-behaved class.

Normally, we study the barometer and listen anxiously to the weather men as Sports Day approaches. The final word, of course, is Mr Willet's, who knows all the local signs of a change. But this year, with weeks of 'Set Fair' and even 'Very Dry' on our barometers we hardly bothered to consult even Mr Willet.

'Might get a bit of wet in a day or two,' he volunteered on the morning of the day, 'but it should hold up for this afternoon.'

'It all looks splendid,' I told him, surveying the course before school began. The grass was still dewy, the sky cloudless. The meadow had been cut for hay a few weeks earlier, and presented a trim face to the world.

'Had a mort of trouble knocking in them posts though,' observed Mr Willet. 'Never known the ground so hard. Better tell the kids to pick their feet up or we'll have some good ol' banged knees.'

Excitement ran high during the morning, and it seemed prudent to let off some of their suppressed steam with number games, and oral work rather than risk bodged pages of written exercises. As always, on these occasions, the girls were much calmer than the boys. The latter seem to have a much stronger

competitive spirit which shows itself in tiresome boasting about their physical prowess.

'Look at my muscles then!' bragged Eric, flexing his arm to his neighbour.

'No bigger'n a sparrow's kneecap,' responded Ernest.

During playtime there was a good deal of sprinting from one end of the playground to the other, and some perilous jumping over skipping ropes obligingly held by the girls. I turned a blind eye to these activities, only warning the infants of tender years, to keep out of the way.

Miss Briggs had thrown herself whole-heartedly into preparations for the day, and had organised most of the timetable, including a mothers' race and a hideously difficult obstacle race for any fathers who were courageous enough to attempt it. As well as a pegged-down tarpaulin, kindly loaned by Mr Roberts, under which one had to wriggle, there were the usual hoops to negotiate, ropes to leap, and a stretch of grass to be covered by means of stepping on flower pots manhandled in a bent-double position. The children were tackling the course themselves, but at half the size and twice as agile they certainly had the edge on their fathers.

Several parents had been coerced into being judges, and keeping the scores of each child. I had been responsible for buying innumerable bars of chocolate, and making badges from cardboard embellished with gold stars. It made a change from making gooseberry jam on recent evenings.

The dinner lady brought us sliced cold ham, jacket potatoes and some salad, for our first course, and a sloshy dish, which she told us was trifle, for dessert. Her offerings were greeted with general approval.

'That's just right for today,' Patrick said graciously. 'Us don't want no stodge and that. Slows you down, stodge does.'

One or two hardy boys professed to despise food altogether

just before racing, but I noticed that they ate as heartily as the rest when it was time to serve out.

At two o'clock we were all out in the sunshine. Chairs had been arranged for the elderly on one side of the course, but most of the mothers, and a sprinkling of fathers who were not at work, sprawled on the grass looking after the many toddlers.

Miss Briggs and I had decided that the first few races should be the straightforward hundred yards (we don't bother with metres at Fairacre) for boys and girls, divided into three age groups. Then came the girls' skipping races, and after that the infants had their turns.

Apart from one of the infants running the wrong way, and Patrick taking a tumble over a tough tussock of grass, and wrenching his ankle, all went beautifully.

Linda Moffat's mother, in charge of the score sheet, was kept busy with a stream of breathless children arriving at her table clutching red, blue or yellow cards for first, second and third places. I had the fairly easy job of being judge for first place in each race, and two brave mothers coped with being judges of second and third positions.

The obstacle race proved to be the most exciting, and the frenzied shouts of the children spurring on the contestants were deafening. Even the cows in the next field came to look over the hedge at the goings-on in their former grazing ground.

Mr Lamb's collie dog had escaped from the Post Office garden and romped energetically among spectators and competitors, licking the children's faces as they emerged from under the tarpaulin, and greeting all with great enthusiasm. It would not have done at the Olympic Games but at Fairacre it adds to the enjoyment.

In the midst of this hubbub, I was surprised to see Mrs Pringle sailing majestically across the grass, wearing her best

navy-blue straw hat decorated with a white duck's wing. Obviously, this was an occasion, and I felt very flattered that she had honoured us with the hat, as well as her presence.

She took a seat on the end chair, and raised a hand in greeting to one or two neighbours. Hard on her heels came Mrs Coggs, the ancient pram making heavy weather of the uneven meadowland.

I was particularly glad that she had arrived in time to see Joseph's age group tackling the obstacle race. He gave her a dazzling smile as he lined up, and whether it was his mother's presence, or simply his own skinny agility, which turned the scale in his favour, no one could say, but he won by several yards and the spectators applauded his success.

The mothers' race was a decorous affair, a straight sprint down the hundred yards. The younger ones took off their shoes, but older ones, like Mrs Moffat, who abandoned her duties to me for this race, rattled along creditably in high heels, and she it was who came in second, yielding first place to Patrick's mother.

I went over to talk to Mrs Pringle when Mrs Moffat returned, flushed and triumphant, to her table.

'I'm glad you could come,' I said, taking the next chair.

'Well, it was a nice afternoon,' said she grudgingly. 'And I guessed I could sit down after my walk.'

'You should have entered the last race,' I told her mischievously.

'The mothers' race? I was a mother too long ago for that lark,' she replied, and who was I to gainsay it?

And now the highlight of the afternoon occurred when seven brave fathers toed the line. Privately, I backed a new-comer to the village, one George Fuller, father of a blonde daughter in Miss Briggs' care. He was slim and lively, and looked a certain winner.

Ernest's father, all of fifteen stone, I reckoned to be out of the

race before the whistle blew, and the other five were fairly run-of-the-mill in weight and athleticism.

Mr Fuller justified my hopes by reaching the hoops first and sliding through them at speed. He also leapt the ropes with the aplomb of a hurdler, and was first to emerge from the confines of the tarpaulin. He was greeted rapturously by Mr Lamb's dog, and the cheers of the spectators.

Now came the flower pot problem, and to my dismay it was quite apparent that balancing with one foot on a flower pot whilst transferring the other by hand a yard or so ahead, was a skill which this young father had never attempted. If he fell off, and he did, he was in honour bound to start the flower pot bit again.

It was here that Ernest's father came into his own. His

struggles under the tarpaulin had been heroic, and the spectators were convulsed with laughter, even Mrs Pringle managing a smirk. Only one father was behind him. The rest had progressed to Mr Fuller's stage of the proceedings.

But despite his girth, Ernest's father had the uncanny sense of balance which so often makes large people excellent dancers. He fairly nipped along with his two flower pots, overtaking all the others, and almost colliding with the hapless Mr Fuller who was returning, yet again, to base.

He won by yards, and Ernest rushed to greet him by throwing his arms round his father's impressive waist, and jumping all over the poor man's feet.

He received the loudest clap of all when he came to receive his chocolate bar.

'He deserved that,' said Mrs Pringle.

And we all agreed.

By the time we had returned the chairs to the school, cleared away the remains of the biscuits and lemonade kindly provided by the Parent-Teacher Association, and carried the ropes, hoops, balls and so on to their rightful places, we were all pretty tired. The bigger boys folded Mr Roberts' tarpaulin with much shouting and falling over, but at length it was done, and dragged into the shelter of the school lobby.

'What about them posts?' enquired one.

'Leave them for Mr Willet,' I replied. 'He will see to them tomorrow.'

The parents drifted away, children darting around them, still glorying in their recent triumphs.

Miss Briggs refused a cup of tea in the schoolhouse, saying that she was meeting Wayne to choose the bedroom carpet.

And so I had my own cup with only Tibby for company, and very peaceful it was after the clamour of the afternoon.

Later that night, I was awoken by the pattering of rain. Mr Willet had been right as usual, and we had got through Sports Day by the skin of our teeth.

17 Off to the Wedding

IT was still raining when I dressed the next morning. It was not the violent torrential downpour which the earlier thunderstorm had brought, but a gentle steady pattering on dry earth and thirsty plants.

The air was mild. It was the sort of day the Irish call 'soft', and it described it well. The downs were veiled in mist, and no doubt the valley of the river Cax, not far from Fairacre, would be just as misty.

It seemed strange to see the children arriving in mackintoshes or carrying umbrellas. For weeks the lobby pegs had held only a cardigan or two, or a floppy sun hat. Now raindrops spattered the floor from the dripping mackintoshes and, true to form, the skylight, so recently renovated, let through an occasional spot of rain near my desk top.

This change in the weather seemed to affect the children in a rather peculiar way. I should have thought that cooler conditions would have enlivened them after the oppressive heat, but the reverse happened. Possibly they were physically tired after yesterday's efforts on the sports' field. There was a good deal of yawning, and a number of children complained of feeling cold. Those that had woolly jackets in the lobby were sent to get them, and to warm and wake the rest we did a few brisk exercises. I cannot pretend that these efforts wrought much change, but at least they were galvanised into taking out their arithmetic books and attempting some work in a desultory fashion.

At playtime I compared notes with Miss Briggs as we sipped

our coffee. Her class too was remarkably soporific and three of the infants had actually fallen asleep.

'I think this place is damp,' opined Miss Briggs.

'It's been that way for over a hundred years,' I told her, 'and unless the stoves are alight, or there is a nice long spell of heat, such as we've been enjoying, the school never really dries out.'

'Time we had a new one,' said Miss Briggs. 'Wayne says this one ought to be pulled down. I'm sure he could build a much better one – and with a proper damp course too.'

'I'm sure he could,' I agreed. 'But with the nation's economy as it is, I can't see our local authority giving him the chance.'

As well as finding the cash, there is another difficulty which is ever present in my mind at Fairacre School. Our numbers have been perilously low for years, and I cannot help thinking that, before long, our little school will go the way of so many more in the country.

It has always been a worry to me. I hate to see these rural schools closing, and yet what is the practical decision?

Parents do not want to see their five-year-olds carted off by bus for a long day some distance from home. Those who attended the school in their own youth are often fiercely loyal, and want it to stay open.

On the other hand, when numbers get into the twenties, or even lower, are the children getting the competition and stimulus they need? The battle continues.

For my own part, the obvious difficulty, in my first few years at the school, was the fact that my school house would be taken from me when the whole property was put on the market. I had no doubt that I should be leniently dealt with, and probably would be offered first refusal, but it was a problem nevertheless. Now, thanks to Dolly Clare's over-whelming generosity, I need not fear the future, but not many school teachers, in the same position, have such comfort.

'Ah well!' said Miss Briggs collecting our coffee cups. 'Only one more week, and it's end of term.'

It was a cheerful thought.

One evening, during the last week of term, Bella George came over to my house after finishing her stint in the school.

The air was still cool. The really hot sunshine seemed to have deserted us, but I hoped that it was only for a few days. We sat indoors, and Tibby, unusually demonstrative, climbed on her lap and settled down, purring loudly.

'You're honoured,' I told her.

'Well, I'm not all that fond of cats actually, and I think they know, so they come and try their luck. Contrary animals, aren't they?'

I agreed.

'The thing is,' went on Bella, stroking the cat, 'Jack's shift's changing again next month, and I can't see how I can keep on with the cleaning indefinitely.'

'We've been lucky to have you for so long,' I replied. 'You've been a tower of strength. How long can you stay?'

'Oh, I'll certainly put the place tidy at the end of term, and if need be, I could come in the day before term starts in September, just to see things are all ship-shape, but I can't do more than that. I'm sorry. I've really enjoyed the work.'

'You've saved our bacon, Bella,' I told her. 'We were really in a desperate plight. I can see I shall have to get in touch with Mrs Pringle and let her know how things stand.'

Bella looked embarrassed.

'I don't know if I should say anything, but she still says she's not going to come back at all. Do you think she's just stringing you along?'

'I wouldn't put it past her. The last she told me was that she intended to come back eventually. When, I don't know, which

is why I shall have to advertise the post in order to have someone here regularly for next term.'

'Shall I let her know you are going to do that?'

I thought for a minute. Mrs Pringle had certainly got us over a barrel, and knew it too. On the other hand, I genuinely hoped that she might return. Better the knave you know, than the devil you don't.

'Leave it for the moment,' I said at last. 'I shan't be drafting an advertisement until after we've broken up, and she may have come forward by then. What a problem it is!'

I accompanied Bella to the gate and watched her wobble away down the lane on her bicycle. She had served us nobly in our time of stress. I only hoped that Mrs Pringle would see fit to take up her duties again with the same dedication.

On the last day of term we had a little ceremony to present Miss Briggs with her wedding gifts and to wish her well.

The vicar represented the governors of the school and made a graceful speech, brief and to the point, and the children tried not to fidget as they impatiently awaited the unwrapping of presents.

Miss Briggs, flushed with excitement at being at the centre of the scene, looked almost pretty. She made a grateful speech to the vicar, and then set about undoing the largest parcel which was from the children.

I had shown them the tray secretly beforehand, and received their commendations. It was an oval one, with splendid gilt handles, and a garland of wild flowers painted on it. The children approved my choice, and now we awaited Miss Briggs' reaction.

It was altogether satisfactory. Her delight seemed genuine, and she thanked the children warmly. They sat, beaming and smug, exchanging congratulatory glances. Weren't they clever, they seemed to say?

The governors had given her a pretty little travelling clock which folded into a scarlet case, and I had put my gift of a Coalport flower vase with the other presents to swell the pile.

The girl seemed absolutely delighted with everything, and when the youngest infant staggered from the lobby with a bouquet almost as big as himself, she was speechless with pleasure.

After more congratulations from everyone, the vicar said grace, exhorted the children to behave well during the holidays, to help their mothers, and to remember to come back on the third of September.

He then shook hands with Miss Briggs and with me, and departed. Within five minutes the school room was empty, except for Miss Briggs and myself.

The girl was busy rewrapping her presents, and when she looked up I was surprised to see that she was very near to tears.

'It all went beautifully,' I said. 'You gave the children no end of pleasure with such a nice little speech of thanks.'

'Not as much pleasure as they've given me,' she responded shakily. 'And you too. It's a wonderful school. I've been so lucky.'

She blew her nose energetically, and I bent down tactfully to lock up the cupboards.

'See you at the wedding,' she said, collecting her parcels. 'I'll give you a ring before then.'

She still looked Mr Willet's 'fair old lump of a girl', I thought, watching her make her way to the car, laden with her bounty, but a very nice one at that.

There was a full week before I needed to set off for the wedding, and I employed it by doing some shopping, which included a magnificent hat to wear with my wedding ensemble, and various other less glamorous items such as grease-proof paper, jampot covers, a new milk saucepan and a new doormat.

The swallows had not improved the latter, and as it had given me many years of service I thought it would be prudent to throw it out at last.

I also brought back from Caxley some patterns of curtaining, wondering if I might get round to choosing something suitable to replace the present shabby curtains in the sitting room.

When I worked out how many yards I should need and how much they would cost me, even without paying for the making up, pelmets, fringe, lining, tape and so on, my heart began to sink. Perhaps it would be wiser to wait until I had returned from my holiday?

A cousin of mine, recently widowed, had begged me to accompany her for a week in Guernsey in August, and to this I had agreed. We rarely met, as she had married a farmer in Cumbria and been much engaged in bringing up a family of boys, but she sounded so pathetic on the telephone, when she

broached the possibility of going with her to Guernsey, that I
was glad to be of some use at this sad time.

It was while I was busy leafing through the pattern book and
wondering whether it would be worth cashing some national
savings' certificates to buy the material and to look upon the
transaction as a wise investment, or whether I should shelve
the whole idea for a time, that Miriam Quinn appeared.

'Lovely to see you!' I enthused. 'It seems ages since we met at
Amy's party. What have you been doing?'

Of course, I rather hoped that she would say: 'Seeing
Gerard' but she did not. Miriam is not one for girlish confi-
dences, for which I respect her. Nevertheless, she looked more
animated than usual, and I wondered if I should learn more. Or
were the village rumours unfounded? They so often are.

'Holding the fort at the Caxley office, I'm sorry to say.
Barney had a business tour in the Middle East, all very
high-powered and lucrative, and he left me in charge for three
weeks. I've hardly had time to breathe.'

I knew that Miriam was private secretary to Sir Barnabas
Hatch, the financier, and that he recognised the value of this
imperturbable and competent young woman. I only hoped
that she was suitably rewarded, and I suspect that she was. If
anyone should appreciate a sound investment it was Sir Barna-
bas, and he certainly had a treasure in Miriam.

I showed her the patterns and explained my problem.
Should I or shouldn't I?

'Let's look at the present ones,' said she practically, and we
went to study the sitting room curtains.

'I should let them do another year,' said Miriam. 'There's
nothing wrong with them. Or do you loathe them?'

'Far from it. And I'm only too glad to take your advice. My
mother used to say that Procrastination was my middle name.
But in this case the thought of finding two or three hundred
pounds is more telling.'

'As much as that?'

'More, probably. I was not going to decide anyway until after my trip to Leamington and then Guernsey.'

I told her about my holiday plans, and she said that she was having a fortnight when Barney returned, and proposed to spend it in Norfolk with her brother Lovell and his family.

'And later,' she added, 'I'm having a week or so, probably in the autumn.'

'That will set you up for the winter,' I said.

'I really called,' said Miriam rising, 'to invite you to a small dinner party I'm giving soon. It's on Thursday week. Can you manage it?'

'Dammit, no! I shall be at Leamington then. I'm so sorry. It would have been lovely.'

'Never mind. There'll be lots of other occasions, and I'll think of you enjoying wedding cake and champagne.'

She waved goodbye from the gate, and I returned wondering, yet again, why it is that one can go for weeks without an invitation to something pleasant, and then when one does arrive it is on the same day as an earlier engagement.

Sometimes life seems as contrary as a cat.

When I set off for my few days in Leamington, the sun was reigning once again, and the weathermen, including Mr Willet, forecast a return to halcyon days.

My spirits were high as I trundled towards Oxford. I had double-checked all switches at home, and left Tibby in Mr Willet's care. He had promised to visit the house night and morning and to see that the cat enjoyed his usual expensive meals.

'Not that it'd hurt him to starve for a few days,' he commented. 'If that cat don't die of fatty heart I shall be surprised. Lives like a lord, don't he?'

In the back of the car was a suitcase with my everyday

clothes and toilet things in it. Another one held my wedding garments. A new cream-coloured silk suit was carefully swathed in as much tissue paper as Amy might have used, and my new cream shoes were my pride and joy, surpassed only, in my affections, by the superb large hat smothered in silk tea roses.

Even Amy had been impressed by this confection.

'Why, you ought to be the bride yourself in that gorgeous rig-out,' was her flattering comment, when I displayed my ensemble to her. This was high praise indeed. I am rarely able to impress Amy, least of all with my clothes, and I made the most of it.

'Though when I'm going to get a chance to wear this lot again, I'm blowed if I know,' I told her.

'They'll never date,' said Amy comfortingly. 'Put them aside for other weddings, or even a garden party. You never know – you may need them for your own wedding, but now that Horace Umbleditch has rushed so madly into that quite misguided engagement, I must admit that the outlook seems somewhat bleak.'

'I'll bear up,' I promised.

'Of course, you might meet someone suitable at the wedding,' continued Amy, brightening at the thought. 'An uncle, say –'

'Or a grandfather,' I put in. 'Or some eighty-year-old friend of the family, creaking along on his last legs.'

'Yes indeed,' agreed Amy, ignoring my sarcasm.

Still, I told myself, as I took the northern bypass skirting Oxford, it was good to have such a lovely collection of matching clothes with me, and I resolved to enjoy the occasion thoroughly.

I approached Woodstock on the dreaded A34 road and passed the gates of Blenheim Palace, recalling the action of the Duchess Consuelo, of American birth, who had had the good

sense to put out the uneaten food from the ducal halls in two containers, one savoury, the other sweet, for the poor of the town. For years it had all been thrown in together, I gathered, like so much pig swill.

My way took me east of Stratford-upon-Avon but I noticed a sign to Charlecote Park where it is alleged the young William Shakespeare did some poaching, and then on to Royal Leamington Spa.

It was early afternoon when I arrived at the hotel, not far from All Saints' Church where the ceremony was to take place. It was in a quiet street of elegant Georgian houses, and I was glad to be shown to my room to unpack and refresh myself.

The next day was free. The wedding was to be the following day, and I spent my time exploring the town. It reminded me of Bath with its graceful terraces, and I did a great deal of window shopping in the Parade. I even tried the water in the Royal Pump Room, and decided that I should never become an addict.

The Art Gallery and Museum was a pleasant haven on a hot afternoon, and I admired some modern paintings and some Wedgwood and Worcester pieces of porcelain which I coveted.

Altogether, I decided, I should come again one day. This visit was obviously going to be too short.

Our Miss Briggs was a wonder to behold as she came up the aisle on her father's arm, and I wished Mr Willet could see her now.

The Caxley dressmaker had created a beautiful dress of white silk, with a short train edged with ruched lace. She carried a Victorian posy of white rosebuds and wore a little matching garland on her head. Two young friends acted as bridesmaids, and were dressed in sprigged voile. The whole effect was youthful and unsophisticated.

The Briggs were lucky enough to live in one of the tall
Regency houses. We walked straight through to the marquee
in the garden where the most sumptuous spread was set out.

Wayne, looking handsomer than ever, gave me such an
enthusiastic hug and kiss, that my gorgeous hat was knocked
askew, but it was a small price to pay for such a warm greeting.
In any case, by the time the celebrations ended, I was past
caring whether my hat was on or off, and by the time I was
safely back in my hotel bedroom all I could think of was the
blessed fact that I could sleep as late as I liked, without
interruption from anybody, and that I had another two days to
enjoy the delectable Royal Leamington Spa.

18 Away From it All

THE sun was setting when I returned to Fairacre. I stopped at Mr Willet's to pick up the key and to thank him for feeding Tibby.

'That cat of yourn don't grieve, you know, when you ain't at home, so don't go thinking you're missed at all.'

'I suspected as much.'

'Golloped down best part of a half-pint of milk, and polished off two saucerfuls of grub a day. Just like them cats on the telly. Which reminds me, we're on tomorrow.'

'On what?'

'The telly. Us. Fairacre. Tyler's Row. Loyshus. The lot. About a quarter past six.'

'Marvellous!'

He walked to the car with me. As always his garden was a picture.

'Alice will be sorry to have missed you. She's over at Springbourne, with her cousin Aggie, on some chapel lark.'

'I hope I haven't stopped you from going too?'

'No, no. It's one of these temperance meetings. Aggie's a great one for abstaining. Well, so are we, as you know, but old Ag's a bit fiercer, if you follow me, and she got this chap from the other side of Caxley to cycle out to give a talk on the evils of strong liquor.'

'Well, I hope he gets a drink of some sort,' I said, 'if he's cycling all that way on a hot evening.'

'Oh, he'll get a cup of tea and a Marie biscuit, no doubt. Maybe a Rich Tea if they start living it up. I think Aggie was

afraid there wouldn't be many attending, seeing as it's August, and most people are busy gardening, or away on holiday. That's why Alice has gone to swell the numbers. Rather her than me.'

Driving home, I pondered on Mrs Willet's outing. It didn't sound like 'a chapel lark' to me.

Tibby ignored my blandishments when we met, and gazed haughtily into the distance.

That would teach me to neglect a cat!

There was a good deal of clearing up to do before taking off for Guernsey with cousin Ruth.

I tackled washing and ironing, a batch of correspondence, and tidied one or two cupboards with some surprising results. The larder yielded a Christmas pudding which must have stood in a dark corner for at least three years, and the landing cupboard had secreted a box of stationery I had been looking for for months.

Also I had to draft the advertisement for Mrs Pringle's replacement, but felt it would be only prudent to check, yet again, that the lady had retired permanently before sending it off.

Meanwhile, I hovered around the television set waiting for the great moment.

It did not come. At least, it did not come on the day appointed. Peter Hale rang me in the afternoon to say that he had been told there was some strike trouble, and that the programme was now scheduled for the following night at the same time.

I switched off and decided to post my letters and beard Mrs Pringle in her lair. But just as I put my letters in the box, the lady hove in sight with one of her own.

'Hello!' I called. 'I was just about to visit you.'

'And what was that about?'

'Frankly, about the advertisement which ought to go in this week if you still feel unable to tackle the work.'

Mrs Pringle bridled, her face becoming suffused with colour.

'Who says I'm unable to tackle the work?'

'Well, are you, or not?' I asked. I felt like echoing Lady Bracknell and saying: 'This shilly-shallying with the question is absurd!'

'I don't say as I'm a hundred per cent fit, and that new doctor don't seem to relish the idea of me working again, but there it is.'

'But what is?' I persisted. 'You know the post is still yours if you want it, but I must know here and now, one way or the other. I expect you know that Bella can't do the job next term, so we must get someone.'

Mrs Pringle looked smug.

'Yes, I did hear as Bella was finding it too much for her. Not surprising, of course. It's too much for anyone, let's face it.'

'Well, what's the answer?'

'I don't think I'm up to it.'

'Right. That settles it.'

'Don't be too hasty though. I'm seeing the doctor tomorrow, and shall we see what he says?'

I hesitated. Clearly, the old scoundrel was enjoying every minute of this encounter, and I determined not to lose my temper. On the other hand, it was imperative to get the advertisement in before I went away.

As usual, we compromised.

'Very well. Come and see me tomorrow evening, and we'll decide then,' I said. 'But I must post the advertisement this week.'

'It'll be after The Programme,' said Mrs Pringle.

'Fair enough,' I said. 'I'll see you about seven o'clock.'

And so we parted.

★ ★ ★

Mrs John and Teresa came the next afternoon. The sun still blazed, and I thought that she looked tired after her hot walk.

I refreshed her with lemonade, and suggested that she might like to tackle the brass and copper cleaning in the garden, in the shade of the copper beech, while Teresa played on the lawn.

I did some ironing and watched the two outside. Teresa was an attractive toddler, still a little unsteady on her feet, but accepting the occasional tumble with great good humour. She had a large ball which she rolled about happily, and a teddy bear which needed a good deal of motherly attention. I only wished some of my infant class were as well-behaved.

We had a cup of tea at the end of her session. I explained that I should be travelling to Guernsey on her usual day, and back from Guernsey the following week.

'So there's absolutely no need for you to come,' I said, 'for two weeks. You deserve a holiday. You look rather washed out, if I may say so.'

'I have been off-colour this week,' she confessed. 'I put it down to this heat.'

I gave her her wages, and the two weeks' money when I

should be away. She demurred, but I insisted, and she seemed grateful.

'Shall I run you home?' I offered. 'I could get one of the boys to push the pram along later today.'

But she would have none of it, and I watched her go towards Beech Green, Teresa waving to the last.

The television programme was highly enjoyable, and Fairacre looked splendid on the screen. The man who played Aloysius looked rather too clean and well-fed, I thought, remembering Mr Willet's description of the poet, but all in all, it was well done, and I could see that the inhabitants of Fairacre would be basking in reflected glory for some time.

Half an hour later, Mrs Pringle arrived, her limp strongly in evidence. My heart sank.

When the lady was ensconced on the sofa, had refused refreshment, and contributed her share of comment on the weather, I felt it was time to come to the point.

'So how do you feel?' I began, and immediately was reminded of television reporters questioning some grief-stricken relatives after various disasters. You know the sort of thing:

'How do you feel now that your daughter's body has been recovered?'

'How do you feel now that you know your leg has been amputated?'

It beats me that none of these pathetic and tragic victims do not turn and rend their interlocutor, or at least snarl:

'How would *you* feel?'

Luckily, Mrs Pringle took my question at its face value. She drew in her four chins and a deep breath.

'I'm sorry to say,' said the lady, 'that the doctor says it still needs care. He said it was up to me to decide about the job, and after a night sleeping on it, I think it would be best to say "No".'

It sounded to me as though the speech had been well rehearsed, but it made no difference to the outcome. If Mrs Pringle did not want to return, then that was it.

I felt a twinge of genuine regret.

'Very well. I quite understand, and of course your health comes first. But I really am sorry. We shall be lucky if we ever get such a marvellous cleaner again. However, I'll post off the letter now.'

Having got the matter over, she took a turn round the garden before setting off to her home.

'There's the end of an era,' I said to myself sadly. 'Come rain or shine, that old terror has kept me company for all my years at Fairacre. How I shall miss her!'

However, there it was. I stamped my letter, and put it ready to post. For good measure, I also wrote out a postcard to the same effect to be put in Fairacre Post Office, by courtesy of Mr Lamb.

Something told me that I was far more likely to get results from this source than the advertisement in *The Caxley Chronicle*.

Two days later, my cousin Ruth and I were in Guernsey.

We put up at a most comfortable hotel in St Peter Port overlooking the harbour. At night we could hear the sea hissing over the shingle.

It was fun to see the steamer coming in daily from Weymouth, and to watch the fishing boats setting out.

The weather was as balmy as it was at home, and I had never seen the sea so blue, not even in Crete where I once spent a holiday with Amy. Ruth's spirits rose daily, and I could see that this break was comforting her after the shock of Bill's death.

It was clear that she needed company desperately at this sad time. She told me how good her sons had been, taking it in

turns to call daily, or to telephone her, or to take her out for a drive.

I remembered Joan Benson talking about widowhood, and how some people just cannot bear to be alone, whilst others – herself included – needed some solitude to come to terms with changed circumstances. At any rate, Ruth seemed to be glad of my company, and it was good to feel that I was of some help.

We did all the things that visitors to Guernsey do. We explored Castle Cornet, seen on the horizon from our hotel windows. We visited the claustrophobic abode of the late Victor Hugo, some interesting galleries and innumerable shops where we were easily tempted by some first-rate clothes and jewellery. Of course, we bought a woollen guernsey apiece, a fawn one for Ruth and a nautical dark blue for me. They would keep out the winds of winter beautifully, we told each other, though even to think of such conditions seemed absolutely impossible, as we basked in the heat.

One of the places we enjoyed particularly was the Fort Grey maritime museum where everything was imaginatively displayed, and the woodwork and brass so immaculately kept that I thought of Mrs Pringle with a sudden pang. How she would approve of such cleanliness!

But I thrust the thought aside. This was my holiday, and I was not going to spoil it by dwelling on future problems. Time enough to worry when I returned.

As we drove home from the airport, at the end of our holiday, we were greeted by heavy rain.

The windscreen wipers were working madly to cope with the downpour, and every car that passed flung up a shower of spray. In places the road was flooded, and for the last few miles we were accompanied by fast-flowing streamlets on each side of the highway.

Mr Willet had thoughtfully left the key in the secret hiding

place known to all, which is under a large stone near the front door. I guessed this meant that he and his wife were away for the day.

The house looked so fresh and clean that I suspected that Mrs John had called in after all to put things to rights.

Ruth was staying the night before setting off north, and we enjoyed our tea in a leisurely fashion with our feet propped up on stools.

I thought of Miss Clare, and her more formal tea time habits. Perhaps I really was a slattern? Nevertheless, it was good to flop back with a cup of tea on a sidetable, with the biscuit barrel handy, and Ruth seemed to be as content with the arrangements as I was.

'This little holiday has done me a power of good,' she said.

'Me too.'

'I do so hope I haven't been a wet blanket. It's difficult to throw off one's cares completely.'

I assured her that she had been the best of company.

'You know,' she went on, 'I think I shall take up a little voluntary job when I get back. We have a scheme at our local hospital where we take it in turns to man the shop or push a trolley round the wards. I rather think the library people are in it too. They've been asking me for years to help out, but so far I've refused. In any case, with Bill so ill I couldn't really be reliable.'

'It sounds just right. I'm sure it would be a great help to the organisation.'

And to you too, I thought. This could be the best bit of self-therapy needed.

'It's always good to feel one is of some use,' said Ruth.

'I endorse that,' I told her.

'You found the old key then?' said Mr Willet when I saw him next. 'Had a good time? You look quite bonny.'

I told him about the trips we had made, and how lucky we had been with our choice of hotel and the weather.

'But we came back to rain,' I said. 'How's it been here?'

'That's our only splash. Came just in time to fill up the water butts again, and plump up the runner beans.'

'Any news?'

'Well now, let me see. Arthur Coggs is due out in a week or two, more's the pity. Mr Hale fell off the garden steps cutting that great hedge of his, and sprained an ankle. Mr Mawne saw some bird that shouldn't be here by rights and wrote to that bird society in London to tell 'em about it. They wrote back to say he was mistaken. *Mistaken*! Our Mr Mawne! You can guess he's been in no end of a taking, and the fur's flying, believe me.'

'The feathers, you mean.'

'Yes, well, maybe. Now what else? My Alice has made sixty pounds of gooseberry jam and forty of raspberry, my marrows are coming on a treat as I've been watering 'em well behind old Ted Bates' back. And they've got the mumps in Caxley.'

'Well, I hope it doesn't spread here.'

'And of course, there's this business of the cleaner.'

I was instantly alert.

'You had any answers yet?' he asked.

'Not one.'

'Not even from *The Caxley*?'

'No. I hardly expected it. I think Mr Lamb's card has more chance of attracting notice.'

'Yes. It's done that all right,' he answered cryptically.

'What do you mean?'

'You'll know soon enough,' he said, making for the door. 'I'm saying no more.'

And the maddening fellow set off for home at a brisk pace.

* * *

For the next hour or two I worried over Mr Willet's enigmatic comment. Had I worded the notice wrongly? Was there going to be a rush of candidates for the appointment? Had Mrs Pringle been putting in her spoke, and warning off would-be applicants with terrible descriptions of the work involved? I would not put it past her.

After a great deal of fruitless anxiety, I decided to pay a visit to Mrs John to see if it was she who had put my house to rights unexpectedly, and to deliver a pot of Guernsey honey and a rather splendid teddy bear, made in the island, and to which I was becoming so much attached that I felt it would be wise to hand it over without delay, to its future owner.

The countryside was looking lovely after the recent rain, and already some of the fields were being ploughed after an early harvest. Farmers did not waste much time these days, I thought, remembering the golden stubble which used to stand in the cropped fields for weeks, it seemed, in the old days.

But already there was a shabbiness about the hedgerows and grass verges which told of approaching autumn. It grieved me to think of the waning of this most glorious of all summers, its joys and its splendours. Well, we had celebrated it, every one of us, and must face the inevitable, I supposed.

Knapweed and late scabious coloured the drying grasses. Already acorns and young conkers were formed, and in the orchards the plums were turning colour, and some early apples, like Beauty of Bath, were being picked.

To some people, autumn is the loveliest of the seasons with John Keats' 'mists and mellow fruitfulness'. But for me, I find it a wistful time. 'The dying fall' presages the chill of winter, and this year, particularly, I hoped that autumn would be late in coming.

Mrs John was delighted with her honey and Teresa with the bear. Yes, she had looked in, she said, almost apologetically, and Mr Willet had unlocked the house for her.

'It all looked immaculate,' I told her. 'But you shouldn't have gone to such trouble.'

'Well, I was going to leave a note, but in the end I decided I'd see you myself.'

'Shall I see you next week? Are you feeling better now?'

'It's about that I wanted to see you.'

She twisted her fingers in some embarrassment.

'You see, the doctor says there's another baby on the way. It's a bit earlier than we'd planned, but we're quite pleased about it. The only thing is I shall have to give up the job, and I did enjoy it so.'

'And I enjoyed having you. You did a first-class job and I shall miss you sorely, but you must do as the doctor says.'

We parted affectionately, and I promised to keep in touch.

Teresa was too engrossed in the teddy bear to wish me farewell.

I left them both with much regret.

So that's that, I thought, as I drove home. Now I must look for another cleaner for my home as well as the school.

I was genuinely sorry to part from Mrs John. She was a fine person, and had looked after me beautifully. While the holidays lasted, and that was not for much longer, I could manage well, but once term started on September the third, I should have to find a help-meet.

Perhaps Mr Willet knew about this too? Next time I met him I must put in some third-degree stuff.

Unfortunately, as I knew from experience, the wily old boy was more than a match for me.

THE last few days of the summer holiday passed with unwelcome rapidity.

Amy called to see me one evening.

'To catch up with the Fairacre gossip,' she told me. 'I haven't seen you since the television programme. I must say they made the village look absolutely Arcadian.'

'It is,' I assured her.

'Oh, come off it! You know there are as many serpents in your Eden as there are in mine at Bent. How's that terrible Mrs Pringle getting on?'

I told her about that lady's vacillations, and my present predicament.

'A pity about Mrs John,' she said, looking closely at the floor and furniture about her. 'She really has pulled this place together. You will miss her.'

I ignored this aspersion on the normal state of my abode, and agreed that Mrs John would be sorely missed.

'I believe Miriam Quinn is in Norfolk at the moment,' she went on. 'Am I right?'

'You are indeed.'

'Well, I asked because I had an extraordinary postcard this morning from Gerard Baker, written from a place called Great Snoring.'

'I don't believe it.'

'Perfectly true, my dear. But it wasn't the address that perturbed me, but the ebullience of the man's message.'

'Tell me more. I'm agog!'

'I ought to have brought it to show you, but the telephone rang just as I was coming out, and I have left it at home, but it was to the effect that he was the happiest man in the world, and what bliss it was to find Fairacre in Norfolk.'

'Good Lord!'

'Yes, you may well say so,' said Amy severely. 'It looks to me as if you have let yet another nice man slip through your fingers. I was afraid from the moment they clapped eyes on each other, in this very room, that no good would come of it.'

'But good *has* come of it, Amy, if Miriam and Gerard propose to get engaged. But somehow –'

'Somehow what?'

'Well, Miriam seemed so very much the confirmed single woman, happy in her work. I wonder if it's true?'

'I can't think of any other explanation, can you? Two people, both connected with Fairacre, now in Norfolk? No, I think it's a case of love.'

'You sound as maudlin as Mrs Pringle,' I told her. 'She's always telling me that it is Love That Makes The World Go Round. Not that she puts it into practice, as you know. I see mighty little love here from that source.'

'Well, there is it,' said Amy rising. 'Let's take a turn in the garden like Jane Austen's heroines, and you can tell me all about Guernsey and the wedding. Was your gorgeous hat admired?'

'It certainly was.'

'And did it attract a flock of eligible men, all soft and wistful in the presence of nuptials?'

'I'm sorry to say it did not.'

Amy bent to sniff at a Gloire de Dijon rose against the wall.

'Never mind,' she said comfortingly. 'There's a lot to be said for living alone in such a heavenly place.'

'I'm always telling you that,' I said.

It was good to have the last word for a change.

<p style="text-align:center">* * *</p>

That evening I was surprised to have a telephone call from Elizabeth Mawne.

'You haven't forgotten our garden party tomorrow, have you? In aid of the Royal Society for the Protection of Birds?'

I confessed that I had.

'No matter,' said she kindly. 'I only rang because you promised something for the cake stall, and I noticed it hadn't arrived.'

'I'll set to now and make something,' I promised humbly. 'Anything to help the R.S.P.B.'

'That's nice of you. To tell the truth, Henry almost called off the whole thing, as he's been having the most acrimonious exchanges with one of the officers about a rare bird he saw up on the downs.'

'How exciting! What was it?'

'Don't ask me, dear. I'm absolutely ignorant of bird life. Some sort of *Lesser Thing*. A godwit, possibly. No, I don't think it was that. He'll tell you when we see you. The man he wrote to told him he was mistaken, and of course Henry was furious. However, I've soothed him enough to have the garden party here tomorrow, but for two pins he would have changed the posters to "In aid of the Cats' Protection League".'

'He sounds as though he's taken it hard, poor Henry.'

'Well, when you are an authority on birds it's rather annoying to be told you can't distinguish between a Lesser Whatsit and a Greater Thingummy, isn't it?'

'I agree.'

'Then we'll look forward to seeing you about two-thirty. With a cake, of course.'

'Of course,' I agreed meekly, and went into the kitchen to make a batch of flapjacks to atone for my forgetfulness. Tibby, expecting supper, accompanied me, and graciously accepted a morsel of cold chicken, before I began my labours.

What a summer, I thought, as I made my way through the village the next afternoon!

Normally, I am full of fears for those organising outside junketings, but this year one just could not go wrong.

The cottage gardens were gay with red hot pokers, michaelmas daisies, pansies and delphiniums. Roses still glowed from old brick walls, and hollyhocks reached to thatched roofs.

Little birds fluffed their feathers at the side of the lane, glorying in their baths, and sending up little puffs of light dust. Cats dozed on window sills, relishing the heat, while dogs had sought the shade, and lay there panting.

Mr Roberts' cows, now restored to our erstwhile sports' field, stood beneath a clump of trees swishing their tails against the tormenting flies, and an aeroplane, leaving trails in the high blue sky, added its distant hum to the somnolence of the summer afternoon.

In the Mawnes' garden, however, all was bustle. I presented my flapjacks to the cake stall, and asked if I might reserve an appetising fruit cake that caught my eye.

'Not until Mr Bradley has made his speech,' said Mrs Mawne, arriving at my side. 'We can't possibly start selling until then.' She hurried off.

'Bossy old thing,' commented Mrs Lamb, who was in charge of the stall. 'Don't you worry. I'll see you get it, Miss Read.'

I expressed my thanks, but moved in a somewhat chastened mood to listen to Basil Bradley, who had mounted a rather precarious stool to make his opening speech.

As always, he was looking immaculate, his wavy hair beautifully cut, his pink shirt and pale grey suit a vision of delight. We are very proud of our local author, and he is generous with his time and money. Also, a great point, he is always brief when speaking, and this has endeared him to us all.

This afternoon was no exception, and within five minutes I had revisited the cake stall and collected my fruit cake. Mrs Lamb was doing a roaring trade, and the blue and white striped pudding basin which was acting as her till, was almost stuffed with notes and silver.

I noticed a particularly luscious chocolate cake, decorated with walnuts, lurking in the shade under the table. Seeing my interest, Mrs Lamb said:

'Put aside for Mrs Mawne,' and rolled her eyes to heaven.

Tea was served at the card tables collected earlier from the village hall, and covered with a fine assortment of borrowed tablecloths. Even on Henry Mawne's level lawn they proved uncomfortably wobbly, but it was pleasant to sit among friends admiring the flowery dresses of the women, and the bronzed near-nakedness of the children.

By four o'clock I felt I had done my duty, and set off for home. It seemed hotter than ever. A few small children, clad only in shorts, were accompanying a man, and were walking towards me.

To my surprise, when they were nearer, I saw that it was Arthur Coggs and all his offspring except Joseph.

He looked rather sheepish as he approached, but we stopped and had a civil word. He looked all the better for his time in prison, I thought, fitter and leaner without his beer, but naturally I did not say so.

'And where's Joe?' I asked.

'Home with 'is mum,' said Arthur. 'Reading some book.'

'He's getting on famously at school,' I told him.

'It's all he seems to think about,' responded Arthur. His tone was derogatory. He might have been saying that the child was hopelessly delinquent from the disgust shown in his manner.

'Good!' I said heartily. 'I'll look forward to seeing him, and the others, next week.'

Mr Lamb was weeding the front garden of the Post Office as I passed.

'Got our old friend back,' he said, nodding to Arthur's departing figure. 'Pity he didn't do his full time. Still, there's a chap at Beech Green has offered him a labouring job on that new building site, and Arthur starts on Monday. If he feels like it,' he added.

'Well, I hope the employer knows what he's taking on.'

'You can bet plenty of people have told him.'

'It's good news for Arthur though. He might go straight for a bit.'

'So might a corkscrew,' replied Mr Lamb.

He came close to his gate, and dropped his voice. 'You had a visit yet about that cleaning job?'

'Not a word. Why?'

Mr Lamb looked furtively about him, and came even closer. 'Well, you know that card you left with me?'

'Of course.'

'While you were away, Minnie Pringle came in for her children's allowance, and wanted to know what it was. You know she can't read?'

I said I did indeed.

'Proper scandal, isn't it? Had compulsory education here for a hundred years, and you get duffers like that Minnie still! Anyway, I was reading it out to her, when in comes Ma Pringle.'

Here Mr Lamb's husky whisper changed to a falsetto.

' "And what may you be doing?" she asks Minnie. "Thinking of going to see about this job," said Minnie, all pert. And Ma Pringle turns as red as a turkey-cock and says: "Oh, no you don't my girl!" and stumps off without buying anything.'

'This is the first I've heard of it,' I said. 'Although Bob Willet did say that that card had caused problems.'

'Problems? Murder, near enough, from what the neigh-

bours told me! When Min went back, the old girl set about her something terrible, and threatened to black her eye if she dared to put in for what she called "her job". Minnie went off home to Springbourne, but she stuck out and wouldn't swear not to apply, and her old aunt is still seethingover it.'

'What a kettle of fish,' I remarked. 'All I know is that Mrs Pringle has said she doesn't want the job, and I'm still hoping to hear from someone, though time's running short. In any case, Minnie is not at all suitable.'

'That she's not,' agreed Mr Lamb. 'Does more harm than good, I should guess.'

'Well, thank you for telling me,' I said, picking up my basket. 'At least I'm prepared.'

The news was disturbing, but I did not intend to let it upset me unduly. Mrs Pringle had had her chance. Minnie Pringle would certainly not be taken on permanently, if she were rash enough to apply, and that was that.

The next thing to do, was to get in touch with dear reliable Bella, and to see if her offer of getting the school in good trim, for the beginning of term, still held.

I determined to see her the next day and went home to follow Mr Lamb's example, and to do some weeding as the evening cooled.

I awoke to another dewy morning, and looked forward to yet another golden day.

Full of good resolutions, I planned to give my house a thorough cleaning, secretly rather stung by Amy's remark about it looking in need of Mrs John's ministrations.

In the afternoon, I proposed to visit Bella, and to tell her how grateful I should be if she would put things straight before term started.

Life, of course, was already waiting with a spanner to throw in the works.

When I was at my most dishevelled, and had spent some time on my stomach attending to dust under the beds, the door bell rang.

Cursing, I ran downstairs. It was nearly half past ten. Whoever it was could have a cup of coffee and then, I hoped, they would leave me to my chores.

Not many people come to the front door. I fully expected to find a gipsy selling pegs, or some earnest soul with a handful of tracts asking if I were saved. Friends and neighbours usually come to the back door and halloo cheerfully to see if I am in.

On wrenching open the door, which tends to stick with infrequent use, I was severely shaken to be confronted by Miss Crabbe and my past assistant Miss Jackson.

'Well,' I said with false enthusiasm. 'This is a lovely surprise!' Sometimes I wonder that I am not struck by a bolt from heaven when I dissemble in this fashion – but there it is. Civilisation rears its head yet again.

'Do come in. I was just going to make coffee.'

The two ladies followed me into the sitting room, where a

full dust-pan lay on the hearthrug, a vase of roses had been upturned by Tibby in his understandable haste to leave home on seeing the visitors, and water dripped steadily, and a few dead leaves had blown in the French windows and added to the general squalor.

'We were just returning from a marvellous course in Dorset, and saw the signpost to Fairacre, and we felt we must pop in,' said Hilary Jackson, teeth and spectacles flashing as brightly as ever.

'I'm so glad,' I said, picking up the dust-pan with one hand, and trying to arrange some stray locks of hair with the other. 'Let me put on the kettle, and then you must tell me all about it.'

I escaped to the kitchen, and did my best to tidy myself. It was a pity that I was wearing a paint-splashed cotton frock, no stockings and sandals with two straps adrift. Minnie Pringle was probably a good deal tidier than I was at the moment, I thought.

I put out cups and saucers, and surveyed the deplorable fragments in the bottom of the biscuit tin. Luckily, I had some oat cakes of Scottish derivation, as hard and gritty as the Grampians, and I added these to my offerings.

The ladies accepted my invitation to call upstairs, and I only hoped that they would not measure their length falling over the vacuum cleaner on the landing. The beds had been stripped, and piles of bedclothes were festooned over the banisters. The whole house must give the impression of total chaos.

However, it could not be helped, and I managed to mop up the water, and straighten a cushion or two, before they returned smelling nicely of my Morny's pink lilac soap.

'We hoped to see you at the course,' said Miss Crabbe, accepting a Scottish rock. 'It was really inspiring, wasn't it, Hilary?'

'Yes, indeed,' said the girl earnestly. She had had the sense, I

noticed, to select half a Nice biscuit from the rubble in the tin. 'It dealt with Difficult Children. Half of them, of course, as we know only too well, are the Victims of Unhappy Marriages.'

'But there are so many other factors,' went on Miss Crabbe, who was gamely trying to chip off a fragment from her oat cake with an eye tooth. 'Unsympathetic Teachers, Hereditary Defects and the Pressures of Modern Life.'

'We had some wonderful lecturers,' enthused Hilary. 'So understanding and really jolly. In the evenings we played old-fashioned games like charades and I-Spy.'

Privately, I thanked my stars that I had not been among those present, and changed the subject by offering more coffee and enquiring which route they had taken to Fairacre.

Miss Crabbe was still fighting her oat cake, and was now attempting to snap it into pieces before transferring the morsel to her mouth. I began to feel quite sorry for her.

'Do leave that if it is too hard,' I said.

'Indeed no! It is absolutely delicious, and full of nourishing roughage,' said the lady. 'I am a great believer in Fibre.'

'I have bran with everything,' volunteered Hilary, who had finished her half biscuit. I offered the oat cakes, but she declined.

Coffee over, I took them round the garden. I do not think they really noticed anything, they were so agog with the mental stimulation of the past course.

However, they seemed to be content to sit on the garden seat to continue their discussion, and I excused myself as the telephone rang.

It was Bella George.

'I was coming to see you,' I said. 'Are you still game to tidy up the school before term?'

'Yes indeed, that's why I rang. But I thought I'd better find out if Mrs Pringle was definitely not returning. I shouldn't like to get across that lady.'

I was in firm agreement with Bella's feelings, and said so.

'No,' I told her. 'Mrs Pringle told me herself that she can't manage the job at the moment, so it will be marvellous if you can help out.'

'You haven't heard about *The Upset* then?'

'With Minnie?'

'Yes.'

'Mr Lamb told me that Mrs Pringle had threatened Minnie when she expressed an interest in applying for the post.'

'That was a while ago. She's been up since evidently, and is still talking about putting in for the job.'

'Well, she wouldn't get it,' I said flatly. 'The work's beyond Minnie, so you need not worry on that score.'

'I see. Well, I'll be along tomorrow and put things straight. I do hope someone turns up for the regular work. What about Mrs John?'

I told her about the coming baby.

'Oh dear! So you're without help too?'

'It looks like it. But I'm not too worried.'

'See you tomorrow then,' said Bella, and rang off.

I took the opportunity of clearing away the coffee cups and straightening the sitting room. Upstairs must wait.

Through the window I could see my two visitors engaged in earnest conversation still. The clock now said a quarter to twelve, and I wondered if I should offer them lunch. And if so, what?

Those of us who live alone do not have cold joints, or large stews standing ready in the larder.

On this occasion, I had one chop which I had intended to grill, with some lettuce from the garden as a side salad. All that I could manage, if the worst came to the worst, was an omelette which should suit Miss Crabbe, the non-flesh-eater, with a somewhat more interesting salad with chives, radishes,

spring onions and any other snippets from the garden added to the lettuce.

I mentally reviewed the bread situation (poor), the cheese situation (disastrous, mouldy cheddar only), the fruit situation (two black bananas, and some sharp apples). Of course, I thought, I could always open a bottle of gooseberries.

I returned to my guests.

'It will soon be twelve o'clock,' I said brightly. 'Would you like to stay for lunch? Or I could take you to the Beetle and Wedge for a sandwich, if you prefer?'

My enquiries were met with a flurry of agitation.

'Nearly twelve? Good gracious, Hilary, we must set off at once!'

Miss Crabbe had leapt to her feet, and Hilary was scrabbling about for her handbag.

'No, no! Most kind of you to offer us lunch, but we have an evening engagement in Cambridge, and must be on our way.'

I did my best to look regretful.

'We are very much refreshed by your delicious coffee and oat cakes,' said Miss Crabbe, as they entered the car. 'By the way, do call and see us if you are ever in Cambridge.'

I thanked her, and helped to guide the car out of my somewhat awkward drive, before returning to my neglected duties.

The lamb chop was delicious, and all the more enjoyed because it was eaten in blissful solitude.

20 The End of Summer

TRUE to her word, Bella appeared the next day and got down to her scrubbing, dusting and polishing.

At mid-morning I went across with our coffee, and we sat on the desks and I admired the tortoise stoves, already gleaming like jet, and the glittering brass rail round the fireguard.

'It looks marvellous,' I told her.

'I like a bit of a shine-up,' she answered, stirring her coffee dreamily. 'I was talking to Jack last night, and he says he don't mind if I want to help out for another week, say, until you get a new cleaner.'

'That's very noble of him. I appreciate that. As a matter of fact, things are slightly more hopeful. Mr Roberts called in yesterday to say that he has a new stockman starting at Michaelmas, and his wife wants a job. So maybe she will take it on.'

'And Bob Willet said he'd do the stoves when the time came, if need be. That's something I really couldn't take on.'

'I've got all my scouts out,' I said. 'The vicar, the Annetts, Miss Clare, Mrs Mawne and Mrs Partridge. Between us all, someone will turn up. Meanwhile, if you really feel you can come after school for a day or two, I'd be more than grateful.'

As it happened, I saw Mr Willet in the churchyard that afternoon, and went to thank him for his offer of coping with the stoves.

'Lord, that's nothing!' he replied, ceasing his slashing at the

long grass, and subsiding on to the flat tomb of Hezekiah
Bootle who departed this life in 1832, respected by all.

'I'll see you and the kids keep warm,' he went on. 'I always
enjoy a nice bit of stoking. Keeps hot, don't it?' he added,
pushing back his cap, and scratching his head.

'A wonderful summer,' I agreed. 'I can't remember a better
one.'

We sat side by side in the sunshine. Bees fondled the clover at
our feet, and a pair of collared doves pattered about on the
gravel path, looking like two curates dressed in clerical grey.
High above us, a flock of rooks winged their way westward,
their harsh cawing muffled by distance.

It was very peaceful. A country churchyard takes a lot of
beating on a sunny afternoon, and I can never understand
people's aversion to such places.

We brooded in companionable silence for a time, until Mr
Willet sighed, and reached for his bill hook.

'No real news then, I take it, about Bella's job?'

I told him about Mr Roberts' new stockman.

'Oh, I knows that couple! Lived over Springbourne way some years ago. Yes, she'd be a bonny worker if she'd take it on. Fat girl. Name of Martha. Don't get many Marthas these days.'

He creaked to his feet.

'Well, I'd best stir me stumps. Don't you worry about this cleaner business. Someone'll turn up, you'll see.'

I roused myself too, and we parted company.

It was the last day of the holidays and it ended very pleasantly for me with a little party at Holly Lodge, where Henry Mawne's nephew David and his wife Irene, sister of Horace Umbleditch, now lived.

The older Mawnes were there, and also David's boy Simon, as well as the vicar and his wife, and a sprinkling of friends from Caxley.

'It's really to celebrate Horace and Eve's engagement,' Irene told me, as she took my coat. 'But they are not here yet. I can't think what has held them up. I do so hope they haven't forgotten. They are so befuddled with love, I wouldn't put it past them.'

Luckily, at that moment there was a scrunching of tyres, and the couple arrived. I made my way into the sitting room, while Irene welcomed them.

'I've always loved this house,' said the vicar, coming up to me with a tray of glasses. 'And everyone who has lived here has enjoyed it. I know Miriam Quinn finds it a real haven after a day's work in that busy Caxley office. You know her good news, I take it? Unfortunately, she is still away, but I think her engagement to Gerard Baker is now general knowledge.'

I said that I had heard something about it, and thought it was marvellous news. Henry Mawne came up at that moment, and said that he had been keeping a sharp look-out in the *Daily Telegraph* for a notice, but nothing had been seen.

'They are keeping it quiet,' said Mr Partridge, 'but the wedding will take place around Christmas, I gather. Miriam wants to arrange things easily for her employer, I know, although she intends to keep on her job after the honeymoon.'

'I like a winter wedding,' announced Mrs Mawne. 'Plenty of fur and velvet. So pretty always. I suppose they will marry at St Patrick's? I always feel a registry office ceremony is rather like a visit to the bank.'

'Yes, yes. The wedding will be here, I'm happy to say,' said the vicar. 'Her brother Lovell will take part of the service, of course. I look forward to meeting him.'

At that moment, the two chief guests arrived, David hastened to greet them, and then made a short but charming speech, asking us to drink to their happiness.

It was good to see Horace looking so smug and cheerful, and his wife-to-be seemed equally content with her lot.

'This is our last fling before term starts next week,' Horace said, in answer to David's speech. 'And nothing could be nicer than an evening with good friends.'

Speeches over, we began to circulate, and I was pleased to see Simon again. He looked much stronger and happier than when he had been my pupil for a short time, and he gave me a cheerful grin as he proffered a tray of tempting tit-bits.

'When does term start for you?' he asked.

'Tomorrow,' I told him.

'Then Uncle Horace has the edge on you. He doesn't go back until Thursday.'

'Lucky chap,' I said. 'And when do you start?'

'Not till the following Tuesday.'

'Hardly worth going back,' I teased him. 'It will soon be Christmas.'

'Stop chattering, Simon,' called David. 'There isn't a nut to be had over here.'

'Back to my duties!' said my old pupil, and departed.

Elizabeth Mawne hove in sight and I enquired politely about the aged aunt in Ireland who had been the unknowing source of my troubles, and Miriam's, with Henry early in the year.

'Perhaps you know I managed to get her into a nursing home?'

I said I did.

'Well, as you might guess, she's taken a great dislike to it, and is raising merry hell according to the matron, and threatening to go home.'

'But can she? I thought –'

'Of course she can't. We sold up everything, and really I'm at my wits' end to know what to do. Henry refuses point-blank to have her with us, and I think he's right. I can see I shall have to have another trip to Ireland to sort things out.'

My heart sank at the thought of Henry left yet again to his own devices. Should I have to be alert for unwelcome visits? Lucky Miriam, I thought! At least, she would now have the protection of a fiancé. It almost made one take to matrimony for sanctuary from lonely grass widowers. However, as Amy had pointed out, with some callousness, Gerard and even Horace were now out of my reach, and I saw no other possibility looming up. On the whole, of course, I was not sorry.

'Old age is a problem,' I said. 'I frequently think about my own, and wonder which will crack first, mind or body.'

'Good heavens!' cried Elizabeth. 'You won't crack at all. Henry's always telling me you are the sanest person he's ever met. You'll go whole and uncorrupted to the grave, believe me.'

I was much taken aback.

'Well, I'm very touched by the compliment,' I quavered, 'and now I must go and see the happy pair.'

Still reeling from Henry's kind opinions, I threaded my way

to speak to Horace and Eve. Perhaps, poor old Henry was not such a bad chap after all, I decided.

Nevertheless, I hoped Elizabeth's absence would be brief.

I walked home through the peaceful village, and encountered Mr Lamb, exercising his dog.

After a boisterous welcome from the latter which left me with laddered tights, and my best fifteen-denier ones at that, Mr Lamb gave me good news.

'I've heard of another likely candidate for the cleaning job,' he told me.

'You are kind. Everyone's been scouting round, and things do look more hopeful. Who's this one?'

'Wife of one of the postmen. They're at Beech Green, and she used to work at that electrical factory this end of Caxley. But it closed down at the end of last month, and she could do with some cash. Nice woman. Plenty of common sense and elbow grease.'

'She sounds marvellous.'

I told him about the possibility of the stockman's wife.

'So now there's real hope of someone soon. I shall miss Mrs Pringle though, awkward though she is. But I can't see her coming again.'

'Would you have her if you could?'

'Yes. She's served the school well for donkey's years, despite being such –'

I searched for a phrase which would be truthful but not libellous.

'Such a wicked old faggot?' suggested Mr Lamb, hauling his exuberant charge away from my ruined tights.

'That's it.'

'Well, now you can have some choice perhaps. I think I know the Springbourne girl, Martha Someone, and I know Reg's missus would work well too. Good luck, anyway.'

He set off at a brisk pace, with the dog panting at the delay, and I went home thinking how helpful my neighbours were in times of trouble.

Naturally, the first day of term dawned as sunnily seductive as one might guess, and it was sad to think of us all confined to the schoolroom when summer remained so beguiling outdoors.

The school looked fresh and gleaming from Bella's ministrations and the children equally radiant from their long days in the open air.

Miss Briggs, whom we now had to call Mrs Richards, was in good spirits, and told me all about the work she and Wayne were putting in on their cottage. It was on the outskirts of Beech Green, and they were lucky to have found it.

'That's one good thing about being in the building trade,' she told me. 'You often get to hear of houses going before they get on to the market. The old couple who had it before us were distant cousins of Wayne's dad, so we heard about it from him.'

I enquired about the house. It sounded as if it were not far from Miss Clare's home.

'That's right,' agreed the girl. 'When we're straight you must come and see it. At the moment it's a proper mess, and we haven't got much furniture.'

'That'll come,' I told her. 'Much more fun to get it bit by bit anyway.'

'My mum and dad married after the war,' she said, 'when things were really tight. Dad always says they set up home with two deckchairs and an orange box for a table. I think we've done a bit better than that, but not much!'

She laughed, and went off to cope with the infants. It was good to see her so content.

Joseph Coggs appeared at my desk, pencil in hand.

'Please, miss, the nib of my pencil's bust itself.'

'So's mine,' chorused three more children.

Term had begun.

Amy called that evening, wearing a most elegant turquoise blue suit and matching hat.

'Heavens, you do look smart!' I cried. 'Have you been to a wedding?'

'No. A rather dreary committee meeting, but all the others always appear dressed to the nines, so I thought I'd better do the same.'

'Well, mind where you sit. Tibby left a mouse on the sofa last week, and it was by sheer chance that I noticed it.'

'You certainly live a primitive life out here at Fairacre,' commented Amy, dusting busily at the seat of an armchair. 'How's term going?'

'Much as usual. Luckily our Miss Briggs, I mean Mrs Richards, is in good form, and I really think I may get a cleaner before long. Everyone's rallying round.'

'Splendid! I came to ask you if you would like to come to the opera with me next month. At Oxford.'

'Lovely! To hear what?'

'La Bohème. Suit you?'

'Perfectly. I can always do with a nice juicy bit of Puccini.'

'Right. I'll fix up the seats. James will be coming too, and we'll pick you up.'

'I shall look forward to that.'

'And the week after, James and I are pushing off for a tour of Scotland, and staying with Vanessa for a few days. I must say, he's being very attentive. I think he fears I might go off on my own again.'

'Well, you gave us all a fright, I must say.'

'Rubbish! And don't expect me to feel guilty, because I don't regret it for a moment. It did me a lot of good, and James too,

for that matter. By the way, what news of that crafty Gerard? I shall never forgive him for throwing you over.'

'Amy, you know there was absolutely nothing in it, and I'm delighted to tell you that, as far as I know, he and Miriam are engaged.'

'Well! I didn't see it in the *Daily Telegraph*.'

'Quite a lot of things don't get into the *Telegraph*. Their engagement was one of them.'

'Let me know when things are a little more public, and I'll write to them. She's a nice girl. I wonder when the nuptials take place?'

'Quite soon, I gather, from the vicar.'

'I shall have to get a new outfit if I'm invited,' said Amy thoughtfully.

'What's wrong with that present get-up?' I asked, waving at the beautiful suit. 'I hope we do get invited. My hat could do with another airing. But somehow I think that wedding will be a very quiet affair.'

'I should hope so,' said Amy sternly, 'after the way he's treated you.'

'Now Amy –' I began.

'What about a cup of something?' she said swiftly, avoiding a scolding, and we went amicably in search of one.

Next day the storm broke, in more ways than one.

The clouds rolled up during school time, and the air became sultry. Distant rumbling could be heard, but we saw no lightning, and luckily the rain held off.

As before, this sudden withdrawal of sunshine made us all feel chilly, although the thermometer registered a fairly high temperature.

The children went home in dry weather, and Mrs Richards and I returned to our respective homes before the heavens opened, as we fully expected.

At six o'clock, the rumbling came nearer, and there was some lightning. Tibby prudently and stealthily crept under the sofa, and I was about to go upstairs to shut the windows when the bell rang at the back door.

On opening it I was confronted by Mrs Pringle. She was wearing her grimmest expression, and her best navy blue hat complete with the white duck's wing.

'Do come in,' I said, my heart sinking. Now what had upset the old curmudgeon? I knew that look only too well. It boded trouble.

'I've been having a word with Bella George,' was her opening remark, when she had settled her bulk in an armchair.

'Oh yes?'

'And I was that taken aback I come straight up here to have it out.'

'Have what out?'

'You knows as well as I do. About my job.'

Mrs Pringle's face was now scarlet, and she leant forward belligerently. I mustered my defences.

'You told me plainly that you did not want the job, Mrs Pringle. Naturally, I've had to look elsewhere.'

Mrs Pringle's ample bosom was heaving up and down with emotion, and I began to wonder how I should cope if she should have a seizure.

'That Minnie Pringle made me see red with her talk of coming for the cleaning, but I soon sorted her out. The very idea! Why, she's got no more idea of cleaning than that cat!'

She glared at poor Tibby who was trying to make a dignified exit from this upheaval.

'Even if Minnie had applied, she would not have been given the post,' I assured her.

If I had hoped to placate the lady, I was wrong. Mrs Pringle's voice now thundered as loudly as the storm outside.

'But what about Martha Ellis, as is supposed to want it? And Reg Carter's wife? Though what good she'd do looking after a school when she's only fiddle-faddled about in Caxley keeping her hands clean, I don't know.'

'They haven't applied yet –' I began, but was howled down.

'And then Bella had the sauce to tell me that Bob Willet had offered to do the stoves, when we light 'em. I tell you straight, I'm not having him crunching coke all over my floors with them great boots of his.'

'But they are not your floors,' I managed to slip in.

Mrs Pringle took an enormous breath. The duck's wing quivered in time with her four chins, and the flash of her eyes reminded me of the Valkyrie.

'They've been mine for more years than I can remember,' she boomed.

'Are you trying to tell me,' I said, as calmly as I could, 'that you are willing to come back?'

'Of course I am! You don't think I'd let that lot of muddlers mess the place up? Bob Willet doing the stoves! A fine old fist he'd make of it. Wait till I see him next!'

'He was only doing what he could to help,' I pointed out. 'You know quite well you let us all down badly. If it hadn't been for Bella, we should have been really in the cart.'

There was no gleam of remorse in Mrs Pringle's fiery eye. Secretly, I was overjoyed to think of my old adversary returning to the field of battle, but she had led us such a dance I did not feel noble enough to forgive her completely.

'I shall have to think about your offer,' I said formally.

'Think what you like,' said she, 'but I'll be coming to work next Monday, and if Bella or anyone else is mucking about in my school, they'll get thrown out.'

'How do I know,' I countered, 'that you really will turn up? We've had quite enough shilly-shallying, and in any case what does the doctor say?'

'It's up to me, he said. Work if I want to, and now I do. I'll be along first thing Monday.'

She began to struggle from the chair, but I waved her down. This was as near as I should ever get to an apology, I could see. The only thing to do was to accept the situation. In any case, it was what I really wanted.

'Very well. I'll expect you then.'

A crash of thunder nearly split our ear drums, and the rain began to fall in torrents.

'I'll run you home,' I said.

'There's no call to put yourself out,' said the lady, but she sounded mollified.

'We'd better wait a few minutes,' I added, as lightning vent the sky. 'Have a glass of sherry now we've settled things.'

She raised a massive hand in refusal.

'You should know I don't drink.'

'I'm sorry. I forgot. A cup of coffee?'

'No, thank you.'

She sat four-square and studied the room about her with an

eagle eye. An ancient beam runs across my ceiling, and this she scrutinised for some time.

'I suppose no one's touched that rafter?' she said.

'No,' I replied, mystified.

'I thought as much. I give it a good rub down each week with a nice soft cloth wrung out in vinegar and linseed oil. And your copper and brass is a disgrace. I'll come as usual and do you now that Mrs John has given up.'

'Thank you,' I said meekly.

'And anyway, we never got down to any proper spring-cleaning this year, as I recall. I reckon the whole house could do with bottoming.'

As soon as the rain abated a little, we drove down through the wet village street to her house. Little was said on the brief journey, but when the car stopped, she thanked me as she struggled to get out.

'I'll see you on Monday then,' I said.

'Be quite like old times,' replied the lady, nodding the hat graciously, as she opened her gate.

As I drove back I faced the fact that Mrs Pringle had easily won this last skirmish. As usual.

But, on the other hand, I was quite content with the outcome.

To my surprise, I had a letter from Miriam Quinn in the next morning's post. It was written from her brother's vicarage, and ran to three pages.

She was obviously very happy, and had postponed her return to the office, with Barney's blessing, as Gerard was busy with a project in Norfolk and they were both enjoying their holiday together.

'We hope to marry early in the New Year, at St Patrick's of course. It will be a quiet wedding, as befits two sober and elderly people, but we want close friends, such as yourself, to

join our families on the day. You shall have a proper invitation when I get back.

'We hope to find a house near Caxley, as we've both made so many friends in the neighbourhood, so look out for one.' .

There followed a eulogy of Gerard, which I am sure Amy would not have endorsed, and she ended with loving messages to her Fairacre friends.

'I wonder if my new hat will look suitable for a winter wedding?' I pondered aloud.

Tibby gave a prolonged and painful cry, but I refused to acknowledge it as a derogatory comment.

'So we've got Madam Sunshine coming back!' said Mr Willet. 'You'll never see the last of her now.'

'It was the thought of you coping with the stoves that really settled it,' I told him.

'I'd have done 'em all right,' he said sturdily. 'The fact is the old girl was jealous of anyone getting in here, and when she heard there might be a rush for the job, she knew it was time to stop malarking about and come up here pronto.'

'Well, there it is. Better the rogue you know, than the knave you don't. I'm not sorry she's coming back, to tell the truth.'

'You're too soft by half. She'll be bossing us all about worse than ever after this.'

'We're used to it, aren't we? In any case, I'm not grieving about it with this sunshine all round us.'

'You're right.' He sniffed the air appreciatively. 'That rain done a power of good. Shan't need to look out for Ted Bates now. Won't want my sprinkler for a week or two.'

We parted company. I was off to take assembly, and he to sweep up some of the coke he would not be allowed to scrunch into Mrs Pringle's floors in the future.

★ ★ ★

It was good to be back to normal, with Mrs Pringle crashing about in the lobby before and after school, and booming awful threats to children who got in her way.

It was even comforting, in a queer sort of way, to have my house turned inside out on Wednesday afternoons, and to be told of the strange articles she had found in the sides of the armchairs, and the deplorable condition of my kitchen equipment.

'Ah well!' pronounced my old tormenter. 'There's some as have their heads stuffed with book-learning, and don't know one end of a duster from another. But I suppose we was all sent here with a purpose. Mine seems to be looking after Fairacre School, not to mention its teachers.'

The golden days passed, and it began to grow chilly. The hedges were dew-spangled each morning, and the berries were glowing red. Before long the Battle of the Stoves would begin, as it had done for so many years.

'I don't like this nip in the air,' I said to Mr Willet early one morning in the playground. 'I can't bear to think of this blissful summer coming to an end.'

'You take a look at the calendar,' advised my old friend. 'It's September the twenty-ninth, Michaelmas Day. The end of summer that is, and we'll just have to face it.'

'Well, we made the most of summer this year, didn't we? A proper celebration. I'll always remember it.'

'Ah! We celebrated all right! Even though it did start with snow on Lady Day. Remember? We've had something to celebrate too, when you think us had weeks without old Sour-face bossing us about.'

At that moment Mrs Pringle appeared in the lobby doorway.

'I want a word with you, Bob Willet,' she said ominously.

'Here we go!' he said, with a wink.